BENJAMIN IRWIN

Cape Contrition

Book One in the Crowley & Iwamoto Files

kindle | direct publishing

For Lauren,
My Brightest Light

Contents

Part One: Between the Devil and the Deep Blue Sea

Prologue

October 6th, 1962

Elvis was crackling and tinny on the radio as Jake Reynolds set his newest *Action Comics* issue on a pile concealing a couple *Playboys*. As he got onto hands and knees to dig underneath his bed, he mumbled along to Jailhouse Rock. The boy cracked a gap-toothed grin as he got a slobbering lick up the cheek from his golden retriever, Oliver. Ollie was ten, like Jake. His mama, Doris, got the puppy a week after he was born. The two of them had grown up together, but ten years showed more on the gray-muzzled Oliver than on Jake.

Sometimes Jake caught himself contemplating how old Ollie was getting. The dog's muzzle was graying, and he fought his stiffening joints sportingly as he kept up with his boy. Jake wasn't one to brood on mortality. What ten-year-old is? He banished the thought and slipped on his battered Chuck Taylor high-tops. His backpack shook with sand as he hauled it up against his shoulder. Ollie still had some bite left in him and could still beg and wiggle like a puppy. Anyone who knew Ollie never would have believed he would abandon Jake to danger.

The boy and his dog were notorious troublemakers and

explorers about town. The residents of Delilah, Oregon, loved and grumbled about them in equal measure. None of them would have guessed they would find Jake's body alone, bloated and drowned in the surf. The same day, Oliver would turn up wandering the beach in confusion several miles north. His leash dragged kelp behind him, all caked with sand.

Open Jake's pack, and you would find a Zippo lighter with a naked girl on it, a few bent, forbidden cigarettes stowed away. Beside them, a folding pocketknife with his dad's initials (E.R.) carved on the handle. A heavy aluminum flashlight sat heavy in the sandy bottom. These were the sum of his inheritance: the only things his pop had left him. Jake clipped on Oliver's leash and slipped out the front door.

He kept singing Elvis between huffing breaths as he plodded over the first knoll of the beach. The wind stirred its balding scalp of windblown yellow grass. Mom was working a double at the diner, so Jake had nothing to fear. The beam of his flashlight on the beach at night was a common sight for the neighbors. Jake liked to run on the hard-packed sand with Ollie, his light cutting through the dark. There is nothing as black as the coast in the dead of night. Beneath your feet, the slick floor of the beach at low tide shines like oily glass all around. The surf roars somewhere out in the nothingness, even the galaxies shrouded in a mantle of clouds.

Jake liked the beach when it was his alone. He loved to walk out in the middle of the coastline desert and shut off the beam of his light. To a watcher from Harbor Street, he would wink out of sight. Jake savored the nothingness. The complete darkness was to him what the Om of a Buddhist monk approached. To tell the truth, it frightened him. His mind echoed mom's warnings of sneaker waves, driftwood

3

battering rams, and worse. To be alone in the vast night with the endless ocean lapping at his feet was a fearsome thing. But Jake wanted to be brave.

Ollie plodded along with his nose to the ground while Jake panned his light along the beach. Nobody. Perfect. His legs pumped the churning sand as the retriever's muscled shoulders strained at the leash. The warm electric light made leering shadows jump off logs of worn driftwood emigrated from some other shore. Oliver sniffed broken crab husks, mussel shells, twisted tentacles of discarded kelp, and saw-bone fish skeletons picked clean by the carnivorous sea. Jake had found many a treasure among the discarded, broken things that wash up on the shore. His nightstand held a glass fishing float that had bobbed across the Pacific Ocean from Japan. His ma told him so. In the imagination of the boy, Japan was a fantastic land of proud samurai and elegant geishas. A week ago, he'd found a dead harbor seal. Chief Blake hadn't found it so interesting.

The surf was roaring ever closer. Jake's flashlight illuminated a bat fluttering low over the sand, catching sand fleas that leapt up inches off the grit. Jake let his beam follow the fluttering wings, and Oliver's jaws snapped after it in vain. He stepped onto salt-eaten rocks covered with clinging barnacles to investigate the tide-pools. Vivid orange starfish, spiny purple urchins, and green anemones glowed in his light like the flora of an alien garden. Tiny sculpins and crabs darted out of the glare or buried themselves in the sand with little underwater dust clouds.

A rush of cold air made Jake shiver as his light fell upon a twisted wooden thing, half-buried in the sand. It sat in the foamy line left where the surf crawled back. The water was at low tide, and Jake glanced up the beach to see he was a long way from the cottages lining the beach. Fearing this curious item would disappear in the next wave, he snatched it as the Pacific crept up to lick his toes. When he shined the glaring light on the smooth shape in his hand, he saw it was a wooden horse. A toy from another time. He felt the smooth carved features, and it was completely dry. The joyous squeal of a toddler pealed out inches away and made him jump out of his skin with fright. The heavy flashlight flashed strobe-like in all directions as it tumbled end over end into the sand.

"Hello?" Jake called as he snatched up his flashlight and slashed its heavy beam to all sides. Oliver let out a menacing growl as more disembodied laughter drifted on the breeze. It was a ferocious rumble Jake hardly knew Oliver could make. Hackles bristled as he hunched his powerful shoulders. Jake glanced back to the distant lights of Delilah. He was farther from home than he thought. As he panned the light over the beach, the beam caught a young girl his age fleeing into the darkness. She held the hand of a tottering little boy. He called out to them, but they didn't respond. Ollie let out several booming, angry barks before laying his ears back and whining. He pulled at the leash, and Jake agreed it was time to turn back.

"This way! This way!" he heard a little girl's voice ahead of him, and he caught sight of her waving for him to follow. He did not get a long look at the children, but their clothes looked like what people wore in old photographs. Like garments from the Pioneer Museum, these were rustic, home-spun, and severe. They also appeared charred and blackened in places. They gave off a strong smell of smoke.

The boy did not follow the beckoning girl, but turned to run the opposite way. Ollie was straining at the leash so hard he was choking himself and coughing. Jake's shoes felt clunky and useless in the churning sand. More children laughed all around him. He lurched away whenever their voices sounded ahead of him, or he caught a glimpse of one in the flashlight. He tried to make plaintive calls for them to stop teasing him, but they acted as if they did not hear. A log snagged his foot, and Jake crashed onto his stomach. The wind shuddered nauseatingly out of him, and he let go of Oliver's leash. At a distance, the dog paced and turned with indecision, fearful for his boy but unwilling to cross back for him. Oliver whimpered for Jake to get up.

The ten-year-old spat gritty sand out of his mouth and dusted off his flashlight before getting up. A little girl stood right behind him.

"I made this for you." She held up a daisy chain bracelet. The girl was horribly burned, with parts of her skin bubbling red, other parts charred black. Half of her face had the skull exposed, but her voice was bright and chipper like she didn't know. Jake moaned in fear and turned once again, flashlight bobbing as he ran frantic after Oliver. The retriever took off at a gallop. Jake's light caught darting glimpses of the little girls and boys frolicking on all sides of them through the sand like they were all playing tag. Home was so far away. For all Jake's twists and turns, it was like he had gotten no closer to the line of houses. It was as if the children were herding the disoriented boy out further from home.

He staggered, heaving and pressing a stitch in his side. Saliva was thick in his mouth, and each breath burned deep in his lungs. There was something worse than burned children out in the darkness. Several times as he ran after Oliver's terrified barks, his flashlight caught a glimpse of a tall woman with her back to him. Her black dress was soaking wet. Long, dark, stringy hair hung out of a wilted black bonnet, lank and dripping about her shoulders. She terrified him most of all. Jake kept running until he collapsed. When his ragged breaths subsided, he looked up to see his home was further away than it had ever been. But he could have sworn he was almost there. Oliver let out several low cries, followed by a frightened yelp.

"Ollie, don't go. Please don't go, buddy." But the dog tucked tail and forsook him. A rush of cold air hit Jake's back, and when he turned around, he saw her towering over him. Her curtains of hair were dark and slick, streaked with seaweed and scuttling with crabs. A red starfish was clinging to the side of her face, and her sickly pallid skin was spider-webbed with lightning cracks of lurid purple veins. She held a belly distended with the swell of child or water. As he stared transfixed into her mottled, terrible eyes, the five burned children gathered around her. They hugged shyly about her skirts. Orange sparks peeled from their heads and shoulders and floated off into the wind. A warm trickle of urine stained the boy's leg, and he wept as he dropped the light and it guttered out in the sand.

Chapter One: Welcome to Delilah

October 8th, 1962

I was driving up the Pacific Coast Highway, hugging the blind curves snaking along the stony cliffs. White bursts of surf crashed against the battlements of rock beyond the guardrail to my left. I engaged the clutch, shifted gears, and flicked the wheel of my Zippo to catch fire to the tip of my cigarette. When the road straightened out, I eased up to 70 miles per hour, took a long drag, and kept an eye out for cops. I'd been on the road a long time, something like two months. I felt my path was going to take me through Astoria, then to Seattle. Even British Columbia and Alaska afterward. Maybe that would be far enough away.

I was forty-seven years old. A runner since high school, I was lean and wiry, my face lined and gaunt. Behind horn-rimmed glasses, my blue eyes were sunken and baggy in the rearview. I parted my chocolate brown hair to the left and wore it up messy, peppered with unfamiliar gray. My hairline was starting to make a concerning sally up the slope of my head, giving me a widow's peak. Only appropriate. I hadn't been too kind to myself in a long time and wasn't in the habit of taking a good look in the mirror. That was always my problem.

This coastal road was making me miss my old Triumph motorcycle. I longed to try the bike on those turns, but it was back home, and home was long gone. Everything I owned was in the back of my blue '58 Series II Land Rover. In the passenger seat, Otis was taking in the briny ocean air with his nose out the open window. Otis was a black and gray mutt I'd found limping on the side of the highway as I was passing through the Rockies in Colorado. He had the creased forehead and barrel chest of a pit-bull, but the beard and shaggy wire-hair of an Airedale terrier.

A car clipped Otis not long before I found him, stitched up his leg, and nursed him back to health. Kid was flea-bitten and half-starved, with part of his left ear missing from a scrap with a coyote or raccoon. Since it was clear he'd been on his own for some time, I claimed him as mine and kept moving west.

The orange cherry at the end of my cigarette smoldered as I inhaled deep and let out a long gust of cloudy smoke. The dark bristles of an eight-week beard were full upon my face, the first I'd worn since my beatnik days. It was grayer now than the last time. Jean begged me to shave it back then. *Jean.* I still couldn't say her name out loud. I saw a flash of tawny blonde in the sun and a come-catch-me smile in my mind's eye. It held for a second as the clouds broke and the sun glared on the windshield.

But it was only a sandy-haired mermaid on a faded gray sign which read, "Welcome to Delilah, Mermaid Cove of the Pacific! You'll be tempted to stay... Population: 5,463."

"No, thank you." I dropped my cigarette butt with the others into the gritty gray water in a paper cup, listening to it hiss and die. With the reflexes of a machine, I lit another without realizing. I rolled through the coastal town without stopping. Delilah was a dying fishing and logging community turning toward the business of tourism and retirement for its own survival. I thought little of the storm-battered, ramshackle collection of diners, canneries, antique shops, vacation homes, motels, and churches. The town spread in a crescent about the arms of a bay on an uneven terrain of sloping cliffs and low beaches. At one point, the main road became a bridge that passed over the mouth of an inlet. Spacious and luxurious cabins newly built as weekend hideaways for city folk huddled about the inlet's edges. They dipped docks into the water like tired feet.

They were soon in the rearview, and I was back to scenic Route 101. The two-lane road hugged the bases of coastal cliffs, treating me to an endless play of gorgeous views. I tried not to lose myself in the rolling sand dunes, forests of windblown Sitka spruce, Douglas fir, and Western red cedar. Most captivating of all were the ancient, monolithic rocks standing knee-deep in the turbulent, moody Pacific. I hadn't thought any part of the country could approach my love for the forests and swamps of my native North Carolina, but Oregon was growing on me.

The towering rocks stood like old gods in the shallows. The ocean must have battered them for millions of years. The environment of the coast was wild and wind-scoured, dotted with isolated and remote settlements. There was something ancient and forlorn about this land. Brooding over all was that beautiful and treacherous mother, the Pacific Ocean. I was starting to understand why so many of the ancients worshiped the sea. The Pacific may as well be God to these people. It is equally vast; as unplumbed and mysterious. They depend on her whims for their food but know better than to trust her.

The fog rolled in, and I lost my train of thought in the struggle to see. I downshifted, de-accelerated, and turned off the blaring rock-and-roll on the radio to focus on the road. As I glanced down to press the button, I failed to notice the massive boulder that leered out of the fog like a thing alive.

"Fuck!" I slammed on the Land Rover's brakes and threw my right hand across Otis' chest. The dog toppled forward, but my grip kept him from slamming into the dashboard. The tires screamed and the whole car shuddered as it lurched to a sudden stop within inches of the massive stone. The smell of burnt rubber was thick in my nose, and my heart was pounding. I felt the singe of my cigarette where it had fallen in the folds of my Aran sweater, and frantically swatted it away like a creeping spider. I cursed under my breath as I stomped it out in the floor of the cab. I opened the door and staggered out to see what I'd almost hit, wiping at the smoking hole and ashy stain on the cable-knit gray belly of my sweater.

I was alone with the boulder and walked along its stolid face to see how it lay across the road from cliff wall to crushed guardrail. It looked to weigh two hundred tons and might have fallen in the last five minutes. As my dizzying adrenaline settled, I staggered back to the cab and dug around for my map. I spread this over the vehicle's hood. Conscious of sitting at a perilous blind turn, I pored over the lines and pinpoints rapidly. My only other route through would double me back twenty miles and take me into the mountains. Towns would be sparse, and I frowned at my gas gauge to see the fuel wouldn't last the detour. Rather than risk running out of gas in the wooded mountains, I resolved to turn back five miles to Delilah. I'd warn the authorities about the blocked road and fill up on gas and coffee while I thought about my next move.

Bacon hissed and spat on the grill over the dull roar of conversation and clinking plates. The air of the diner was rank with the smoke of grease and tobacco.

"Biscuits and gravy?" the pretty young waitress asked. She balanced a heavy-laden plate with a hot pad on one hand while she carried a steaming pot of coffee in another.

"Yes, Ma'am," I smiled as she set before me a steaming plate of biscuits, hash browns, and scrambled eggs drowned in sausage gravy. She refilled my coffee without asking: my fourth cup. The gravy was too peppery, and the biscuits were burnt. I choked one down to be polite and ignored the other. At least it was good coffee. The Thunderbird was packed to the gills for breakfast and running short-staffed.

A bop record was crackling and crowing over the speakers. Some leather-voiced artist I'd never heard before, but I liked him well enough. I lit a smoke at the breakfast bar before taking another swig of bold, rich coffee. There was a woman in her late thirties seated next to me. Her curly red hair was in a short, bouncy bob cut, and she wore thick-rimmed glasses. She was smoking menthols and sipping Earl Grey tea as she read... *Coal Train Coming* by Joseph Simon Crowley. *Well, how about that,* I smiled as I took a drag from my cigarette. It was an invigorating reminder: I was more than an unwashed vagrant in a diner. I had once been the man who wrote that book, and a few better ones. Maybe I could be him again. The unexpected reminder of my past life brought a painful sting and a surge of confidence.

"Hey," I ventured, though it was unlike me to approach a stranger. "What do you think of the book?" She gestured that she was only a third of the way through, and I recoiled with a twinge of regret. But she was likely accustomed to being clumsily flirted with by aging tourists. I couldn't blame her for not wanting to put up with it this morning. I turned back around and took a few contemplative puffs off my cigarette before stubbing it out in the ashtray.

"*American Quixote* and *Appalachian Queen* were better," she said, once she finished the page she was on and marked her place. "The quality of his prose has slumped in this one, and the plotting is a little chaotic, but the characters make it adequately readable. I don't know a lot of male authors who write as vulnerably as him. Seems like there's a sensitive guy behind all the tortured artist bullshit."

"I agree. *Coal Train Coming* was never my favorite either. Still, I like the way he encapsulates the American experience. My favorite review of that book said Crowley was the Fitzgerald of our generation."

"Well, I don't know if I would go *that* far. He's no Jack Kerouac. The Beat Generation has produced better." She stoked a little fight in me once she realized I spoke the King's English and didn't drag my knuckles on the ground or carry a club.

"Oh, come on. I was starting to like you," I laughed with a pained wince like I had been stung. "And Kerouac would be flattered to hear that. I'll have to tell him you said so the next time we talk. We send one another our work from time to time, but I haven't had anything to send him lately."

Her green eyes widened for a moment as she flipped to the last page of the book and looked over the old black and white photograph of the author. The picture was all the way back from '48, but even through the intervening years and thick beard, she saw right through me.

"Shit," she laughed, covering her white grin with embarrassment, "Well, if it isn't Joseph Simon Crowley." She shook my hand.

"My friends call me Joe. But I'm undercover as a hobo, so try not to blow my cover, Miss...," I smiled, searching for her name with my eyes.

"Gwen Christiansen. I own a little bookstore in town, on Conch Street."

"I'll have to drop by and see what you've got."

"You haven't written anything in a while. Been pretty reclusive for what..."

"Eight years." Jesus, it was eight, wasn't it? I had really let myself go.

"What brings you out this way? Are you roving across America for inspiration, *Mr. Kerouac?*"

"Why? Do you know where I could catch some?" She knew I was flirting, but I couldn't tell what she thought of that.

"Well Joe, I'll think about it. Right now, I've got to go open the shop so I can afford to keep indulging in my habits." She held up the book and cigarettes in the same hand.

"Alright, well, it was nice meeting you."

"Say, before I take off. Have you heard of Usher's Fall?"

"Should I have?"

"It's a local curiosity. Maybe a little darker than your usual tourist trap. Someone with your grasp on American tragedies and family sagas might find something poetic about it. Most outsiders are more interested in resorts and casinos. The old families around here stay clear of it. It's about three miles up 101, on Cape Contrition."

"Thank you. I'll have to look it up," I smiled as I watched her go, remembering a turn-off I'd passed a few minutes before the boulder. An elderly man with a potbelly, paisley bandana, and braided gray beard stole my attention with an angry call to the waitress.

"How much longer is my slice of Marionberry pie gonna take, Darlin'? I been waiting twenty minutes!"

"And you can wait five more, Ed," she snapped back as she bussed another table. "We're running short-staffed today."

"Well when's Doris coming back to work? Place ain't the same without her." The bell tied at the door rang, signaling another person had walked in.

"Jesus, Ed. What the hell is wrong with you, anyway? She just lost her son," came a deep, withering reply from the man who had entered the Thunderbird. I looked back to see a tall, broad-shouldered police chief wearing a bomber jacket, cowboy hat in hand and a big revolver hanging at his hip. He looked to be in his late thirties. He wore a thick mustache and a full head of curly brown hair, flattened from his hat. He had the air of an ex-high school quarterback past his glory days, but it was clear the people of the town revered him. His midsection was padded with a gut gained in recent years, but his back, chest, and arms were still as strong as ever. The man was big enough to hunt bear with a stick and give the stick to the bear.

"Aw hell, Will, I was just funnin'. I know it's awful what happened to her boy. But maybe she should've been looking after him instead of letting him run wild all over town.

Everyone's thinking it."

Police Chief Will Blake flicked open his Zippo and lit a cigarette as he walked to the bar and stood next to me.

"Betty, Darlin', get this hillbilly asshole his bill and his pie, *to go*. Then kindly tell him to clear out before I put him through a window."

"Oh, Chief, not again!" called the Thunderbird's owner from the back, where he was frying hash browns.

"And I'll have some coffee, when you ain't too busy," Will said kindly as he took a seat. Betty smiled at him and whispered "thank you" as she passed. The old biker took his pie and decided it was a fight he didn't want to pick. As Betty set the steaming white mug in front of the Chief, she took the cigarette out of his mouth and stole a puff of it before returning it to his lips.

"Hey Tom, what is this shit, anyway? Put the Hank Williams one on when you get the chance." As if Will owned the place, the sound of the jazz band immediately ceased with the abrupt sound of the needle scratching as it was clumsily lifted off the record. In a few seconds, Hank was twanging and baying on the speakers. Chief Blake took a satisfied drag and a swig of coffee before murmuring along, a little off tune, to I'm So Lonesome I Could Cry. He turned, as if noticing my presence for the first time. "Oh, sorry, were you listening to that?"

"I can dig Hank Williams fine," I answered diplomatically, signaling I was ready for a to-go box and my bill.

"That's a nice dog you've got out there. Why don't you bring him inside instead of leaving him cooped up in your car?"

"I'm not sure that's allowed. Besides, I'm about to take

off."

"Hell, do you see the Health Department here? Tom don't mind, do you, Tom?"

"You better not be letting any more gol-durn hound-dogs in here, Will," the still disembodied voice of Tom called out from the back.

"Right. Well, like I said, I think I'll just go on." I slid the waitress a wad of cash as I boxed up my leftovers.

"What's the matter, Stranger?" Will leaned in close. His growl belied his smile. "You seem nervous. Don't like cops?" As a general rule, I don't.

"Look, John Wayne, this ain't an Old West saloon. I'm only passing through town to eat some breakfast. Is that illegal here?"

"Guess not, but vagrancy is," Blake curled his nostrils like I carried an offensive stench. It was a possibility. "Best you move on someplace else, before you get yourself in trouble."

"Oh, I'm good at trouble, Sheriff. Are you?"

"Chief, actually. And you don't want to find out. Safe travels, now, Carolina. Whatever you're running from back there, don't bring any of it here." Will gave me a strong pat on the back before downing the rest of his coffee, slipping Betty two dollars, and heading out the door.

"Asshole," I muttered as the bell rang and the Thunderbird's door swung shut. I grabbed a copy of the local newspaper on the way out. Otis beat his bony tail against the seat and gave me kisses on the cheek as I opened the car door and sat. The dog took some rapid, eager sniffs of the bag as I opened it and let him dig in. While Otis happily scarfed down what remained of the worst biscuits and gravy I'd ever had, I rolled down the window and lit a joint of reefer. In my mind's eye, I imagined the whine and flash of a camera in the spark of my lighter's wheel. As I leaned back against my seat's headrest and took a drag, I could see the picket signs waving outside the courthouse, and hear the shouts. **MURDERER. HOW COULD YOU? JOSEPH CROWLEY WILL BURN IN HELL.**

My hand trembled, so I grasped the steering wheel until my knuckles turned white. My breaths focused into slow gusts of smoke. The pot took the edge off, but my mind was full of my wife and daughter, and a house in Chapel Hill, North Carolina. I tried to distract myself with the local paper, but it was no good. *TRAGIC DROWNING OF CHILD SHOCKS COMMUNITY*, ran the headline. A ten-year-old boy named Jacob Reynolds, found dead on the beach. The article examined the tragedy, offered condolences, and warned readers not to go onto the beach at night, or turn their backs to the ocean. Next page was a fluff-piece on some local millionaire named Rupert Wycliffe, CEO of Cascadia Lumber: the biggest logging company in the Pacific Northwest. I gave it up and turned the ignition.

The blue Land Rover rolled up the incline of a winding two-lane road which split off from Route 101 a few miles from where the boulder fell that morning. The fog had cleared and rain was falling in a drizzle. The road wound through a thick forest of towering firs, needles and rocking branches heavy with raindrops. The wind was howling and turbulent, and I swerved into the empty oncoming lane to avoid a fallen branch. I passed a mossy boulder on the roadside, broke out of the trees, and started onto a modern two-lane bridge of steel and concrete. As the heavy curtain of woodlands gave out, light poured into the vehicle from the open sky. Sidewalks and squat barrier walls of stone three feet high lined the bridge.

Two bronze gargoyles in the shape of calling sirens capped the parapets at either end of the bridge. Their wild hair billowed over their thin shoulders and bared breasts, mouths twisted in painful howls. Serpentine fish-finned tails coiled around the wave-battered rocks they sat upon.

Across the bridge, my road shifted into a mild decline to a small visitor parking lot. It stood empty except for one sleek black 1928 Mercedes-Benz SSK with its convertible top up. I let out a wolf whistle as my eyes roamed over its long, curvaceous body.

I parked, killed the engine, and set the emergency brake. The mutt scampered out behind me as I took in my surroundings. From where I stood, I commanded an impressive panorama of scenery. Immediately beyond the parking lot was the golden beach of a wide half-circle cove which framed the low evening sun. The drizzling sky was yellow and streaked with lavender, pink, and orange. The fiery glimmer on the rolling jade waves was breathtaking.

The shallows held jagged rocks shoulder-deep in water. Out beyond the arms of the cove were towering stones with seagulls, cormorants, and puffins buzzing and nesting about their crowns. Fat, spotted harbor seals reclined on the laps of these monoliths. I let Otis off the leash and watched him buzz a flock of dirty gulls on the beach.

To my left, I got a better look at the bridge from the underside. It spanned six hundred feet across two cliffs. Two-hundred feet beneath it, a small creek ran over jagged rocks before opening out into the ocean. The bridge was in the style of a Roman aqueduct, with a single parabolic arch spanning half its length. To my right, across the cove, I saw Cape Contrition striking out into the sea. A narrow dirt trail snaked up into the thick cover of woods before ending at the lighthouse itself. The sixty foot tower glimmered like ivory in the sunset. The lighthouse loomed lofty and alone atop a towering cliff, whose stoic face dropped right into the sea itself and stood armed to the teeth with bristling rock formations against the heaving siege of the waves.

I whistled sharply and the mutt snapped into a gallop after me. As we started toward the trailhead, I tried to get another glimpse of the lighthouse and stopped in my tracks. It appeared to be ablaze with a terrible fire. There was something foreboding about that confusing sight, and I stood staring at it for a long minute. I felt drawn into the raging torrent of flames roaring around the tower in the distance, but not consuming it. As I watched entranced, I could almost hear the crackling roar, and the tortured screams.

"St. Elmo's Fire," declared an amused voice that startled me into a jolt, for I thought I was alone. I turned to see a man who had appeared at the mouth of the trail. The stranger was rounded with the paunchiness of age, but his high cheekbones and a pointed jawline gave the impression of a man who had been strikingly gaunt in earlier years. His beady, dark eyes were highly intelligent, and there was a crafty smirk about his thin lips that gave the impression he was in on a joke others could not perceive. His dark mustache and thick-lensed spectacles gave him the look of Theodore Roosevelt. A tailored, old-fashioned beige suit and straw boater hat lent it a splash of Jay Gatsby.

"It is a weather phenomenon which occurs in a highly charged atmosphere: when luminous plasma is created by a coronal discharge from a tall, pointed object. Like a ship's mast, or a lightning rod."

"Or a lighthouse?" I asked.

"Very good, sir! Old-time fishermen would say you saw a good omen! Perhaps it does mean the spirits are watching over us here."

I had heard of St. Elmo's Fire, but never witnessed the phenomenon. I imagined it would have looked different. But when I glanced back at the lighthouse, it stood white and cold without a trace of the roaring inferno. The newcomer had a well-bred air of sophistication and the clipped, nasally, archaic transatlantic accent once taught in American boarding schools and used in radio and film in the '30s and '40s. There was no mistaking he was the owner of the pristine '28 Benz. This was one of the old counts of the dying American aristocracy. As I took in this apparition of history, my mind drifted back to the article glimpsed in the paper earlier.

"Rupert Wycliffe?" My lips broke into an uncertain smile, and he bowed.

"Why, the very same! It is a pleasure to meet you, Mr.," Rupert extended his hand to shake and searched my eyes inquisitively.

"Joe." I returned the handshake with a firm grasp and maintained eye contact. Certain men discern all they need to know of another man in that primate ritual of the first meeting. "Joe Crowley."

"*The* Joseph Crowley? Author of *American Quixote* and *Look at all the Flowers*? You snatched a Pulitzer for that last one, I believe?"

"You caught me."

"Well, it looks as though I am not the only one whose reputation precedes him! I must confess, this chance meeting is a treat for me." Rupert gave a jolly chuckle.

"You know my books?"

"I have been waiting for your next one for some time now!"

"You sound like my agent. I'll give you his number so you two can commiserate." As I said it, I remembered my agent and I had parted ways years ago, and he was dead.

"Very good, Mr. Crowley, I am honored to meet you."

"Likewise. I hear you're quite a titan in this region."

"Bah, my forefathers were the titans. I have never chopped down a tree in my life. Have you been to Usher's Fall before, or is this the first time?"

"First time in the state, actually."

"Ah, a man like you would find something inspiring about that site. Well, I sometimes like to give tours of the grounds to interested visitors, but I was just leaving. With my poor health, I do not have it in me to make that hike again after coming down."

"Is it closed for the day?"

"Oh, well, you would not be able to enter the house or the tower, but you are free to walk the grounds. But it is not every day I meet one of my favorite American novelists, and I would have loved to show you around the place myself. I must confess, I am disappointed by the missed opportunity."

"It doesn't have to be missed. Perhaps we could do it another day?"

"Oh, Sir, you are most obliging. But I have inconvenienced you, for you wished to see the lighthouse this evening. Please, Mr. Crowley, as my apology and a consolation, I must insist you come to my house tonight for dinner. I would love to pick the brain of a literary man such as yourself. You would not believe how starved I am for intellectual discourse in a backwater like this. It has made me quite needy, I am afraid. I would have to go at least as far as Portland to have a conversation of any real significance. And my Latin and French have grown dreadfully rusty."

"What are we having?"

"Oh, you will come, then? Excellent, Sir, excellent!" Mr. Wycliffe grinned, showing his brilliant tombstone teeth. "Since you do not know the area, would you like to follow my automobile?"

"Unless you want to trade cars for the drive."

"You are a funny man, Mr. Crowley, but that car is one of fewer than eight surviving original models in the world. I had it brought over from Germany before the War." Rupert Wycliffe directed an unimpressed look at the blue Land Rover stained with the dust and crushed bugs of a long Odyssey. "Oh, but I have been rude. What is the name of your friend here?"

"This is Otis," I said as the scruffy, musclebound mutt sat back on his haunches and tried to give the wealthy gentleman a handshake. It was not reciprocated.

"I have always loved dogs. What is his breed?" Mr. Wycliffe looked over the animal with trepidation before patting it timidly, as if it was a tiger. I had trouble believing Rupert Wycliffe had ever been around dogs.

"He's a Heinz."

"Some breed of wire-haired German terrier, I imagine? I cannot say I am familiar with the Heinz Terrier breed."

"No, Heinz as in *57 Varieties*," I chuckled, but my counterpart didn't understand the joke.

"Quite." Mr. Wycliffe took his hand away with disdain when he realized he was touching a mutt.

"Well, should we follow you?" I tried to move past the

moment.

"Certainly, Mr. Crowley," Wycliffe said, his amiable smile and jolly manner restored.

Chapter Two: The Timber King

October 8th, 1962 (Cont.)

I followed Mr. Wycliffe's car along a darkening wooded road. Why would a man whose industry clear-cut forests for a living choose to live surrounded by them? The rain was picking up again. Otis looked out the windows and laid his ears back, whimpering.

The prospect of a fancy dinner with a polished old dinosaur like Rupert Wycliffe piqued my interest. I call him a dinosaur, but we were close to the same age. Hard living may have worn me down in recent years, but Rupert Wycliffe seemed as though he had been middle-aged his whole life. It was as if he'd never left the forties. His appreciation of my work appealed to my vanity. Still, I was not without my trepidations. I may have passed for an intellectual worthy of Wycliffe's company, but was a decidedly working-class man. As were my novels, for all their acclaim. It's hard to see what he loved so much about my books. I wasn't writing about the same America he lived in. If I wasn't a famous writer, he wouldn't even acknowledge me in the street. My time in the Beat counterculture gave me a natural aversion to stuffy, rich capitalists. My rural southern upbringing gave me an aversion to anyone who was rude or dismissive to my dog.

Wrought-iron gates opened before the grille of Wycliffe's automobile. In the dark, the looming shapes of several old trees and a marble fountain dotted the verdant lawns. The manor house was a log cabin built on the scale of a castle. I parked behind Rupert and killed the engine. Otis scampered from the car and ran to the polished door at my side.

"This was my father's house, you know," Rupert said. "Built in 1915, out of Oregon timber and Oregon stone."

I didn't know how to admit I was currently homeless, so I kept it to myself. A Japanese butler opened the front door and ushered us into a vaulted entry hall.

"Hayato," Rupert addressed the butler with circular-framed eyeglasses and black hair parted in the middle, "Would you go and check with May to see if dinner is ready? Tell her I am hosting an unexpected guest. Her portion will have to go to my friend here." Hayato bowed and strode away toward the kitchens, and Rupert commenced to give me a tour of the house. My guide showed me through disused extra bedrooms with posh Roaring Twenties furniture, drawing rooms bedecked with Turkish rugs and couches, a private library and study where I could have passed the winter in a leather armchair with a stack of old books by the fireplace, and a cigar room with a wall-to-wall humidor cabinet and an old-fashioned gramophone. *Maybe the capitalists don't have it all wrong.*

Hayato escorted us into a dining room warm with a roaring fire in the hearth. A long rectangular wooden table stood set for two at one end, and I wondered what a man with such a table did with so few friends in this lonely place. A light salad was served first beside a creamy lobster and tomato bisque.

"So, how is the next book coming?" he asked before taking a spoonful of bisque. I swallowed some crisp leaves of romaine lettuce dripping with balsamic vinaigrette and washed them down with water before replying.

"It isn't, to be honest. I've started and stopped a few times, but haven't committed to working on anything in some time."

"Do you fear failure?" Rupert took a sip of water and trained those penetrating, snakelike eyes on me.

"Why do you ask?"

"Well, your memoir was your most successful book yet. It did win you the Pulitzer Prize, after all. You left yourself with a tough act to follow, as they say in show-business. Maybe that is why Joseph Crowley's fifth creation has passed such a long gestational period. And there was the film adaptation! Gregory Peck was a revelation in his portrayal of you, Mr. Crowley. And Grace Kelly as your Jean? I don't mind telling you I wept, Sir, when the two of you were reunited at last."

"So, will I," I murmured, taking a stiff drink of water. He went on, oblivious.

"It must have been a real privilege to have Orson Welles direct such a triumph. How exciting for you, my friend!"

"To be honest, I haven't kept up much with how the picture turned out. I'm sure Welles, his cast and crew did an incredible job with whatever script they got, but I never got around to seeing it. My involvement with that picture was minimal at best, beyond writing an early draft of the script."

"Sharing your creative work with others must be difficult."

"I've never been one to write on a team. And if I did, I would choose to write with other writers and not businessmen. No offense."

"None taken, Mr. Crowley. I appreciate your candor."

In my mind's eye, it was five years ago, 1957, and I was in a fancy L.A. restaurant forty minutes late to a meeting. I burst in to find my long-suffering literary agent, Larry Filbert, sitting at a table near a large bay window with Mr. Welles, a producer whose name I couldn't remember, and a quiet young man with glasses and curly hair I had never met. None of them looked happy. The gleaming dome of Larry's bald head was dripping with sweat. His suit was soaked through. I've never seen the domed minarets and palaces of Istanbul and Baghdad, but I've seen his head, and I'll have to content myself with that small wonder. He looked to me with relief.

"Jesus, Joe, where have you been?" he hurried over to me as if I needed to be braced up for support. I was in sorry shape; hadn't shaved in days, eyes red and sunken, and I was already tipsy. More than tipsy.

"I forgot this was today. Got here as fast as I could from the hotel. I'm sorry, Larry. I'll make it up to you," I mumbled, taking my seat.

"Yeah, we'll see if you still can, buddy," Larry muttered.

"Hey, sorry I'm late, everyone."

"Well, can we get you something to eat? Some bacon and eggs, friend? Black coffee?" Larry gestured impatiently for a waitress. His mood was optimistic, ever the peacemaker and the smooth talker. But he was all out of excuses for me.

"Bloody Mary," I muttered to the waitress.

"Ah, *hair of the dog.* Of course," Orson rolled his eyes. The waitress stiffened but tried to keep her winning smile as she said,

"Sir, I am afraid this establishment has a two-drink limit."

"What are you talking about? I just got here."

"Yes, but Sir..." she leaned in and took a confidential tone, "it appears you have had enough to drink already. And in the interest of keeping a quiet family environment-"

"Oh, you think I've been drinking? Are you a cop, sweetheart? Are you going to make me walk in a straight line now to prove I'm sober? Pour the fucking drink!"

The restaurant turned silent as the grave. The young waitress took a step back with a pained sigh as she tried not to cry, before turning and hurrying away. I took a calming puff of my Benzedrine inhaler and a long swallow of ice water before rubbing my throbbing forehead. My eyes were sensitive to the light of the Southern California morning. Behind each eye it felt like there was an egg-sized tumor of pulsating pain. Several of the restaurant's patrons looked over to our table and muttered to themselves.

"Christ alive, Crowley, are you drunk?" the producer asked. "It's not even ten in the morning. Pull yourself together, man."

"Look, I'm fine. I was up late working on the rewrites for the script, that's all. I'm tired and cranky, not drunk."

"And what was that inhaler you flashed?" the producer asked.

"Don't you know? I'm asthmatic," I lit a cigarette and inhaled a deep breath of smoke. "Anyway, I was up late and lost track of time. Overslept this morning."

"You have lost track of a lot of things in the last year, Joseph," Orson Welles shamed in resonant tones.

"I know, but I think I've found it. I was on a roll last night."

"A bender, more like," the producer leaned in to Larry's ear and murmured loud enough for me to hear. I ignored it.

"If you give me a few more days, I'll have a script like you wouldn't believe."

29

Orson Welles crossed his arms across his massive chest, looking down at the other men at the table from his imposing height to see what they had to say. The producer grimaced with simpering dissemblance.

"Listen, Joe. About the rewrites. We know you have been working hard, and you know we all love the work you have done in the past. Adapting a novel to film is hard when you are so attached to it, and already have such a creative vision in place. They're different mediums. Some things won't translate."

"What, you don't like my ideas for the picture about my own book?" My temper was flaring up again, and Larry was glancing about like he feared another scene.

"We have decided to take the film in a different direction. We are going with someone else." The slight man with glasses who sat next to me stiffened at this, and my heart sank. "This is Mr. Hank Richards. He is going to be handling the script from here on out."

"It's a pleasure to meet you, Sir. I am a big fan of your work!" Hank tried to keep a positive face on things as he extended a genial hand.

"So he *can* talk." I took another puff of my inhaler. "What, are you fucking kidding me with this?" I shooed away the kid's hand. "What's he written? How old is this kid, fourteen? I'm not convinced he has *pubic hair*, much less a Pulitzer."

"Mr. Crowley, there is no need to be crass," the producer started, but Hank sat forward to speak for himself.

"I'm twenty-two. I've had one screenplay go to film so far." He shifted in his seat, not looking me in the eye. "And I have pubic hair. -Sir."

I laughed and tried to read the faces of the men at the table for some twitch of a smile.

"Come on, you guys are jerking me off here, right? This is some kind of joke."

That was when smooth, amiable Larry finally had enough and boiled over.

"You know what, Joe? You're the fucking joke. You miss your deadlines, you come into meetings drunk. You're drunk right now! Your prose is lazy and careless. Everything about your script is cynical and insulting toward everything and everyone concerned."

"It's a damn war movie, isn't it? More war pictures ought to be cynical. You think star-spangled John Wayne is going to show you what it was like over there? But I'm sure HUAC and McCarthy would have a few things to say about the undertones."

"-Dammit, Joe, this isn't about ducking the blacklist by sanitizing the message of your book. The brilliance of your novel was how through all the darkness, you never lost sight of the light. Deep down, the guy who wrote that book was a romantic and a humanitarian. He saw the concentration camps and *still* had hope for the world. But these scripts and their re-writes are shit! They're shit, Joe. And you know why they're shit? Because you aren't the same guy who wrote the 'novel of a generation' three years ago. And frankly, I am tired of waking you up, pouring you coffee, fixing your tie, and hoping you will stay artificially alive long enough to make it through your next meeting without embarrassing yourself. I'm done being your mother, and I sure as hell know Jean is."

"The fuck did you say?"

"I'm done waiting for the Joseph Crowley revival that's never going to happen, and I'm done with you. This is

31

finished."

I leaned back in my chair with a snarl of disdain and betrayal, and felt the manager of the restaurant come to stand behind me. The little waitress from earlier was standing in his shadow, and he postured protectively to keep me away from her. The knight in shining bowtie.

"Sir, I am going to have to ask you to leave. You are disturbing my customers."

"Alright, keep your shirt on," I growled, getting up. "And as for you guys, good luck with the kid. I'm sure he'll come up with something completely forgettable." I shook off the grip of the restaurant's manager on my shoulder, muttered "don't fucking touch me," and staggered out on my own. The stares and whispers were all around as I burst out into the blinding light of Los Angeles, and the euphoria of the Benny washed over me. Then I heard Mr. Wycliffe calling in the distance.

"Well, how is your family, Mr. Crowley? Have they been supportive during your spell of writer's block?"

I shifted in my seat and glanced at the fire. Another intrusive thought confronted me with the sudden image of a house outside Chapel Hill, North Carolina, consumed in flames belching black smoke into the sky.

"I haven't been home in a long time." My mind played a tortuous film reel of scenes. My wife Jean with daisies in her flowing lion's mane of thick blonde hair, laughing and urging me to come in after her as she ran into a field of tall sunflowers. Another flash, I saw her smiling and trying to follow along as I taught her Woody Guthrie songs on the guitar. Then a tiny five year old girl was trying to flip a pancake in a skillet while her beautiful, tired mother watched. That same girl, six years later, was beaming with braces and orange freckles as she held up the largemouth bass she caught with me. Then that little girl was at college so many miles away, and Jean and I were screaming at one another before I slammed the door, flicked that damned cigarette, and got in my car. Then that car was all I had left. And I was hungover, walking in the charred black frame of my ruined house, touching twisted and burned relics still dripping with water from the fireman's hose. My mind was so full of that woman, I could smell her perfume and my eyes burned with the threat of tears. All those yellowed love letters, vinyl records, the books we read and the ones I wrote when I should have been spending time with her. And all my fucking liquor. Did those typed pages, those weathered guitars, and the library of books we had talked through together over sixteen years kindle the fire of our home to burn any more brilliantly? Did the words of my love letters feed the smoke that suffocated you in bed as you slept?

"My wife is dead." It was the first time I ever said the words, and I half choked on them. "But you knew that, didn't you?"

"My God, no. I am so sorry for your loss, Joseph. I had no idea. And your daughter?"

"She is at college in Boston. We don't talk. Her decision, not mine."

"Pardon me, Sir, if it is rude to ask. But how did your wife d-"

"No." There was a dangerous edge in my voice. "We will not talk about her. You will not say her name-" I cut off when Hayato leaned in to take the remains of the salad and soup away. The chef came out with two steaming plates which looked like loaves of mud and set them before us. A small hammer and chisel were set beside each plate. I looked uncertainly at the dish, but Rupert laughed, the tension of a moment ago seemingly forgotten.

"It is rainbow trout from the Columbia, wrapped in lotus leaves and baked in a shell of clay that hardens around it in the oven, as in a kiln." He took his hammer and chisel and cracked open the shell of his own, breaking it into large pieces and smiling at the rising steam from the fish inside as he pulled the crumbling shell away. Watching him, I got the feeling he was trying to do the same to me. I picked up my own hammer and broke apart the hard layer of dark clay before tasting the scrumptious meat of the trout itself.

"And paired with it, we have a Dry Riesling which should complement nicely." Hayato produced a dusty bottle from the cellar and poured it into his master's cup. My pulse quickened as I lifted a hand to signal Hayato not to pour.

"I'll just have water, thanks." Mr. Wycliffe did not appear to notice or take offense, but I was learning he missed nothing.

After a dessert of crème brûlée and rich Turkish coffee, we walked to the cigar lounge. Mr. Wycliffe busied himself with getting two Romeo y Julieta cigars from a box at the top shelf of his humidor. I froze when I noticed a dust-coated old bottle of caramel-brown liquor. Two squat tumblers sat beside it. A part of me saw the bottle as if it was a rattlesnake, and I broke out in a cold sweat as my heart spiked. But my mouth was watering, and my desire to pour a stiff glass and sample the aged liquor was powerful. Just a taste. That could be all, right?

"Ah, I see you have noticed the treat I had Hayato set out

for us. How would you like to try a bottle of pre-Prohibition bourbon? Bottled in 1919. My father hid it in his safe and took a stiff drink of it when the Tillamook Burn nearly sank us, but otherwise kept it preserved. When my father died, this bottle came down to me."

I swallowed and stumbled over my words.

"I don't drink. I... I'm a recovering alcoholic. I haven't had a drink in three weeks."

"Oh dear," Rupert cooed with concern, moving the bottle and cups and putting them out of sight in a cabinet. "I apologize, my friend, I didn't know."

I suspected this millionaire *did* know about all of it. Several times throughout the evening, I noticed a cruel smile glinting about the man's lips. His beady, bespectacled eyes evaluated everything he saw. I was beginning to think my encounter with Rupert Wycliffe was not a chance meeting at all, and the entire evening was orchestrated to rattle me and test my limits. I have never been a churchgoing man, but if I were to meet the Devil, he would remind me of Rupert Wycliffe.

"I was a sickly boy," Rupert announced, "and had three older brothers. They were the fighters, the athletes, the ones who didn't mind cutting timber with the common men. When the War came, they all went to battle as officers, but I was too frail to join. I lost Francis at Guadalcanal, Martin in Algeria, Christopher in Italy. While all the heirs to the throne were fighting overseas, I was at home learning my family's trade, rising to the top of my father's kingdom." He took a cruel pride in this that made me sick. I didn't respond.

"What was war like for you?" Rupert tossed the question like a dart before he lit his cigar with a cedar match and puffed it into life. I lit my own cigar before speaking. The pure, premium tobacco was sweet and fragrant, and I savored the blue-gray smoke before answering.

"You read my book. That's how it was for me." But it was evident Mr. Wycliffe wanted the horse's mouth. This eccentric timber king wanted to plumb the depths of my past trauma and see what sort of man I was. But for what?

"I was drafted in '42 to fight the Nazis. I was twenty-seven, a Duke graduate, a new father. Emma had just been born, but I wasn't ready for that. Then they made me an officer. In French Algeria, I killed my first man. I was out of ammo and cut off from my men, so I beat him to death with a shovel. It was hotter than hell, with sandstorms like you could never imagine. When the Kraut planes screamed overhead, there was no place to hide. Italy was the ugliest fighting I saw. We stacked corpses in piles and used them for sandbags. When the wheels of a Jeep drove over a person's skull, it made this... this popping sound, I'll never forget. In France, I was sweet on a girl named, oh, what was it... Sophie. She taught me a little French. I tried to find her again, after, but never could. I never told Jean about her. I killed more than forty men during the war. When I was twenty-nine, and a Captain, I got shot three times through the thigh, chest, and abdomen. I got an honorable discharge, received a Purple Heart and a Silver Star, and got to go back home when better men didn't. I never forgave myself for that. Published my first book, met my daughter, and married Jean. Those were some good years.

"From '51-'53, I was a journalist who braved the wrath of generals and bombed out battlefields to tell America the real story of how its sons were being killed in a pointless, unwinnable war on a foreign battleground where we had no business being. I was writing because I knew the cost of war, and I wanted it to end so we could spare some more of those boys getting killed. But when those boys got home, you know what my ethical concerns and in-depth journalistic coverage of the war did for them? Nothing. America moved on without them, fat and happy, forgetful they were even at war for reasons they couldn't explain, in a country they couldn't find on a map. Korea was messy, complicated, and inconvenient. The vets returned home to a hard-luck economy and the apathy of their neighbors. A lot of people couldn't look them in the eye. I blamed myself.

"So I started drinking. And I wrote this acclaimed book that made me rich and famous so I could afford to drown my guilt in more booze. My bitterness and alcoholism ruined my prospects of writing a script for the film adaptation. I wasn't the same man who had written the novel anymore. And all this was ending my marriage. Jean and I fought all the time, and the last night we fought, I went out on a bender all night while a freak accident caused my house to burn down. Fire department said the fire began with a cigarette I hadn't properly disposed of right before I left. I was acquitted of manslaughter in the eyes of the law, but I still know it was my fault. That cigarette was the spark. It started the fire that killed my wife. And the only person left I care about in this world is my daughter Emma, and she can't even look at me anymore, because I killed her mom. So... is that what you wanted to hear?"

Mr. Wycliffe paused as he puffed on his cigar, mulling over my words.

"I see I have upset you, Mr. Crowley. This was not my intention."

"Yeah, I'm finding that pretty fucking hard to believe. From reminiscing about the war to talking about my tarnished career and desecrated family, to leaving that bottle of bourbon out when my name is more tied up with alcoholism than fucking Hemingway's. If you read my books, you knew how I felt about the Great War and Korea, and what I went through over there. You knew I struggled with drink, and you knew bourbon was my poison of choice. And a guy like you, I bet you knew about my writing prospects and the death of my wife, too."

"You must believe our meeting earlier at Usher's Fall truly was a happy coincidence. I would have had no way of knowing you were in town or would have been there. But yes, Sir, my every move since then has been... calculated. Such is my nature."

"Alright. I'm going to collect my dog and get the hell out of here." I started to leave, whistling for Otis.

"I was trying to see what sort of man you were. Artists tend to have pretentious, fictive public personas, but your writing always struck me as genuine. I wanted to see if your persona was real: if you really saw the world the way you write about it. And yes, I wanted to test your limits."

"Give me one reason not to walk out the fucking door right now."

"How about the story that will save your career? Please, Sir. I understand your mistrust, but you ought to sit down." I obeyed. He had my attention. "It is time I tell you the real reason I invited you here tonight, Mr. Crowley. I was familiar with your troubles. I followed your manslaughter trial and was relieved to learn of your acquittal in the eyes of the law... and unfortunately *not* in the eyes of your loved ones and neighbors. I assume you have been keeping a low profile since then? Moving from place to place? Living like some sort of hobo, punishing yourself? Looking for healing and inspiration? I never thought I would meet you, of course, but you have been on my mind. And now that you are here in Delilah, I wish to help you."

"You aren't going to fix my bridges with Hollywood or my publisher. And you sure as hell won't bring Jean back or convince Emma to pick up the phone. How can you help me?"

"As I said, I want to give you a story, Mr. Crowley. I believe it is the one you are destined to write: your magnum opus, your rebirth. Picture, if you will, a tragic family saga of isolation, religious fervor, abuse, suspicion, and betrayal on the haunted, stony coasts of the Pacific Northwest. A novel to restore your name and reputation in the eyes of the world. I am prepared to set you up in a quiet house far from prying eyes where you can continue to work on your sobriety, rest and heal from the hard life you have led the last few years, gain perspective on your grief, and catch some peace and quiet. But most importantly, you will be researching and writing the story that will become your greatest triumph. I am prepared to pay you the salary of a live-in attendant, but the only real work you would be doing is writing. Think of it as an extended sabbatical, with me as the patron who will pay you to paint your *Creation of Adam* on the Sistine Chapel ceiling."

"What sort of book are we talking about, here? I don't collaborate, and I don't ghostwrite for others, if that's what this is."

"No, no, nothing like that. You will receive all the credit due to your name and talent. For years now I have had a pet

39

fascination with a strange and terrible event which occurred more than forty years ago in the place where we met."

"Cape Contrition."

"Exactly. That place figures in much of Delilah's folklore, but is little known outside the county line. The most disturbing and infamous legend associated with Cape Contrition is the death of the Usher Family. The Ushers were an isolated, clannish lot with a grim reputation in town as some sort of incestuous, abusive religious cult. They tended the lighthouse out on the Cape until April 8th, 1919, when the family perished in a great fire under mysterious circumstances. The affair was swept under the rug with the easiest explanations at hand. The people of Delilah didn't care to examine the case any closer, and police investigations were not what they are today. I want you to solve the mystery of what happened to them. Really solve it."

"You know I'm not a detective," I sighed, skeptical of this plan already.

"No, but you are a student of history, and a former journalist. I have read your historical fiction. You not only have a head for scholarly research and a keen investigative mind, but you also possess deep empathy and moral conviction. Your characters are complex and written with a compassionate hand. I believe you could write the narrative in a way that does it poetic justice and is honoring toward those it concerns."

"What's in it for you?" I was immediately suspicious. But I had to admit, the prospect sounded better than anything I could have hoped for. I resentfully conceded Mr. Wycliffe spent a significant part of the evening guiding the conversation to make it clear I had no other prospects in life but to accept his offer.

"Besides getting to be part of the comeback of the great Joseph Simon Crowley? To be the patron of his most anticipated novel yet?"

"Besides that." His dissemblance was giving me a headache.

"I have a deep personal interest in the story whose full truth I am hoping you will uncover. To finally have some answers to this enigma will be a significant incentive. And, as the owner of the humble tourist attraction of Usher's Fall, I have some small profit and pride to derive from your next bestseller telling the history in my own backyard."

"You want to bump up the entrance fee on your creepy lighthouse?" I took a long drag off my cigar.

"Oh, come now, Joseph, don't be squeamish. We're talking business, are we not? A pittance like that would be of no concern to me, but have you taken a look around this place? Delilah is dying. The lumber and fishing jobs that sustained it are disappearing. The young are moving away." Rupert flicked off the white chalk of ash from the tip of his cigar and puffed once before speaking again on the exhale.

"I know you are somewhat *allergic* to money, but of course I would grasp at any straw that would put my community back on the map. I am getting older, and my thoughts turn to legacy and posterity. But you must understand I am mainly doing this for your benefit."

I was simultaneously liking this man less and less by the minute, and becoming convinced taking his offer was my best and only play.

"How much do you know about Usher's Fall?" Mr. Wycliffe asked.

"Apparently, Oregon's best kept secret? A curiosity."

"*Curiosity.*" Rupert smiled as he took a long pull from his cigar and exhaled a swirling fog of thick, rolling smoke. The cloud twisted and climbed around his face like he was a fire-breathing dragon, and his dark eyes glinted like Satan's in the haze. "Tell me, Mr. Crowley. Do you believe in ghosts?"

"If I were to believe in ghosts, I would need to believe in the human soul." I flicked off a fat stub of ash from the end of my cigar before stoking it back to life. "I didn't see any human soul on those battlefields. The scientists have spoken. We're just apes with big brains, and when it comes to killing one another, you see it yourself and find out we're only so much blood and meat. So no, I don't believe in ghosts any more than I believe in God or angels or saints. But what I do believe is that the things people do have unforeseen ripples through time. The sins of men haunt their children down through the generations. The Bible at least had that right. And if you go to some places, you can feel that the stones you walk on hold onto the atrocities people committed there. Tainted land. Have you ever been to Dachau or Auschwitz, Mr. Wycliffe? Or any of the old slave plantation houses of the South?"

"No, I haven't."

"Well, you would know what I meant if you had. I believe in ghosts in the sense that I believe in history. The sins of our forefathers don't rest in the past. We're still paying for them today."

"Very good, Sir!" Rupert smiled, amused. "What I have in mind is for you to spend some time plumbing the sins of the past: in a place where you can feel them in the very stones, as you say. For the next year, you are going to be living in Usher's Fall. I want you to research and experience the daily life of a lighthouse keeper. And I want you to write about the last family who tended that light: the Ushers. You will find theirs was a sad and sordid tale worthy of Poe or Hawthorne. Currently, their story is without an ending. I want you to see if you can solve the mystery of what happened to them on the fateful night of April 8th, 1919. If you can uncover the truth of what occurred, I am prepared to pay you an additional bonus of $20,000, in addition to the $2,000 per month stipend totaling $44,000 you will receive for a year living in the keeper's house. I can have my lawyer draw up the contract in its particulars tomorrow. That should be plenty to allow you to live comfortably and accumulate some savings before you have even sold the first copy of the book which is sure to be your salvation."

"That does sound appealing." My funds were miserably depleted. Still, money was not attractive enough to woo me for its own sake. "But if you are going to put up all that money, it is only fair to insist once again that I'm not a detective. Even though I studied history and write historical fiction, I am not a proper historian either. You need to be prepared for the possibility I will not find anything."

"I've already spoken to local historians, and to detectives. But you understand human beings, Mr. Crowley, perhaps more keenly than they. I see an opportunity for you to look upon this with fresh eyes. These are characters. Know and empathize with them, the setting in which they lived. Piece together their story, and tell it as well as you can. You have a keen eye for that. You know how to commit to extensive research, your writing humanizes and fleshes out the complexities of the people who came before us, and most importantly of all... You are familiar with the darkness of man... Are you not?"

"Yes. Alright, let's see if we have a story."

"For many centuries, the headland where the lighthouse was eventually built was considered a foreboding and bewitched place. The Coos, Umpqua, and Siuslaw Indians who lived nearby kept a reverent distance from it, though some chose it as a destination to commit suicide. The Indians did not name the headland, because they did not wish to acknowledge it. It was a place of despair for them. The rocky cliffs of that promontory and the cove it shelters were especially treacherous to sailors, and on a foggy night they would seemingly rear up and attack out of nowhere. White men called it Siren's Head, because sailors reported becoming disoriented and turned around in that region of the coast, drawn in toward the cliffs on dark nights even when they tried to navigate away from them. Even their navigation equipment became confused. We now know a high concentration of iron in the rocks there disorients the needle of a compass, and the rocks were simply in need of illumination.

"A lighthouse was needed to warn ships away from danger there. But the construction of the place was plagued with difficulties even from the beginning. In 1892, a surveyor was swept out to sea. In 1893, a group of quarrymen, stone masons, and carpenters were nearing completion of the tower and cottage, but they all disappeared. A dozen of the sixteen men washed up on the shore. The other four were never seen again. The ocean does not always give back what she takes. It was a disaster. My grandfather, John Franklin Wycliffe, was overseeing the construction. He had to replace the entire crew at three dollars a day more than their unfortunate predecessors. In 1894, Siren's Light was at last completed. Of course, today we know them more infamously as Usher's Fall.

"My Grandfather founded Cascadia Lumber in 1868, and by this time was both the mayor of Delilah and the foremost employer of her men. From the tip of the Headland, the oil lamp of the lighthouse gave off a blaze visible ten miles out at sea. The shipwrecks ceased. But the life of a lighthouse keeper was a solitary one, especially in such a remote place. The house lies three miles from Delilah, the nearest town, but the terrain connecting the headland to the countryside was impassable with steep cliffs and ravines. The road from Delilah to the Headland and the modern Siren Creek Bridge were not built until 1932. Before then, the Headland was only accessible by boat, and the jagged coasts made that a job for an experienced mariner.

"Siren's Light was a self-sustaining farm. The daily life of a family who lived out there revolved around tending the light, cultivating crops for their own table, and raising livestock. But raising enough food to feed one's family was a constant struggle against the rains and winds that beat upon the cliffs from the Pacific. Many storms batter the headland. The farmhouse has undergone constant repairs throughout its history. The only contact the keepers of Siren's Light had with the outside world occurred once a month, when a boat from Delilah would come with essential supplies, news, and conversation. If the people of the lighthouse were in need of anything, that was the time to ask. You can imagine it wasn't an easy life. Few were drawn to it, and few of the would-be keepers could stick out the isolation for long. One after the other, they abandoned their post. But then there was Henry

45

Ahab Usher.

"He was a pioneer from the Eastern States. A religious fundamentalist in the extreme, but what his beliefs were, well... That was a bit muddled and unclear. He was a Southern Baptist in his youth, then spent some time with the Holy Rollers or some other such group of charismatics. He was run out of Salt Lake City in Utah because his views were too vehement and radical for the Mormons. It appears he got himself a wife before he left. When he came to Delilah in 1910, it was with a quiet young woman named Rosemary Annabel Usher. They had a seven year old daughter named Rebecca, a four year old daughter named Anna, and Rosemary was pregnant with her third. Rosemary and her little girls were terrified of Henry, and they kept close to him while saying nothing and making eye contact with no one. He was an Old Testament man. There was no gentle Jesus informing his treatment of anyone. It was unclear what Rosemary and Rebecca thought of the townsfolk, but Henry was none too impressed with them. He attended one service at St. Nicholas Episcopal Church, the town's oldest parish, and swore he would never return. The women of that congregation were a little too free-spirited and open for someone of his sensibilities, and the children too silly. He worked on the docks, but despised the rough folk who worked with him, with their drunkenness, whoring, and vulgarity. They took to calling him 'Preacher,' and not kindly.

"When he heard of the need of a new lighthouse keeper on Siren's Head outside of town, he jumped at the opportunity. And so, in 1910, Henry Usher, his wife, and his little daughters put their belongings on a local boat and moved out to the lighthouse to begin their isolated existence there. On the boat ride, Henry raved about distancing themselves from the ways of the world and preparing their family and their piece of ground for the second coming of Christ. Though it was both out of date and outside his religious upbringing, he dressed himself and his family in simple, homespun black and white clothes, and made them live like the old Puritans.

"Henry Usher attached a holy significance to the way people who went near the promontory often reported experiencing overwhelming feelings of guilt and remorse for the sins of their pasts. He said the power of the Holy Spirit was convicting their hell-bound souls, and renamed the headland Cape Contrition. For the next nine years, the Ushers lived alone on the promontory, isolated from the world and ruled by their increasingly unhinged patriarch.

"Rosemary had her third daughter, Ruth, not long after making the move to the house. Over the course of their time on Cape Contrition, she had three other children: Peter, Elizabeth, and Nathaniel. The children were never allowed into town, studied at home, and knew nothing of the world beyond the Cape. The only ones of them with any memory of life off Cape Contrition were the eldest, Rebecca and Anna; but their memories were the dim, dreamlike flashes of early childhood, most of them fraught with the terror of their father. On those monthly visits from the local sailors, Henry was aloof: disapproving of their loose-living and rough language, and jealous of the way he imagined Rosemary looked at them. He accused her of having affairs with the sailing men, but this was impossible. He needed the supplies the mariners brought, but resented the passing influence they had on his household, and the glimpse of worldliness they showed.

"Over the years, he became more and more antagonistic, and the obligatory trips to check in on the Ushers became less frequent. The family developed a dark reputation around town as an incestuous cult of neo-Puritan lunatics ruled by a wicked and dangerous man. The nine years spent in isolation on Cape Contrition pushed Henry further and further over the edge. He began to tell his family he was the Son of God and they were to tend their Eden for him. Cape Contrition, cut off and isolated from the world, was his own kingdom. His wife and children were his creations, and he was their god, father and husband. He also suffered spells when he claimed he was being possessed by the Devil.

"April 8th, 1919 was when it all ended. The next day, the people of Delilah saw a terrible fire raging on Cape Contrition, and sent a boat out to investigate. The lighthouse burned to the ground, but a blackened lock was found in the ashes where the door had been, giving evidence it had been sealed shut. The fire was determined to be arson when evidence was found that the insides of the tower were doused in the whale oil used to feed the light. Charred bones and ash were all that remained of the Usher children, found in the ruins of the tower. The fire raged so hot for so long, assembling and identifying six complete skeletons would have been impossible to do. All six of the Usher children perished in the lighthouse fire. Rebecca was sixteen years old, Anna thirteen, Ruth nine, Peter seven, Elizabeth five, and Nathaniel two."

"God damn," I muttered.

"They found Henry locked inside the storm cellar of his house, stark-raving mad. He was possessed of incredible strength and feral aggression, as lunatics sometimes are, and it took four men to subdue him. Rosemary's body was never found. Teams searched the Cape for days, but there was no evidence of a recently dug grave or a body in any crevice where one might be hidden. Authorities thought Henry might have eaten her. He never spoke of what happened that night, and it was decided Henry Ahab Usher murdered his entire family in a fit of cabin fever."

"But I'm unclear about one thing," I said. "You're talking about a mystery to be solved, but... It sounds like the police had a strong consensus about what happened that night. The authorities consider the case closed."

"Perhaps they should consider the matter of the locks. That is the piece the police narrative does not account for: the part which has tormented me for years. The lock on the lighthouse door was bolted from the *inside*. They were not trapped in against their will. They had the power to unlock the door and leave, but instead they burned. Why would children do such a thing? And there is the padlock on the cellar door, where Henry was locked inside. It was locked from the *outside*, Mr. Crowley. His fingernails were all gone and the tips of his fingers were bloody stumps. The hatch had claw marks on the inside, and I have seen them myself."

"So you're saying the children were not chased and forced into the tower by someone they feared. They were shepherded in by someone they trusted and gave themselves to the fire willingly: a group suicide. And you're saying Henry, the obvious suspect, understood in the eyes of the law to have murdered his family... Was actually trapped inside his own storm cellar by someone else at the time his family died? Why would Henry have been convicted for murder if the evidence suggests he was incapacitated at the time of the lighthouse fire? That's a strong alibi."

"The direction in which the doors were locked was either not known, or was dismissed as not being enough by itself to exonerate Henry Usher. The good people of Delilah were disturbed by this whole incident, and in no mood to scrutinize it. You must remember violent murder of this kind, if it was a murder, was virtually unheard of then. One involving a cult family, with shocking rumors of incest and cannibalism to sensationalize the story? No one was in a hurry to look too closely at this. It was hard enough for most of Delilah's residents to even admit the fire was not an accident. The details were too ghastly to speak of, and some would rather be mystified by the weirdness of the family's end than have it explained. The only one who knows what happened that night is Henry. If that knowledge still exists in his diseased mind, he has not offered a hint of it to anyone in more than forty years. The locks do not necessarily disprove Henry was responsible for the murder. But they are an incongruous detail which doesn't fit the narrative. Every case has one or two of those. But this one has gnawed at me for some time. It was not enough for the Delilah police in 1919, but perhaps it is enough for a private sleuth to look into today."

"Did anyone consider Rosemary?"

"What? A quiet little woman overpowered her towering bear of a husband, trapped him in a cellar, murdered her own children, and disappeared without a trace, never to be seen again? I dare say no one thought the old girl had it in her at the time. But I suppose it is a theory worth examining."

"What can you tell me about the place since then?"

"It became evident a new lighthouse was needed, but no one wanted to live on Cape Contrition anymore after the Ushers. During the absence of a lighthouse atop the cliff, numerous shipwrecks occurred between 1919 and 1931. In an effort to prevent further tragedies, Usher's Fall Lighthouse was built on the site of the original at Cape Contrition. It was raised in 1931, and fixed with automated electric lights. The need for a live-in keeper disappeared, and the new beam could shine twenty miles out at sea. In 1932, the Siren Creek Bridge was built and Cape Contrition was opened to anyone curious enough to come visit in an automobile. Usher's Fall, as it was known by that time, was renovated with new furniture, indoor plumbing, modern appliances, and electric lights. Most of the personal effects of the Ushers were preserved. Since John Franklin Wycliffe was the original builder of the house and owned the land, my father saw fit to preserve Usher's Fall as a tourist attraction and historical landmark. Actually, he opened the old house as a boarding house when the work finished in '33.

"It became a destination for honeymooners and couples on their anniversaries. But guests reported strange things. Items rearranged in another room while they were gone, without it being clear who moved them. Sometimes food would spoil the day it was bought even though the refrigerator was working. Sometimes people heard children or farm animals about the grounds when there was no explanation, or thought they saw glimpses of people dressed in outdated clothes. The footpath through the woods was without forks, only half a mile from the parking lot to the lighthouse. But people would get turned around and get lost in the woods for hours. Others reported chills, sudden onsets of overwhelming depression, or the sensation of being watched."

"You mean people felt chilly and depressed at the Oregon Coast?" I gave a sarcastic smile. "Come on. These are the kinds of things you hear all the time. People hear about an old house marred by terrible murders. The owners of the boarding house play up the legend to attract curiosity. Visitors who already believe in the paranormal go in expecting to see something to confirm those beliefs. They get jumpy, interpret innocuous, mundane things as hostile; tourists on the grounds they can't see making noise, misplacing items. Kids get high and can't find their way out of the woods. The part about the people in period clothes is interesting, but with superstition doing so much of the work for them, a few pranksters could have a hell of a time with this place. People have been getting conned out of their money by promises of spiritual activity since the dawn of civilization. We are skilled at fooling ourselves into seeing what we want to see, Mr. Wycliffe. Is Usher's Fall still a boarding house?"

"No. We were forced to close in '49."

"What happened?"

"An elderly couple, Tom and Mabel Waters, hanged themselves from the rafters of the master bedroom on their fiftieth wedding anniversary. They were, by all accounts, happy and wholesome folk; still deeply in love. Their families maintained for years they were actually murdered and never would have killed themselves, but this was politely ignored as the denial of the bereaved. That was the first time anyone killed themselves in the house, but you should know between 1932 and 1960, twenty-six people have leapt from atop the cliff at Cape Contrition." I could not believe what I was hearing.

"What could cause so many people to do something like that in this place?"

"Why do so many people kill themselves at the Prince

Edward Viaduct? Aokigahara Forest at the base of Mt. Fuji? The Golden Gate Bridge? There are places all over the world that become magnets for unsettling numbers of suicides. It is hard to puzzle out exactly why. But when you hear how many people have committed suicide at Cape Contrition, were overwhelmed with depression, or driven into crippling mental illness from being out there too long... You see why I was testing how tight a leash you have on your demons. If you are going to take on the task of living at Usher's Fall and writing the story of the Usher family, I need to be sure you are not at risk for suicide."

I considered that for some time. The history of this place was magnetic to me. And I could feel in my bones Wycliffe was offering me a story to change all my prospects. Besides, what options did I have? My home was gone. Jean was gone. My professional relationships and publishing contacts were gone. I had no friends anymore. The last thing my daughter said to me was the wrong parent died in the fire, and she was right. The media in North Carolina portrayed me as a drunk, reckless bastard who caused the death of his own wife, and they were right too. After living like a fugitive for the past two months, a chance to lay low, work on my sobriety, and write in peace didn't sound like the worst course of action. I was a tough, intelligent, contrary son of a bitch, and I didn't believe in ghosts.

"I'm your guy." I mustered a winning smile and extended my hand to shake with Mr. Wycliffe. "Let's get to work."

Chapter Three: Elephant Dream

October 9th, 1962

I had been here before. It was France during the War, in the Orleans Forest. I awoke on the cold ground in the pre-dawn twilight. My back was stiff and I shivered in my jacket, breath fogging in the still air. Several of my men were asleep around me, with few blankets or sleeping bags to go around in the dead of winter. Sergeant Norris was on sentry duty, and glanced over when he heard me stir. I rubbed the numbness out of my dirty hands and struggled with frigid fingers to light a cigarette. The dense trees crowded around us, and a thick fog rolled low over the forest floor. Spotting any Krauts in this mist would have been damn near impossible, but we scouted out the area. We were well-concealed, confident Adolf's boys were holed up far enough away to give us a few hours of sleep.

Some twigs snapped in the trees, and Norris bolted to attention with his M1 Garand. I stubbed out my cigarette so the light wouldn't give us away and raised my rifle as well, trying to pierce the fog. We saw a large silhouette loom in the shadows, indistinct and improbable. Norris and I rousted the others from sleep. In seconds, a dozen rifles trained on the heaving bulk in the mist. Branches snapped as it moved.

"Is it a tank, Cap?" Private Perry asked, a little too loudly. He was a nineteen-year-old good-ol'-boy from eastern Kentucky, and he would be dead in a week.

"Hush up, Pear," I muttered. "We see them, but they don't see us. But no, I don't think so. It's big, but... No sound of treads. And even though it's shaking trees and snapping branches, it's moving among and between them. Panzer couldn't do that."

"It's alone, too. Even in a thick-fuck haze like this, you can tell," muttered Private Crabtree.

"Wait for my signal," I murmured. Perry's startled rifle cracked alone in the stillness and I cursed under my breath when I heard the last sound I could have expected: the lonesome, pained trumpet of an elephant.

"The fuck was that?" Horse asked, and the behemoth leered out of the mist, shouldering between two trees and staggering into our small clearing with a pained grunt. Her trumpet came strangled and pitiful.

"Not the first time you got excited and shot too quick, eh kid?" Crabtree chuckled at Perry, somehow jaded enough to be unsurprised by the sudden appearance of an elephant in a French forest. I ignored the remark and stepped closer, and my heart sank when I saw the blood ooze thick and flow free. The elephant had stepped on a landmine and lost her right forefoot. She cradled the stump of her leg to herself, and I got close enough to see bewildered, frightened tears running down the deep cracks of her wrinkled face. Her bumpy head hung low with exhaustion, and her flappy ears lay back against her neck. She was covered in white dust, and had been walking for a long time. My eyes burned with gloss as the Asiatic elephant cow let out a plaintive trumpet, crying

55

out for her family a world away, as alone and out of place in the French countryside as I was. I still wonder where she came to us from, what jungle she was born in, and if any of her family are still out there.

"There ain't elephants in France, right, Cap?" Perry asked.

"No, dumb-ass," Crabtree piped up.

"Can it, Crabtree. Lay off the kid." I turned on him with a glare. "My guess is it escaped from some zoo or circus that got bombed in this godless fucking war. But it has to have come a long way. Horse, Norris, help me." I saw her totter and threaten to collapse. She was too big to steady: we had to give her room to fall. I cradled her massive gray head in my arms and comforted her as our sleepy medic reluctantly did what he could. She assented to the medic's care, but had marched a long time and lost a great deal of blood along the way. Perry managed to hit his target for once because there was a bullet wound in her side.

I looked into her frightened, intelligent eyes, petted her rough hide, and talked to her until we watched the sunrise together. My uniform was stained with her blood. When she died, I was inconsolable. I buried my face in her wrinkled neck and wept. Crabtree had joked I wanted to bring a three ton pet home across war-torn France, but when she died, for once, he couldn't say a word.

But in my dream, the elephant lifted her trunk and beckoned to me before turning her massive head and wandering back into the still forest. I followed her alone into the dense foliage. She limped, and the stump dribbled blood on leaves, mushrooms, and soil. I walked at her side with my palm resting on her immense shoulder. As we moved, a song was playing all around us. The lyrics sent a cold shiver up my spine.

It was Hymne à l'amour by the great French singer Edith Piaf, in English titled "If You Love Me (Really Love Me)." It was my wife's favorite song: a piece I had not been able to listen to since her death. But the words sounded so clear now. They pounded in my ears like an accusation.

As we walked, the Forest of Orleans was changing little by little. The trees transformed from the beeches, oaks, and elms of the Loire Valley to the pines, flowering dogwoods, sugar maples, and sweetgum trees of North Carolina. Spanish moss hung lank from the branches. A creek babbled nearby. I smelled smoke in the air. The elephant led me into a clearing of the forest, and I saw a large Tudor-style house in Chapel Hill, North Carolina. It was burning in the midst of a sea of dirty, discarded glass bottles. The hellish inferno belched a column of black smoke into the air, and I became numbly aware I heard my wife's screaming inside. The elephant held something out to me, wrapped in its serpentine trunk. It was a bottle of bourbon.

I woke with a jolt, surprised to find myself on a comfortable leather couch in Rupert Wycliffe's library. A plaid quilt covered me, and Otis was curled up asleep next to my head. The warmth of him, his porcine snores, the rise and fall of his woolly chest, my responsibility and love for him, brought me back to myself by degrees. There on my finger was the worn, plain gold band of my wedding ring. Sometimes I forgot I was still wearing it, but I could not bring myself to take it off. I was still her husband.

Otis followed as I walked barefoot through the halls of Wycliffe's mansion, searching its unfamiliar corridors for the smoking room. My mouth tasted stale and acrid from the previous evening's cigar. I was ashamed to admit it to myself, but I was hunting that priceless bottle of liquor. The nightmare rattled me, as did the disturbing account of Cape Contrition whose details swam in my groggy mind. My self-control was not as strong that morning. I would have given anything for the comfort and calm one taste of that pre-Prohibition bourbon would bring. As I turned a corner, my futile search ended when I found myself face to face with Wycliffe, already dressed. He smiled with surprise to see me awake this early.

"Good morning, Mr. Crowley!" he beamed, "Looking for the bathroom?"

"Yeah, sure."

"Down the hall there, third door to the left. I had Hayato lay out some toiletries for your convenience. We thought you might like to freshen up a bit before we embark for the Cape."

I nodded, taking the hint. It was a few days since I had taken a proper shower. The bathroom was pristine, polished white tile and porcelain. As I took off my shirt, my eyes lingered on the name "Jean", tattooed in cursive script over my heart with a thorny rose, still vibrant in its red petals and green leaves. Other old army tattoos included an eagle, a galloping horse, and a pin-up girl. I ran my fingers through the coarse bristles of my thick beard, and after a moment's hesitation, dove into the work of shaving it all off.

After cleaning up the tumbleweed of discarded hairs, I looked myself over to make sure I hadn't missed a spot. I hadn't seen the squared angle of my chin or my gaunt cheeks in a long time. A splash of aftershave burned and reminded me why I was an infrequent shaver. After brushing my teeth clean and taking a long, hot shower, I changed my underwear, pulled on my jeans and worn leather wingtip shoes, buttoned a red-checkered flannel shirt, and a gray wool aran cardigan. I sprayed on some expensive cologne I found on the counter, which smelled of sandalwood and leather. Taking a long look at the expensive bottle and breathing in the aroma, I glanced shiftily about and pocketed it for myself.

After a sumptuous breakfast of salmon eggs benedict and roasted russet potatoes laid out by Hayato, Wycliffe and I piled into our cars and drove in caravan out to Cape Contrition. We made the hike along the steep switchback trail leading out to the top of the cliffs at the end of the Cape. The heavy clouds of the morning broke as we quitted the trail, and it was in the light of the glorious morning sun that I got my first glimpse of the house which was to be my home for the next year. It was a white, gray-shingled, two-story farmhouse with a wraparound porch on two sides complete with a hanging swing. Not far from the old house stood a collapsed, forsaken barn, at the edge of the forest and already being reclaimed by it. Near the edge of the cliff stood the towering white lighthouse: pale and desolate. The homestead stood on a clearing of verdant lawns, and low iron railings screened the abrupt edge of the cliff. At several places, benches were set up to afford tourists a comfortable view. Bronze plaques inscribed them in memory with the names of the people who had thrown themselves from atop the cliff.

While I walked through the grounds of Usher's Fall, Rupert clutched a stitch in his side and winced, winded from the hike. The frail, bookish man wiped the sweat from his brow and mounted the steps of the long porch, fumbling with a jangling ring of keys. A thick, heavy door of planks with no knob stood stolidly shut, painted white and blending in with the house's façade. It swung open to reveal a smaller, more traditional front door behind it, with an elegantly carved surface and delicate panes of glass. This first barrier was a rustic storm door in the event of a tempest. That was when I noticed the thick defensive qualities inherent in the open wooden shutters. Once inside, a person could close mighty boards over every vulnerable window, blocking out every prying eye. As I stood on the lawn and marveled at the historic cottage, Wycliffe turned his key in the old lock and swung the front door open. Otis whined and strained forward, eager to investigate. As I followed him inside, Rupert tossed me a small ring of three keys.

"That one is for the farmhouse, the other for the lighthouse, and the last one for the storm cellar. They're yours for as long as you stay here. As you can see, the place comes furnished, so you won't have to worry about lugging a couch or a bed up that trail. Sorry, but the visitor lot at the bottom of the hill is as close as you'll be able to get a car. Do you have anything else to move in besides what you brought with you in your automobile?"

"No," I said, walking through the low-ceilinged, cramped rooms of the cottage. Usher's Fall was harshly utilitarian in its room size, as if built for ancestors smaller in stature than their modern descendants. Though claustrophobic, the rooms were charming. Rupert flicked the light switches in each room on and off as he entered, testing them, along with the faucets in the sinks and bathroom. The electricity, bathroom, and running water were a modern renovation. At the time the Ushers inhabited it, they kept a privy out back and made do with kerosene lamps. The furniture was pleasant, with beds, couches, and chairs dating back to the '30s or '40s.

Some articles of wooden furniture looked as if they dated back to the 1910s or the turn of the century, used by the Ushers themselves. Perhaps handmade by Henry. There were several shelves in strange nooks of the house lined with crumbling old books and other oddments of decoration. A glass fishing float, a small cast-iron anchor, seashells and sand dollars; a stuffed pufferfish.

Rupert showed me the fireplace and a wood-burning stove for the winter, murmuring there was a stack of firewood covered up in the barn if I should need it.

"The house has old fuses, so the lights tend to flicker, and the hot water can come in stops and starts. The house is not equipped with a telephone or radio."

"Good, I don't want them."

"Are you sure? You're three miles from Delilah, and it can get lonely out here."

"I'm sure. The peace and quiet is nice. Besides, no one would have any calls for me."

"Very well, Mr. Crowley. I will leave my telephone number in case you wish to call me from town, and do-"

I was faintly listening, but my attention leapt to the appliances and rustic wares of the kitchen. I was already looking forward to plying my hand at cooking some of my native Southern soul food. On my second entrance to the sitting room, I spotted a gramophone from the roaring '20s, and an acoustic guitar sitting in the corner. I hadn't played one in months. In my roving journey across America, I had picked up a few vinyl records, and was glad to see I would have such a specimen to play them on. Otis sniffed about and patrolled the rooms before trampling a little nest and curling into a ball on the sofa as if glad to be back in his own familiar home.

"We'll take it," I smiled as I shook Rupert's hand. My new artistic patron flashed a grin of horsey teeth beneath the thick whiskers of his mustache.

"Sold!" He said jovially. "Well, I shan't keep you long, for I am sure you are eager to explore. Here is my business card with my address and telephone number if you need to get ahold of me. Do think about having a telephone installed, Mr. Crowley. I would sleep much better at night knowing you could get someone on the line if you found you needed help. I suppose the last thing will be for me to give you this." Rupert handed me a crisp check. "I thought it would be good to give your first month's wages in advance to help you settle in with whatever you might need." The aging millionaire gave me a firm handshake, affirmed once again it was an honor to be my artistic patron, and quietly slipped out at last.

I had few possessions left in the world. Two suitcases full of clothes accumulated over two months of travel, a small bag of toiletries, a couple pairs of shoes, a box of records, a few books, a heavy Smith Corona typewriter circa 1946, a Louisville Slugger and heavy flashlight I kept in my Land Rover, a kennel, and a few items for my dog. All this I brought up in four trips from my car at the bottom of the half-mile long forest trail. As I heaved the last box onto the porch, I collapsed on the step and felt my heaving chest with a muttered curse.

Gripping the worn railing of the porch steps, I hauled myself up and went into the house. Peeling off my stifling clothes, I went to the bathroom and drew a shower. The hot water was finicky, but I was too exhausted and overheated to mind the occasional stops and starts of cold.

I gulped down two tall glasses of cold well water and took a moment to bask in the nearly forgotten comforts of running water, electricity, and a place that was mine. After setting up Otis' kennel in the mudroom, I coaxed him into it. The young mutt sighed and looked up at me with pleading dog-pound-eyes, and I reassured him I wouldn't be long before locking the front door of Usher's Fall and turning to make the hike to my car. As I stepped out on the porch, I was surprised to see a woman standing out near the edge of the cliff with her back to me. She wore a modest black dress that blew in the wind along with the curls of her black hair as she gazed out at the ocean. Somewhere near the barn, I heard a child's squeal of laughter. I shrugged and started off down the wooded trail, remembering Wycliffe's reminder that my new home was an occasional destination for sight-seeing tourists. By the time I got to the bottom of the trail, I had forgotten all about them.

Rain drizzled as I drove into Delilah. After setting up an account with the local bank and cashing my first Wycliffe check, I swung by a modest grocery store to stock up on food. Having formerly loved to cook with beer and wine, I lingered over a bottle of cabernet sauvignon to pair with the steak and ground beef I was purchasing, but decided it was too risky for someone of my tenuous sobriety and set it back.

As I was driving through town, I noticed a weathered sign for Lost Cove Books, and remembered Gwen from the diner. I stopped my Land Rover at the curb by the door and decided I could use a couple new books to while away the hours at Usher's Fall. A soft bell tinkled as I opened the door into the little book store. The place was warm and cozy, painted with soft blues. Bookshelves loaded with dog-eared, used paperbacks with faded spines loomed on all sides. A small staircase led to an upstairs reading loft with a coffee maker. I breathed in the comforting odor of old books and listened to the soothing sounds of folk music on vinyl. Gwen came out of a back room and dropped the book she was reading with surprise when she saw me there.

"Joe! Hey, welcome! I didn't expect to see you again."

"Yeah, I guess I'm living here now," I smiled as she stooped to pick up *Coal Train Coming* and adjusted her glasses.

"Well, that's a bit forward, Joe. You might have to ask my father's blessing," she crinkled her nose mischievously.

"Ha, I didn't mean, uh, that is," I stammered, trying to find my words. "It's a weird circumstance. You know that lighthouse you were telling me about? Well, I met the owner, and he's a fan. Of me, I mean."

"You met Rupert Wycliffe? What's he like?" Gwen took a seat behind the counter by the cash register.

"Uh, kind of like the love-child of Jay Gatsby and Vincent Price. But Wycliffe hired me to write a book for him. A novel about the last family who lived there. I'm setting up at Usher's Fall, at least for the winter; maybe longer."

"Well, well. Joe Crowley comes out of retirement right here in my own town." Her tone mustered up the appearance of happiness, but there was an unmistakable crack in her smile.

"You're disappointed. What's up?"

"No, it's nothing like that. It's just, well, how much have you heard about that place? It gives me the willies."

"Wycliffe told me the whole story, as much as anybody knows. I'm there trying to find out the rest. I know there's an ugly history, but it's just a lonely old house, without any close neighbors. Actually, it's pretty peaceful out there. I'll be fine. In fact, it'll be nice to write and not worry about anyone else for a while. I don't mind being alone."

"Oh, right." Gwen's countenance fell a little more.

"But, I don't mean- Uh... You should come up there some-time. I don't like to brag, but I'm a pretty good cook. And we could put on some records."

"A sock-hop at Usher's Fall could be groovy. I didn't mean to be a wet blanket, it's just... Well, that place can mess with your head. People get lonely out there. Don't be a stranger, okay? You can come here any time."

"I think I will... Well, in the meantime, I'll fight off the Oregon Coast Blues with some good literature."

"Yeah, knock yourself out." I browsed a while, taking my time edging between the close shelves and ducking the low ceilings in the back as I scanned the cracked spines. I ended up picking Tolkien's *Lord of the Rings* Trilogy, *The Sea Wolf* by Jack London, *For Whom the Bell Tolls* by Ernest Hemingway, and *The Razor's Edge* by W. Somerset Maugham.

"I'll call you," I said as I took my paper sack full of books. I was to my car when I realized I had neither a phone or her number.

The rain picked up as I parked in the empty visitor lot on Cape Contrition, and I hurried to the shelter of the trees laden with five heavy paper bags threatening to disintegrate into pulp. When I neared the top, I heard sharp, pitiful cries from the house. It could only be Otis. I ran with my heavy-laden bags, setting them down on the porch before trying the door. The wire-haired, shaggy pit bull mutt was trembling and whining in his kennel, and had made himself as small as possible to shrink away from its walls. I opened the door and soothed the dog. When I brought my hand back, it was streaked with blood. Otis had given himself a cut on his creased, heavy forehead, now inflamed and bruising. It looked like he had been banging his head against the bars of his kennel. His bedding was torn to shreds of cloudy cotton.

"What's wrong, buddy?" I whispered, rubbing Otis behind his ears. Otis crept out of the cage, head bowed and whining. He was usually calm in the kennel and had never injured himself before, but I chalked it up to nerves his first time alone in a new house. I hugged the mutt close and murmured in his ear that everything was going to be okay as I clipped on his leash and led him outside.

The sun was setting over the Pacific. I walked the sulking, anxious dog about the grounds, giving him the chance to do his business and explore. Otis was a dog who needed much reassurance and affection. He could become anxious when separated from me, but he never displayed this acute level of anxiety before.

When we got back into the house, I tended the dog's wound. As I worked, his soft whine turned to a low, threatening growl, rumbling in his barrel chest. He pulled his head back and bared his teeth at me.

"Hey. Stop it. You put those away." I looked Otis in the eye and bared teeth as he put his away. "This is for your own good, Beast." Otis submitted to my hand as I finished disinfecting the cut, bandaged, and wrapped it. When it was finished, I kissed him on the cheek and remembered the groceries set on the porch. When I came back out, several of the bags were ripped, and food was strewn about on the boards of the porch. None of it appeared to have been taken, at least.

"Goddamn raccoons." After cleaning it up and stocking the cupboards and refrigerator, I walked over to the old gramophone. For a moment, I touched the Edith Piaf record with the song on it: Jean's song. Jean's record burned with her in the fire, but I found this one at a flea market in Omaha. I still could not bring myself to listen to it, but I kept it safe and secret, like the idol of a family god. After flipping through the small collection, I put on a Billie Holiday record, poured dry kibble into a bowl for Otis, and set to work in the kitchen.

While Billie sang, I set to work in the kitchen steeping a pitcher of sweet tea and getting dinner ready. Soon, the old house was alive with the sizzle of oil, the smells of frying chicken, roasted vegetables, and rising biscuits. It was a tradition of mine and Jean's for me to cook fried chicken our first night in a new home. When we moved into our first apartment, I started a small fire that scared the living daylights out of us and set our daughter wailing. Jean teased me about it for years. The memory of that kitchen grease-fire was less funny now.

By the time I picked my plate clean, it was dark outside. The rain was still falling, pelting a soothing rhythm on the roof. I turned on the porch light, took the old guitar from the living room, and brought it out there to sit with me in a wicker and wood rocking chair. My hands ran with tender familiarity over the hollow body, frets, and tuning pegs as I sounded each out-of-tune string and adjusted it in turn. With a quarter from my pocket as a pick, I strummed and plucked. After sounding out experimental notes into the night, I soon hit my stride. My hands plucked out a melody. I had not sung since Jean died, but soon my old voice was finding its way back to me in its raspy baritone.

I played for the better part of an hour as the rain pelted on the porch's shingled roof. Otis pushed the door open with his bandaged head and curled at my feet, seeming more like his old self. I played until my fingertips threatened to crack open on the strings and longed for my old calluses as I played through a whirlwind of old songs I knew by heart. When I was about to call it a night and take the guitar back inside, I heard a twig snap out in the tree line, about fifty yards from the front porch and beyond range of the light. Otis jolted to attention and rumbled with a low, terrible growl. The wiry hair of his back bristled as he lowered his head with a bared snarl and assumed a threatening posture with his heavy shoulders thrown forward. I set the guitar down and peered out into the rainy darkness, trying to listen. Otis let out two threatening barks. I had learned the gut reactions of dogs were rarely wrong.

"Hello?" I called out, trying to see into the night. I was met with silence, and out beyond the range of the porch light was only blackness. Somewhere among those vague shapes, I thought I saw movement. Another branch rustled. I moved slowly, whistled low for Otis to slip into the house, and followed him back inside, locking the door behind us. I hurried into the bedroom for my baseball bat and picked up my heavy flashlight in the mudroom before stepping back out onto the porch. My bare feet were cold and wet on the grass as I walked out onto the lawn and directed the powerful beam into the edge of the forest. Otis was snarling and barking behind me as I panned the light over the trees. I almost dropped it when I caught a glimpse of someone in the woods. I sucked in a deep breath and rallied myself as I settled the beam of light on the distant figure. Standing between two fir trees was a large man in a black pea coat, with a sandy beard and a wool newsboy hat dripping with rain. In his hands was a long, archaic Winchester lever-action rifle. The man stood still at the edge of the tree line staring at me and the house.

He did not move to avoid the beam of light, and he did not speak. He just stared out from the woods, his face a twisted mask of abject hatred and contempt.

"What is it? What do you want?"

I had seen that look in the man's livid eyes before, in other men on the other side of the world. The unforgettable red glint of murder. I didn't know who the man in the woods was, or why he was standing in the dark staring at my house with such vicious hatred. But I knew how to deal with people like that. I wasn't all guitar strings and books, after all. Knowing I couldn't fold, I stepped forward with the bat in my hand, keenly aware of how alone I was out here, if anyone meant me harm.

"Hey! Do you hear me? I'm talking to you. What the fuck are you doing out here?"

The man was silent. He panted and bared his teeth in a leering snarl.

"Clear out. Go home. Concert's over. What, no comprende? I have a gun in the house." This was not true. I hadn't fired or owned a gun since the '50s and had developed a distaste for them. "Want me to go get it?" Still silence. I kept my voice even and my tone stayed aggressive, but it masked fear. It was like the man was staring through me and didn't even notice I was there.

"You trying to scare me? If you pick a fight here, you should know I killed more than forty men in the war. Want to try your luck? Step into the light, you fucking coward!"

A gust of wind picked up, and the breeze slammed the front door of the house shut as loud as a shotgun blast. I turned, startled, and saw Otis take off at a run from the porch, galloping valiantly toward the woods. Though he'd been terrified out of his mind earlier, he resolved to be brave for my sake. With frantic speed, I turned my heavy flashlight back where the man had been standing, but there was nobody there.

"You do not get to keep this house! You do not get to keep this family! Not after what you've done to her!" the voice called from the trees. "You know who's come for you. Come into the trees and face me like a man!" I ran forward with the bat in hand, panning my shaky light stream over the trees, but caught no trace of anyone fleeing. Otis snarled and paced back and forth at the edge of the forest. The dog let out several low, grumbling woofs under his breath, as if he were muttering to himself.

"That's enough, boy." I breathed heavily as I passed my light among the trees with trepidation. "He's gone. I think he got your message. Good job." Otis warily loped back in the direction of the house, where the door stood shut. In case the man in the woods had an accomplice who entered Usher's Fall while my back was turned, I kept the bat close. The wind and rainfall increased as I opened the front door and let Otis inside. The dog patrolled from room to room with me in search for intruders, but there was no one there. It was late, but the unwelcome sighting had me wide awake.

After checking the dark corners of the unfamiliar house with my flashlight and confirming I was alone with Otis, I closed the heavy storm shutters over the doors and windows. I let out a long, tense breath. I had scared off whoever was watching the house from the forest, but now I feared going to bed. The bizarre threat he shouted from the trees repeated itself in my mind. Something about me not deserving to live in this house, not deserving to have my family, after what I did to 'her.'

I replayed a thousand handshakes and greetings in my mind, trying to remember the face of everyone I had ever met. His face was unknown to me. And if he knew me, or knew Jean, how could I not recognize him? And how could he possibly know I was here, when no one but Wycliffe and Gwen knew I was in residence? My only conclusion at the time was that I must have a stalker, maybe some crazed fan of my work, or a nutcase who fell in love with Jean's picture in the paper and had taken it upon himself to avenge her.

I thought about the man's challenge to follow him into the woods, ashamed I was too scared to do so. *Don't be ridiculous. You stood your ground on the lawn with a baseball bat against a man with a gun. Of course, you didn't follow him into the woods to be shot in the dark.* But another thought intruded on my reason, calling me coward and telling me I deserved to be shot in the woods for who I was, what I'd done to the woman I'd loved and the life we had built. I couldn't think of any clever counterpoint to that.

I lit a cigarette with a trembling hand, breathed deep of the acrid smoke, took a seat at the kitchen table before my Smith Corona and loaded a blank sheet of paper into the machine. God, I needed a drink. My life had been threatened by a gunman who may still be out there, and all I wanted to do to calm down was get blind drunk. Stupid. I deserved to die. I cursed my weak-willed longing for booze in times of stress, the old soldier in me saying if I were to drop my guard now and get loaded, I deserved every bullet. I quieted the arguing voices of a veteran lost in waking nightmares of the last time he'd had guns waved at him, a feckless drunk who wanted to drown his anxiety and damn the consequences, a coward who was afraid to go outside, a raging beast who wanted to charge out and kill that man for daring to threaten him, and a lost, broken man who pleaded to let himself be killed. Several long drags off the cigarette clouded me in a swirling smog before I flicked the ash into a tray and wrote the first words of my manuscript. The title had already come to me. *Between the Devil and the Deep Blue Sea.*

Chapter Four: First Clues

October 11th, 1962

Even though it took until close to three in the morning to fall asleep, Otis woke me before dawn for a walk. After a sleepy shuffle around the grounds by the illumination of my flashlight, we crawled back into bed and slept until close to ten in the morning. I was spared the vision of the elephant, but dreamt of Jean. I could still hear the anger and disappointment in her voice as she held up an empty bottle of vodka in front of my face. "You're drinking again. I found the others, too, in the woods out back. Did you think I wouldn't find out? Jesus, Joe. This has to stop." When I awoke, I closed my eyes and ran a finger over my wedding ring. My silent apology was choked and fervent, but too small and too late. *I'm trying to get better, Jeanie. Wherever you are, I hope you see that.* I didn't *believe* she could see anything where she was now, but it made me feel better to think of it. Even if part of me criticized that as childish. For someone who didn't believe in spirits, I talked to her a lot.

As I rolled in bed and glanced up at the low ceiling, I realized the stout support beam over my head must have been where the elderly Waters couple hanged themselves on their wedding anniversary in 1949. Shaking the visual out of my eyes, I got up, put on some red running shorts and a Duke University T-shirt, and grabbed Otis' leash. I locked the house tight behind me, and the two of us went out for a run in the gray half-light of morning. The sky was threatening rain. We ran for close to an hour down the switchback dirt trail through the forest, over the blacktop of the visitor parking lot, along the hard-packed, wet sand of the beach where the surf rolled in and the gulls fought for overturned crabs. My chest heaved. The muscles of my calves and thighs burned like they were pumping with acid as I rested on a spongey rock at the end of the cove. When we turned back, the first raindrops were beginning to fall.

The public library of Delilah was a squat two-level building of red brick with a totem pole out front. A small atrium with musty armchairs and a reception desk opened up into a single room, walls lined with wooden bookshelves. There were chairs and tables attempting to answer the space, all unoccupied. A narrow stair led to a close, stifling attic level. The whole library was hot and musty, as if they calibrated the thermostat to drive away loiterers. But the creatures who tended the books seemed immune to the humid suffocation in the air. A lanky Japanese-American girl sat at the front desk, a pink headband keeping her thick, silky black hair out of her brown eyes as she flipped through a *Spider-Man* comic.

"Let me know if you have any questions," she mumbled, not looking up. Otis sauntered in behind me, unnoticed by the girl. I no longer felt comfortable leaving him alone in the house.

"Do you work here?" She glanced up, rolled her eyes, and

gestured that she was, in fact, sitting behind the front desk.

"Okay, I see you're sitting there, but I mean, are you a paid receptionist? You're just a kid."

"I'm fourteen. I help out here and get paid in books, as patronizing as that is of Mr. Mast. Maybe I should negotiate a raise soon. Are you with the Department of Labor?" she asked.

"No, smart-ass. And it's 11:00 in the morning. Shouldn't you be in school?"

"Are you with the schoolboard?"

"Thanks for all your help," I smirked, rapping knuckles on the reception desk before strolling into the library.

"Mister, you can't bring that dog in here."

"I'm blind. He's my seeing-eye dog."

"No, you're not." But she gave up and returned to her reading. I saw a middle-aged man with stringy, thin hair and a paunchy belly on a ladder, returning books from a creaky cart back to their places on the shelves.

"Hey, are you the librarian?"

"Lower your voice. This is an environment of study," he said without looking at me, continuing to push books back into the gaps on the shelves.

"Sorry," I whispered, even though no one else was in the library.

"Dogs aren't allowed. It's against the rules." The librarian glanced at Otis with distaste.

"He's a therapy dog." The librarian didn't seem to be able to tell if I needed a therapy dog and dropped it. "Hey, listen, you've got to do something about that kid. She's rude for a receptionist. Like Genghis Khan."

"Your line of personal questioning was boorish and impertinent. Not to mention unseemly, when directed at a child by a stranger. This is a library, Sir, not *the Tonight Show with Johnny Carson*. No interviews." He spoke without turning aside from his work to make eye contact.

"Fair enough. I don't know if you've heard of me, I'm Joe Crowley."

"Crowley, Joseph Simon. Born August 8th, 1915 in Raleigh, North Carolina. Age 47. American novelist, former journalist, and World War II veteran. Graduate of Duke University. Notable works: *American Quixote*, 1946, *Coal Train Coming*, 1948, *Appalachian Queen*, 1950, *Look At All the Flowers*, 1954..."

"Okay, so you *have* heard of me," I interrupted. The encyclopedic, detached recitation of the highlights of my life wigged me out.

"Don't mind Mr. Mast. He's not like other people," the little girl explained. She set down her comic book and walked into the main room.

"What was that about?"

"It's not like he's obsessed with you or anything. He can do that for any author who has books in our library. Watch this. Hey, Herman. Ernest Hemingway."

"Hemingway, Ernest Miller. Born July 21st, 1899 in Oak Park, Illinois, died July 2nd, 1961 at age 61. American novelist, short story writer, journalist, and World War I veteran. Notable works: *The Sun Also Rises*, 1926, *A Farewell to Arms*, 1929, *For Whom the Bell Tolls*, 1940, *The Old Man and the Sea*, 1951."

"That's some trick."

"It's not a trick. He just has some funny ways about him. I'm Hana Iwamoto, by the way. Are you really some famous author?"

"Was. Just moved into town the other day. I'm researching a tragedy from about forty years ago. The deaths of the Ushers. You know that one?"

"Everyone in town knows that one."

"Do you have any old newspapers or records here I could examine?"

"*Grisly Slaying of Usher Family Shocks Community*, Silas Egerton, *Delilah Caller*, April 11th, 1919. *Death on Cape Contrition*, Edgar Scott, *the Oregonian*, April 13th, 1919." Herman Mast continued to rattle off newspaper headlines, but Hana took me by the arm and led me up the stairs, murmuring he would be at it for a while. Hana Iwamoto led me into a close, dingy attic level. She told me to wait while she opened drawers and flipped through organizational index cards. The kid searched through filing cabinets and flipped back into the old newspapers and local records, fluently navigating the library's organizational system. In a few minutes, she walked up to me lugging a heavy box of material.

"These are the local primary sources we have on the Usher Family slaying. Or at least everything I could find in a pinch. I could do some more digging later. You carry this. I'm just a kid, remember?" I accepted the cardboard box as she ushered me impatiently down the stairs. Soon, I was sitting on an old couch thumbing through yellowed, fading newspaper clippings and other tattered papers.

I looked through the collected materials for hours, reading each newspaper article about the Ushers. I was struck in my initial research by how cruel, vapid, and prattling the people of Delilah were. In the official reports by the media and the dialogue of the townsfolk, the burning of the Ushers was not the heartbreaking, tragic death of six children and their mother after years of extreme social isolation and unimaginable abuse. It was another picture at the theater, a sordid dime-novel. Something to gossip and speculate about, bored housewives making up bogus insider information they had supposedly learned from a close source; drunk men giving their hot takes at the tavern for anyone who would listen. The Ushers weren't people to them. They were pariahs, bogeymen out beyond the edge of town for grandmothers to scare their little ones with. When I saw the utter lack of sympathy in the source materials I was reading, I felt anger toward the people of Delilah who had known something was unspeakably wrong out on Cape Contrition and did nothing about it for years, only to speculate and swap shocking details for months after their deaths. The absolute isolation of Rosemary Usher and her children three miles away came into new focus.

I went through a whole pack of cigarettes reading all the available materials about the trial of Henry Ahab Usher. Articles speculated almost gleefully about incestuous abuse of the children, of his supposed cannibalism of his wife Rosemary's corpse, of his sundry religious delusions. I learned his lawyers went for a plea of insanity. Henry himself appeared to take no interest in his own defense and remained silent throughout his trial. In 1920, Henry Usher was sentenced to life in prison. The most recent sources I could find at the library indicated he had been placed in the custody of the Oregon State Hospital, but that happened in the '20s. I did not know if he was still living, and was not eager to meet him for an interview.

At this stage, I was not looking seriously for new evidence in the case of the Usher family slaying. For my part, I thought it most likely the official story on the murder was the right one. Henry Usher was a monstrous, unthinkably abusive religious zealot. Men like that murder their wives and children every day. The only alternative I could see to Henry Usher having killed his wife and children was the improbable theory that his wife had locked him in the cellar, burned her own children, and leapt to her death. But I didn't have much confidence in that scenario. Nobody in town knew much of anything about Rosemary. By all accounts, she was a small, timid woman, little more than a child bride when the Usher family came to Delilah. She stayed cowed and quiet by Henry's side, held completely under his dominion. I doubted she would be able to physically overpower her husband, by all accounts a mighty man, and lock him in the cellar. And even if she managed to do it, why not run with the children, flee the Cape, and make a better life for them somewhere else? Why would she burn all her children alive and take her own life at the moment when she might have been able to free them and herself at last? If that was the only alternative possibility, I thought it a weak one.

Tragic and fascinating as the Usher saga appeared, Rupert Wycliffe's pet obsession with his theory that the police had taken the wrong man was not my obsession. He had me chasing shadows, and whether I was being paid to chase them or not, I still saw them as shadows. I doubted I would uncover anything about a forty-three-year-old murder no one else had noticed already. My purpose at this stage was to familiarize myself with the Ushers themselves; anything to help me tell their family story better. While I read, Hana came around and set a steaming mug of coffee on the table in front of me.

"Can I have one of your cigarettes?" She asked.

"You're too young to smoke."

"How old were you when you started smoking?"

"Your age. Younger, maybe." I kept reading.

"What are you looking at that stuff for?"

"Kid, I've read the same sentence about ten times now." I took a sip of the coffee and it was good, so I decided I ought to be friendlier. "I'm trying to see if I can learn anything from newspaper articles of the time, but these people knew less about the Ushers than I do." She glanced over the articles spread before me, and scratched Otis behind the ears.

"Well, it looks like all these articles are from right around the time of the fire. With such a sensational case and the whirlwind of speculation surrounding it, you aren't going to find any clear answers or new revelations there. Have you considered looking back further? The Ushers lived in town for a few months or so before cloistering themselves on Cape Contrition. Maybe they're mentioned in older articles from back then. What year do you think that would be?"

"1910 was when they started tending the light. Do you have materials from then, or from '09?"

"I'll check." Hana set her comic on the couch and ran upstairs. Hana Iwamoto conscripted Herman Mast into helping her lug several cardboard boxes full of periodicals and public records down to the couch. I was struck by how good she was with him. They made an odd pair, but Hana seemed to be the only one who knew what made Herman tick. For much of the afternoon, I stayed on the couch flipping through the materials before me with Hana's enthusiastic help. Little by little, she became acquainted with who I was and what sort of book I was hoping to write. She revealed nothing about herself, despite my own occasional questions. I didn't get the feeling this was from mistrust or spite, but rather from a comfort in remaining mysterious.

The reading was deadly tedious, and hours passed without a hint of the Ushers at any point. I was about to give up when I glimpsed a small personal advertisement in one corner of a yellowed page of community announcements. Amidst the usual gentleman-seeking-lady, lost dog, automobile for sale, etc., one announcement caught my eye:

Family newly arrived in town seeking permanent accommodations: man, pregnant woman, and two young daughters. I have little money but can work for my keep. I am experienced in farming, carpentry, and construction, and am no stranger to hard labor. Good and godly people, in need of a windfall and a chance. Contact Henry Ahab Usher at the Whispering Conch Inn.

It was small, but it was something.

"Whispering Conch Inn. Is that still around?" I asked.

"It's on Broad Street," Hana said, taking the leash and hooking it to Otis' collar. "Come on, I'll show you."

"Young lady, you are still on the clock," Herman Mast protested.

"Take it out of my book stack, Herman. I'll be back in a bit."

The Whispering Conch stood within sight of the ocean in Delilah's downtown. A hundred years ago, it had been raised as a saloon and inn, and these amenities were kept intact as the owning family expanded the old building and attached an upscale seafood restaurant to it in the '40s. I tied Otis' leash to a shaded tree near the front door. The restaurant was nearing its evening rush, and the black-clad staff were rushing to keep up.

"Table for two?" A bright, smiling hostess asked as we walked in.

"You hungry, kid?" I asked.

"Gee, are you sure? I mean, I could eat, but-"

"Yeah, table for two. Is the owner around?"

"She is, actually. She's managing in the kitchen right now."

"I was wondering if I could speak to her when she's free."

"I'll let her know. What name should I give her?"

"Crowley. Joe."

"Right this way, Mr. Crowley. I'll bring her out as soon as possible."

The kid ordered fish with chips and a root beer float. I had a chicken Caesar salad, an appetizer of shrimp cocktail, and ice water. She inhaled her meal at an unsettling pace. She must have brothers. The hostess pointed us out to a dark, beautiful woman a little older than me, in a black turtleneck sweater and skirt. She walked over, and I gave Hana a light kick under the table to watch her manners. She set her finished float down with a gulp and wiped the ice cream and foam mustache from her lip when I gave her a covert signal to do so.

"Naomi Friedler," she announced with handshakes to us both, "pleased to meet you. Mr. Crowley, is that right?"

"Yes, ma'am, thank you for taking the time to come to our table."

"Was everything to your satisfaction?"

"The food was great!" Hana declared.

"Thank you. Your daughter is too kind. Is there anything I can do for you?"

I explained who I was, what I was writing, and how her

inn came into it. I asked if she still had guest records from 1909-1910.

"Well, I'm afraid I can't give you access to guest records. Even if you were policemen, that would be a touchy issue. However," she sat in our booth next to me and spoke low, "I may as well tell you the Usher family lived here for a period of several months during that time. The wife, Rosemary, was confined to her room with the children while her husband spent all his time trying to find work or rambling about town. That was during my grandfather Erasmus' time as the innkeeper. He was murdered in 1909. The word *Jew* was written on the outside wall of the saloon in his blood, over where his body was found lying against the wall. No one was ever arrested for his murder, and my grandfather was... Little loved."

"Are you saying his murder wasn't investigated thoroughly because he was Jewish?" I asked.

"And because he was a usurious, cruel, abusive-" she stopped short of swearing, for the benefit of the kid. "Well... He gave our family a bad reputation I am *still* working to wash out. But for all that, he was still my grandfather, and he was still murdered outside this very building. Though we have carved out a successful family business in the Whispering Conch, we have always had our vandals and detractors. Times are hard in Delilah, but we have always been as hardy as any of the other families here. Hardier. My son is talking about going to Israel. With the troubles there? This is *my* Promised Land. My father added this restaurant to his father's saloon and inn. In the next ten years, I will add a casino and resort onto his restaurant.

When the fishing and logging jobs that fed the families who

wanted us out are gone, we will still be here. Their sons and daughters will be working for me."

"Forgive me, Ms. Friedler. I can see you are upset. I did not intend to bring up any ugly memories."

"If you are writing a book on the Ushers, bringing up ugly memories is all you will do. I am sorry, I... I must go back to work." Naomi Friedler rose from her seat and walked away, the lines of her face etched with subdued emotion.

"Wow, call the men in white coats. What was *that* blow-up about?" Hana asked in low tones.

"Shush." I signaled a waitress and paid the bill. "I didn't bargain on upsetting her. But Ms. Friedler knows more about the Ushers than she's letting on."

"Obviously," Hana rolled her eyes. "So how are we going to put the thumbscrews to her and get her to spill the beans?"

"Who are you? Grab your coat, kid. I'm taking you home. This job requires a softer touch."

"Aw, come on. You can't pull me off this now. I'm on the case."

"There's no case. I'll know where to find you if I learn anything. Now come on, it's getting dark out."

After driving Hana back to her family's house and foisting Otis on her for the evening, I sat at the bar in the Old West saloon of the Whispering Conch. I pulled at a bottle of Coca-Cola and thought long and hard about getting something stronger. Waiting for this woman in the bar was a bad idea. Country music was playing on the jukebox, and an old cowboy was dancing with his wife out on the floor. I was about to give in to the temptation to order a glass of bourbon when Naomi Friedler walked through. Her lip curled in a questioning smile when she recognized me.

"Mr. Crowley! I didn't expect to see you again. Can I get you anything stronger to drink?"

"Probably shouldn't. I'm a recovering alcoholic."

"A twelve-stepper. I admire your honesty. But isn't it a little dangerous to be hanging around with your demons?"

"Maybe, but I'm not here for them. I was hoping to talk to you some more."

"Well, I'm off work now, but I'm not sure how much help I can be. I don't know much more than I told you earlier."

"But you were upset earlier. Can I ask why?"

"Do alcoholics have any compunction against buying drinks for other people?" she pulled out a stool and sat next to me.

"You've got to pay for drinks in your own bar? What's the point of having a bar, then? Sure, sweetheart, what's your poison?"

"A French 75." I signaled the bartender. I was sweating, and my hand was trembling, but I didn't want her to notice. Obviously, I couldn't order a cocktail after admitting I had a problem. Maybe that was why I did it. The barkeep handed Naomi a tall flute of bubbling golden Champagne, gin, lemon juice, and sugar. She sipped and smiled at the tangy kick of the mixture. I reached for my cigarettes. All out. She looked damn good enjoying that drink.

"Nervous?" she smiled at my fidgeting.

"Just not as strong as I thought I was."

"Here, maybe this will help," Naomi reached behind the bar for a box of Lucky Strikes and pulled one out for me. She struck a match and held the flame for me while I puffed it to life. "Your hunch was right, detective. I do know more than I was letting on. I didn't think it was appropriate in front of your daughter and was too irritated to get into it; but I could now, if you wanted."

"Hana? She's not my daughter. I mean, I *have* a daughter, but... That was just a penniless street urchin in need of a hot meal. I'm a charitable guy."

"Well, the penniless street urchins do need all the help they can get, I suppose." She smiled, taking another sip of her bubbly cocktail. "But you are married. I noticed the ring when you lit your smoke."

I pushed twin jets of burning smoke out of my nostrils and looked down at the bar for a moment. "I'm a widower, actually. Still can't take it off. Old habits and all that."

"You poor man. Now it's my turn to be sorry for bringing up painful memories." Her tone simpered and sympathized, but her eyes betrayed relief that I was single. I didn't know whether that made me randy or angry. I took a swig of coke and inhaled bitter smoke, feeling the cloying syrupy sweet and acrid tastes blend in my mouth. "A few years ago, I was overseeing some maintenance when an old journal was discovered hidden beneath a loose floorboard under the bed in Room 9. The journal was written by Rosemary Usher."

A stub of ash fell on my arm and started to smoke and burn on the fabric of my cardigan, but my attention was on her surprise revelation. I cursed and swatted out the orange firefly buried in the folds of wool when I felt it touch my skin, and Naomi laughed as she took my arm, rolled up the sleeve, and examined the tiny burn.

"The lifestyle of a writer is more dangerous than I imagined."

"You're saying you found the diary of Rosemary Usher, and kept it a secret?"

"My grandfather was also in there, Joe. He shamed me in those pages, and I couldn't bear to let anyone in town have more evidence of his disgusting acts to throw in my face. What's more, without coming right out and saying it, the journal paints a pretty clear picture of who Rosemary believes killed Erasmus. It was 1909... Most everyone the journal mentions must surely be dead by now, but I still couldn't give Erasmus' ghost in Hell the comfort of knowing his murder was ever solved. Even if there was no one left to arrest, I didn't even want to give him that. Is that crazy?"

"No." I stubbed out my cigarette. "Do you have the journal?"

"It's back at my place." she laid an inviting hand on my wrist. "If you want it... Come and get it."

Chapter Five: Storm Cellar

October 12th, 1962

Morning found me alone, naked and tangled in the blindingly white sheets of a strange bed. Naomi had gone to work without saying goodbye. We'd had our fun, and neither of us expected it to be anything more than that. But how do you explain what it's like to feel alone when you're inside someone? I still felt like Jean's man. Being with Naomi was infidelity. A message was written in blood-red lipstick on the mirror of her vanity. "Good morning, Joe." And next to those words was the blooming red print of her lips on the glass. A worn leather journal was sitting underneath the mirror. I opened it carefully. The first page bore these words in a slanting, faded script:

Diary of Rosemary Annabel Usher, 1909

It was a thick volume, with sporadic entries of varying length and frequency kept in 1909 and 1910. From what I could tell at a glance through the pages, the entries ran from the time of her leaving Utah with Henry to right before they moved their belongings to Cape Contrition to tend Siren's Light, as it was then known. As far as I could tell, it was genuine. The brown leather cover and brittle, yellowed pages were undeniably old. The characters of script held to consistent trends in their slant, shape, and size that made me sure the whole diary could be authenticated as having a single author. I am not a forensic specialist, but have studied and handled enough primary sources to know what to look for. I checked the form of individual letters against one another in entries written months apart in different hued ink and found them to be the same.

Sometimes whole pages were filled with trivialities of daily tedium. Other times the entries were monosyllabic but shocking. There were weeks where she picked up the habit again and wrote almost daily, other times she would lapse for months without touching the thing. Most remarkable of all, the diary appeared to be a secret from her husband, which may have explained why she had to abandon it at last in 1910. Though the entries conveyed a wide range of emotions from naïve optimism to wounded terror, every syllable betrayed her loneliness.

I brewed a pot of coffee and started reading the journal at Naomi's kitchen counter. I lifted the mug to my lips, savoring the smell as it steamed my glasses. Before tasting it, I realized I'd left my dog with Hana overnight without a word of explanation. Cursing myself, I left the coffee untouched, pulled on my clothes, tucked the diary in the pocket of my black pea coat, locked up the handsome Friedler beach cabin, and drove like a maniac over to the Iwamoto house. The sky was dark for morning, and the wind was cutting in cold from the bay. Of course, I was so caught up in the discovery of the journal, I had no idea the coast was about to be hit by the most infamous windstorm in eighty years. When I dashed to the front door and opened it, Hana was standing in the landing with her hands on her hips, backpack slung over one shoulder.

"You had sex with that woman, didn't you?" She let me have it as soon as I opened the front door.

"How do you even know about- ...Don't they wait to tell you that stuff?" I asked.

"I'm not stupid. I know what it means when you're wearing the same clothes this morning you wore last night. And you haven't shaved."

"Kid, if you knew me, neither of those things would stand out."

"Point taken. Your dog is safe and well-fed. You're lucky I'm not a cannibalistic murderer or something."

"Look, Hana, I'm sorry about this. Things, uh, got out of hand last night. I meant to come back sooner, I just got caught up."

"You're so disgusting. Here's your dog, I have to go. I don't even care if you found anything out about the case while you were giving her the time."

"Are you going to school? I could give you a lift for your trouble."

"It's Columbus Day. So obviously there's no school today."

"Obviously. Okay, see you around, Iwamoto. Otis says thanks."

"There's a storm coming, Crowley! Get Otis to shelter. You I don't care about so much."

"Will do. Thanks for your concern."

Dark clouds were building on the horizon, and the wind was picking up fierce as I drove through town. The radio whined with static. As the reception improved, I heard an emergency broadcast coming through about a terrible windstorm coming to sweep across the region. All I wanted to do was find a café and read the journal, but the broadcast was warning everyone to stay indoors and seek shelter. As Main Street cut along the bay close to the marina, my heart dropped into my stomach. The docked boats were tipping and heaving ominously, crashing into one another, ripping off their moorings, and pitching into the splintering docks like a capricious toddler's playthings on the surface of a bathtub. With the howling winds came pounding fists of waves. I saw an immense wall of water heave against the warehouses, canneries, and restaurants in its wake. Thirty feet high, the terrible wave crashed into the four-story beachfront hotel shielding me. With a squeal of tires, I turned the Land Rover through a side-alley as a seething swell of water swept over Main Street and burst through storefront windows.

There were several people running who were shoved off their feet by the flood across Main Street, and as the water pulled back, I saw its strong current seize an old man who thrashed and screamed as he was drawn back inexorably into the bay. The ocean grabbed several people that day, and the storm was so extreme, no search party could be safely mustered to search for them. They were just gone. The maelstrom flooded two city blocks before I could even believe it was real. Other automobiles sped frantically, and I had to swerve hard while shifting gears to avoid hitting a motorist as reckless with fear as myself. While people battened down the hatches or fled to higher ground, I rocketed through downtown Delilah, rejoining Main Street in time to veer onto Highway 101 out of town. In the rearview mirror, it was like God was smiting Delilah from the earth.

As I fled down the road, the fir trees were rocking. Branches flailed like the arms of a tightrope walker clawing for lost balance. Terrifying, immense waves were still battering the shores, and on long stretches of coastal highway, avoiding them was impossible. Heavy blankets of spray blinded my windshield for terrifying moments before the wipers swept it clear. My tires slid on flooding roads as they kicked up large walls of water and I struggled to keep control. At several points, I feared my engine would stall or my automobile would be swept away, but I kept on moving as fast as I could toward Cape Contrition.

I looked out at the churning gray ocean to see a log barge had broken apart in the storm. The rolling mass of trunks was tumbling onto the highway like an avalanche of timber from the ocean, battering rams carried on the crest of a wave. I slammed on the gas and shifted gears, roaring to eighty miles an hour in the blind, driving rain while immense tree trunks spilled over one another across the road behind me. Rain pelted onto the car sideways, and as I started the Land Rover across the Siren Creek Bridge, the gale picked up to about ninety miles per hour and rocked the car. The ocean heaved against the stony ramparts at the base of Cape Contrition.

Rain bolted like bullets as I pulled the car into the guest lot and put it in park. Siren's Cove was awash, and the seething rush of booming waves was spilling over the low stone wall into the parking lot, like water cascading over the rims of an overfull bathtub. The parking lot was an empty lagoon. I was nervous about flooding carrying away my vehicle, but there was no other place to park. The dirt trail leading through the woods to Usher's Fall was too narrow for my Rover to navigate. Before I got out of the car, I remembered the diary of

Rosemary Usher, and checked my coat pocket for it. The diary was gone. Cursing aloud, I patted down the other pockets of my coat and pants and twisted around to check the floor of the cab. After checking underneath and behind seats and popping open the glove box, I began to panic. The missing piece in my puzzle, only just found and not yet even read, had disappeared. I wanted to search more, but if it wasn't in the car, it was soaked through on the ground somewhere outside the Iwamoto or Friedler house. The rising storm reminded me I was out of time to search for it. If I turned back, I would be caught in this maelstrom. I was in it already. Cursing my luck, I got out of the car and splashed in water up to my ankles. Cape Contrition was like a castle under siege. My black pea coat and scarf whip-cracked around me as I urged Otis onto the forest trail. Hurricane force winds were blowing, and the trees creaked and cracked all around us. Great limbs of trees fell perilously close to us on the path. We were barraged with small debris: little branches patchy with quills of fir needles, twigs, and pinecones. Otis barked and yelped, looking about frantically when tree limbs fell. His muscles bulged out at his shoulders as he hauled me up the trail on his leash. As we neared the house, an epiphany struck.

The old house had a storm cellar. The same one in which Henry Usher was driven mad. The same one where he maybe butchered and ate his wife after burning their children alive.

We burst out into the green clearing of Usher's Fall. The automated electric light blazed out into the churning cauldron of the sea. Its tower stood white and lonely out on the edge of the Cape, steadfast against the wind. The old house creaked and shuddered, and even as I watched, a window in the second

93

floor shattered and several shingles were ripped from the roof. I urged Otis, and we ran around the side of the house with its wrap-around porch. My hair was soaked down to my skull. The heavy wooden double-doors of the cellar were set at an incline into a square of the foundation. Otis pressed his front paws on the worn wood, whining and clawing at their surface, impatient for shelter.

I scrabbled at the padlock and heavy rust-spotted chain, remembered the key in my pocket, and jammed it home with a forceful turn. The stubborn lock chucked open, the chain slinked apart and hung limp like a dead snake, and I cast it aside. I closed my eyes and hesitated when I laid hands upon the doors, mind still spinning with instinctive fear, doubts of my own sanity, and dread of entering this darkened basement of madness when my nerves were already so fraught. But as the wind shrieked with claws grasping over the Cape and thunder boomed low and menacing, I realized I had no choice. A twisted weathervane from the highest peak of the roof crashed down and half buried itself in the dirt not five feet from where I crouched. I braced myself and flung wide the doors.

The cellar was silent and choked with dust, the darkness impenetrable beyond the shaft of murky light from the top of the stairs. As I stood there at the entrance to the deserted basement, Otis peered in with me and balked at the safety he had been hoping for moments ago. He huddled behind my legs with low whimpers. I was unsettled to notice long scratches in the wood of the inside surface of the doors, like something from the walls of a gas chamber. I put my hand to the claw marks and saw they were made by larger hands than my own. The cellar was quiet and musty, with no electric lights. I decided to keep the top hatch open just long enough to find a lantern, candle, or torch.

The stairs were stone set into hard-packed dirt, unyielding and secure under my feet. Damp and heavy air filled my nostrils, choked with dust and the sweet stink of earth. Old tools lined the walls, rusting and neglected. They clinked against one another in the wind like tetanus-laden chimes. Rat droppings lined the edges of the earthen floor. In the darkness, silhouettes of piled and forgotten furniture loomed, draped in protective white sheets. I moved past a broken spinning wheel, disused farm equipment, and a shelf of ancient pickle jars encased in dust. Most of the things shoved into this darkened corner of the house had belonged to the Usher family. As I glanced about the room, a darting movement caught in my peripheral vision, like a small animal that was startled and bounded off. A flutter of pages rustled like wings as a book fell from one of the forgotten heaps. I moved to the part of the basement where the noise had come from, eyes trained to the dimness and darting about warily. I saw a small leather Bible on the floor, fallen from its perch on the edge of a full wicker basket, and slowly crouched to pick it up. It lay on its crumpled pages with covers spread, open to the underlined passage of Deuteronomy 18:9-18:12:

"When thou art come into the land which the LORD thy God giveth thee, thou shalt not learn to do after the abominations of those nations. There shall not be found among you any one that maketh his son or his daughter to pass through the fire, or that useth divination, or an observer of the times, or an enchanter, or a witch, or a charmer, or a consulter with familiar spirits, or a wizard, or a necromancer. For all that do these things are an abomination unto the LORD: and because of these abominations

the LORD thy God doth drive them out before thee."

I let the book fall. Otis sniffed about the ground and patrolled the narrow paths between piles of looming refuse, growling as he went. While I was on one knee, the hairs on the back of my neck stood up as I heard the unmistakable sound of children's feet hurrying through the room, accompanied by a whispered "shhh!" The sound echoed in the close room.

"Hello?" I asked sharply, drawing up to my full height and searching about the room. The basement was packed with junk, but small enough to be sure I would see anyone who was in there with me. But while my eyes told me I was alone, my ears told me there was at least one child hiding in the room, perhaps two. The steps were solid enough to be climbed in silence by a stealthy foot, but I had seen no one on the grounds. Otis was perceiving the sounds as well but wasn't confident he had found anything. My thoughts raced as my mind struggled to make rational conclusions from the evidence of my senses, which I increasingly couldn't trust.

"Someone down here? Kid, come on, I heard you." I felt silly, speaking out when I could just be falling victim to an overactive imagination and a primal fear of dark, abandoned rooms. As I tentatively addressed my unwanted visitor, I crept about the room, occasionally lunging around a pile of chairs or a wardrobe to try and catch someone hiding there. I came to a halt when I saw a clearing in the corner of the room. Antiquated toys were arranged haphazardly in the scattered circle of open floor space, the way a child would as she was setting up some imaginary scene. There were several dolls made of porcelain and dressed in hand-sewn clothes, painted features faded and chipping. Some of the dolls were made from straw and cloth, with facial features and buttons stitched onto the garments. I saw farm animals carved from wood: two chickens, a goat, a sheep, and a pig. These antique toys were all positioned around two toy structures: a small box crafted to resemble an old farmhouse, and a model lighthouse beautifully carved and painted.

Five little dolls were placed about the house and grounds. Something about the dull expressions on their porcelain and cloth faces was lost and scared. In the front yard of the house, a straw and cloth doll of a man stood around the animals. Since his legs weren't rigid, he leaned like a drunk against the house itself. In his hand was an axe, and his features gave me pause. The doll wore faded black clothes and a dark beard. If stitches and buttons could make a dour and cruel face, they did on this doll. The black bearded man stood with his axe over a doll of a chicken laying on the floor with its head torn off, and stuffing sticking out. And... No, it couldn't be. I got down on my hands and knees and touched the ruby droplets on the floor where the toy chicken was slaughtered. I put it to my nose and smelled the iron tang of it, removing all doubt it was blood. The thick, gleaming drops were still wet.

Aloof from all the toys and standing propped against the small lighthouse was a doll of a woman in black. Her porcelain face was shattered like an eggshell into a gaping hole.

I felt my hands tremble and my pulse quicken as I took in the disturbing scene and considered its implications. The cellar door with its rusty padlock looked as if it had not been opened in years, but someone had been playing down here. The deep red drops had to have been spilled onto the floor minutes ago. As I took in the scene, I noticed the toy house's roof was attached on hinges. The worn brown corner of a book's cover was peeking out from underneath its eaves. As I carefully

97

opened the roof and took out the small book, I realized it was a lid and the toy house was a music box. Clockwork wheels wound up and a soft tinkling melody began to play. I did not recognize the tune, but the chiming tones haunted me as I watched a porcelain ballerina spin in place. The music wasn't exactly the same, but the tune reminded me of another song. The one by Edith Piaf that haunted my dreams.

Her movements stuttered in their turn as the old wheels caught. As I listened to the haunting song and watched the tiny dancer rotate, I remembered the leather-bound book in my hand and opened it.

It was the same journal Naomi Friedler left me and I lost on my way to the house. Beyond all doubt, it was the same. A chill stole over me as I looked at the crabbed writing of Rosemary Usher, the tinkling song ended, and the ballerina wound to a halt.

Like the jarring spring of a jack-in-the-box, the cellar door slammed shut with a thunderous crack, and the feeble shaft of light from outside was closed out.

Panic seized me as I rushed for the hatch, tripped over the leg of an overturned chair, and crashed heavily onto the floor in pitch darkness. My shoulder took the impact on the hard-packed dirt floor at the same time as I twisted my ankle in the limbs of the chair, and the corner of a table punched me in the ribs so hard I thought I broke one. I choked and sputtered with the wind knocked out of me, gulping in the mildewed air as fast as my ragged, hissing breaths would allow. As I crawled, cursed, and scrabbled blindly in the dark, I heard a few things toppling around me. I did not know if my fall set off a chain reaction in the crowded cellar, or if I was not alone after all. I felt the unshakable conviction hateful eyes were watching me in the darkness. A presence was standing so close I might touch it by accident. Sometimes I felt movement, the unmistakable instinct of a large body shifting stealthily right by you. The sensation of a lion brushing the thin cloth wall of your tent on a safari. I gasped with relief as my hand touched the bottom step of the stone staircase, and I dragged myself to my feet with a wince. I threw myself into the closed cellar doors with the aching shoulder I had fallen on, but it was locked. From the outside. Otis was barking frantically out there, snarling with wrath. I hadn't seen him slip out of the cellar while I was exploring it. Along with my own fear, I was protective of my mutt. As I struggled with the door, I heard a terrible scrabbling and scratching sound against the wood on my side. It was a desperate, disembodied sound.

My grasping hand blindly found a shovel hanging from a hook on the wall, and I heaved its spade into the door like a battering ram. I felt the darkness and the ineffable presence of hate closing in on me and cursed my aching rib as I heaved the shovel's head into the door again and again. A beam of clouded daylight streaked in as I speared the head of the shovel through the worn wood panel of the cellar door. I stabbed again, punching open the hole with two heavy thrusts so it was large enough for my arm to reach through. Intrusive thoughts crawled over my mind like spiders in the dark. I shook off the guilt and fear that came on so strong they were almost crippling, and my desperate grasp found the old orange and brown-spotted padlock on its chain. It was bound around the handles of the doors again. I pulled as hard as I could on its loose chain, bringing the padlock through the hole into the cellar where the doors were still clawed by unseen hands. Fumbling, I tried the keys on my ring one after another until one shoved into the stubborn lock and turned. I felt the rusted chain rattling to the ground and burst through the cellar doors out into the storm.

There was no trace of whoever might have restored the padlock and chain to its place behind me. The grounds were flogged with driving winds and stinging hailstones. In the distant dark over the ocean, the heart-sinking spiral of a cyclone was reaching down into the water like the finger of God. Windows shattered in the farmhouse, and shingles were ripped from their places to hurl through the air. Otis trembled up to me and wagged his tail as he licked my fingertips, and I knew he was urging me to leave the cellar now that we were reunited. But the sight of the cyclone convinced me I had no choice but to turn back inside. There was nowhere else to go. It was a shelter built for this very eventuality. I set my teeth and ran into the house, only long enough to grab a lantern and close every window-shutter which hadn't already been broken. With the lantern in hand, I sealed the heavy storm door of Usher's Fall, ran back around the side to the cellar hatch and flung it open, commanding the reluctant Otis to bow his head and creep inside. Fearing another trick of an unseen captor, I grabbed the rusted chain and padlock and cast them down the stairs into the darkness of the cellar. With a heavy heart, I closed the hatch behind me and latched it securely from the inside against the baleful roar of the hurricane.

The experience of hearing children and seeing darting shapes ended, but the sensation of being watched did not. Nor did the hair-prickling feeling of solid shapes moving close at hand. The building itself was growing increasingly resistant to my presence, as if it felt me prying into its secrets and resented it. Like white blood cells attacking a virus. I passed a long sleepless night huddled with Otis in the protective yellow circle of lamplight at the bottom of the stairs, afraid to close my eyes even for a moment. Imprisoned in this low-ceilinged dungeon for the storm's duration, I flipped open the journal of Rosemary Usher and started reading.

The early passages began with Rosemary's departure from Utah and the red rock canyons of her birth. She was the youngest of six daughters and three sons sired by Abraham White, patriarch of one of the most influential families in Salt Lake City. Though polygamy was officially outlawed by the Mormon Church and the United States government before the turn of the 20th Century, special arrangements were not unheard of in some fundamentalist families. The Whites were one such family. When Rosemary was a young girl, a stranger arrived in town, and gained employment as a carpenter in her father's shop. He was a gentile, but a hard worker, a charismatic Christian, and a winnable case for conversion. The handsome, swarthy lad of nineteen quickly ingratiated himself to Abraham White, and was a regular presence at their supper table. It took me a few pages to recognize this charming craftsman with a preacher's passion as the megalomaniacal killer Henry Usher. Inserting himself, mockingbird-like, into the position of an adopted son, Henry was a godsend to be married to one of Abraham's brood, but for one problem. Henry was already married.

At nineteen, Henry Usher was married to Catherine Clayton, a New England woman of twenty-five. Catherine was kept under close watch, a prisoner in her own house. Her husband was free to roam, and people commiserated with him over his mad, barren wife. They had never seen her but knew her to be such by reputation. And Henry was her lonely, long-suffering keeper.

Rosemary was twelve years old when her father gave her to Henry in marriage. She'd had her first period a month before. Henry frightened her even then, but she was drawn to his dark intensity and passionate sincerity, and he awakened desires she had never known. In the tragic pages, Rosemary confided she was clumsy and frightened when she lay with Henry for the first time. She wondered what she could give this man that the beautiful Catherine could not. She soon learned the answer: sons.

Like a wife of King Henry VIII, the sheltered child felt the pressure to provide her dread husband a male heir. In these years, she lived in the glare of Henry's dowager wife Catherine, who only stayed her hand for fear of her lord husband. Like every concubine, Rosemary learned the lady of the house cherished a deep and abiding hatred for her. When Rosemary's first daughter, Rebecca, was born, Catherine attempted to murder the baby with scissors. She was disarmed and thrown across the room with a sweep of Henry's arm and locked in a cupboard for three days.

When Henry Usher finally hitched up his wagons and left Salt Lake City to seek his fortunes further west, his little wife had borne him two daughters, and Catherine was quietly divorced and committed to the Utah State Mental Hospital. It turned out she was right to fear being replaced. But as Rosemary left the community of the Saints behind, her most private confession was that she too feared the day she would be cast aside for a younger bride. At seventeen, she was already too old for her husband's perverted desires.

In the crossing of the Owyhee Desert in Nevada, Henry

howled at the moon and cut himself with stones. It was one of the first fits when he warned her the Devil was in him. His voice was black as the pit when he commanded Rebecca and Anna to watch as he had their pregnant mother underneath the stars, hands caked with blood and filth against her milky skin. Rosemary saw the way his manhood grew when he looked upon his children and sated his hunger in the ways she had been taught. She was enough for his lust that time, but she feared the day she wouldn't be. The poor child wondered what Catherine would say if she could see them now. Why could she not just have the man she loved? Why did he have to have the Devil in him? Did God get taken over by the Devil on occasion as well, and did such a black whim preside over the day this man first stole into her father's house?

The version of Henry she loved returned to her when they reached the Pacific; lifted her in his arms with his great booming laugh. Rebecca and Anna giggled as they all sang hymns on the beach and waded into the surf. But Delilah was no New Eden. It was a storm-battered town of hard men and grim women who made their living pulling fish from the deep along the stony shores or felling huge trees in the woods. The rain was constant. At night, the taverns overflowed with lost men reeking of smoke and liquor. They toiled at the saw or the nets all day long and at nightfall spent their money at iniquitous card games or carousing with whores.

They lodged at the Whispering Conch Inn until they could find more permanent lodgings, but this would take months. Rosemary passed long hours with her children in their small room, forbidden to leave. She hardly saw Henry, who was sometimes absent for days at a time, spending all his waking hours looking for work or doing God knew what to console himself. The children grew restless and mischievous, and Rebecca's willful disobedience and callousness in causing pain to her toddling sister Anna made her mother believe she had more of her father in her than she'd known. Rosemary's isolation from Henry exposed her to the unwanted attentions of Erasmus Friedler, the lustful and avaricious innkeeper who complained of them constantly, imposed ever-mounting fees, and watched her through hidden peepholes with hungry eyes.

Henry was barely able to keep up with the innkeeper's bill, and when he could make up the money, Erasmus complained of their keeping bothersome children and threatened to put them out anyway. One day while Rosemary was supposed to be napping, she heard the hushed tones of an argument between Henry and Erasmus. Filthy words about her vagina and what Erasmus planned to do to it bled through from the next room before Henry slammed him up against the wall.

Knowing what the repulsive weasel wanted, Rosemary quietly told her husband later that night she could do it if he needed her to. If it alleviated the burden he bore and allowed him more time with the girls... Henry struck her across the face when he realized what she was proposing.

Rosemary's third birth was five hours of clenching, bloody agony. She was alone with her girls and no doctor came. Henry was away. Rebecca and Anna did not understand why their baby sister did not cry. She came out cold, gray, and still. A tiny little thing. On some intuitive level, Rosemary had known the child she was carrying was dead. She had not felt movement in her belly for two days when she began to bleed and go into labor. She wrote,

"I am desolate, wretched beyond the description of words. I am struck by the poverty of the English language for words of anguish."

Henry was cold and distant when he found out. Alone and ashamed, Rosemary stripped the bed and buried her little swaddled stillborn in a potter's field. With no one to share her sorrow with, the young woman sank into a dark pit of depression, unable to stir from bed as her remaining children pleaded and pulled at her.

Not long before the turn of 1910, Erasmus at long last tried to force himself on Rosemary when he caught her alone. Rebecca ran for help, and a kind-hearted sailor named Caleb rushed to her defense, beating the man bloody and throwing him out of his own inn. While the villain vomited blood in the street and picked up lost teeth, Caleb saw to Rosemary's hurts and comforted her. When Henry found out about the affair later, the Devil was on him, and he stormed out into the night. The next morning found Erasmus sprawled dead outside the saloon. His neck was broken, he had been beaten to death, and the word "Jew" was written in blood on the wall. As Rosemary silently washed the blood and broken glass from the cuts on her husband's knuckles, he mentioned he had found them a house.

Chapter Six: Wreckage

October 13th, 1962

It was a long and restless night in that cellar, reading Rosemary's words by the uncertain light of the lantern. The wind rattled the doors and shook the house overhead. Otis relieved himself in a corner, and the stench was inescapable. It was impossible to tell the passage of time. We waited for the gale to stop whistling through the hole battered in the door. The fear of things watching and moving in the dark did not pass. Eventually I was too exhausted for it to matter and slept for hours on the dank floor. When I finally awoke, all was still. Otis whined and pawed at the hatch, and I rose slowly, stiff from my repose on the hard-packed earth, to unbar and heave open the doors.

The storm passed over us at last to ravage the rest of the state. It left ruin in its wake. Shingles, glass shards, protective shutters, branches, dead seabirds, and splintered railings littered the grounds. The porch swing was flung across the yard. The heavy storm door held, at least. The power was out in the house, and in over three quarters of Delilah. The lighthouse remained curiously untouched, but it was better built to weather such storms than the old cottage. The forest trail was a disarray of toppled trunks and snapped tree limbs. The Land Rover's windows were mostly shattered, the roof partly crunched in. A branch speared the automobile right through the windshield, impaling the backrest of the driver's seat now covered with broken glass. The parking lot had flooded and partially drained again, but when I opened the driver's side door, sea water a foot deep cascaded out from within the cab.

I whistled low at the damage and hauled the broken top of the tree off where it leaned against the back of the Rover. Next, I grasped the branch speared into the driver's seat and set my teeth as I strained to draw it out. I set my worn leather shoe on the front bumper for support as I pulled. The branch came loose with a rending groan and a tinkle of falling glass, and I heaved it aside, hands sticky with sap. Wrapping my sap-stiffened hand in my scarf, I carefully brushed the broken glass off the seats and out of the floor, careful to make sure Otis didn't step in it. The whole cab was still dripping damp and stank of seawater. I laughed and smiled with relief as the damn thing started, and I resolved to take it to a mechanic in town and visit a hardware store to begin repairs on the house. But most importantly, it was past time to contact the police.

"And you said he was dressed... Like a sailor? The little hat, the blues and everything?" Police Chief Will Blake asked. He was sitting at his desk in the bullpen of the Delilah Police Station, making a big show of writing notes in a small pad. He wasn't taking me seriously, but I was too rattled and exhausted to care about how crazy I sounded. The building's lights were only on by grace of an emergency generator.

"His clothes were dark and plain. I couldn't get a close

look, but yeah, they looked like a well-worn historical period costume. Practical and demure. And he wore one of those wool newsboy caps.

"Demure..." Blake scratched the word out on the pad. His every movement was dripping with sarcasm. "Say, you mean like those hats golfers wear?"

"Yeah," I said, running fingers through my messy hair and massaging the headache forming behind my left eye. "Like golfers."

"I can guess you think of us as 'Mayberry', Mr..."

"Crowley."

"–Like the occultist. English guy. That's right."

"No."

"Well. If he's trying to spook you on a historical site, dressing like Popeye doesn't make a whole lot of sense. What do navy-men have to do with that place? It's out of place with the history, an anacon... Shit, what's that word?"

"Anachronism," I answered wearily, "There were a lot of shipwrecks there, so it isn't a stretch. But who cares? I'm not saying he's a fucking historian. I'm saying he's wearing antiquated clothing to add some kind of effect when he watches the house. With a gun. Which is really a bigger concern to me than what kind of outfit he's wearing."

"Okay, okay, simmer down," Blake chided, raising a hand in surrender and sipping lukewarm black coffee from a green enamel mug. "Hey Cody," he called to another officer at a nearby desk. "We've got an important lead here. Call the Pioneer Museum and see if any of their old sailor mannequins got stripped naked in the night."

Officer Cody chuckled and Chief Blake's earnest demeanor cracked into a charming, insolent grin. They don't believe a word of this. He glanced back at my tired, cold eyes and averted his own, tucking his pencil behind his ear and clearing his throat.

"I'm not joking around here, Andy Griffith. But if you're going to jerk off and waste my time, I'll take care of this creep myself." I got up to leave, but Will raised a hand and stopped me.

"Alright, alright, I deserved that. Sit back down, now. I need to ask you a few questions." I stonily returned to my seat.

"So this sailor. Big guy. Mean. About 6'1", 180 pounds, with sandy hair and a thick beard, right?"

"Yeah."

"And you said he was holding an old musket, too? Flint-lock?"

"More like a cowboy Winchester. Lever action."

"Well, the good news is, it's an old-as-shit gun. Probably more for show than anything. Old West collectible like that would be as likely to blow up in his face as hit you."

"I'm relieved. Thank you." My tone dripped with sarcasm.

"Obviously, a guy baring a gun at you is a threatening gesture no matter what kind of gun it is. Now you said he closed your cellar door behind you while you were down there and locked you in right before the storm. Has he ever laid hands on you before?"

"No." I reluctantly relaxed. Despite the initial screwball attitude, it seemed Chief Blake was actually listening to me now, but I was still on my guard.

"And he hasn't broken into the house before?"

"I haven't seen him in there, but maybe. Things have been moved out of place a few times. And I found toys set up in the cellar. Between that and him locking the padlock, he has to have a cellar key at least. But... I think he has children with him, maybe. Some of the things that have been moved out of place... It just feels like kids are around." It was a distinct and familiar feeling all parents know.

"Children..." Blake wrote the word down, underlined it, and narrowed skeptical eyes at me. "How many? How old?"

"I don't know." My mouth went dry. "I've never seen them." Christ, I sound like a lunatic.

"So, you haven't seen any kids snooping around, or seen them with this man."

"No."

"Okay. So, back to the man. He's mostly just watching the house and glaring at you, making sure you can see him do it? Maybe poking around in the place when you're not there? And he hasn't stolen your possessions, left a threatening note... taken a shit on your car, or anything like that."

Officer Cody buried his face in the crook of his arm as he tried to strangle a choking, high weep of a laugh. His shoulders shook with the effort.

"Jesus, Cody, I'm conducting a serious investigation here," Chief Blake rounded on his officer with straight-faced but feigned indignation and threw a spinning pen across the room and hit him right on top of the head.

"No, uh, nothing like that," I said, trying to rein the kids in a little. "It feels like stalking, though. Something uglier than a practical joke. Something that might escalate."

"Stalking is often motivated by a personal connection to the victim, with strong mixed feelings of anger and desire, love and hate. Are you sure you haven't seen this guy before?"

"I don't know him, but I'm also famous. Couldn't this be

some kind of deranged fan or something?"

"Maybe, but my understanding is you haven't had a permanent address in about two months, and nobody knows you're here now except for a few residents. So it doesn't sound like anyone from your old life or your fan club would know you're here."

"That makes sense." I stewed over how paranoid these questions made my fears seem.

"So he hasn't spoken to you, hasn't written you any message. Hasn't appeared to be following you anywhere off Cape Contrition. Just watching the house: the historic landmark and tourist attraction, open to the public."

"... Yeah."

"So you see my problem. Oh, and as to the things getting moved around in the house. You ought to know, kids come up there to neck in the woods. That's no secret in these parts. A few probably used the house over the years. Winos and hobos too. Might be a couple of them broke in before they realized it was occupied. Then there's all the crazy jumpers."

"*The people* who committed suicide."

"Right. Anyway, your sailor... The most I could do at this point is get him for trespassing. We don't have much else at this point."

"So we'll wait until after he cuts me into little pieces. Great."

"If you're afraid for your safety, I can send one of my boys there tonight to keep an eye on the place. See if your spook makes another move, and we can scare him off. But I can't arrest someone for something they haven't done yet."

"Right. Okay."

"On the other hand, this is the West. If someone means to

do you harm, it is your right as an American to stand your ground and defend yourself. That is, if you can hit more than typewriter keys."

I gave a wry, tired smile.

"Guess we'll see."

"Oh shit, Chief. We've gotta go, man. It's Jake's thing tonight."

"Alright, let's move out." Chief Will Blake donned his cowboy hat from where it rested on the desk and got to his feet.

"What's happening?" I asked.

"Jake Reynolds. He was a good kid. Drowned on the beach here in town a few days ago."

"I read about that in the paper."

"Well, his wake is tonight. We're going to pay our respects. We'll send a squad car over later."

"You know the house isn't accessible to cars, right?"

"That's why I'm sending someone else. How's your porch?"

"Wraps around two sides of the house, has a couple nice rocking chairs, good vantage point on the property, and your officer is welcome to whatever I cook for dinner. I usually eat late."

"Cody," Blake called to his officer as he was disappearing out the door. "That schoolteacher of yours still not calling you back?"

"Not yet. She'll be back, though. The silence feels like it's coming to a head now. Like it'll be over soon."

"But not tonight, right?"

"Why do you ask, Chief?"

"You're babysitting Hemingway tonight. He's cooking

steaks."

"Out on Cape Contrition, Chief? Come on. What am I gonna do out there?"

"Eat red meat. Sit and think, read a book, watch the waves. A whole list of things that'll do your goofy ass some good. That's an order. I want our new friend to feel safe and welcome here in Delilah."

Delilah was hard hit. Many of the buildings along the ocean-front were battered and flood damaged. The harbor was a desolation of smashed docks, capsized vessels, and splintered masts. Huge tree trunks carried on the ocean spilled across roads and crumpled parked cars like tin cans. The beach was strewn with debris, and survivors were grieving loved ones dragged into the Pacific, racked by uncertainty and denial in cases where no remains would ever be returned to them. The city was dark with the power lines severed, but many windows flickered with oil lamps: their wicks kept ready by folks prophetically skeptical modern electricity would serve them when they needed it most. When the storms came, Delilah coped in the old ways, as her pioneer forefathers had taught her.

Later that evening, I sat in the back pew of the Delilah Baptist Church while the community gathered in candlelight to grieve, console one another, and try to make sense of the tragic death of a little boy who got too close to the water. It seemed cruel how this tragedy had been so overshadowed by the mayhem of the storm. I felt a little guilty for being there as a stranger. As the congregation tearfully sang The Old Rugged Cross, I sat and reflected on the contents of Rosemary's journal for the first time since that horrific night passed in the storm cellar.

Immersed in reverie, I mechanically shuffled out with the crowd at the service's conclusion and tucked forty dollars in the collection for the kid's mother. As I headed out into the parking lot, I caught a glimpse of a verbal altercation between the bereaved mother and a man in the parking lot.

"It's not true!" Doris sobbed. "My boy did not kill himself on purpose. I don't care what the autopsy says, you hear me? He was ten years old! Oh, sweet Jesus, my boy was ten years old!" She pounded fists into the big man's chest, and he pulled her in close, holding her and stroking her dark, mousy hair as her shoulders heaved with wretched sobs. I gathered he was the boy's father and discreetly stepped into my vehicle to give them privacy. An overheard secret, a ten-year old's accidental death determined to be suicide. I couldn't stop thinking about that as I made the long, lonely drive back to Cape Contrition with a new 12-gauge shotgun and two boxes of shells in the passenger seat.

The old house gave off an aroma of seared rare steaks and fried potatoes as I cooked dinner and ate with Officer Cody Mitchell on the porch. We listened to the distant crash of waves against the jagged rocks at the base of the cliff over one hundred and thirty feet below us, and the occasional hoot of an owl high in the firs. Cody wasn't all too bright and had little perspective on anything outside his county line but was a gifted conversationalist. He knew how to keep an amiable, surface level dialogue rolling, and since I was a mere stranger to Delilah, Cody got to be the expert. He took pride in that.

After a while, I brewed a pot of coffee, brought out a steaming enamel mug to my watchman, and retired inside to read by lantern, chain-smoking cigarettes at the kitchen table. The night was quiet and still. The Sailor wasn't making an appearance. Cody was strumming contemplatively and clumsily at my guitar when I went to bed. I was embarrassed the night I had all but insisted on police protection was completely without incident, but my protector made no complaint and didn't insinuate a peep that his presence was a chore. I slept longer and more peacefully than I had since the strange incidents began. When I awoke to find dawn breaking over the forest and Cody sleeping soundly at his post, I gently woke him up and sent him home. I apologized for the slow night and assured him I wouldn't need protection again. If my stalker made another appearance, the shotgun would have to be enough.

The following week passed without incident. I continued to be nagged by depression and guilt, and my nights were frequently disturbed by dreams of my wife, or scenes of slaughter and holocaust in North Africa, Europe, and later in Korea. I combated the darkness of my thoughts by striving to improve myself every day. Each morning I woke early and went for long runs with Otis. I felt my body growing leaner and stronger, and every time I ran, I pushed myself a little farther down the coast. As a recovering alcoholic chasing the distance running stamina I'd had in high school, my life is guided by a mantra that is simultaneously a hope and a warning: If I was the guy who could do that once, I could be that guy again.

Work on the house kept me busy, setting new windowpanes, repairing shutters, and replacing shingles torn off in the Columbus Day Storm. I tore through the books bought in Gwen's store, reading as much as five hours a day. By night, I was poring through the journal of Rosemary Usher, documents, periodicals, and books on local history borrowed from the library, and writing on my Smith Corona. The initial fear and anxiety I experienced during my first few days in the house wore off. My mind was quickly comforting and deluding itself with rational explanations for the strange phenomena which had already occurred. I grew to like the stillness and solitude of my coastal home, and took advantage of the chance to grieve and process the rough few years that led me here.

My primary focus was working on my sobriety and health, but I was also hard at work on *Between the Devil and the Deep Blue Sea*. I had struggled for eight years to accomplish any sustained writing, started and crumbled up a hundred aborted stories, and smoked through dozens of packs of cigarettes while staring in frustration at a clean white page. I'd lost a part of myself, for how could I call myself a writer if I couldn't write? It was as if the fog had lifted. I could write for hours, look on my work, and feel it was my best. Usher's Fall became such a boon of feverish creativity, I couldn't even see how it was also slowly killing me. It was difficult for me to see how depressed and isolated I was becoming, how little I was eating.

Even though I was improving and healing myself, the tragedy of the old house with its long history of isolation, abuse, incest, murder, and suicide formed a larger part of my thoughts than I was aware of. Even beyond the strange and unwelcome happenings, the madness and death of so many screamed from behind the walls and thrummed underneath the floorboards. You could smell the depression and loneliness in the briny air, the earth and the trees. What a place for a person to choose to live in. As the week wore on, I began to relax in the old house, and to second-guess my initial misgivings.

Chapter Seven: Sunflower

October 20th, 1962

I was driving into the sunset, a sheen of gold glowing over the world. On either side of the car, fields of bright sunflowers danced in the wind on stalks seven feet high. Northern Virginia in June of '48. Jean was in the passenger seat, wild blonde hair blowing all around her face from the open windows. This was the height of the brief span of years between my return from fighting in the War and my departure to write about the next one as a journalist. Our lives were intertwined, off and on, from '39 to '61: twenty-two years. Married for fifteen. Happy? Smooth sailing? That part was more like five years. But we had a moment there from the end of the Second World War to the early days of Korea. It was the best of my life. I had never loved someone like that. I had never loved myself like that: who I was, what I was doing. With two published novels, I was on the rise as a recognized author. My daughter and I grew close. And I was driving through sunflower fields in Virginia with Jean. She wore a daisy-chain like a crown.

"Look at all the flowers! You would think it was all of them in the world."

"If I pulled over, how would you feel about walking through these with me?" I asked. The sun glinted on her sunglasses as she broke into a grin.

"Joseph Simon, you know we wouldn't be allowed to do that."

"Oh, come on. Who's gonna know?"

"Well, now that you mention it, I was having similar thoughts. But not about walking."

We exchanged a glance, she laughed, and I kicked up a shower of dust as I laid on the brakes and skidded over to the side of the road. She leaned in close and her full lips brushed my ear as she said in a husky voice,

"Come find me, Joe." A kiss on the cheek and a mischievous laugh and she was in the wind, bounding through the stalks of sunflowers like something elemental. I tore off after her, crashing through the stalks and trying to see through them to her.

"Jeanie? Darlin'?" I called out as I tried to pierce the thick growth of green stalks, sunlight filtering through a canopy of yellow petals overhead. I found a yellow shoe, and a few feet away there was another. I picked them up, calling her name again. There were hose strewn on the ground, then a polka-dot sundress blowing in the wind like a flag. My heart beat faster as I felt the soft fabric, hearing a giggle and another invitation to keep looking. There was a brassiere on the ground, and a pair of panties. I loosened my necktie and hastily unbuttoned my shirt.

"You're almost there! We'll be together soon." Her voice carried through the sunflowers.

"I hope we never leave." I cast my shirt aside and fumbled with my belt next. I stepped out of my slacks and into a clearing in the field... And an old house from Chapel Hill, North Carolina was there, engulfed in flames, billows of inky smoke spilling into the sky. The trampled clearing beyond the edge of the sunflowers was littered with empty liquor bottles. The elephant was next to me, and she reached out her trunk to pour whiskey into a glass held by my daughter.

"What's wrong, Daddy?" she asked as she handed me the glass. "Who did you burn?" Inside the house, the screams built to the wail of a hurricane. Time slowed to a crawl as I dropped the glass to shatter on the ground.

I woke up screaming in the pitch darkness of my room. Otis barked and stirred from his sleep with alarm, rushing to my side and licking my face as the tears fell. I was soaked in sweat, chest heaving. When I checked the clock, it was after midnight, but I wasn't going to sleep again. I wanted to die, overwhelmed by the ruin of my life. Instead, I put on my clothes, staggered through the woods to my car, and threw away my first whole month of sobriety in years so I could feel nothing instead of the crushing weight of my guilt.

The roadhouse was near empty when I walked in and stole up to the bar, trying to keep my hands from shaking. Country-western music was playing. The only ones in the place were a lovely bartender in her thirties and a pair of dirty old men, passing the time by flirting clumsily with her and trying to work out how to get as drunk as possible without spending a cent more than they had to. I resented them for being there. I had no business being in that tavern either, but felt like there was still time for me. These men were well into their seventies. If they had nothing better to do than hound dog a barmaid near one in the morning when they should have families somewhere... The more I thought about it, the angrier I got. What if I got to their age and was still so lost? What if I never figured it out?

"What'll it be, handsome?" the bartender asked.

"Got anything with sunflowers in it?" I replied dryly, unable to make eye contact.

"How do you mean?"

"Ah, never mind. Bourbon, please. Neat."

Chapter Eight: The Priest

October 27th*, 1962*

The last few days had been quiet save for the usual chills, fitful electricity, and melancholy, but the weird and troubling things I was experiencing were beginning to outrun my logical explanations and beggar reason. I threw myself into research at the Delilah Public Library, focusing at first on books of psychology, treatises on hallucination, fugue states, and delusions. Despite my skepticism, I gradually felt the nudge toward books dealing with séances, Spiritism, mediums, demon possession, poltergeists, hauntings, telepathy; all the topics I had spent years scoffing at as con-artistry and paranoid superstition.

I spent most of the day learning about psychological and paranormal phenomena, making liberal use of the coffeepot and eating sandwiches brought from the house. I was looking without knowing exactly what for, finding no satisfactory answers in tomes of science or superstition for the things happening around me. I had been at it for hours when I noticed a tome on one of the lower shelves. A colorful hand-written sign said "Hometown Author!," and pointed to several dusty identical hardcover copies of The Lost Soul by Thomas Forester, published by a small Pacific Northwest press in 1950. I ended up completely engrossed in it, devouring the introduction and first three chapters in a little more than two hours.

Thomas Forester proved to be both a captivating writer and a remarkable scholar, an enviable double-threat. He possessed a multifaceted knowledge of beliefs regarding ghosts and the immortal soul in many cultures throughout time. Though he examined the diversity of human belief in spirits, he avoided the heavy-handed conclusions and zealous certainty favored by other authors I had been perusing. Thomas Forester stood out from the herd of paranormal theorists as an intellectual and a scholar of some merit.

"Usher's Fall is haunted, isn't it?" Hana materialized at my side, as if from nowhere.

"Can you stop with the sneaking up on me?" I'd jumped out of my skin.

"It's a library. You're supposed to be quiet."

"What makes you think it's haunted?" I whispered.

"Is it?" she pressed with a hiss.

"No. Maybe. I don't know anymore. I never believed in that stuff. Don't believe in it now. Places like Usher's Fall develop reputations and paranoid, superstitious people see what they want to see because they're already expecting it."

"But you weren't expecting it, and whatever you've seen has you looking up... demon possession, poltergeists, astral-projection..." she listed them off as she handled each of the books in my stack in turn. I turned to her with a hard frown, deciding how much I wanted to tell her.

"Look, Usher's Fall is a place where disturbed people go to die, and where teenagers go to... Well, to park, or spook one another in the woods. There's a dangerous man I've seen there who carries a gun. I think him and some kids have ways of getting into the house and moving things around."

"And you've spent the afternoon reading about spirits, not pranksters and gunmen. So there's a part of you which doesn't accept that explanation."

"Maybe. But maybe the isolation of being out there with my own demons is chipping away at me. I don't know how to explain everything I've seen, not yet anyway. I'm trying to see if there's any substantial explanation, even if it's from a quarter I previously wouldn't have considered."

"You should let me help. I'm a ghost detective. I know all about this stuff."

"How many ghosts have you uh, detected?"

"Well, none yet. But this could be my big break!"

"On to the next thing, then. What can you tell me about Thomas Forester?"

"He's the bee's knees! His book is great, if you get a chance to read it. You might say he got me to where I am today."

"And he's still local?"

"He works at St. Nicholas."

"Alright, I'm going to head over. Watch Otis, okay?"

"You can't keep pawning your dog off on me."

"Here's ten bucks."

"Well, in that case."

St. Nicholas Episcopal was an old stone church with a high belfry and beautiful, stained glass windows depicting scenes of storm-tossed ships, lighthouses, and leviathans of the Deep. The red front door creaked as I stepped out of the rain into the wood-paneled, brown carpeted foyer. The cavernous sanctuary was lit only by beams of rain-sprinkled light filtered in blues through stained glass windows. The ceiling was ribbed with support beams like the belly of a capsized ship, and at the end of the rows of polished wooden pews I caught the dull glint of brass implements upon an altar, and a towering pipe organ decorated with an immense wooden cross hung before its metal tubes. The building reminded me of the sailors' chapel from the beginning of Moby Dick. Though the door was unlocked, the place appeared to be empty. The only sound was the soft patter of rain on the roof.

"The Lord be with you," a regal, cavernous voice said with the audible curl of a smile in it somewhere behind me.

"I hope so," I replied, missing the cue to respond 'and also with you.' The voice belonged to a black man perhaps twenty years my senior, with soft gray hair turning white, like a cloud that might rain on a whim. His face was kind and intelligent, with pronounced cheekbones and shining brown eyes marked with the crow's feet of frequent laughter. He wore a thin gray mustachioed goatee, the black shirt and white tab collar of a priest.

"Good afternoon, Father." I shook his hand. "My name is Joe Crowley."

"You don't need to call me Father. Thomas will do."

"Thomas Forester? I'm actually here looking for you. I saw your book in the library and had some questions."

"That old thing?" He chuckled. "I almost forgot they kept any copies. There aren't many around anymore. You're a fan?"

"I've been reading it for hours. You're a remarkable writer. Forgive me, sir, but... You aren't quite what I expected from the text."

"Because I'm a priest, or because I'm black?" his frankness was intoned with an easygoing smile.

"Both, I guess. I've been doing some reading on... Spiritual activity, you might say. Your work stood out to me because I'm inclined to doubt this stuff. Your work indicated you felt the same. You approach ghosts as an academic, not as a zealous believer. But you don't seem entirely dismissive of the notion either."

"The notion that we have immortal souls? Well, I'd have to check with the Diocese, but I might be out of a job if we didn't have souls." He smiled. "But I appreciate the compliment. The only ghost I'm sure about is the Holy Ghost. And there are days I doubt if He's around too. There are so many opportunists and conmen, and so many gullible, desperate people who need to believe in a hereafter. Is that shocking for a churchman to say? I've seen a lot of people get robbed by smooth-talking grifters: psychic mediums and pastors alike. I seek to guide my own parish in a gentle way, as a fellow admirer of the holy, but not as someone who can sell them all the answers. I try to teach the people in my care how to live at peace and love their neighbors in this life. I talk some about what may come next, but many preachers are too certain about Heaven and Hell and all. The Bible says little about that, and much less literally. Their orientation toward it is all wrong. Heaven isn't something to escape to, it's something to be: here, right now. Dying isn't the point, living is the point. If we go to a nice place after we die, it should be a pleasant surprise after living a good and upright life: not the sole reason you lived a good and upright life. That doesn't sound too good at all. Ah, but the more I learn, the less certain I am about anything. I just hope I'm doing what's right. I take it you're the same?" I nodded, glad to meet this kindred spirit. "If you don't mind my asking, Son, did you fight in the War?"

"I was an army captain. Any chance you were there?"

"No, but I was barely more than a boy when I served in the final months of the First World War. 'The War to End All Wars,' that was what it was supposed to be. If only. Sadly, the generations of American men can be categorized by which war was theirs."

"I know it. Say, do you do confessions?"

"Have you ever been to Confession?" he replied, bemused.

"No."

"Well, our confessions tend to be more communal. We don't do the booth or the Hail Marys. We read a prayer from the Book of Common Prayer together and try to mean it. But if you have the time and need to get some things off your chest, let's walk to my office."

I must have asked him three times if he was sure it wasn't a bother as we walked down a dim hallway to his cramped private study. He took his place in a chair by a roll-top desk against one wall, and I took my seat across from him. Rain continued to patter against the glass of his window. The room was plain and clean, decorated with various mementos and curios from his long life, two of its four walls taken up with bookshelves of mostly theological works. I don't know exactly how long we sat there, but I hadn't realized how much I needed to talk to somebody, how lonely and aggrieved I was. Once I started, everything poured out. He took it all in attentively without interrupting, breaking focus, or looking at his watch. Occasionally, he would ask clarifying questions, for me to go back to an old detail for a moment, or expound on a certain remark. When I finished, he took it all in for a few minutes, formulating a careful response as we sat in silence.

"So, you believe you might be having encounters with a ghost? Maybe several?"

"I don't know. I'm considering it, but I'm having trouble accepting it. I thought you would have some answers for me."

"Well, Cape Contrition and the lighthouse have a chilling reputation, to be sure. But I haven't seen what you have seen there. All I can say is your complaints bear much in common with things people have reported experiencing there for decades now. Maybe those stories run together because people are experiencing the same supernatural phenomena. Maybe people are experiencing what they expect to experience based on the local legend. But Joseph... Have you considered that the house isn't what's haunted, but you are? I don't want to make light of what you are feeling. The isolation and depression a place like that can bring on is real, and it has made many men before you unravel. But have you considered how much the mystery you are investigating may connect to unresolved trauma from your own life? As you told me, your own father was abusive to you, and his reign of terror in your childhood home was bolstered with religious dread and shame. Just like Henry Usher in his own household.

"Henry Usher was a failure as a father and husband, ultimately responsible for the destruction of his family and the death of his wife. Destruction wrought by fire. Forgive me, but don't you fear you have done the same? I know this is the greatest pain of your life I am speaking of, so I strive to be gentle, but... Perhaps you are too close to this case, and as you try to solve it, you are also on some level trying to understand how your own life ended. And perhaps, the deeper into this story you get, the more it's killing you. I don't want to discount completely that there are malevolent forces at work in that house, and I hope we will speak more in the future as you learn more. But in my experience, people are more haunted than houses, and you, Mr. Crowley, may be the most haunted man I have ever met."

Chapter Nine: Asylum

October 30th, 1962

Something was different at the Thunderbird. As soon as the bell rang behind me and the door closed, a hush fell over the old timers who filled the room. Heads all over the place bobbed back to gawk my way while some muttered darkly to one another.

"Morning, folks." I lit a cigarette and exhaled a swirling cloud of haze into the awkward silence as I added, "Didn't check the mirror this morning. Did I grow a second head or what?" The people who had been staring turned back around, determined to ignore me. "Okay," I murmured as I sidled between broad plaid-shirted backs crossed by suspenders and overalls, making my way through the crowd. There was a single seat open at the counter, and a squat toad-like woman hurriedly shoved her purse and bundled shawl into it, while the person on the other side turned away.

"You oughta be ashamed of yourself!" she snarled.

"I was a Southern Baptist as a kid, so they made sure of it. Tom, how the hell are ya?" Tom's voice squawked disembodied from the kitchen.

"Joe, that you? Ain't servin' you no more. Now scram!"

"Not you too. Why is everyone treating me like a leper? Let's get to the bottom of this over bacon and eggs, sunny side up. Sourdough toast, please. Black coffee with two sugars."

"Crowley, I'm not kidding. You've got no business where people want to have your guts for garters."

"This is a real hoot. Just bring me what I ordered." Though I was continuing to deflect with humor, something was terribly wrong. I'd been coming into this place since I moved in and enjoyed a pleasant relationship with Tom and his staff. Most everyone else left me alone. Gwen was wearing a gray knit sweater and navy-blue chinos, with the sun blazing her bob of curly red hair in a window seat. She waved me over and I squeezed into the other seat at her table.

"What the hell is going on here? Everyone is looking at me like I stole the Lindbergh Baby," I asked her under my breath.

"Have you seen the paper today? You're the front page." Her voice was subdued.

"What?" I cast about for a newspaper and apparently even though everyone in the diner had read it, no one had one out. The food came fast, and when the waitress plopped the plate aggressively onto the table, I noticed Tom stubbed out two cigarettes into the runny yolks of my eggs. The orange filters with their charred stubs leaned like twisted towers, black ash running into yellow yolks. The words "FUCK YOU" in ketchup cursive on the plate.

"Wow, you've done it again. My compliments to the chef," I told the waitress, who turned on her heel without a word. I finished my cigarette and stubbed it out in the eggs with the others. There was a garbage can in the corner behind my chair and I dumped the meal, plate and all, into the trash. At a far table, I saw an elderly man holding a spread newspaper inches away from his ailing eyes, squinting through coke-bottle thick glasses. He was one of the ones who'd been muttering about me as I came in. I got up, put a dollar bill on the table for his trouble, and pulled the paper out of his hands before turning around and going back to my seat. The old man sat flabbergasted, still holding two torn gray tufts of newspaper in his hands. The front-page item of today's Delilah Caller:

Acquitted Murderer and Disgraced Novelist
Laying Low on Cape Contrition

The piece was a hatchet-job written by one Edwin Gaines, no relation to the American murderer and body snatcher Ed Gein. I didn't read the whole thing and won't repeat the text of it here. Suffice to say, it was a sensationalized retelling of my acquittal, and contained a great deal of speculation about what depraved meddling I might be up to. Of course, if he had talked to me about my acquittal, he would have known I already blamed myself for the fire and believed I didn't deserve to live after the ruin I'd wrought with a cigarette flicked in anger. If Gaines bothered to ask me what I was doing in town, we might have talked. Instead, I stewed that he would have the gall to write it.

"Have you read it?" I asked.

"Along with the whole town."

"So, are you going to grab your torch and pitchfork with the others?" It came out more accusingly than I meant.

"Should I? Look, Ed is a jackal journalist. Maybe he's got enough clout to poison some locals against you, but everyone knows he's a libelous parasite. I know you well enough to know you're not a murderer. Oh, go ahead," she said as I took a small sip of her tea without asking and mulled over what she'd said.

"Okay. Thank you."

"You didn't... Right?"

"This is not how I wanted to have this conversation with you, okay?" I was getting agitated, but there was no getting out of this. Every bum from sea to shining sea could curse me for a murderer, but she had to know the truth.

"My wife Jean was the best woman I ever knew. Smart, kind, constant, nurturing, self-giving, funny. She was a force of nature. Jean was the only light I ever saw. I loved her more than any words I could compose would ever convey. But she wasn't enough. I don't know how she and Emma, the fame and success, none of that was enough for me. I was so lost. The things I experienced in the war ravaged my mind. I couldn't sleep without hearing myself lie to friends of mine as they tried to hold their guts in, telling them everything was going to be alright. I saw concentration camps, piles of bodies frozen together, stiff and pale with lifeless eyes staring like fish in a market. The faces of men I'd killed, twisted masks of fear, agony, hate. I say men, but many of them... Boys really. Barely eighteen. I hardly slept for years. Patrolled our property at night with my gun. A car could backfire, and my ears would be full of the boom of shelling, the roar of planes. Sometimes I can feel the bullets punching into my body like it just happened. The worst part isn't the way it rips through you. It's when it comes to a stop in the meat of you and sits there burning, like a hot coal burrowing into your muscle. A part of me never came back from over there.

"How could I talk to Jean about that? She'd never beaten someone to death with a shovel. She'd never... I couldn't explain to her what I'd done, so I kept it to myself. I resented her for not understanding the thing I didn't know how to say, and I felt isolated from her because of a wedge I was pounding between us. Writing helped me get the poison out, for a time. We had some good years. But writing wasn't enough either. One day I found I couldn't make myself do it anymore. It went like that for years. The reason I didn't talk to Jean about the war, the reason I pulled myself away from her and was such a difficult son of a bitch to live with was this: Jean was a good person, and I wasn't. I went through life terrified she would learn the secret, that I wasn't worthy of her. And when she learned the depth of that unworthiness... I didn't believe she could want to be with me. After all, I didn't want to be with me. So I lived in fear I would screw it up and she would leave, until the prophecy fulfilled itself.

"I drank myself half to death, tried to drown the depression overtaking my mind and pulling me out of my life, but it was a bottomless hole. I didn't see how deep I was digging myself until I was so far down, Jean didn't know who I was anymore. We were fighting constantly. I hadn't written a word in years and burned every bridge I ever built. On the night of July 7th, 1961, she asked: 'Did you ever love me?' And the last thing I said to her was, 'I don't think I love anything.'

"That night I went on a bender. Didn't come back until late in the morning. Firefighters said the cigarette I flicked near our porch before I stormed off caught fire on some dry brush. That fire hit a stash of whiskey bottles I'd stowed under the porch, and the conflagration spread to consume the entire house. Whole place was a damn tinderbox. She had a remarkable talent for going to bed angry. I never got the hang of it. We could scream at one another and she would be fast asleep five minutes later while I stayed up fuming all night. The smoke... suffocated her in her sleep, before the flames got there. Firefighters said she probably never felt a thing. Probably. But when I dream, I hear her screaming. There was almost nothing left of her. The house in which we had built a life together was four blackened stilts and a desolation between. It was my negligence that destroyed my family and my marriage, long before I flicked that cigarette. I squandered everything.

"So yes, if you want to walk any deeper into the mire of my life, you should know Jean's death was my fault. I left Chapel Hill because there was nothing left of my life there. Spent two months running down the highways, trying to find where I'd lost track of who I was. I didn't know if I would stop and settle down somewhere, or find a place to die, but I could never go home again. I was just passing through Delilah when Delilah decided she was going to keep me here awhile. That's it, that's everything."

Gwen sat for a while and lit a cigarette.

"Thank you. That took guts to say. I hadn't known how... damaged you were."

"Does it scare you?"

"I'm not afraid of you, Joe Crowley." She flicked ash onto her finished plate with a sardonic smile. "Maybe I'm damaged too." She looked like she would confide something to me in turn, but didn't. "I'd better get to work." She picked up her book and cigarette case. "What will you do now?"

"It's early yet. Think I may find out what happened to the Ushers. And I believe I know just who to talk to." I unfolded a square newspaper clipping from my pocket and showed it to her.

No Parole for Usher Family Slayer

A dark pall of heavy clouds loomed overhead as I crossed the Pacific Coastal Range, and my two-hour drive to Salem through farmlands and forests was made in a downpour of chilly rain. I stopped over in Eugene for a burger, and it was close to two in the afternoon when I crossed into the clean, manicured capital city of Oregon. After stopping long enough to see the stately marble capitol building and the well-tended lawns of the capitol mall, I got coffee at a place not far from the corner of Church and State. On the pretense of sightseeing, I stalled until I mustered the gumption to drive to the Oregon State Hospital. The immense asylum's rectangular Kirkbride building loomed with broad shoulders at the end of the long, straight drive. In the clouded foreboding of the storm, its ruddy Italianate façade, sharp High Victorian Gothic angles, and the spire of its white cupola and steeple towered with menace. After walking through the pouring rain with a small valise over my head, I found myself in a wide atrium where several orderlies and a secretary were smoking.

"Welcome to the Oregon State Hospital, Sir. How may I help you?" the front desk secretary asked between chews of gum, adjusting her cat's eye glasses.

"Good afternoon." I set my wet briefcase on the floor. "My name is Joseph Crowley."

"Like the magician?" She blew a large pink bubble and popped it before slurping the garbled mess of gum back in her mouth.

"Like the writer. I'm staying at the coast working on a book, and was hoping to interview one of your patients, if it would be possible. I thought he was dead, but recently learned he is still here."

"Name?"

"Usher. Henry Ahab Usher." Another bubble popped as she looked at me with surprise. She wadded the gum and threw it in the trash before saying,

"I think you had better speak with his doctor."

The long white hallway smelled of piss and bleach. Gray daylight filtered in through barred windows as Dr. Holland Anders walked me through the hospital for the insane. Over-worked nurses and orderlies in stark white uniforms stole smoke breaks amidst long hours in the overcrowded and underfunded mental hospital. Abuse and squalid conditions were apparent. Inside dim, padded rooms behind heavy doors, the afflicted gibbered and howled like the damned. A young woman patient with dirty, straw colored hair turned her uncannily gleaming eyes my way in a clairvoyant, unsettling look, and she laughed knowingly as if at some secret joke. A large bald man was thrashing violently ahead of us in the corridor, and when two orderlies body-slammed him into the green and white wall, he yelled,

"The dark mother! The Drowned Woman. She walks these halls too! Soon! Soon!"

"You can imagine my surprise, Mr. Crowley, when I heard which of our patients you were here to see. Mr. Usher has been with us over forty years, but you are his first visitor." Anders was a cool, easygoing psychiatrist in middle age, with neat blonde hair and thick spectacles. He showed all the Zen of a Buddhist monk in the bedlam around him.

"What can you tell me about him, Doctor?"

"He was moved here in '21, because his madness was too severe for him to cope with a normal prison. His case required full-time psychiatric observation. He beat another patient to death in '26. In '47, he bit off most of a nurse's nose, disfiguring her for life. She hanged herself three years later. In forty-one years, he has attempted suicide twenty-eight times. But he has been so closely monitored, especially since his violent incidents, he never had much chance of succeeding. Mr. Usher is a paranoid schizophrenic and manic depressive, given to violent mood swings, almost constantly perceiving powerful auditory and visual hallucinations, and suffering from profound delusions. Many of his delusions have a religious focus, as we often see. One day he would be Jesus Christ, and the next..."

"The Devil," I finished.

"So your research has told you something of what to expect. In his heyday he was a mountain of a man. In fits of rage, it took up to six orderlies to subdue him. A lucid man of his size is strong enough, but when stripped of all inhibition by mania, one can become truly herculean. But he's seventy-nine years old now, greatly diminished in strength and bearing. Eight years ago, at long last, he received a transorbital lobotomy. He has benefitted greatly from the procedure and is much more compliant."

"I'm sure."

"He was one of the last people in the United States to undergo the procedure. If his doctor at the time had waited just a few more months, he would have been able to manage Henry's symptoms with Thorazine, which is how we treat patients in his condition today. Some luck, eh? Oh, and one more thing... You should be warned he is also a rare sufferer of Cotard's Delusion."

"I'm not familiar with it."

"The simplest way to put it is he believes he's already dead. When he sees himself in the mirror, he sees a progressively rotting cadaver, and understands this place as some sort of purgatory."

"If he believes he is dead, why does he attempt suicide?"

"Mr. Crowley, I studied psychiatry at Johns Hopkins, and have been here for sixteen years. And the truth is, you cannot try to interpret the behavior of a maniac with a rational mind. It defies all logic. But delusions are not necessarily constant things. They can be broken through, or fade for a time, and return with full force. Perhaps we could say he periodically wakes up to his reality, attempts to free himself by suicide, and falls back into the comfortable delusion of being dead in order to preserve some part of himself comforted by that notion. After all, the mind's powerful ability to delude itself, warping reality into something we can cope with, is a defense mechanism for our own survival. But here, this is his room now." We came to a halt beside a heavy white door with a metal lattice of wiry bars across a rectangular porthole of thick glass.

"Thank you for your time, Doctor." I moved to shake his hand.

"My apologies, Mr. Crowley, I thought you understood. You cannot be alone with him. Lobotomized geriatric or not, Henry Ahab Usher is the most dangerous man in my charge. And furthermore, for my own curiosity, I would not miss your interview with him for the world."

"Very well." I steeled myself. "Let's meet the man." The door swung open at Dr. Anders' touch, revealing a Spartan cell with padded walls, a simple bed bolted to the floor, with a chamber pot underneath. No sharp corners, electrical outlets, or anything else that could be used to a violent end. A tall, broad-shouldered black orderly sat comfortably in a folding chair against the wall reading a book, keeping one experienced eye on the man in his charge. From the diary of Rosemary Usher, I expected a towering bull of a man, swarthy and black-bearded, with a wild gleam in his eyes and a fierce zeal in his powerful voice. A part of me also expected to see my fiery deacon father, who could throw me across a room one handed and, on several occasions, beat me to unconsciousness.

The person I saw was anticlimactic by comparison. Small, withered, snugly wrapped in a straitjacket, a beard and long, thin wisps of iron-gray hair showing a greenish, sickly scalp beneath. His face and neck were scored with jagged scars he'd made himself. The most striking was a slashed and puckered scar stitched vertically down the left side of his face from temple to jawline, with another scar like it starting at the bridge of his nose and snaking up jaggedly through his brow into his thin hairline. His body was presumably also a tapestry of slashes. Often in elderly men, after the body fades, the eyes still gleam with the mind of the young man behind them. But Henry Usher's eyes were cloudy with cataracts, lifeless and cold. The eyes of a cave serpent that has never seen the sun. One look in those eyes could tell, no one was home. Like an abandoned lighthouse, Henry Usher's fire had gone out. He sat still as a statue, staring lidless out in front of him, through us, not even registering our arrival. He was seated at a chair with a green folding card-table before him.

"Jerome, how is our patient today?"

"What you see now is all there is to see." Jerome closed his book after marking his place. "He's been catatonic like this for three days. I've been here long enough to see plenty of stiffs, but this is uncanny."

"Catatonic?" I asked, unfamiliar with the term.

"A state of psychogenic motor immobility and behavioral abnormality manifested in a statuesque stupor. In his case, his catatonic fits seem to be part of his delusion of living death. Electroconvulsive therapy has been helpful to alleviate these symptoms, but Mr. Usher has become so frail, we must be careful how we administer such treatments. But I'm afraid if he is like this, you will have little hope of getting anything out of him. He will not speak to anyone. He may not be aware we are here at this very moment."

"I've come an awful long way not to at least try. Do you... Do you think I could try to speak to him?"

Doctor Anders nodded.

"You can certainly try." I got a freshly bought tape recorder from my briefcase, set the large unwieldy machine on the card table, and switched it on. The reels of magnetic tape hummed into their steady rotations, and I adjusted the microphone before him.

"Mr. Usher. My name is Joe Crowley. I'm the person who lives in your old house. How do you feel about that?" A pause, nothing. "Do you remember the old house out on Cape Contrition? You gave Siren's Head that name when you moved your family there. Do you remember your family?" I shifted uncomfortably, meeting his dead, milky eyes. "I came here today because I am trying to find out what happened there, the night of the great fire. Do you have anything to say about that night?" The silence and stillness of the man made me feel foolish. The rebuke of a brick wall. "Sir, my research has led me to think you may not have actually killed your wife and children all those years ago. Does the possibility of your vindication hold no interest for you?" I let the question hang in the air before averting my eyes from the ruin of his face with a sigh. "It's no use. His mind is dead. It just forgot to tell his body."

The air was split by a woman's wail, horrific in its shrill agony. All of us but Henry jolted at the sound. She screamed and screamed again. A man roared and her voice cracked and shook, breaking into an agony of moans. "She told me to! She told me to, hahahahaha! The Dark Mother!" I heard the man cackle outside while several footsteps thundered and squeaked down the marble hallway. There was a dull thud right outside the door, and a splash of blood spattered against the glass of the porthole.

"Oh my God. Oh, Jesus," Doctor Anders shuddered as he ran outside, and Jerome followed him. Through the closing door I saw a man's skull crushed in a widening sanguine pool on the floor. A nurse moaned as blood poured down her face and her eye dangled from a red socket by the ropy thread of the optic nerve. The old instincts of my war service were firing up, and the terror of life and death struggle washed over me, but as my heartbeat rose to a pound and my limbs went weak, I realized I couldn't follow them. It was as if I was paralyzed by my fear and could only huddle in the padded room to avoid the screaming slaughter outside. Anders and Jerome fought to restrain the murderer, but I was shut out from their struggle over the gory scene, as the door of the cell closed on its own between us and left me alone with the catatonic Henry Usher.

When I turned back around to him, a chilling gleam came to his eyes, and movement returned to his limbs. Was his glassy-eyed catatonia some kind of an act, held until he had me alone? Had he known I was coming and held up this façade unwavering for three days?

"Not your house," he murmured in a hoarse, excited whisper. "Hers. All hers now."

"Whose? Who in God's name are you talking about?" I whispered too, though I didn't know why.

"There is no God. Only the Woman. I've never seen God, but I've seen her. She has spoken to me here twenty-eight times. Twentyeighttimesnowtwentynine. She is here now." His cloudy eyes widened with horrible recognition as he gazed over my shoulder into the space behind me. The room grew cold and the lights flickered with a fitful hum. I sat paralyzed, terrified to look behind me. He is hallucinating. This isn't real. There is no one there standing over my shoulder. But another part of me felt a powerful and malevolent presence. That part of my brain screamed for me to keep my eyes locked on Henry, not to look behind me at any cost. How could I feel the presence at Cape Contrition in this very room? Henry's face flickered with so many emotions in the span of a few seconds. Its fissured wrinkles and craggy features showed hate, anguish, despair, and resignation, then eagerness.

"Twentyeighttimesnowtwentynine," he chanted. "She has come for me now. She will come for you too, Joe Crowley."

"Who?" I shouted. "Who is she?" He broke his eyes off from their stare over my shoulder to settle them on me as his mouth smirked in a bemused smile.

"She told me to drown." Henry Usher stuck his long, pointed tongue full out of his mouth and down his chin, his face a twisted mask of mockery and disdain. That demonic, terrible face with dark scars and jutting tongue reminded me of a Maori warrior dancing the Hakka to intimidate his enemies. I didn't realize what he was doing until he slammed his chin as hard as he could on the card-table, and his decaying teeth bit clean through his tongue like a guillotine. When his chin hit the table, he let out a determined groan through his clenched, bloody teeth. When he lifted his head high, his tongue remained sitting like a dead slug on the table. A thin spittle of red droplets peppered the spinning wheels and buttons of the tape recorder, as well as my own face. On the lenses of my glasses was a vision in carmine.

His gaping, red mouth gushed a bubbling froth of blood and he smiled with sick abandon as he threw himself backward. The chair toppled back with him, and on his back upon the floor, he howled, coughed, and sputtered as he drowned in his own wicked blood. The twisted mockery of his snarling face through the gushing froth will forever be seared into my brain. The door flung open behind me and the feeling of the other malign presence in the room vanished as Doctor Anders and Jerome burst in, their clothes spotted with blood. The two men rushed, frantic, to Henry's side. Nausea took over, and the initial terror of the hallway scene fused with Henry killing himself before my eyes to send me into a paralyzing war flashback. All sound turned down to a heavy pressure and dull murmur as if I was trying to hear underwater, and time crawled around me. I sat on the floor, face splattered with Henry Usher's blood, watching in disbelief as Jerome and Anders tried and failed to save his life. Henry's ghoulish, red-grinning head lay back in his own blood on the floor, and he was dead. I was dimly aware Anders was shaking me, and the sounds of the world turned back up.

"Dear God, man, what happened? Mr. Crowley? Mr. Crowley! What did you do? What did you say to him?"

My words poured out in a jumble, and I was unaware of

what exactly I was saying. He gathered Henry had not been catatonic, and made some mocking, darkly cryptic references before biting his own tongue and choking to death on his own blood. The rest is a blur, but Dr. Holland Anders gave me his own handkerchief to wipe the blood from my face, before quickly ushering me out of the hospital and onto the front steps. I stood there in a daze of horror, shuddering and trembling until the chill rain soaked me to the bone. I forgot my boxy recording device, and they did not return it to me.

I was back in Delilah, six or seven drinks in at a run-down bar, maybe more, when Gwen found me late that night. I'd lost track of time and drank more than I had money to pay. My face was numb, I was sweaty and red, and could hardly see straight. My mind was still full of that blood.

"Gwen! What a surprise! Come sit, have a... Have a drink!" I shouted, forgetting I'd had the bartender call her.

"Gwen, you know this louse?" The pony-tailed, balding bartender asked, thick mustache set in an annoyed frown.

"What does he owe you, Lenny?"

"Seventy-eight dollars, and that includes a broken stool and two shattered glasses. Gwenny, just get him out of here, or I'm gonna call the police."

"Big Chief Blake! Take the bad medicine away." I let out a war whoop broken up by clapping my hand over my mouth, the way boys do when they play cowboys and Indians.

"Hey, cut that shit out, I'm a quarter Chinook," Lenny said.

"Joe!" Gwen turned and snapped, shutting me up completely. "It's almost midnight. I have to work in the morning, and don't make enough money to support your habit. Are you done now?" She opened her purse and took out a fold of bills, counting out eighty dollars and handing them to Lenny, murmuring her apologies. I drunkenly and profusely thanked her as she braced me with her shoulder, wrapped an arm around my waist, and led me staggering out of there. When she finally tumbled me into the car, climbed into the cab, and slammed the passenger door, she groaned,

"Why did you call me?"

"Who else did you think I could call?" It was pathetic, but true. She looked as if she would scold me further, but relented and started the car. I remember little from the drive back to her house. Only how as we drove, my account of the horrific thing I saw that day came pouring out of my mouth, and when she saw how pitifully alone and miserable I was, her anger softened and she was gentle with me. When she tumbled my dead weight onto the couch, I looked at her with a sleepy smile and said,

"Thank you, Jeanie." I only realized my dead wife's name slipped in place of hers after I said it. She paused for a moment and lowered her eyes: the look a person gets when you accidentally spit in their face.

"I'm sorry, I –Gwen," I tried to recover, but it was too late, and I was too drunk.

"It's fine. She, uh, meant a lot to you and you're pretty drunk, so. Of course, you'd be thinking about her." I didn't have anything to say to that, and soon drifted off into a heavy sleep.

Chapter Ten: The Shipwright's Widow

October 31ˢᵗ, 1962

I knew I was dreaming when my old agent Larry Filbert joined me in my living room at Usher's Fall. He didn't know where I lived, wouldn't have spoken to me if he did, and was dead to boot. Larry leaned forward in a wicker armchair, training a hard, disappointed look on me. The gleaming Taj Mahal dome of his bald head had broken open like an egg, streaming blood, brains, and skull fragments from the top. In the dream, I did not find this to be alarming or strange. After all, word got back to me that my career's downfall coincided with his. After a few other bad investments brought him to financial ruin, he put a gun in his mouth in '59.

"Look at this place," he said, glancing around. "Unbeliev-able. Why does a guy like you get to put his feet up in a beach house like this? You should be dead and in Hell with me, not on vacation."

"I'm not on vacation, Lar, I'm working out here. The next novel is well on its way."

"Oh, I've heard that one before. That's just great. Of course, you couldn't be bothered to squeeze through your creative constipation when I was going bankrupt waiting for you."

"You can't know how sorry I am about that."

"Yeah, pal, you're sorry about a whole lot. You're a real piece of work, you know that?"

"I'm out here because I'm trying to get better. Working on my sobriety, the book, processing what happened to me, what I did."

"Working on giving the time to that bookstore broad too, huh? So, you'll get it all back. The writing dough, the career, the replacement wife. So there really is no God. Unbelievable, the kind of luck you have. You know what? You've lost more than I've ever had. I would've killed men with my bare hands to have your life. But you tortured artist types... standing waist-deep in money, fame, the love of a good woman, and you're still so god-damn miserable. It's maddening, Joe! I loved your wife; did you know that? Hell, you probably did. She only had eyes for you. And your little Emma was like a favorite niece to me. Loved that kid. What the fuck did you have to be so depressed about? So daddy beat you. Lots of kids get beat by their dads. You saw some hard shit in the war. But you survived it when how many millions didn't, a decorated hero and all. You've met presidents and Hollywood actors. You had a beautiful family. How could you have had Jean, Emma, and all that success and it not be enough for you? Joe Crowley, you had everything I ever wanted and still hadn't found what you were looking for. You know how that feels? That's why I ended it, Joe. You squandered everything God ever gave you. And damn it, Joe, that's why I've come back. I'm here to drag you to Hell where you belong!"

"I'm sorry, Larry. I know it's not enough, but it's all I've got now."

"You've got so much more than that, but you can't see it.

Now, all you're gonna have is this." He lifted a snub-nosed revolver to my forehead and squeezed the trigger. I snapped awake with the sound of the pop still ringing in my ears, sweating and panting on a corduroy couch. A thick Indian blanket was thrown over me, and I was in my skivvies in a strange room where I'd never been. My head was full of the dull throb of a hangover headache, and while my aching eyes tried to figure out where I was or how I'd gotten there, I asked myself why people can't see themselves die in dreams.

The smell of baking was heavy and cloying in the air, and warm morning sunlight filtered through the blinds, enough to illuminate the cluttered living room without overwhelming my light-sensitive eyes. A fat orange and white tabby cat padded lazily across the carpet, lifting its quivering nose to smell my face and purring in my ear. I lifted a hand to scratch the cat behind the ears, and saw my hand was bandaged with linen. Dimly I remembered crushing a glass in my hand, blood dribbling on a barstool the night before. Gwen came in, whisking something in a large bowl.

"Oh, good, you're awake," she said brightly, leaning against a wall and continuing to whisk the contents of the bowl.

"What are you making?"

"Lemon meringue, for a pie. Would you like coffee?"

"Sure." I sat up and feebly wrapped the blanket about myself. I wondered if she'd noticed the puckered bullet scars or was shocked by my tattoos. The corduroy pressed long lines into my skin over the side of my face and thin body.

"I have a plate of bacon and eggs ready, too. Protein should help with that hangover."

"What did I do to deserve you?" She wouldn't say. "Did we...

149

" I started to ask, but she shook her head, smiling privately to herself as she averted her eyes into her mixing bowl.

"No. I wouldn't take advantage of you. But your clothes had some blood on them and smelled like beer, so I helped you out of them before you spent the night on the couch. I would have given you the bed but couldn't get you that far. Anyway, your clothes are in the wash. In the meantime, I laid something out for you." Next to me was a folded red flannel shirt and a pair of blue jeans I cinched up with a belt before putting on my own crusty socks from the day before, and my wingtip shoes. When I finished dressing, she stifled a laugh at how enormous the clothes were on me but looked pained as well to see them.

"You look good," she snickered, putting a brave face over that flash of a grimace.

"Whose clothes are these?"

"My husband's." she glanced away to get my plate. "Ex-husband. He left about five years ago, ran off with some schoolteacher in Florence. The one in Oregon, I mean."

"I'm sorry that happened to you, Gwen."

"Me too. I have to run, Joe, but you can hang out here for the morning if you want and pick up your clothes when they're done drying on the line." I was ashamed of myself in the face of her kindness. My mind flashed with pictures of all the times Jean walked me up the stairs of our house, tumbled me into bed, and gently tucked me in while I was drunk, cuddly and fussy like a sleepy toddler. She did that long after it wasn't cute anymore.

"Thank you. I know I wasn't fun to be around last night, but I needed this."

"Try not to make it a habit, Joseph. You're better than this."

"I'm trying to be." Unexpectedly, she kissed me on the cheek before she left. I lived on that for the rest of the day.

Otis and I passed the drizzly day in town after I picked him up from the Iwamoto house later that morning. I was eager for quality time with him and wanted to avoid being cooped up in Usher's Fall: especially on Halloween. We walked all over Delilah, browsing shops decorated with black cats and Jack-O'-Lanterns, lounging in cafes, and chasing one another on the beach. My thoughts still swirled with the ghoulish red mouth of Henry Usher and the carnage of the hospital hallway, but my shaggy mutt's wide smile, lolling tongue, and simple joy were bringing me back little by little.

Eventually, we found our way to the waterfront district. Warehouses and canneries gave the area a fishy odor, and we walked docks crowded with gillnetters, trawlers, crabbers, small personal outboard motorboats and sailboats, and the occasional humble pleasure yacht. Out in the bay, long, low barges drifted by. Seagulls hovered like kites on the wind before snapping into sudden dives with the simultaneous hive-mind of bird flocks, bolting after a single splash on the water's surface.

We saw fat, sleek sea lions lounging on the dark rocks of a jetty. Others loudly barked and bellowed while they jostled with scarred shoulders, heaving bulk, and bared fangs for coveted positions on the end of the dock. Occasionally one small opportunist would launch himself out of the water into the wriggling mass of his kind, only to be shouted down and heaved back into the water. Otis barked and snarled at the creatures with mingled fear and wonder. We lingered there for a while, watching the endless argument of the bellowing animals, each jealous for their rights and none willing to listen. A position on the dock couldn't be enjoyable if they had to spend the whole time fighting and howling for it.

In another time, Henry Usher had roamed these same docks looking for any work he could find. I thought about the sea lions on their jetty and the Ushers on their Cape for some time as I walked Otis along, and soon found my way to a shipwright's workshop huddled at the far end of the marina. A cowbell hanging from the door clattered as I opened it. The place had fallen on hard times. The smell of sawdust and mildew hung in the air. In the center of the workshop was the unfinished, ribbed wooden hull and husk of what promised to one day be a sleek little handcrafted yacht. But the project was abandoned and unnamed, the haunt of a bony Calico cat and a shaggy Maine Coon the size of a bobcat. The Calico hissed and spat at the sight of Otis with her back arched, but the wizened Maine Coon sized him up where he was lounging and was unimpressed.

An elderly woman came out from the back, wrapped in a thick navy blue cardigan and holding a steaming white porcelain mug. Her iron gray hair was once black, tied in a messy bun with a pencil through it, and her jaw was set with a firmness that gave the impression of a stubborn streak. She had the jowls which often form with age, lending her a bulldog's surly aspect. Her pale blue eyes held a haunted depth: a cold dullness indicative of woundedness. Hurt people have a mysterious way of recognizing one another. All I can say is this old woman's eyes reminded me of the eyes of men I'd fought the War with, and of my own in the mirror.

"What can I do for ya?" she asked, setting her mug on a counter by a cash register and shooing away a long-haired Siamese that immediately hopped up for a sniff.

"I don't rightly know. Just found myself here."

"We don't let dogs in. You've upset Leeland." One of the three cats, but I didn't ask which.

"Sorry, Ma'am, I wasn't thinking. He goes where I go." She chewed on that for a moment.

"All the same."

By the time I tied Otis up outside, came back in, and closed the door on his whines, she had another mug steeping with tea for me.

"You take chamomile? Can't do coffee this late in the day."

"Chamomile's fine."

"Storm's coming." She wrapped the cardigan close and shivered as she glanced outside the window behind me. "Can feel it in my bones. I've got the arthritis. Rheumatoid, real bad. What about you? You're not old enough, maybe."

"I've been spared that so far, but I'm sure it's coming. I'm a typist and guitarist, so the fingers will go; my ankles and knees won't be long in following from running."

"Typist, guitarist, runner," she smirked, keeping track on her fingers. "And you're not local."

"No, ma'am. I'm new in town, working on a book. Joe Crowley." She shook my hand, and replied,

"Alice Cole. Will you be here long?"

"A year, at least, I expect. But I'm taking to the place. Could end up settling here."

"What's your book about?"

"The Ushers, out on Cape Contrition. You're familiar with them?" She got quiet and her pleasantness dropped for a long moment before she remembered to reply.

"Everyone in Delilah knows them now, or thinks they do. Might be if they'd bothered knowing them at the time, it would've turned out different. But who are they to you? And why is the only thing you want to write about my town the worst thing that ever happened here?"

"The father of that family reminds me of my dad. He ruled our house with a Bible and a leather belt, and I guess remembering him makes me pity the woman and her children. But more than that, well, I guess you could say I relate to them because we're both outsiders here."

"Mm," she nodded, unimpressed but too polite to say so.

"What about you? Do you have any memory of them? You must have lived here back then when you were young?"

"Aye. But like I said. Ushers kept to themselves out on the Cape. Delilah folk had few dealings with them. My husband Caleb might've been able to tell you more, but the ocean took him from me, seven years gone."

"I'm sorry to hear that."

"He was a good man." Her lips turned in a smile that showed the old girlish love of a younger woman, unchanged by the passage of time. "I miss 'im. This old place was his, you know. I just keep it up with a carpenter and mechanic. I picked up a little of the trade over the years, but none of us are shipwrights proper. That yacht was going to be his life's work, and now look at it. The *Cat Nest*."

"Can you tell me anything about what Delilah was like back then?"

"Much like it is now. Places like this don't change. But it looks like we may have to. The trades that sustained this place are dying out, and people are talking about replacing fishing and logging with, what... gift shops, resorts. Whole damn place is prostituting itself to stay alive, forgetting what it's supposed to be."

"And the people? I guess the more I learn about the Ushers, the harder it is for me to believe no one here did anything to help them."

"You aren't that naïve, Mr. Crowley. When it comes down to it, most folk are in it for themselves. They keep their heads down and don't rock the boat. Most people care more about their own peace and quiet than they do about justice. Maybe that's what's wrong everywhere. Delilah folk are no different. They sweat in the fishing ships, the lumber yards and canneries, maintain their little lives, drink and play cards of a night and forgive themselves when they play church on Sunday. They jostle for their place, gossip with cruel delight at their neighbors' misfortunes, and roar their petty feuds, blind to anyone else... like those sea lions outside, matter of fact. Happy, barking little fools..." she paused, and looked out the window with ancient, keen eyes.

"What Delilah folk all know and pretend they don't is this little rock of theirs ain't so wholesome. They're hard working people and all, doing everything an American ought, each thinking they've got a righteous and good little town here on the brink of the old ocean. But towns have secrets, just like men. Ours is what happened to that poor family out on Cape Contrition, the way everyone knew what was happening to them for a decade and nobody lifted a finger. That was the day we were all damned. Only time will tell to what. We thought we could ignore the past because it was dead. But dead things can still haunt."

She fell into a reverie for a long moment, and I wasn't sure what to say. For a minute, she looked as if she might say more, and I was afraid to even breathe in a way that would chase her next statement off. An old journalist's twitch told me she was about to drop a line I would need to hear, but she changed the subject instead.

"Well, Mr. Crowley, do you fish?"

"A few times a year. I enjoy it when I do, but I'm no virtuoso."

"You good in the water?"

"All Southern boys can swim, Ma'am."

"What about boats? You're in a boat shop, after all."

"To be honest, I don't know what I'm doing on a boat."

"Well, you look like a sharp lad. We can fit you up with an easy one. Ain't right that a man who lives in this town wouldn't have a boat." I don't know how she talked me into it, but when I drove out to Cape Contrition at the day's end, a little outboard motorboat was in tow on a two-wheeled trailer behind me. I piloted the little boat out of Siren's Cove and beyond the tip of Cape Contrition that evening with Otis struggling to keep his feet. Together we watched the most brilliant sunset, sky a swirl of gold, orange, lavender and pink. The water glimmered peach and cherry blossom, and I was careful to steer around the knuckles of stone jutting out of the water as we made our way out onto the open ocean. I laughed and stood up in the rocking boat, whooping like a boy with Otis barking and struggling to keep his balance. To watch the sun sink into the Pacific when you're out on the water was to feel the illusion of being so close you could sail into it. The sprawling canvas of soft color and glowing light was all around us. We were no longer spectators, but participants in the sinking of the sun. It was a perfect end to the most peaceful and serene day I could remember in a while.

I had cleaned my dinner plate and was strumming my guitar on the porch when I saw a new man lurking in the woods. Like the Sailor, he wielded an archaic, rusted rifle. He would not step full upon the lawn or approach the house, but merely lurked among the evergreens. He stared with eyes full of hate, but held back, as if restrained or afraid. At first sight of him, I set down my guitar with a discordant jangle of sounding strings and picked up my shotgun so he could see me holding it. Like the Sailor, he did not appear to be intimidated by any show of force on my part. Something was keeping them from entering the house and walking the lawn, but it wasn't me. This new gunman was a head and a half taller than the first, a towering bear of a man, swarthy, black-bearded, and almost simian in his facial features, like a ruthless Cro-Magnon ancestor of humanity. His forearms were thick with black hair and muscle, like a gorilla's, and he clothed himself in a wide-brimmed black capotain hat and a drab, puritanical outfit. When he drifted back to disappear in the trees, I took Otis inside and locked the door behind us.

The first panicked fever of my thoughts was that there were two of them now, and I knew I could not go to the police a second time after crying wolf with my strange tale already. I could already hear Will Blake's sarcastic questions about the man dressed up to meet Squanto for Thanksgiving haunting the woods of Usher's Fall. But as my first fearful impression settled, another suggestion came to me. A month ago, I would have scoffed at it, but it came to overtake all other possibilities. While I had no basis for recognizing the Sailor's face, the Pioneer was uncannily familiar to me already. I had met him in the pages of a forgotten journal, and seen him as an old man, watched him die only a day ago. There was no room for me to doubt it. The second gunman was the Preacher of Delilah's sordid docks, the keeper of Contrition's light, and the red-grinning ghoul in the asylum. I was seeing Henry Usher again. He was appearing on Cape Contrition for the first time in over forty years because he had been alive all this time, and some part of him was bound to this place now that he was dead.

Chapter Eleven: The Attack

November 9th, 1962

   Chilly wind cut across the secluded estuary as I heaved a crab ring into the churning water with a splash. The netting and rotting fish bait slapped the surface and dropped to the depths, lost beneath the green churn of the waves. Later, we would return to the buoys, drawing the slick wet ropes hand-over-hand quickly enough for the force of the pull to draw up the concentric rings of the traps from their flat resting place into a rigid circular wall of nets, racing for the surface. Otis would huff and stare as I picked through the netting, prizing apart the pincers of small crabs clinging to the ropes and tossing them out over the side. Often, the male Dungeness crabs large enough to keep crouched protectively over the stinking carrion bait in the bottom. I checked their pale underbellies for an obelisk shape indicating males, tossing the females whose undersides bore a beehive shape. Even after the rapid rise to the surface, they were still tearing greedily at their last meals with their pincers, pulling shreds of rank meat into the open shutters of their alien mouths. I collected the six big eligible bachelors of the day in a deep bucket. They snapped, quarreled, and writhed spiderlike on their backs on top of one another, shells ruddy brown, purple, and green. Several had broken claws, missing limbs, and scarred carapaces from their gladiatorial lifestyles.

The sun was setting in the distance beyond Cape Contrition when we returned there, and in the last gasp of fading daylight, I made the hike up the wooded path to the old house, heavy bucket in one hand and taut leash in the other. Rose gold beams of fading light filtered through the firs. The sloping backs of two chubby raccoons passed behind a moss-covered log, and the pure blue wings of California scrub jays flitted in the branches as they passed questioning shrieks back and forth. My hands were rope-burned and pinched, my back was aching, and it was the perfect day.

That was when a patch of bark on the tree right next to my head exploded into a burst of wood-shards and dust, and the jarring crack of the rifle-shot sounded half an instant after.

I swore, dropped the bucket, and ducked. The dog triangulated the direction of the sound a moment before I did. I followed his gaze to see a plume of smoke curling in the air, and the immense figure of the Pioneer in his wide-brimmed capotain hat stepping out from behind a tree off the trail fifty paces to my left. My theory that this man was the ghost of Henry Usher vanished as he cranked the lever-action of his Winchester again and raised it to his shoulder, leveling the long, rusting barrel dead at me. For a split second I crouched paralyzed, making eye contact with him like a petrified buck. An instant's flash of fire from the bore and I tore off again, a hot whining whistle of metal streaking down and exploding a clump of earth by my feet. My heart thudded in my ears as I left the overturned bucket of live crabs liberated in the middle of a forest and ran for my life with Otis galloping beside me.

Old war instincts kicked in as I zig-zagged off the trail, trying to keep my eye on the Pioneer and put the cover of trees and boulders between us. A third shot burst a shower of bark dust and jagged splinters of wood over my shoulders, and I glanced out to see this one was fired by the other, the Sailor. So they were both making their play. My legs pumped as I tore through the undergrowth, leaping over logs and twisting around trunks in the deepening gloom, seeing an occasional flash of fire and smoke behind me as another bullet whistled past. Every time a gun went off, my panicked mind scanned over myself for a wound, and glanced at Otis for the same. I knew from experience my adrenaline was throbbing so high, it was possible I could not immediately notice a hit.

Night was coming on fast, and I got disoriented in what was normally a breezy hike along a straightforward switchback trail. These weren't woods you could get lost in, but my breath was rattling in my chest, and my terrorized mind couldn't interpret up from down. Keeping track of one of them as I ran was doable, but with two, I had no idea where the next gunshot would come from. With my sense of direction clouded, I feared I might dive between two trees and end up with one of their bores right in my teeth. Their shouts sounded guttural and ugly, hate-filled barks over the gunfire. Shots burst with bullets that passed nowhere close to me, and it almost seemed as if they might have been shooting at one another the whole time.

All higher thought was expelled, subservient to the instincts of fight and flight. I ran as fast as I could until I burst out through the edge of the tree-line and fell on my face upon the green lawn of Usher's Fall. The ground knocked all the wind out of my desperate lungs. I sucked a moaning, shuddering gasp of air as I tore up clumps of dirt and grass with clawing hands that launched me back onto unsteady feet. Otis' leash was no longer in my hand, and the barking dog galloped with his tail between his legs, leaping onto the porch and clawing at the front door. Two more gunshots sounded on top of one another as I flung open the door and threw myself into the darkened house.

A few seconds later, I flooded the yard with light from the porch and house, and burst out through the mudroom with a 12-gauge at my shoulder. Rather than wait to be besieged in Usher's Fall, I ran across the lawn into the forest. Every step I was conscious of Otis' shrill barks locked in the house behind me, and my vulnerability in the yard. When I melted into the tree-line, though, my body was in command of its fear. Time rolled back twenty years, and I was a Captain again, a specter in the shadows of the huge old trees. I was good at this part. The question was, were they? I crouched behind a tree with the gun at port arms across my chest, keeping my breathing slow and even, strangling the rise of coughs and gasps after so much frantic running. Visibility had gone to near pitch-darkness, but I could still hear their yells and shots, less frequent now than before, and getting farther away. In my pocket was a heavy aluminum flashlight, but I dared not use it and risk giving myself away. Careful to move from one point of cover to another, I followed the sounds into the woods.

The forest was larger than it should have been. Over the rise at my back, I saw a faint hint of all the lights on in the house through the trees and tried to keep it as a point of reference. I heard a gunshot ring out close, within only five yards of me, but it was one of the men aiming at the other. The light of the muzzle-flash aimed away from me, and he did not know I was there. As soon as the jarring blast thundered, I ducked behind a mossy boulder in a crouch. I was confident I would get the drop on my man, and a glance from my cover told me it was the Pioneer himself. He grunted in pain from a glancing gunshot wound to the midsection. Doubled over, he groaned and cursed the son-of-a-bitch. Overhead, the clouds parted from the moon long enough to filter some of its silver light through the treetops. In the moment of illumination, I caught a wet glint of blood where his hand pressed his abdomen, and he cursed to see it painted carmine.

Twigs snapped as he turned and staggered forward. He was only paces from stumbling right over where I was standing. Steeling myself, I turned a smooth pivot and stepped out from behind the boulder with my gun leveled. The clouds plunged everything back into utter darkness as my shotgun heaved a deafening blast and fire flashed from its muzzle. As soon as my first shot cleared, I racked the action and squeezed the trigger a second time, spraying another burst of buckshot over where he had been standing. The twin blasts were deafening, and my ears rang with the shock of them, more jarring than I remembered from the decade since I last fired a gun.

As the boom of the second shot rattled in my eardrums, I strained my eyes to pierce the darkness. There was no sound or sight of a falling body I could perceive among the two bursts, and the possibility of seeing the corpse stretched out on the forest floor would have been hopeless this late at night. I could barely see the muzzle of my gun in front of me. But at the same time, even rusty, I was always a capable marksman. And marksmanship didn't enter into cutting a man in half at five yards with two blasts from a shotgun. I'd struck him twice, in rapid succession, and knew it for a fact even in the stygian gloom. I crouched and blindly felt the forest floor in front of me, pawing at the brittle pine needles, snaking tree roots, gobs of sap, and moist, cool dirt under my fingertips. But my touch found no body, even when I crawled well beyond the point where I knew he must have fallen. With extreme hesitation, but the absolute need to know the score, I clicked on the flashlight, holding it in my right hand with my elbow cocked out and the barrel of my gun laying poised across my right forearm. The beam hit the ground like a spotlight, and I was immediately self-conscious of how blazingly my position had been revealed to the other gunman. But I had to see. I had to know. And when I cast my flashlight's beam over the earth, there was no body, nor was there even a drop of blood from the wound he already had before I fired at him. The Pioneer had vanished without a trace.

"Fuck," I muttered. Immediately I clicked off the beam and tried to quell the riotous pitch of my panicked heart, forcing myself to relocate to higher ground. My soldier's mind knew the Sailor would have seen my flashlight and would be making for the spot. And if I hadn't hit the Pioneer with those two shots, he could be within a couple feet of me at this very moment. I turned and bolted uphill. If the Sailor and the Pioneer were still close, they weren't firing anymore, and I was running alone through the trees. In my mind, I was back in the War. My mind's ear echoed with the scream of Luftwaffe planes overhead, the hulking crunch of lumbering tank treads, and screams of wounded men. The Pioneer and the Sailor had vanished, but now there was a Nazi behind every tree.

The light from the clearing at the end of the Headland was shining brighter through the trees than I remembered, but I followed the beacon through the blood-rush of traumatic adrenaline and tore out through the tree-line onto the grounds of the homestead. What I saw made me drop my empty gun in the grass. The lighthouse was a pillar of swirling flames. A column of black smoke was winding into the night sky. Ashes and glowering sparks drifted on the air around me, and children were calling out inside. At first, I didn't know what I was hearing, but the high small voices joined in raising an old hymn. The sound was nearly lost in the dragon's growl of devouring fire. The song was breaking into shrill, terrified screams. The radiance of that blazing tower in the middle of the absolute coastal darkness was blinding, the air choked with the heavy fumes of wood smoke and the inky smog of burning oil. The sheer heat was overpowering and forbade approaching further, and yet there were children inside, screaming in the excruciating agony of the stake.

I cursed at the thought of facing this fire that had appeared out of nowhere. I swallowed hard as I remembered Delilah was three miles down the coast, and no one came out to Cape Contrition the night of the original lighthouse fire in 1919. By the time anyone else came along to see what was amiss, the tower would be a blackened skeleton dripping with rain, and there wouldn't be enough left of the ones inside to bury. Like a house in Chapel Hill, North Carolina.

"Hold on!" I shouted, throwing myself forward when every instinct screamed to run. Thoughtlessly I grasped the brass knob of the door and screamed as my hand enclosed on the glaring brand. I smelled my flesh cooking as the skin of my palm split, melted, and crackled on the metal. I bit my tongue so hard, my mouth filled with blood, and choked down a seething hiss as I looked at the deep burn and brand of the doorknob's keyhole in my palm. It was a scar I would carry forever. Blood dribbled down my chin with an involuntary thought of Henry Usher's end. I screamed and threw my shoulder hard against the crackling wood of the door while squeezing my burnt hand as tight as I could. Even weakened by the fire, the heavy oak door did not budge. I tried to stave it in a second time by throwing my shoulder into it with a running start but sank to the ground beaten. The screaming was over, and this was not a comfort. As I stepped back to see if there was any other way into the fortress of the lighthouse, an oil-fire explosion burst in a gushing inferno that threw me several feet backwards, rolling and coughing on the ground as I frantically swatted out the flames clinging to my clothes.

Curiously, the structure of the burning tower was undamaged by the burst that blew me backwards, and I felt the same unreality as when the Pioneer vanished without a trace in the woods after I fired my gun. As in dreams, I could not begin to consider I was seeing an illusion. The heat that branded my hand with the pattern of the doorknob *had* been real. The bullets exploding into tree trunks inches from me *had* been real. And yet, as I looked at the lighthouse again, I saw how it flamed and was not consumed, like the burning bush from Exodus. Through the inky smoke and bellowing whirlwind of fire, the lighthouse was unchanged. As my panicked, adrenaline-high mind struggled to make sense of this inundation of extreme, dangerous circumstances of dreamlike unreality, I glanced out beyond the fire. I glimpsed a woman in black, standing with her back to me as she stared out at the ocean. Her hair and dark, modest dress whipped about in the gale, but she stood right at the edge of the cliff unmoved and unafraid, beyond the guard rail. She did not appear to be aware of the hail of gunfire in the forest, or the burning lighthouse, though the light of it was what illuminated her to me. As I watched, she took a step closer to the precipice.

"No! Hey! Don't!" I shouted, running toward her. I drew up so close I might have reached out and touched her shoulder. Her belly was swollen with child. She did not budge. As I came close to her, my instincts flared with the innate command: *Don't look! Don't look!*

"You don't have to do this. Believe me, I... I've thought about it. But whatever it is that brought you to this cliff, it doesn't have to kill you. You can come back from it. It's damn dangerous out here. There are men with guns, and the fire, don't you see? Come on, I've got a storm cellar we can hide in. We can get you warm and dry and talk about it-" She stepped out beyond my grasp and leapt from the cliff without a word.

"No! Please!" I cried, throwing myself out after her, but she slipped right through my fingers like a cold wisp of silk. I collapsed on the ledge, blindly grabbing the rail for dear life with my burned hand. I gritted my teeth in a pained snarl as my branded palm protested with lightning bolts of pain firing up my arm, threatening to spasm open my grip. In my desperation to catch the woman, I nearly followed her off the cliff. I clung to the metal rail and the mossy rocks, craning out over the edge as far as I dared to peer down. But piercing the night over Cape Contrition was hopeless, and a hundred and thirty feet below, white waves boiled and churned. There was no trace of the woman. I squinted into the abyss for a glimpse of her dress billowing in the water, her broken form twisted upon the rocks. But she was gone. The wind threatened to send me after her, and I cursed myself for failing to save her. Had she too been an illusion? I asked myself if I was hallucinating, losing my mind. My brain was bruised with sensory exhaustion and boiling in the acidic corrosion of panic. The terrors were piling on wave after wave. Though my mind echoed with instinctive notions I was seeing an illusion, as the mind sometimes sleepily half-realizes in an absurd dream, this was not enough to quell the terror. Rational thoughts could not gain the foothold to draw me out of the paralyzing mist of war trauma brought on by the firefight in the woods, or to dismiss the overwhelming evidence of my senses.

I pulled myself to my feet and ran for the house, frantic to collect Otis and race to town. The fire, the woman. I had to notify the police, useless though they were. We had to get boats in the water to find the woman, fire engines to douse the burning lighthouse. I collapsed on the porch stairs before throwing open the door and falling into the darkness of the house. Otis' heavy shoulders bowled me over onto my back in the landing, and he wiggled and whined with a beating tail. Like a drunk, I staggered into the kitchen and ran the faucet with cold water, moaning in pain as I plunged my red raging hand into the chilly jet. The tap dulled the feeling of writhing coals inside my palm, and I held it there for a couple minutes, shuddering.

I wrapped my hand in a paisley handkerchief, and as I walked through the creaky stillness of the house, I realized for the first time all the lights were off. But I'd turned every single one on before charging into the woods with the gun. As I crept into the living room, a voice made my blood run cold.

"You're drinking again." her back was to me, long waves of blonde hair tumbling down her shoulders. She'd been crying, I could hear it in her quivering voice.

"Jeanie," I gasped, taking a hesitant step forward.

"I found the others, too, in the woods out back. Did you think I wouldn't find out? Jesus, Joe. This has to stop."

"I know, baby." I got on my knees. "I'm trying to get better." She turned around and her face was puffy and red from crying, but she was still entrancingly beautiful in her wild way. She was wearing a thin, pale nightgown that clung and left little to the imagination. Her eyes had an unnatural, discordant glow, like the gleaming pinpoints of a wolf's at night. The tired, instinctive warning was tugging desperately at me. *Don't look. Run.*

"You can barely stand," Jean said, her tone disappointed but concerned, motherly in its gentle scolding. "Are you drunk right now?"

"No." I looked up at her from my pleading tableau, "someone tried to kill me, and then, and then there was a fire, and someone jumped from the cliff-"

"Why didn't you?"

"What?" *Run! Fuck, Joe, get up now! Don't look! It's not her!*

"Why didn't you jump too? You're not getting better, Joe. You're all alone in the world, don't you see? And if you do find anyone, you know you'll just kill them, like you killed me. You get so wrapped up; you can't see how you're losing yourself in this book. It's going to kill you, you know, writing this. Look at you. You aren't eating, you aren't sleeping; just wasting away, and driving yourself insane with loneliness. There won't be a comeback. There won't be any redemption.

But you don't have to live on punishing yourself. Jump. Then, we can be together again. Don't you want that?"

"More than anything in the world." Tears ran tracks down my face. I was losing my resolve, her cloying sweet promise pulling me in. My mind still screamed for me to get away, but my feet were heavy as lead. "You're the one I want."

"Come find me, Joe. Come find me at the bottom of the sea." *'Come find me, Joe.' A kiss on the cheek and a mischievous laugh and she was in the wind, bounding through the stalks of sunflowers like something elemental.*

"But you didn't drown, baby... You burned. You're not down there."

"I miss you, Joe. Please... We can be like we were, before we lost it. It would be so beautiful, in the After."

"The After. Is that what they call it? No Heaven, no Hell?"

"Just us, and a new start. I'm not in pain here. You won't be either. The dead ones, they're all at peace."

"No." I got up onto unsteady feet. "Not all of them."

Her face lit with ecstasy as she talked about the After, but when I got to my feet and took a step back, her face twisted into a forbidding look, those eyes still glowing in the thick mass of her flowing hair.

"Where are you going?" Her voice tinged with anger

"I can't," I faltered, fighting against my weakening resolve. "I have to go tell someone about the woman who jumped. I can't be with you yet. I need to learn how to be with *me* first. And I need to finish this book. People need to know what happened here. I need to know."

Crocodile tears started in those eyes which glowed like predatory coals.

"I'm cold. Hold me. Don't leave me alone."

"No, I... I have to go." I turned and grabbed Otis' leash. He was huddled by the front door, ears laid back against his head as he watched Jean.

"Of course," she snarled acidly at my back, "Go choose your book over me, *again*. Run away from your family and hide in your writing."

"It's not like that. I just have to go. I'm sorry." As I collected Otis and was walking out, she was screaming now. The shouts at my back were in two voices, laid over one another. Beneath Jean's screaming was something wild, roaring, and guttural as a pit.

"If that's really what you're doing. If you're not running around town drunk and sniffing at some slut! You think I don't know? **YOU THINK I DON'T KNOW?**"

I shuddered as I slammed the door on her screams and heaved myself across the lawn, breaking into a run. But as I came to a halt on my wobbling knees at the edge of the forest, I realized leaving Cape Contrition would mean plunging back into the trees where the danger was. A last glance was all I allowed myself before disappearing into the woods.

The forest was silent and still. The confusion of earlier was gone, and even in the darkness, it was a simple matter to navigate the trail to the parking lot. With each step downhill, I became clearer and calmer by degrees. The Pioneer and the Sailor, whoever and whatever they were, had vanished. At long last, the slick black asphalt of the parking lot spread before us, and the battered blue '58 Land Rover sat alone. Otis leapt inside when I opened the door, and I followed him in with frantic speed, turning the key in the ignition, switching on the lights, and lurching the vehicle in reckless reverse before shifting gears. Tires squealed. Straining, sloppily shifted gears rattled and chugged as I peeled out and picked up speed, racing over the winding road like a bat out of hell. The twin beams of my headlights cut down the black highway as the dashes of the white central line jumped along in a blur. In the middle of the night, nothing at all of the country on either side of the road was visible, only the vague menace of the towering trees with their grasping branches and bristling crowns against the starless sky. The arms of the small clock on the dashboard told it was after 11:00 at night, and the speedometer was mounting from eighty to ninety miles per hour. As the car careened along the empty road, I tried to think of what I would say to the men at the station; whether or not they would believe a word of it; how quickly they would mobilize.

I was glancing back to calm Otis as he whimpered, and that was when a pregnant woman in a black dress stepped out into the road and squared up against the onrushing headlights of the Land Rover, staring right at me through the lank curtains of her sickly dark hair.

"Fuck!" I screamed when I looked up and glimpsed the shape of her standing alone in the midst of the highway. Her sudden appearance was alarming, but in the moment of seeing her, I was overwhelmed by an onrush of overwhelming remorse that defied explanation. The black wave of depression screamed for me to die. But seeing her in the road, feeling the existential terror, and reeling to avoid her all happened in less time than it takes to write it down. There wasn't time for that sensation to wash over me and take hold. My hands and feet were automatically responding with evasive action.

I slammed my foot on the brake, and as the car lurched and squealed, I jerked the wheel to avoid her. As my Land Rover careened off the road, the bouncing beams of the rattling headlights framed the trunk of a massive tree the moment before I slammed into it. The last sounds I heard as my face slammed into the steering column were the screaming twist of metal, the shattering of glass, and the clipped whimper of my dog.

Chapter Twelve: Broken Glass

November 10th, 1962

Cold rain was tinkling through the gnarled metal and busted glass of the cab when I woke the following morning. Smoke was still curling out from underneath the crumpled hood. The front end of the car had smashed like an accordion against the stolid trunk of an ancient fir. The cool droplets ran into eyes crusted shut with dried blood from a gash in my brow. When I opened my eyes, the left lens of my glasses was a kaleidoscopic spiderweb of cracks. My breaths rattled with dull agony, and I was trapped in the collapsed cab. Part of the tree had broken off and fallen on top of the car, and its needles were heavy and fragrant, dripping with the morning drizzle. Otis lay crumpled in the floor of the backseat and gave voice to a weak whimper that seemed to be all he could muster. Broken glass covered my clothes like a dusting of diamonds. As my brain swam with incomprehensible glimpses of the horrors that led me to this, a flashlight clicked on and glared in my eyes.

"Joe? God damn, is that you? You alive in there?" Will Blake. His mustache frowned beneath the wide brim of his Stetson.

"My dog," I murmured, trying to point to the backseat. That was when I saw crushed bone spearing through my right forearm, gory with a thick jelly of dried blood.

"Paramedics are on their way. We'll get your dog. You should be more worried about yourself. Your arm is broken, and your collarbone. We'll see what else, you're beat up pretty bad." He tore my glasses off and shined his irritating light in my eyes again, checking their dilation. "I'd guess you have a concussion too. And you were here like this awhile before anyone drove by and found you. It's about ten in the morning now, and this happened late last night, right? Were you drinking, Crowley?"

"No," but I could tell he didn't believe me. "There was a woman, she jumped from the cliff. The lighthouse was on fire, firefight in the woods. I fought men with guns, and, and the woman from the cliff. She was there in the road! I almost hit her-" the account of what happened was drooling out of me, delirious, each part coming out hopelessly wrong and unbelievable. He knocked aside the last crooked teeth of broken glass from the window with the butt of his revolver before giving my shoulder a comforting pat.

"You're in shock, Joe. Take it easy. We'll get you to the hospital."

"You have to... Believe me! Send your men. You have to."

"Oh, we'll check it out. We'll be looking into what happened with you very closely." I heard the warning in his tone, laid my head back against the seat and closed my eyes, drifting out of consciousness.

When I awoke, I was in a hospital bed wearing nothing but a flimsy gown. My right arm was stiff in a plaster cast and immobile in a sling, and there were stitches and bandages for dozens of small cuts on my face, scalp, chest, and arms. The worst was a slash to the bone in my left brow, which would remain as a ropy scar. My body was a battered patchwork of bruises and cuts. Gwen was there, and her face beamed when I came to. Otis was sitting at her side with his own front right leg in a cast, and several shaved patches of pink skin in his thick fur where ugly cuts were cleaned and stitched up. He wore an Elizabethan collar. Very fashionable. His bony tail beat ecstatically against the wall when he saw I was waking up.

"Hey," she smiled, setting down her book and adjusting her glasses.

"Hey yourself." A pained grimace that tried to be a smile. I turned my aching head to the side, said, "hey, good boy," and Otis' tail beat to a fever pitch as he stood on his hind legs and his cone-framed face descended. The dog covered my face in heavy licks, his mustache and scraggly beard tickling my stubble.

"You've been in a car accident, Joe. They said you might've been driving drunk. Is that true?"

"No. I haven't had a drink in ten days, I swear." She looked at me with a desire to believe tempered with mistrust, and the idea struck that I may not have been the first alcoholic in her life. "There was a woman on the road."

"You said that. When you were asleep, you kept talking about a drowned woman."

"Drowned woman?" I asked with surprise. But the image of the pregnant woman in black standing dauntless in the middle of the road flashed through my mind, cold and menacing in the glaring rush of my advancing headlights. At the thought of her, I could hardly breathe, and felt I didn't deserve to.

"The police are here, Joe," she murmured, leaning in close. "They think you had some kind of nervous breakdown and hurt somebody. Is that true?"

"Well, everyone here seems like they're waiting for that to happen. Aren't they?" I replied moodily, remembering the swirl of gossip.

"That's not fair," Gwen reproached, looking wounded. "They said your hand was badly burned, like with a brand. They can't account for how that would have happened in the car accident."

"Burned?" The realization of what she said sat with me. Gwen looked as if she might say more, but Chief Blake was leaning in the doorway, wearing a bomber jacket and his beige Stetson. He hadn't shaved in a couple days and looked like he was in bad need of some coffee.

"Gwen, darlin', could you give us a minute?" He stepped out of the doorway for her to leave.

"Of course, Officer." Gwen traded an apprehensive glance with me before stepping out into the hall. Blake came over and sat.

"Car's totaled. You probably guessed that." Damn. She'd been a fine ship. I'd loved that car since the day I'd bought it, and she'd taken me all over America. Losing it was like losing an old friend.

"We followed up your uh, claims, about what was going on out on Cape Contrition. Since we found you six hours ago, my boys have been combing the headland, and searching the waters at the base of the cliffs. Those waters, by the way, are not easy for a boat to navigate. One of those dumbasses went and beached himself between two rocks, and had to be

177

rescued. Another of our police boats was scuttled. You were going on and on about a Drowned Woman. It was all you wanted to talk about. There is no drowned woman. A lot of people have jumped from those cliffs, and I've pulled a few of them out of the water myself. We didn't find a body."

"And do you find them every time?"

"I guess that's impossible to know. That drop is 130 feet. The fall alone would kill most people, but that alone isn't fatal every time. Many break apart on the rocks. The ones that don't, well, they drown; the waters stay frigid year round. It's a rare person in rare circumstances who can survive that fall and swim to safety. The dead ones? They frequently stay on the rocks, get sucked into tidal caves and little nooks in the headland, or wash up on the beach of Siren's Cove. That rock formation, well... It keeps them. But people who jump don't exactly sign a guestbook, so if some of them wash out to sea, I would have no way of knowing."

"So you can't know for sure whether or not I saw someone jump."

"That's correct. I guess I'm just wondering why *you're* not sure you saw someone jump. Did you know the suicide rate in Delilah is nine times the national average for small towns?"

"No, I can't imagine why," I answered dully.

"Well, people jump. That's just how it is. Place is a magnet for it, and someone jumping isn't your fault just because you're living out there. But after your erratic behavior last night, and the way you were ranting about the Drowned Woman, you better believe if we find a body, I'm going to be investigating for the possibility of foul play."

"Do what you have to do. The reason I wasn't positive about what I saw was there were a lot of things happening at once.

There were the men with guns, and the lighthouse burned–"

"I'm going to have to stop you right there. We went to Usher's Fall, Joe. The lighthouse is still standing, completely unharmed. Cold to the touch. We found a shotgun laying in the grass not far from it. Yours?"

"Yeah." That news took me back, especially when taken side by side with the news that the doorknob disfigured the palm of my hand.

"I thought so. Juan told me he sold you one in his shop. I took the liberty of stowing it under your porch. Big old boom-stick like that shouldn't be laying around for some kid to pick up. Those grounds are open to the public."

"Right. Sorry."

"As to the period-costumed assailants with cowboy Winchesters. My boys went through the woods along that trail. No bullets took chunks out of trees, no shells on the ground, except for three of yours. Unless your triggermen went through those woods in the middle of the night and picked up every single shell they fired, I'm going to have to hazard a guess the only person unloading their gun in the woods last night was you."

I had no response ready and felt like a fool.

"So what the fuck happened last night, Crowley? Are you smoking marijuana?"

"No, Officer," I lied dutifully.

"Your crying wolf wasted my time, and the time of eight of my officers who spent the day searching the length and breadth of the Cape. Is that a joke to you?"

"No, Officer." Stonily this time.

"Apparently the doctor cleared you of boozing. His theory is you saw an elk and veered off the road. But don't waste our time like that again. Because when I do catch you doing something wrong, I'm going to nail your ass to the wall."

"Thank you for your help, Officer," I replied, looking him in the eye and waving him off with my burned hand. As he turned his broad back to me and stormed out of the room, I laid my head against the pillow and fell asleep.

Chapter Thirteen: The Call of the Void

December 9th, 1962

The weeks were crawling by. The finished books of other writers built up like sandbags around my Smith Corona typewriter, with its smug blank page taunting me as I smoked and sulked on the couch. The sea wind blew hard, and the old house trembled like a leaf as the briny, scouring gusts whistled through every crack. I leaned back as Otis curled up on the couch next to me and laid his head in my lap, scratching him behind the ears as I inhaled smoke from the orange glow at the tip of my stubby cigarette. Calm resignation washed over me as I released a long, even exhalation of bluish smoke and crushed out the last of it in an ashtray.

I was slipping away. Depression isolated me not only from the few people I knew, but from the only interests that helped me to function. In idleness, my mind turned often to self-bullying spirals of poisoned thought. Nightmares of concentration camps, deafening explosions and red abattoir scenes of war, old arguments with Jean and a million regrets of a misspent life filled my nightmares more now than ever. Run ragged with miserly sleep over months, my chronically exhausted brain was beginning to devour itself like the empty stomach of a starving man. The house no longer needed to terrify me, only to isolate me from help so I could mentally torture myself to death. And death was the end the presences of the house intended. Of that I was sure.

This was the first time since my arrival in Usher's Fall that I contemplated suicide. The seed was planted with my first fleeting glimpse of the Drowned Woman's face. After learning I had given her this name in the delirium following the crash, it stuck. I hadn't yet advanced to the stage of actively planning when and how I would kill myself. It was only a morbid and intrusive suggestion. These spontaneous self-destructive impulses, such as the sudden nudge to swerve your automobile into oncoming traffic or leap from a tall precipice, are what the French call 'L'appel du vide': The Call of the Void. I wasn't on the ledge to jump yet, but I'd climbed onto the roof.

On this Sunday afternoon, I was becoming overwhelmed by my own self-cannibalistic thoughts. My desperation to escape them finally propelled me out of the house and down to the salt-eaten, bulbous, rusted red 1950 Ford F-3 pickup truck I'd acquired. It was a long walk. The woods were terrifying to me after my firefight with the Sailor and Pioneer, which I still struggled to accept was some kind of illusion or waking nightmare. Freezing rain was pattering hard, carried sideways on the cutting coastal wind, and the parking lot was enshrouded in a thick fog that drifted in from the cove. I turned up the collar of my heavy black pea coat, and smoothed out the folds of the scarf coiled about my neck. The old Ford sat alone in the parking lot, but as I walked out to it, I heard laughter and the drifting calls of children. To my right, two small shapes darted past in outdated, handmade clothes. I'd seen them in my peripheral vision so many times, I was no longer surprised. But they were still unnerving.

"They're not real," I reminded myself as I let Otis climb into the cab, followed him in, and closed the door. The Drowned Woman drifted in the fog with her back to me, overseeing the children as her hair blew around her head in the wind. I ducked down in the cab as she wandered out of the fog into my headlights, but she seemed to be unaware of me. To look upon her was undeniably captivating. Her hair appeared stirred by the breeze, but it waved slowly and against the wind, dark wet tendrils rising and falling like the slithering mass of snakes which formed Medusa's hair. The locks spread and danced more like hair underwater than hair in wind. I remembered the glimpse of urchins, barnacles, and starfish clinging to her sodden dress and purple-veined, translucent skin in the pale flash of my headlights and forced myself to look away. I sat with my head pressed against the steering wheel for several minutes before finally turning the key and driving away. When I raised my head, the shapes of the Drowned Woman and her playful familiars were gone. Still, I feared every moment her terrible face would suddenly materialize out of the mist until I was well across the Siren Creek Bridge.

The icy rain pounded on my windshield and was swept aside in a steady rhythm by my wipers. Through the streaming rivulets and fog, I watched the sloping heaths of scrubby bushes and twisted, windblown little Lodgepole Pines, patchy yellow grass, towering rocks, shell-littered beach, and peaceful surf roll by. I didn't know where my aimless drive was taking me until I finally pulled into the parking lot of St. Nicholas Episcopal Church.

The service was over, the last parishioners drifting out

to their cars underneath the canopies of black umbrellas. Thomas Forester was smiling wide and shaking hands with folks as they left, still dressed in his flowing alb and purple stole. I sat and watched the people leave, remembering my own childhood church services of fear and fervor, fire and brimstone. I doubted any such terrifying sermon would be preached by a gentle and gracious intellectual like Thomas Forester. But still, the memory of stiff-necked fundamentalists and segregationist evangelicals poisoned my whole experience of religion, and there was no other shade of stained glass through which I could see it. What did the people of Thomas' church get out of those services? Why did they linger so long after they were over? Part of me longed for the community and hopefulness they had. But I couldn't make myself walk in the door until the place was empty at last. When the old priest saw me coming, he smiled and walked down the steps.

"Joseph, welcome. What can I do for you?"

"Sorry I missed the service," I felt obligated to say, even though I never went. But he waved it off as if he thought nothing of it.

"Wasn't going to shame you."

"I'm going out of my mind. I need some counsel." Why was I drawn to this old man's quiet presence if I was so cynically dismissive of the things he believed?

"Of course. Have you eaten?"

"No."

"Then we'll go to Melville's. My treat."

"Please, let me. We'll call it a long-lost tithe." Forester walked me to his gray 1940 Oldsmobile Series 70.

"How do you drive stick with one arm anyway?" He opened

the passenger door for me and let Otis in the backseat.

"Very carefully, and not well," I answered. Thomas Forester closed his umbrella and set it in the backseat before climbing in, starting the engine, and cruising out of the parking lot.

The wipers were beating back the rain steadily when it turned into a rattling hail of icy pearls. We drove for a while in silence, listening to the pelting bullets and watching the huddled shops drift by.

Melville's turned out to be a pub, and it bore the dreaded white whale Moby Dick on its sign board. As Forester put the old automatic in park, he stopped and put a wrinkled hand over his mouth.

"Joe, I'm sorry, but I wasn't thinking about this being a pub."

"It's alright, most people don't have to worry about something like that."

"Should we go someplace else?"

"Nah, you'll keep me on the straight and narrow. Besides, I want to see what ol' Herman has been up to." Otis whimpered in the back when he realized he wouldn't get to go inside, so I kissed his forehead and murmured goodbye as his bearded muzzle quivered against my cheek. As soon as we were inside, we were greeted by a portrait of the old writer himself, distinguished by the square angles of his great beard. A waitress recognized Thomas and smiled as she waved us in out of the chilly rain and told us we could sit wherever we wanted. The old pub was rustic and dim, walls decorated with ships' wheels, oars, boathooks, harpoons, netting, floats, stuffed fish, framed photographs and paintings of ships, and beaming navy sailors on old wartime propaganda posters.

We sat at a table made from an old cask by a large porthole window framing the swell of the ocean in the rain. Over the next hour, as we dipped into bowls of creamy clam chowder and lunched on rockfish and salmon, I told him everything of the weird and terrible on Cape Contrition. As in our last meeting, he listened attentively. Between bites, I detailed everything for which I struggled to find a natural explanation, from the mundane to the horrific. The children, the gunmen, the Drowned Woman, the terrible night passed in the storm cellar during the Columbus Day storm, the suicide of Henry Usher, the spontaneous attack of November 9th, the persistent nightmares and the growing depression that seemed not only to be a condition of my mind, but something the house itself was cultivating. When I finished my account, he sat and sipped his ice water, contemplating it all.

"What are you hoping to hear from me?" he finally asked, and my heart sank when I feared he did not believe me.

"Do I strike you as a dishonest person?" He quietly said 'no.' "Do I strike you as a crazy person?"

"Troubled, yes. But 'crazy' is not a word I would use to describe anyone. I believe you to be of sound mind, despite the traumas you have experienced and the burdens weighing on you."

"And when I tell you there is something evil on Cape Contrition... Do you believe me?" As I said this, I opened my left palm before him to show the circular burn scar with the mark of the keyhole in its center. He held my hand in his own and felt the pink, raw lines with his fingertips, and I realized how similar the action was to the Biblical scene when Thomas the Disciple personally inspected the nail wounds on the palms of the resurrected Jesus of Nazareth.

"Yes, I do." He crossed himself by impulse.

"I read your book, Thomas, but that was theory. I need to hear what you make of this. Diagnose it."

"Usher's Fall and Cape Contrition are haunted by a number of spirits. The smallest and least threatening are the Usher children. These ghosts are not necessarily evil, but are rather playful and mischievous. The early disturbances you experienced in the house may have been pranks on their part, attempts to confuse or rattle you. It sounds as if they are not always visible, and much of their tricks sound like activity attributed to poltergeists. Then there are your gunmen. Since the Pioneer bears such a strong likeness to Henry Usher and did not manifest himself until after his death, I would say you have his identity figured out. Who your Sailor is, I have no idea. Another suicide? Or potentially the true assailant, since you have come to believe Henry Usher was not responsible for the death of his family. His identity needs to be established. From what you have said of their behavior, it sounds like these two spirits are particularly wrathful, but are forbidden from entering the house itself or walking on the lawns. And the one who forbade them entry and consigned them to lurk in the forest is the true mistress of Usher's Fall..."

"The Drowned Woman."

"From what you have described, she's the real danger to be reckoned with on Cape Contrition: a uniquely powerful and malevolent spirit, and the others who haunt the headland are subservient to her will. From what you have described, it sounds like the other beings exist in fear of her. The Pioneer and the Sailor do not dare cross the tree-line but stare out with loathing at the house they are forbidden to enter. The children are afraid of her as well."

"The way they cling to her skirts and are never far from her have led me to guess the Drowned Woman is Rosemary Usher. She has to be their mother. Rosemary's body was never found. She simply vanished from the Earth, and an extensive search could uncover no explanation. But if she leapt from the cliff, there is a chance her body would never have been found..." I paused, trying to find my words, my excitement mounting as I put the pieces together.

"It would explain her appearance. It is said, the ghosts of those who died particularly grisly deaths bear the marks of what happened to them. What I am curious about is how a woman who was, by all accounts, meek, submissive, and docile, became such a powerful revenant in death. For Henry Usher's ghost to hold Cape Contrition in his grasp as he held it in life would make sense. For his ghost to be bent to the will of his wife's ghost is a reversal of the living power dynamic, and that I can't explain."

"What do they want? How do we... exorcise them? Have you heard of such a thing?"

"Most people consider ghosts to be troubled spirits bound to this world, unable to pass on fully to the afterlife. The reason for this depends on your source. Perhaps the departed left a crucial task undone, or a secret buried. If that is the case, you must finish their quest. Uncover the truth of their lives and their spirits will be put to rest. You have been attempting to do this since before you suspected the house was haunted. The closer you come to finding the answers, the more violent the spirits of the house are becoming. This brings me to another potential reason the souls of the dead could be forbidden from passing on into the afterlife."

"What's that?"

"Something has enslaved them to its will and holds them in its power."

"And that something is the Drowned Woman herself."

"If that is the case, you should be extremely careful. A being like her, with the level of influence she exerts over both the living and the dead, is not simply a 'ghost.' Maybe the others on the headland fit that description, but she is something else, something worse. Tread lightly."

"I saw her this morning by the cove, but she wasn't aware of my presence. And even when the Sailor and the Pioneer stared at the house, it sometimes seemed as though they were not staring at me but through me. Like I was the ghost and they were real. When they were shooting in the woods, I thought they might have been shooting at one another, rather than at me."

"It is important to remember ghosts do not exist in the same way you or I exist -within time. They are trapped in a nebulous middle-ground between the past and the present, our own plane and theirs. They are one foot in, one foot out of this world, and so they exist and perceive the world around them in a fragmented and disjointed way. One might compare the gaping holes in the consciousness of a ghost to the perception of a person with advanced dementia. The ghosts of Usher's Fall are not always aware of your existence. When they are, perhaps, sometimes they see you as Joe Crowley in 1962, and other times they mistake you for one of their own contemporaries in the 1910s. It's possible some of their anger has been because you are intruding in their domain in the present day, and at other times their anger has been because they mistake you for Henry Usher: the man they most feared in life. And with that broken understanding, sometimes they must believe themselves to be alive, and to be who they were when they were alive, and sometimes they might know they are wraiths of departed beings. It must be a bewildering and terrifying experience to be a ghost.

"Some of the things you witnessed might be called *astral replays*: living memories held within Cape Contrition itself. These events from the lives of the Ushers are reenacted like a vivid motion picture projected all around you, but the players are unaware you can see them, for they are unaware they are even moving through events that already unfolded decades ago. These are traumatic events a spirit is stuck in, and they keep going back to them. It could be, if you witness these scenes again, they will unfold in the same way. You could follow them and see for yourself some part of what happened that terrible night in 1919."

"At the risk of seeing the Drowned Woman again."

"Just so."

"And these living flashbacks you're talking about... They're just complex illusions? They aren't *happening*, they just... *happened?*"

"Are you asking if they could harm you in the physical sense? Hard to say. But from the sight of your branded palm, I would say if you find yourself between those men shooting at one another in the woods again, it would be best not to test it."

"Fair enough. So you think ghosts exist partially in the world around us and partly in our own minds?"

"I don't know what I think, but it is a possible explanation. Make no mistake, though: their existence within our thoughts makes them no less dangerous. If something is real within the mind, it is real enough to cause harm. This would explain why the vivid things you have witnessed are not only visions of the Ushers, but also flashbacks of the War, visions of your late wife. Sometimes the paranormal forces at work in your mind and your environment show you things of the Ushers unconnected to your own experience, but other times you see things that are intensely personal and private, such as visions of your wife reciting things she said while she was alive: things only you would know. The malevolent power at work on Cape Contrition paints your dreams and waking sight not only from the palette colored with its memories, but also your own. It can draw out your darkest thoughts and most private regrets and display them before you as if they are real. But you need to recognize these for what they are: attacks on your own sanity to demoralize, isolate, and exhaust you, ultimately to drive you to death at your own hand. When you spoke with your wife in the house, it was a fraud. That thing contained no more of your wife than it could find and piece together from your own tormented memories. It wasn't her, Joe. You need to know that. The Drowned Woman was wearing your wife's face like a camouflaged predator, trying to lure you into its grasp."

"I can't get her out of my head. I see her every time I close my eyes now. In the moment I saw her before the crash, all I could think was nothing would ever be good in my life again, and the only way to make the pain stop was to die."

"The Drowned Woman is the being who concerns me the most. Ghosts themselves are alarming, but rarely malevolent or capable of harm. Like what people say of spiders to comfort their children: they are probably more afraid of us than we are of them. But this mother in black... I need to do some research, see if any sort of equivalent to her might exist in folklore we might learn from. The Ancient Hebrews believed a person who even laid eyes upon the face of God or one of his angels would be struck dead instantaneously. The thing we are disconnected with in the modern world is that spiritual beings are terrifying: even the ones we hope are fundamentally good and on our side. And it sounds like you've found something else entirely. Something demonic."

"Is there a way to make contact? Reason with it?"

"For centuries, spiritists and self-described psychic mediums have held séances in which they claim to facilitate contact with the dead, but... I'm inclined to be skeptical about whether or not something like that would work. In their heyday, Spiritists employed many of the same tricks as stage illusionists and were largely conmen grifting the bereaved and desperate out of their hard-earned money. The most famous example of this would be the Fox Sisters. They gathered huge crowds to witness them communicate with the dead, who responded with strange knocking noises the secretly double-jointed women were making themselves. Besides, I'm not sure we want to be inviting something like this Drowned Woman into our midst. That sounds far too dangerous."

"Is there any way to fight against a ghost or repel it somehow?"

"You mean like holy water and crosses? Some garlic cloves?" he asked, amused. "Unlike other undead creatures of legend, ghosts are most frequently understood to be unable to harm someone in their wraithlike state. There is one thing, possibly, but it would involve getting close to the Drowned Woman, and because of the risk, I would only suggest this as a last resort. A common thread throughout folklore in many different cultures is that some measure of control or advantage can be claimed over a demon or evil spirit by learning its true name and declaring it in its presence. The belief goes that if you can identify the being's true name, you can articulate enough of its essential nature to bring it under your control –though the extent of this would vary from one story to another. In Ancient Egyptian mythology, Isis learned the true name of the god Ra through a trick, and used his name to gain power over him and put her son Horus on the throne. The Ancient Hebrews believed God's name was so potent, the invocation of it could confer tremendous power over Creation to the speaker. For this reason, speaking the name of God has always been blasphemous in Jewish circles, and this taboo was passed down to Christians. I am not overly eager to test this theory out, and this is all hypothetical, but... there is a chance, by declaring to the Drowned Woman that she is Rosemary Usher, you might gain some measure of advantage over her. If we can use the Séance to make contact and speak her true name, we can attempt an exorcism of the house."

"And this is all we have to go on? Myths and legends?"

"What else did you expect? These things aren't supposed to exist. I study belief systems regarding the paranormal as a pet hobby, but I've never encountered a ghost. I'm disinclined to believe in them. So we're both amateurs at this. Were you expecting me to be your Dr. Van Helsing?" Thomas took a long drink from his sweating, clinking glass of ice water. We sat there in silence for some time as our finished plates were taken away and I paid the bill. As we were getting up to leave, a parting thought came to him.

"You know, it isn't understood to be a ghost story, but

the way your Drowned Woman's glance causes people to feel overwhelming suicidal urges reminds me of the gorgon Medusa, who could turn people to stone with a glance. Both of them horribly wronged women, transformed by supernatural means into terrifying and extremely powerful beings, living in isolation by the sea. Perhaps the legend of Medusa has its origin in another being like the one we are faced with, sequestered on an island in the Mediterranean thousands of years ago."

"How did they kill Medusa again?"

"Perseus went into her lair with a mirrored shield before his eyes and cut off her head."

Chapter Fourteen: You Should

December 23rd, 1962

The lampposts were hung with wreaths, and a festive banner across Main Street declared it would be a Merry Christmas. Delilah got a fair dusting of snow that morning, the rooftops of downtown coated in a fine, powdered-sugar coat. Shoppers in coats and scarves browsed and pulled their bundled children past window displays of gingerbread men, bauble and tinsel-laden Christmas trees, elves, and reindeer. The white streets were rutted with crisscrossing tracks, and low, blackened drifts of dirty snow formed along the curbs. Otis limped along at my side with his nose quivering to the ground, frosting his mustache white. I shivered in my pea coat and stopped at one of the shop windows to see a frosted alpine village with light spilling from tiny windows onto the porcelain faces of miniature children petrified at play. Horse-drawn buggies carried fares in the tiny streets. A mechanical toy train circled on its track through the village square before disappearing into a tunnel through a snowy mountainside. Another shop displayed hand-made dollhouses of remarkable detail, and an array of snow globes with miniatures of Usher's Fall Lighthouse trapped within their glass spheres and coats of settled flakes waiting to be stirred up again. I bought one of these and tucked it into my coat pocket.

I had just picked up my new glasses from the optometrist when I bumped into Gwen. She was huddled under an awning sipping hot apple cider from a paper cup, and a rolling coil of its steam rose to fog her glasses as she caught sight of me.

"Ah! I'm blind!" she laughed, "Hold on, Joe. Hi."

"Hi," I smiled as she held out her drink for me to hold. When I took it, she wiped the lenses of her thick-framed glasses with a handkerchief before resetting them on the aquiline bridge of her nose. Her green eyes stood out, magnified by the lenses, and the red curls of her hair peeked out from underneath a blue knitted cap.

"That's better," she said, looking down to Otis while I stole a hot sip of her cloyingly sweet cider. "Hello!" she squatted in the sidewalk and offered Otis a handshake, which the dog accepted. "His beard is so snowy," she beamed. "How are you both?"

"We're good. Stocking up on a few necessaries before we get snowed in out there." There was a powdering out on the Cape, and the forest was heavy with icicles, but it wasn't going to stay cold enough for it to last. If any more precipitation fell, it would likely turn to a slushy rain.

"So, you like snow globes?" she asked awkwardly, and I realized the wide base of it was hanging out of my coat pocket. I plucked it out with a smirk and gave it a shake, watching as white flakes flurried in all directions, swirling about the white tower at the edge of the cliff and the cottage beside it.

"It's funny, how small and safe it looks like this."

"Please, don't tell me you're spending Christmas alone in

that dreadful old house."

"Alright, I won't tell you," I smirked as a family impatiently sidled around us on the sidewalk, the mother grumbling about clearing a path.

"No family coming to visit?"

"No. Doesn't look that way."

"Oh, Joe, I'm so sorry." She took a sip of her cider before offering it to me. I tilted the paper cup back and felt the thick molten-gold liquid roll on my tongue with relish in the cold.

"Don't be. Not your fault. What about you?"

"My mom and dad are up in Astoria, and I'll go visit them. My brother might be coming back from San Francisco, and I haven't seen him in ages."

"That sounds nice."

"You should come with me! The Christiansens throw quite a Yuletide party. But I'll warn you, they can go a little hard on the alcohol this time of year. My father home-brews mead every summer so he can give it to his friends and relatives at Christmastime, and it's potent. His way of pleasing his Viking ancestors, he says."

"Well, mustn't forget them. Are you sure I wouldn't be imposing?"

"Of course. My parents would be aghast if I didn't bring the mysterious out-of-town man I had dinner with tonight."

"Oh, is that what we're doing?" I smiled.

"Unless you have any better offers?"

"I'd be glad to." Otis encircled our legs to sniff and lick at the faces of some passing toddlers and his leash buckled the backs of her knees. She started to fall forward, but I caught her in my good arm and tried not to show my pained grimace as she fell against my sling. As I moved to catch her, the snow globe dropped from my pocket and burst open on the curb, spilling Cape Contrition and its snowflakes into the dirty gray drift of the roadside.

"You trained him to do that one," she blushed as I set her back upright and untangled her legs.

"I swear I didn't." I offered her my arm. She took Otis, and he almost dragged her behind him as we both laughed and left Usher's Fall upside down in the street gutter, so small and trivial a thing it now seemed.

Freezing rain started to come down as we drove back to her house. By the time we pulled into the driveway, it was clear the roads would soon be glossy sheets of ice. The house was still and peaceful with its corduroy furniture, mustard yellow wallpaper, and brown carpets. Gwen immediately set to cooking while I made myself comfortable in the living room.

"I was thinking about tortellini, is that okay?" she called in from the kitchen as she readied pots and pans and pulled things from the refrigerator.

"Sounds great." I found her record player and thumbed through a box of vinyl in colorful sleeves.

"I haven't cooked dinner for anyone else in close to a year, so you better like it." I found a Miles Davis record called 'Round About Midnight, its cover art a red-washed black and white photo of the man himself in thick sunglasses, trumpet across his chest. I carefully slid it out of its covering before placing it on the turntable and setting the needle.

"Good choice!" Gwen called in as the hard bop rhythm and blues crackled and rolled over the speakers. She was starting to bounce and shake her head a little as she worked. While the music played and the living room filled with the creamy smell of alfredo sauce, I stoked a blaze to life in the fireplace with logs from the screen porch. When I looked up from my work, I saw the kitchen was empty, and the heavy pot on the stove was rising to a boil.

A door closed down the hall, and Gwen stepped out of her bedroom in a light blue, sleeveless summer dress printed with irises. Her bare arms and collarbones were freckled and pale, and from her waist, the bouncy skirt fanned out to her knees. Her bob of ginger hair hung in light curls. Behind the lenses of her glasses, her delicate brown eyeshadow and mascara brought out her striking green eyes. Her lipstick was a blushing pink, and she wore no jewels but a simple locket on a thin chain around her neck. As she walked up to me, I drew her in close and slowly inclined my head to hers. She lifted her own chin with closed eyes and parted lips and pulled me in the rest of the way by my collar. We lingered there in a long, slow kiss. The light slip of her tongue in my mouth made me want more, and when we parted, our eyes were both lit by a new smolder in the flickering firelight.

A small table was set with a checkered cloth and two tall candles, and we cracked the window so some sound of the heavy rain could come in over the music. The tortellini dumplings were stuffed with prosciutto, served with green peas, mushrooms, and smoky Canadian bacon, dripping with rich, creamy Alfredo. Alongside this was a light chicken Caesar salad, and we sipped water from glasses dripping with beads of condensation. As I blew gently on the first bite and tasted it, she looked on expectantly.

"What do you think?" she asked. I paused and closed my eyes for a moment as I chewed, and swallowed before making eye contact with her and reassuring,

"It's delicious." She smiled, and with a tone of amazement, I asked, "Where did you come from?"

"Astoria, but my father emigrated here from Denmark during the First World War."

"You have me at a disadvantage, do you know that? You know a whole lot more about me at this point than I do about you."

"Well, what do you want to know?"

"Everything."

"Well, I was born in '23. My father's name is Erik, and he was a carpenter. My mother Gladys mostly stayed at home with the children but took on work as a nanny when she needed to. I have one older brother named James. We fought like cats and dogs growing up but get along fine now. I went to college at Berkeley, like my older brother, and studied American Literature. The summer before I went off to school, my dad and I finished rebuilding a little Norton motorcycle, and I rode it solo down the coast all the way to the San Francisco Bay. That was the best, scariest damn thing I ever did.

"After college, I met a man here named Mark. We had something good, once, but... We lost sight of it, you know? Mark, he really wanted kids. I like kids, but never saw myself settling down and being a mother. I don't tell many people, because most folks you tell aren't too impressed... It all became quite a scandal with the hens in town when they found out. I did try, for Mark, but it just... I'd lose them somehow. I had three miscarriages in my marriage to him. People in town said it was my fault, and eventually Mark got around to believing that too.

"He left in the night five years ago, and I found out he

shacked up with a teacher down in Florence. The last I heard from him was when he got around to divorcing me. That was three years ago. He left me the house since they have their own. I guess that was the decent thing to do," she scoffed and looked down for a moment as her voice faltered. She paused, squeezed her eyes shut for a moment, and resumed where she'd left off.

"He doesn't mean anything to me anymore, or anything like that, Joe. But it still hurts. People in town pretend like the whole marriage never happened, at least to my face, but I know they talk about me like I'm some kind of eccentric spinster. That's the thing about people in this town. Everyone wants to convince everybody else they live in this happy little Norman Rockwell illusion. The house, the picket fence, the car, the well-behaved children, the good job, the devout church involvement, the big family dinners. The American Dream, you know? But nobody has that life here, everyone must know it on some level, but nobody talks about it. Sure, they cluck their petty little gossip about other people, 'thank God our family isn't like them', but you never see folks look at the skeletons in their own closets. And every family here has them, everyone. But when people could comfort someone, or say 'I've been there too', they clam up or ignore it. And when that hurting person turns their back, they tell themselves that at least they're more righteous or fortunate than that poor fool." I remembered the old woman Alice Cole's comments, and how even the moldering journal of Rosemary Usher communicated that same spurned resentment close to fifty years ago.

"Most folks just want to pretend. Maybe they're hurt by the hypocrisy of that when they're young and swear they

won't turn out the same way; but somewhere, they forget."
She seemed to appreciate the sentiment, but I could tell she
couldn't keep talking about it without working herself up
more.

"Okay, your turn," she said.

"Well, I was born in Raleigh on August 8th, 1915, and grew
up in a house on the outskirts with a few acres of woods and
creeks to roam in. I had an older sister named Beth when I
was little. I only have faint memories of her. She used to sing
to me, and we played with dolls. She was kicked in the head
by a horse when she was nine and I was four, and it took her
almost a week to die."

"Oh, my God. Joe," Gwen said, hand over mouth and eyes
wide, "I had no idea."

"I haven't told anyone about Beth in a while. I always felt
like there was a hole in my life where she ought to be. People
didn't understand, since I couldn't even remember her face
or anything more than a few indistinct images. My dad asked
me once, 'how can you miss somebody you barely even got to
know? You couldn't miss her like I do. You were just a little
boy.' I have a younger brother named Frank, but we never got
along well, and he's eight years younger than me. We don't
talk much anymore. My father was a Southern Baptist deacon
and mechanic named George. Pretty much the only thing I
could get him to talk about was baseball, which I pretended to
be interested in for years so we would at least have something.
Occasionally he'd let me help him work on a car, but that never
lasted long before he got mad and sent me away.

"He had the quickest hands I've ever seen if you stepped out
of line. He beat me and my mom, and everyone knew, but no
one bothered. His house, his rules. He told me he didn't know

any better way to raise me, and I guess that was true, but it didn't make it right. My mom's name was Agnes. She was a good woman, kind, thoughtful. It was her who taught me how to read and first introduced me to poetry. Her favorite was Walt Whitman. She started me writing and read the first book I ever published but didn't live to see the second. I'm pretty sure my father has never read one of my books, and he's still alive, but we haven't spoken in four years. I got out of that house the first moment I could and never looked back. Worked on cars for a few years in Raleigh until I started at Duke University in '36. I was 21.

"In 1940, I graduated from Duke with a B.S. in History at age 25 and broke up with Jean Elizabeth Townes, my girlfriend of one year. At the time, neither of us knew she was pregnant. In '41 she called me and let me meet my daughter. Her name was Emma Christine Townes. Jean and I didn't immediately get back together, but I wanted to be close and present in my newborn daughter's life. I fell in love the first moment I held her, just like folks say. As we were reconnecting, I was drafted. I already told you what the war was like. Once I got back and convalesced, I married Jean and published my first novel, *American Quixote*, in the same year. To tell you the truth, I couldn't decide which of those things made me happier. Jean and I settled in Chapel Hill, North Carolina, I had her and our little girl, made enough money to write full-time... Those were good years. But the last few years haven't been so good. And you pretty much know all the rest."

"That's not the rest." She looked into my eyes with intention. "That was a horrible few years. But it doesn't have to be the end for you, Joe. You get to come back from that. You're a good man, even though you can't see it. You deserve to be happy and will be happy again."

"I don't think deserving enters into it. But I hope you're right." She leaned in and kissed the wrinkles on my forehead before getting up. The music stopped, and the needle list-lessly thumbed at the center of the spinning record. Gwen changed it over to something else before clearing the finished plates and silverware away. As I sat and listened, I remem-bered it was a hit when I came back from the War. I sat and closed my eyes as I listened to Harry James' waltzing trumpet over the clink of lifting plates, trying to forget.

I bowed my head and squeezed my eyes shut as Gwen moved around me, feeling the taunting certainty in my burning eyes that I was soon going to cry. My shoulders trembled as I tried to hold it in and take my mind to another place. Her fingertips brushed the inside of my arm, and she was tugging at my hand as the band launched into the chorus. I don't know if she knew what she was pulling me out of. She kicked off her shoes as she pulled me to my feet, and soon we were swaying slowly to a song I hadn't heard in almost twenty years.

"Where did you go just then?" She put her arms around my neck and played lightly with my hair.

"I don't know, I just get lost sometimes."

"You need to relax," she smiled, pressing her forehead against mine for a moment.

"I'm trying it on." I lifted her arm and twirled her. She moved readily and easily, responding to my touch and going where she was needed. My leadership was far from pristine, and it had been years since I danced, but she was gracious and gentle. "You're a much better dancer than me."

"You're doing fine." We danced for a few more songs, picking up rhythm and fluidity as we grew more comfortable.

When the record ended, she put on some Elvis and we bounced to the rock and roll, smirking and trying to imitate his scandalous, gyrating pelvic thrust. At last we fell into one another's arms, red-faced and laughing. When we could breathe again, I looked into her eyes and said,

"Thank you. I haven't been... very kind to myself. In a few years now." She looked at me thoughtfully.

"You should."

Otis was curled by the smoldering coals of the dying fire, quivering and woofing softly in his mustaches in the midst of some dream. Gwen's tabby, which by way of cruel Steinbeckian irony was named Lennie, was head-and-forepaws plunged into the kitchen sink. With splayed-out clawed toes gripping the counter and tail flicking in the air, he at last stole the opportunity to lick the Alfredo sauce and salad dressing left on our stacked plates. Billie Holiday was playing on the record player. The rain picked up to a downpour, the roads were thick slabs of black ice, and I was kissing Gwen Christiansen. There was hunger in our hot and feverish kisses. As I pressed her in close to me by the small of her back, she was quickly unbuttoning my flannel shirt. Her voice came hot and husky in my ear as she whispered she wanted me, and my lips and tongue felt the racing pulse of her throat as I kissed her there. She was gentle with my arm in its binding sling and cast as she shrugged me out of my shirt.

She paused for a moment over my tattoos and the puckered bullet scars on my torso, and I was painfully aware Jean's name was tattooed over my heart with a flowering rose. She caressed the pale stars of scar tissue with soft fingertips and touched the etching of Jean's name with respect. She shrugged off the straps of her dress and I covered her freckled, bare shoulders in kisses as I pulled the cold zipper down her spine. As her floral dress slipped down her ribcage, she guided my left hand to cup one of her small breasts. As the momentum of lust carried us past the hall to her bedroom and instead to the living room floor before the fireplace, my long-suffering dog grumblingly gave up his seat and sauntered off with head bowed to sulk in a quieter part of the house.

Gwen stepped out of her dress and unbuckled my belt, and when our clothes were discarded on all sides, I laid her on the floor. She groaned softly and pulled at a fistful of my hair as I kissed the hot, moist flesh and downy orange hair of her mound. She had me take her from behind in the firelight. When I slowly pushed myself inside of her, she groaned sharply and arched her back, reaching over behind her head and pulling me in close. I shuddered in her ear as she writhed and pressed me deeper inside of herself, my heaving chest against her pale back.

When it was done and I achingly pulled myself out of her, she guided me to the couch and crawled between my knees, taking me in her mouth until I was ready for her a second time. Drunk on one another, heady with the first real intimacy either of us had felt in some time, she led me back into her room and put me on my back on top of her made bed. She groaned as she lowered herself onto me and pushed me up inside of her. Her flushed chest heaved, and her glasses fell askew to the floor as the headboard struck the wall. We took our time now, pleasure throbbing and aching as our voices mingled in the dark. I cried out loudly when she rode me to climax a second time. When she too had her fill, Gwen swore like a sailor as she collapsed quivering and sweating on top of me. Our grinning mouths found one another in the dark as we held one another close and drifted off into a contented sleep. Outside, the storm of freezing rain made the roads slick and impassable, and all the people of the town were vexed except for us.

Chapter Fifteen: Come Find Me, Joe

December 24th, 1962

On the morning of Christmas Eve, we walked to Gwen's bookstore through the slush of ice. The hilly roads were still a nightmare to travel. Gwen was learning Otis didn't leave my side if I could help it, but she was taking a liking to the mutt, even if she was more of a 'cat person'. She laughed and steadied my arm as the wire-haired terrier pulled me along like a sled dog on the slick sidewalks. We passed by several automobile accidents where cars backslid down ambitious slopes or spun out of control in intersections. Crunched bumpers and broken glass steamed in the morning air as motorists bickered and gesticulated. That day, I helped with the last-minute business, manning the cash register with an inexperienced hand while Gwen passed out paper coffee cups and helped tourists find paperbacks for their vacation reading. Because the roads were slick, the only business Lost Cove Books saw was from people within walking distance. When six o'clock came, we locked up the shop for the holidays and walked over to Melville's for fish and chips.

That night, we returned to her house together, listened to the radio, and talked by the fire until we crawled into bed together. As I dozed with my face buried in her red curls and breathed in the scent of her, I knew I never wanted to go back to Usher's Fall again. Rupert Wycliffe could roll up his checks and sit on them. That night, I dreamed of my wife. As I lay in Gwen's bed, conscious of the fact she was next to me, Jean walked into the room with her wild, leonine hair down and only a thin nightshirt on. The garment clung to her hips and thighs, and her eyes had a hungry, unnatural glow in the darkness. I started to ask what she was doing, but she put a lone finger to her pursed lips to shush me.

"Baby, what are you doing?" I slurred thickly as she climbed onto the bed. "No, you can't." She crouched at the foot of the bed and looked up at me with mischievous eyes. "I'm with someone in here."

"I know." And she was pulling down the waistband of my boxer shorts, kissing the trail of curly brown hair before putting my penis into her mouth. She slurped and sucked as her head bobbed and I lay stiffly, trying not to make a sound. Every second I was terrified Gwen would roll over and see us. She was so close I could feel the warmth coming off her body.

"Why haven't you come home to me?" Jean asked between my legs. There was a jealous, territorial edge in her voice. She asked too loud, unafraid of waking Gwen, daring her to turn over and see. I was terrified but couldn't move. A part of me didn't want to. "Don't you miss this, Joe? Is it this good with her?" She went down again, and I suppressed a groan. Then she was hiking up the skirt of her nightgown and squeezing me inside herself. I heard her groan as she worked herself up and down on top of me, thighs hugging my hips. I gripped the headboard and looked over to Gwen with fear. Why wouldn't she wake up? Jean's fingertips scratched at my neck and chest, and cotton ripped as she fucked me and tore at my thin white tank top, revealing her name tattooed on my chest. Jean rode with reckless abandon, getting louder. I lay stiff underneath her gyrating hips, barely remembering to breathe, simultaneously thrilled and terrified by the possibility of Gwen seeing us.

I was overwhelmed. I could not deny I longed for her and missed her, and what she was doing felt intoxicatingly real. But she was dead, and everything we had was ashes. For the first time since her death, I was trying to let her go and fall in love with someone else. My eyes rolled back in my head as I tried not to moan, and she let her head and shoulders fall over mine as she kissed my throat and gyrated. But as heady as the pleasure and longing was, another thought was screaming in my brain. *It isn't her. It isn't her. She's dead, this isn't real. You are fucking a corpse.* Dread was rising, and I was paralyzed in my sleep, unable to cry out or to move a muscle. I didn't want it, but I was powerless. There was the cold sensation of a powerful body sitting on my chest, holding me down. When my body at last shuddered in a painful, intense orgasm, I opened my eyes. The hair brushing my face was not the sunny gold of my dead wife, but inky black and smelling of seaweed and death.

She crouched over me in the dark, and I was still inside her, but the visage of Jean and all the mixed feelings it brought were gone. Her hair hung lank over her facial features, but I caught a glimpse of one predatory eye shining catlike, and her translucent pallor gleamed in the blackness. As I lay terrified and immobile beneath her, I realized a distinct sensation she felt young – too young. Younger than my daughter, a teenager. And her pale belly bulged with advanced pregnancy. I saw the fetus' outstretched limbs pushing out against the walls of her flesh. I was full of such shame I wanted to die. She climbed off me, and in the darkness, I saw her walking away. When she turned around, her voice was my dead wife's voice.

"Come home. Come find me, Joe." An image of Jean's smiling face as she climbed out of my car and disappeared into a field of sunflowers. The dark-haired, pale slip of a naked girl stepped into the wall and disappeared through it.

When I woke, I could hardly breathe. I choked and shuddered in the dark and grasped for the lamp on the nightstand. The first thing I saw was the tumble of Gwen's ginger locks on the pillow beside me, the gentle slope of her figure beneath the blankets. I thanked God and closed my eyes, telling myself it was only a dream. Of course, a widower would feel conflicted and guilty as he steps into a new relationship. Of course, I would have a confusing dream about my wife. But it wasn't my wife. I centered myself and steadied my breathing, rising from bed. My shorts were sticky from nocturnal emission, and I remembered the intrusive horror intermingled with shameful pleasure as I stumbled in the dark to the bathroom and flicked on the light. I saw claw marks on my throat and chest, and my undershirt was ripped open to bare the tattoo on my chest. I grimaced and grasped the cold porcelain of the sink as I rested my forehead against the mirror, trying to stay calm.

A rush of nausea overcame me, and I heaved a sudden slop of vomit into the sink. It was fishy and acidic with potato starch. After coughing and spitting, I ran the tap and guided the clumpy liquid down the drain, wiping my clean-shaven chin and trying not to cry. With one last, unbelieving look, I looked at the raw red gouges of fingernails in my flesh and read Jean's name in the curling brown hairs and goosebumps of my chest. I balled up the torn shirt, used it to clean the rest of the vomit, and threw it in the trash. I never told Gwen. I couldn't go back to sleep and passed the small hours of the morning shirtless in the living room at Gwen's typewriter. I smoked cigarette after cigarette and tried to write but couldn't focus long enough to put down a sentence. My head sank to my chest and my shoulders shook as I pressed my forehead into the keys and wept.

Chapter Sixteen: Astoria Noel

December 25th, 1962

That morning over breakfast, Gwen asked how I'd slept, and I only told her I'd had a nightmare.

"I didn't do that the other night, did I?" She gestured to the scratches on my throat and chest.

"Must have done it in my sleep," I lied as I pushed scrambled eggs around my plate with a fork.

We packed up her olive green '49 Volkswagen beetle and worked as a team in the slush of the driveway to lash chains to the wheels. After leaving food and water out for Lennie and cramming ourselves with Otis into the car, we drove out to Cape Contrition so I could pack a bag. We walked hand in hand along the forest trail up the slope, like any sightseeing couple. I was trying not to let my anxiety show. I hadn't told her the house was haunted. She knew what all the locals knew: it was a troubled place, magnetic for suicides and shipwrecks, and people who lived there could become isolated and depressed. Her fears for me were merely psychological. I feared she would never believe the truth of this place.

The snow over Delilah was fading fast, so it was more of a gray than a white Christmas in town. Oregon's coastal climate is too temperate for heavy, lasting snows. The forest floor was wet and mostly bare, but the trees still held a dandruff of snow, melting icicles tinkling like chimes in the silent wood. A lumpy, tattered inch of snow lay upon the lawn. Unoccupied for days, the house stood silent and cold with its roof in a thin blanket of white. I popped the collar of my pea coat and gave my scarf another wrap about my neck before jangling out my keys, stepping onto the creaking porch, and opening the door.

Gwen had never been inside and explored the old house as I packed a small valise with essentials. We were coming up to her parents as a surprise. In preparation for typical Christiansen hospitality, we planned to stay until New Year's Day.

When we got back onto Highway 101, the drive was tense and silent. With a steady hand and the windshield wipers slapping away the inundation of rain, Gwen guided the beetle on the winding roads hugging the cliffs. We rattled over a web of cracks and broken pebbles in the asphalt, as if some god fell from the sky there. I remembered how a fateful boulder blocked my road on an October day that now seemed ages ago, turning a single pass through Delilah into a semi-permanent residence. Of course, they still hadn't bothered to repave the road where the boulder crashed. It wasn't long before the road conditions improved enough that we were able to pull over and remove the chains.

Passing on from the cliffs and their foam-spattered rocks, we drove over sloping heaths of tangled, scrubby bushes and the crouching forms of balding Lodgepole Pines. Plains of swampy yellow grass rolled by with inlet streams of shimmering indigo cutting through. A bull elk waded through the wetlands. At the edge of the field was a backdrop of towering spruce. Lofty above them, the wooded crests of prehistoric hills were wreathed in mysterious gray fog. Out on the distant horizon of the west, chilly rainstorms were hazy streaks of vaporous cascades rippling down, as their clouds hovered over the face of the waters.

After covering seventy miles in three hours, we pulled at last into the port of Astoria. The lamp posts and shop windows were alive with Christmas cheer, and the sleepy town lolled contented in the cool ocean breeze. Construction had begun on the Astoria-Megler Bridge, a sloping cantilever through truss bridge which would come to span four miles across the mighty lower Columbia River, replacing decades of ferry service to connect the rugged corners of Oregon and Washington.

The Christiansens lived in a white two-story house with a wraparound porch on two sides and a faded white picket fence enclosing its overgrown yard. The house peeked out from a cluster of trees at the top of a steep gravel driveway, high upon a green hill in a picturesque old neighborhood overlooking the ocean at a distance. As soon as we opened the front door, we were met with the mirthful Viking roar of a huge red-faced man in a gray aran sweater, with white hair and beard. Gwen squealed when this bear in a sweater hoisted her off the ground in an alarming hug before setting her down. Otis stepped into the house with wagging tail and ears laid back, wiggling happily about the man's legs as he roared again and rubbed heavy hands into the dog's shaggy coat.

"Papa, I want you to meet somebody," she said, but the big man anticipated her words, and was already turning his attention from the dog to me.

"Hello, who is this?" the old man asked as he crackled my knuckles, enclosing them in his own meaty paw.

"Joe. Joe Crowley, sir." I looked Erik Christiansen in the eye and didn't give him the satisfaction of seeing my pain in his aggressive male primate greeting ritual. I don't care if you're 17 or 47. Meeting your girlfriend's father for the first time never changes. The gruffness of the man melted away as he got to know me, and his bombastic company soon became a delight; as did the gentle sarcasm and self-deprecation of Gladys, Gwen's mother. Gwen's brother James arrived hours before us from San Francisco, where he worked as a reporter. Since this was a former career of mine, we meshed easily over the kinds of shop-talk unacquainted men in the same field of work stick to. He asked me some apt questions about my upcoming book, and I spoke of it as if my work was going well. I couldn't tell him by this point I was no longer working on it and hadn't gotten around to informing my artistic patron and employer.

I was quickly accepted into their family with easy welcome and bountiful hospitality and was rarely conscious I was spending Christmas with complete strangers. The Christiansens had a gray-muzzled golden retriever, and though he befriended Otis, the younger mutt tired him out with endless wrestling and chasing. It was amazing to see the way the dog's broken limb in its cast did so little to slow him down, when my own threw me into such a pit of inactivity. After helping to pass out the presents, eating dinner, and helping Gladys do dishes in the kitchen, I had to duck an offer of home-brewed mead from jolly Erik, who was sampling his own wares and drunk as a lord. But I did take him and James up on smoking pipes on the porch after sunset. We savored the sweet, odoriferous smoke and made easy conversation until late into the night, and I realized I'd never been enfolded this easily into a lover's family. The realization came with a twinge of grief for the aged parents of Jean in Tennessee, who were once dearer to me than my own parents.

Chapter Seventeen: Ransacked

January 1ˢᵗ, 1963

We stayed in Astoria until New Year's Day, and I looked forward to the bright new year of 1963 with all the optimism of a holiday vacationer. Usher's Fall and the stalled novel were impossible to think about in this place. The warmth and inclusion a troubled old cynic like me felt, wrapped in a strange family's wholesome holiday gathering, was like the end of a Christmas story. My relationship with Gwen was in those thrilling early stages of learning everything about one another when everything was new. Our time together was still colored with a nervous desire to impress and excite one another. It was a path I had not walked since my early twenties, and it made me feel young all over again. True to my new-adopted age, I was falling for her with an ease that alarmed me. I had not dared to say it in words, but I didn't need to. Our every look, smile, and touch said it. *I'm learning to love again.*

When we arrived back in Delilah on the afternoon of New Year's Day, Gwen and I said our fond goodbye in the lighthouse's visitor parking lot. It was to be our first time returning to our individual lives and sleeping in separate houses in over a week. It felt like we'd been going steady for months. *Going steady.* The thought brought a smile to my face. I was trying to act casual and easygoing, rather than show my looming despondency. The realization was gnawing at me that the life I was returning to had so much less joy and peace in it than her own. I did not want to seem clingy, but I also knew any time we spent apart would pass far slower for me than for her. And though I nearly started to at several points, I still hadn't told her what I would be returning to at Usher's Fall.

Broken bones aching from prolonged sitting in the cramped Volkswagen, I clicked my tongue at Otis and we started up the path together. The dog limped along at my side with head bowed, stopping only to dutifully mark the same trees which had gone a week without his spoor. The snow was melted and the earth was wet, the forest still dripping. The air was cool, rich, and thick with moisture and brine. The coastal air always made me feel alive, as if its molecules were richer with life than the stale, paltry stuff that passed for air in other places. As we made it to the house and stepped out of the trees, I would not have guessed anything was amiss.

But when we entered the house and my shoes crunched on broken glass, I saw the house had not taken kindly to my abandonment. The place was ransacked, as if by a bear and a hurricane. Otis growled and ruffed low as he padded into the house, but with so much broken glass about, I hauled him back into the small mudroom. He yelped and clawed at the door when I shut him out to survey the damage myself. I stepped gingerly over a strewn mess of stuffing from clawed apart pillows, shattered plates and glasses, bent silverware, and shredded garbage confetti. Food was dragged from the refrigerator and dumped all over the ground floor. It was all moldering and blackened to an impossible degree, after a week on the floorboards of the drafty, cold house. On several parts of the walls, the rotten guts of exploded apples and tomatoes clung to the patterned paper in the midst of the acidic splashes of their juice. The noisome odor pervading the ground floor was enough to gag me. The hot, trapped stinks of rotting food and raw sewage are so similar when you realize they amount to the same thing.

Pages of *Between the Devil and the Deep Blue Sea* were gaily cast all about the house, intermixed with typed passages of vulgar, unhinged mania running on like the rants of one possessed by a demon. The couches of the living room and my bed upstairs were overturned, most of the pillows and cushions ripped open with stuffing scattered about. The contents of every drawer and cupboard of the kitchen were upturned and spilled out onto the floor, along with the drawers themselves. A crude array of steak knives were stuck inches deep in the kitchen wall. Nailed up by one in the center was my only remaining photograph of Jean and Emma. They held one another in the center of a pumpkin patch in a balmy Carolina October, black and white faces frozen in laughter. But the eyes of the photographs were scratched out, replaced by vicious, forceful scribbles of black pen ink.

The house sat and watched with an air of smug self-satisfaction and petulant jealousy, waiting for me to explode. *Look what you made me do. See what happens when you try to leave.* I did not disappoint. For several minutes I stood seething, fists clenched at my sides as I trembled, and Otis clawed at the door off behind me. Breaths rattled hot and angry as my brain boiled and screamed like the steam from a teapot.

"FUCK!" I roared until my voice broke and echoed back at me mockingly from the corners of the house. I fell to the ground in the broken glass and rotting food, groaning in pain as I instinctively caught my fall with my broken wing in its clumsy plaster cast. My foot struck out of its own accord and crashed through the wood panels of one of the lower cupboard doors. I raged and gasped on my back with one foot lost in the cupboard before pulling it out through the jagged hole I had made. I got to my feet on wobbly knees and thought for a second the rage was out of my system, but my arm in its cast swept all the broken refuse from the counter onto the floor, and I kicked the wall so hard I nearly broke my toe. I bellowed and staggered back as I clutched at my foot in its worn leather shoe, hissing in red pain and lifting a long middle finger to every corner of the house. For a few minutes, I crouched low to the floor like Gollum amidst the ruin, struggling to breathe as the rage crackled through me. I felt in that moment like the bestial energy channeling through my body could power cities or destroy them if it only flowed within a vessel that could properly harness it. But my vessel was weak, and so I stewed in the mocking stillness of the tossed house. I knew the impotence of my powerlessness, the pointlessness of my childish temper tantrum. As my equilibrium resettled, I limped on my throbbing foot to the mudroom, stroking Otis' head reassuringly as I grabbed the broom and dustpan and set to work.

The clean-up lasted until sunset, and the work was made even more enervating by the fact I had to do it one-handed. I clumsily swept all the refuse with the broom pressed in one hand, heaved all the furniture upright and put my back and shoulder into sliding them back in place, and scrubbed the walls with a soapy rag that did little to remove the corrosive stains of fruit juice left for a week. I set the kitchen drawers back into their tracks and removed the kicked-in cupboard door from its hinges. I pulled each of the knives out of the wall and plucked down the picture of my girls like a sacred family idol that had been desecrated. I stared at the savage blots of their scratched-out eyes for several minutes before sighing and consigning the photograph to the trash pile. What is a portrait without eyes?

Outside by flashlight, I made a small ring of stones by the base of the lighthouse and set up a pyre of split logs from the dilapidated covering provided by the ruins of the barn. I had never been in the collapsed structure, which was being dragged with clinging ivy and constricting vines back into the forest. A sapling was growing up from the killing floor toward the jagged hole in the ceiling which seeded and watered it. Just outside the barn was a low, jagged tree stump with a heavy axe buried in its many rings. As I looked at the dull steel wedge of the rust-spotted blade, I felt a strange foreboding. My mind whirled with images of Henry Usher's hairy arms hefting that axe to split wood or slaughter livestock. As my eyes hung glued to the axe in the stump, noises came to my thoughts with such reality, I almost looked about for their source. A goat's anxious bleating, the squawking of chickens, and the groans of a girl as her father beat her and worse.

I found a decaying old wheelbarrow with a rattling wheel, filled it with split logs, and precariously steered it out to the fire circle I'd made. The hole-pocked, rust-eaten barrow was so vexatious, the twenty-yard journey made with so many stops and starts, when I finally overturned its payload into the circle of stones, I just left it there. With one last careful examination of the house, I saved everything that could be saved and dragged the rest out to be burned at the base of the lighthouse. Lighting the damn pile in the wind at the edge of the cliff took several tries, but with the rolled tube of the rambling nonsense papers for kindling, I nursed the blaze to life. The fire picked up and consumed the refuse in a towering gout of flickering yellow and orange, showing weird shadow-puppets against the cold face of the lighthouse. I stood and panted with the labor. In the light of the stirring bonfire, I saw the blowing hair and dark dress of a woman in black standing with her back to me, beyond the tower at the edge of the cliff. I could only just see her at the edge of my view, but I knew who she was and looked away. That little trick wasn't going to work again. Let the bitch fall. The blaze crackled and growled, and with the flickering light playing shadows on the lines of my gaunt face, I glared up at the lifeless white tower like the general of a besieging medieval army, taunting it with a prelude to its own fate.

The lighthouse stood silent to the challenge for a minute, but as night fell and the world dimmed, a dull hum of electricity whirred to life as if in answer. I shivered in the wet grass by the wind-tossed fire, furiously sucking down a cigarette and hissing out snakes of blue smoke as I watched the pale beam of the tower's magnificent searchlight pan heavily across the dramatic turbulence of the black ocean. The warning it gave to turn away could be seen by sailors as far as twenty miles out at sea. If only I had listened.

Chapter Eighteen: The Madness of Joe Crowley

January 13th, 1963

The doorbell sent a clamor through the house, reverberating off the thin old walls. The noise jolted me from a deep sleep only just achieved. In the bleariness of waking, I realized I hadn't even known what the doorbell sounded like. This was my first visitor. With a groan, I hauled myself up and stepped into a pair of pants. What time was it? I pulled apart the drapes to see the beam of the lighthouse like an eye in the heavy blanket of fog enshrouding the grounds. The bell rang again as I was running down the stairs, haphazardly buttoning my shirt.

"Yeah, yeah, keep your shirt on," I muttered before I opened the door to a couple in their early eighties. The man stood shivering with hands in his overall pockets. His wife looked up with a kind smile of horsey dentures, clutching her tiny purse to herself.

"Good morning, young man," the old woman beamed with bright eyes.

"We didn't mean to wake you, Sir," her husband stepped between us and shook my hand like a man embarrassed by his wife's insistence. "I apologize for the early hour."

"What can I do for you?" I shivered in the morning cold and pushed the last two buttons of my shirt into their holes.

"We're in town for the weekend, celebrating our anniversary. It's our fiftieth, can you believe it?" the woman replied, looking at her husband with the giddy adoration of a sixteen-year-old.

"Oh, that's swell," I covered my mouth as I yawned. "Well, congratulations."

"Tom heard about this lovely little boarding house, and we just had to come see. Are you the host, or a guest? Is there still a room to let?"

I looked slowly between the two of them to make sure this wasn't some kind of joke. Usher's Fall had not functioned as a boarding house since 1949, when-

"No. I'm sorry folks, but this house hasn't been open to guests in years. I'm the only tenant." The woman smirked, as if to say *oh, I don't know about that.*

"Oh, darn," the old woman snapped her fingers, and as she turned to her husband, her private, bemused smirk of a moment turned to a disappointed grimace. "Well, it's a beautiful old house. We just had to check. It seemed like such a pleasant place to die." She said it so offhandedly I almost didn't notice.

"What did you say?" My voice trembled as I stepped out onto the porch after them.

"That's enough, Mabel." The old man turned his wife around toward the porch steps and guided her away. She was so frail, she needed to hold him for support as she walked. As they turned on their heels, they were walking into a pair of nooses hung neatly side by side at head-level from the eaves of the awning over the porch steps.

"Hey, wait!" But the nooses slipped easily over their heads, and when they stepped off the porch, it was into open air. The steps disappeared. My stomach roiled as they dropped, and the ropes went taut with the simultaneous wrenching snap of their necks. I dropped to my knees in horror and awe as I watched them twitch and sway from the porch gallows. The slip-on flats and dead, hosed legs of the woman kicked and scuffed against the boards as her nerves played out their last trauma. Her name was Mabel. And he was Tom. No, this wasn't right. It wasn't the porch, they had hung from the... bedroom. Waters. Fiftieth anniversary. My eyes misted over with tears and I put hands to my knees as I struggled not to throw up. I closed my eyes against the scuffling dead spasms of their shoes against the edge of the porch. I opened my eyes and looked up to them. The ropes creaked and the hanged pair brushed softly against one another in the cool morning breeze. Dead, blueish fingers brushed clumsily against one another like the awkward first teenage attempt at holding hands.

The body of Mabel Waters turned on its rope like a ghastly marionette, and I saw the black neck, purpling swollen face, distended tongue, and glassy dead-mackerel eyes. These were displayed in all their ghoulish parody of the sweet, wrinkled face I could hardly recognize. As I watched, the dead eyes settled on me and the mouth moved. The woman's voice spoke unbelievably through the crushed windpipe and garish mask she now wore, and she said,

"Don't you think so, Joe? Isn't that why you're here?"

I plunged wide awake into consciousness with a sucking gasp, and lay panting for several moments before knowing it hadn't been real. But the first thing my gaze settled on was the stout rafter where the Waters Couple suicide occurred. Otis snapped awake with me, and his nose came quivering with hot sniffs as he investigated my heavy breathing. Pushing him off, I staggered in my underwear to the bathroom as I shook off the dream. The day before, I had finally gotten my sling removed and received the good news my collarbone was healed at last. The arm would take more patience, and so my itchy cinderblock limb remained. When the cast was finally due to come off, I was told to expect a regimen of calisthenics and other at-home exercises to build back my atrophied strength and coordination. I stopped by Lost Cove Books and invited Gwen to dinner at Usher's Fall that night, as a celebration of my recovery.

I wheezed through my first run since the car accident and cursed shins threatening to snap beneath my weight. My heavy swinging forearm cast slowly nudged me off balance as my legs pumped down the forest trail, and by the time I reached the beach of Siren's Cove, I admitted defeat. With heavy, clumsy jerks, I tore off my red running shoes and socks. I perched them on a rock before wiping my hands on my running shorts and walking out to our beached boat, which was nestled far back from the grasp of the tide. Half-buried in the sand and sheltered from view by tall yellow grass, the boat's metallic hull and bulky motor squatted like a mechanical tortoise in the fog.

While Otis wallowed in the sand and smiled at me upside down, I overturned the fishing boat and plowed it through the gritty sand. Plumes of dusty cloud stirred in the murky, greenish water and were swiped away by the surf as I toed the cold, marshy sand with bare feet, guiding the motorboat out into the shallows. Otis snapped to his feet, tearing up sand and water as he barreled through the surf and threw himself into the boat, forgetting how anxious he always became once we were out to sea. Water dripped from his beard and mustache, and I shooed him out of the way before climbing into the boat and jerking back the line of the outboard motor.

For the better part of two hours, I chugged around the cove heaving crab rings into the water, marking the location of their buoys. After they sat for a bit, I'd haul them up hand over hand and pick through their snapping, angry carapaces for a suitably large male. Then, it was throwing the rings back and starting again. It was soothing in a way only laborious, repetitive work can be. The fog burned off at noon, but the day never warmed with the emergence of the sun, so the only way to avoid the chill was to keep moving. By the time I hauled the last crab ring into the boat for keeps and was ready to turn back, only four eligible crabs were brooding in the bottom of the bucket. But four was enough. I lamented the bucketful I lost in the woods when the Pioneer and the Sailor came out shooting.

The shower was cascading over my head in a steaming gout when the doorbell clanged throughout the house. The sound alarmed me with memories of the morning's disturbing dream, but I thought it must be time for Gwen. The moment the bell sounded, Otis let loose a torrent of howling barks, sounding the alarm and galloping for the door. I hastily twisted the shower knobs so the spray guttered and spat to a trickling halt.

"Just a minute!" I called as I stumbled out of the shower, wrapped a towel around my waist, and my bare feet slapped wetly down the old steps to the front door.

"So, this is the date, huh? You just get right to it," Gwen smirked over the frames of her glasses when I opened the door naked and wrapped in a towel.

"Sorry, I lost track of time," I panted, dripping with water and smiling, "Unless you're into it."

"Go get some clothes on, Slim." I leapt to the second step to dodge a slap at my ass. Otis wiggled between us as Gwen squatted with chipper hellos.

"I think you like him more than me," I called from the top of the stairs, and she called back,

"Why do you think I came over?" She took the dog outside to run and play in the yard while I finished getting ready, and when I came down in fresh clothes, the three of us chased and wrestled in the grass until we were breathless and wheezing with laughter, and evening was coming on fast.

The air was fragrant with smells of butter, paprika, peppercorn, and garlic as the crab boil stewed in a tall steel pot. Gwen and I nursed newly bought enameled tin mugs of coffee at the kitchen table while the boil continued, reconnecting as I cut red potatoes, andouille sausages, ears of corn, and onions at the counter.

"New plates, new mugs... You didn't get all new dishes for this, did you?" she asked later when I shoveled the crab boil onto two brand new dinner plates and set the table.

"No." The question caught me off guard. "I had to replace a lot of them recently. I've been pretty clumsy with just my left hand free."

"You're left-handed."

"And clumsy," I parried, a trifle touchier than I meant to.

"Did clumsiness scar up that wall with holes, and put all those dark stains on the living room wall?" Damn, she was good. It was like talking to Sherlock Holmes!

"Man, you are not letting up about this. Can't we just have dinner? I caught these myself."

"I can eat fresh-caught seafood anywhere in town. I'm here because I care about you. You cleaned up, but this place was wrecked, and it's obvious. Should I be worried?" I looked at my untouched heap of steaming food for a moment, caught with nothing to say but the truth, and unable to give voice to it.

"You don't have to worry about me." A feeble deflection.

"Really? Because I don't think that's true. You damn near killed yourself and Otis in a car wreck two months ago. You're all alone in this depressing house three miles from anybody else. I know you haven't been writing or exercising. You never come into town anymore or leave your castle up here. We had this beautiful week together and I introduced you to my parents, but now I've hardly seen you since we got back..."

She kept going, and every word of it was true, which only made it all seethe worse in me.

"You don't tell me what you're thinking, you've been through a lot since you lost your wife-"

"Don't talk about my wife," I snarled so suddenly it brought her up short, and her eyes widened with fear and anger behind her glasses.

"We've both been married before, Joe, and we've both suffered. We've talked about it before. I thought-"

"-Well, we can't, okay?" I interrupted, and we stared at one another across the kitchen table in barbed silence for a long minute. Finally, she broke her gaze and gathered her purse and coat.

"Like I said, I didn't come here for the crab boil. I want to share more than meals with you. If you want that too, you know where to find me. But I'm not twenty, and I'm not going to sit and eat a fucking seafood dinner while we pretend nothing is going on with you."

I cursed under by breath as she walked off, and the slam of the door rattled the frame. Did that just happen? I had whiplash from how rapidly the argument exploded, seemingly out of nowhere. But it wasn't out of nowhere, I admitted to myself. The house gave off clear warning signs, and I dropped off the map after we got back from Astoria. What did I expect? I hadn't been fair to her, and she knew she deserved better. We were too old to play boyfriend and girlfriend. I cared about her, and our relationship was the greatest joy of my life in Delilah. I had not been honest or attentive to that relationship, and now she was walking out the door. And yet, even as I got up to follow her, another part of my mind reminded me: *what, are you going to tell her you're being driven to the brink by a house full of ghosts? She'll never believe you.* Maybe she wouldn't believe the whole thing, but I had to tell her the part of the truth I could bring myself to say, at least.

She was halfway down the trail when I caught up to her. The forest air was balmy, full of birdcalls and shafts of golden light.

"Gwen, hold up!" When she turned around on the trail, I could see tears flushed her cheeks. I lifted my hands in surrender, ready to bargain with what truth I had to give away in exchange for her company. "I'm ready to talk. Just... Don't go, okay? Come on up to the house."

"What happened up there, Joe?" Her arms crossed stiffly

231

over her chest and refused to budge. My mind worked fast as I decided what partiality of the truth would be enough.

"You're right, I've sealed myself away. And I haven't been talking to you about what I'm going through. We've shared so much recently, but when I got off on my own, my brain sort of... attacked itself. I didn't want to be a burden to you, so I didn't talk about it."

"But Joe, do you understand you aren't a burden to me? That I want to be here for you and help?" I could see pity softening the anger in her eyes.

"There's knowing a thing and *knowing* a thing. I can know our relationship is a good thing for me and still feel I don't deserve it, like being with me is only going to hurt you in the end."

"Is that what you think? You haven't talked to me since New Year's because you're afraid if you're with me, I'll end up like..."

"Yes." The word was heavy with the quiver of suppressed tears. I was being torn apart inside by the whole truth I was strangling, but... She would never understand the ghosts if I tried to tell her. She didn't have to live with them.

"The truth is, I smashed up the house. Every mug, every plate, all the food, the furniture. I had a nervous breakdown and tore the house apart. I didn't want to scare you."

"I told you before. I'm not scared of you, Joe." But I could see in her eyes it wasn't true, even if she wanted it to be. She stepped closer. "But I'm scared *for* you. It's not right for you to be alone here for so long. That would do things to people with far less to overanalyze than you. I warned you the first time we met. This place... People aren't meant to live like that. *That's* what happened to the Ushers, and that's what's happening to you.

"I'm drowning, Gwen. And I don't want you to drown with me. What we have, it isn't going to work. I'm not easy to be with, and you won't be happy, because deep down, you're a good person. And deep down, I'm not." She stepped forward and took me in her arms, and I buried my head in her chest like a little boy, shoulders trembling with tears. The forest was still. The distant croaks of ravens were the only sound besides my own heaving. After a few minutes, Gwen spoke softly.

"The people I really mistrust are the ones who say they don't have any demons. It's the good people who are all killing themselves with guilt. The evil ones? When night comes, they sleep just fine. If you were as wicked and undeserving as you think, you wouldn't be living like a penitent over it."

By slow degrees, my outburst was forgiven, and our whispering embrace turned into a slow walk back to Usher's Fall. The food was growing cold, but we ate our fill of it, and for the next two hours we listened to records by a crackling fire in the living room and talked. Guilt nagged at me for my inability to open up to her about the ghosts, the way I had to Thomas Forester. I almost told her several times, but how could I say it without sounding crazy? *Tell her about us and you'll scare her away. And you'll only have me for company. What do you think happens to you then?* I banished the guilt, pulling myself out of my mind to be present with Gwen.

When I listened to her speak and heard her hopes and desires, I believed she could cure me of my madness and make me a better man. But I knew this was me medicating and putting the burden of my healing on the shoulders of another person, and that was wrong. Bitter experience reminded me it wouldn't work in the long run. No matter how happy I was when she was with me, when she left, the ghosts would come back. My brain would commence to attack itself. And after this went on long enough, my despair would continue regardless of whether I was alone, or she was at my side. It would make me feel isolated and unrelatable to her. I would close myself off and in turn resent the distance I unwittingly created. Given enough time, this would kill us. It had happened before. It was unfair to make her my answer when I needed to find that within myself. When our time together was through, it would be up to me to save my own soul. If she would walk with me on that road, I needed to tell her everything. But I didn't know how to accomplish complete truth or self-salvation. Instead, I wished the night would go on forever and hoped in vain this remarkable woman would never leave me alone.

Night closed in, and we were reclining loose and contented by the fire, talking and passing a cigarette back and forth. I lost all track of time until I saw the silvery disc of the three-quarter moon through the window, looming low and large over the bladed canopy of the evergreens. As I stubbed out our cigarette in the ashtray, I asked if she thought she better go home, and she started kissing me, smoky and heavy. Perfumed red curls tickled my nose as her whisper brushed hot and intoxicating in my ear.

"I think I'll stay." When her soft fingertip tickled and traced up the palm of my left hand, I closed my hand in hers and let her lead me to the bedroom. We kissed on the stairs as we went, like teenagers pouncing at the opportunity of an empty house at last. But when she got to the landing, opened the bedroom door, and flicked on the light, her breath sucked in a terrible gasp as if she was choking on her heart. A terrible moment passed as I raced up to the landing, and her voice found itself in a trembling moan of fear as I looked past her into the room. Over the neatly made bed, hanging evenly spaced from the heavy support beam of the ceiling, were two nooses.

"Oh my God," I murmured. Gwen shoved me backward against another door with all her strength and was tearing off down the stairs as rapidly as she could. *Oh no, oh no, oh no,* my mind panicked as she slammed the front door. The fear in her eyes the moment she pushed me from herself was mortal. Three seconds was all it took for her to get from the second-floor landing to the front porch. Her flight could only mean one thing. She believed I set the nooses for us and planned some sort of murder-suicide for the evening. What explanation could there be? I had said nothing to prepare her for any other. *Stupid, stupid, stupid.* The preparation of the nooses was disturbing and insidious, but I was inured to such horrors. My disturbance was far more in Gwen's terror of me. Hardly knowing what I was doing, I charged after her, tearing out through the door and barreling into the woods after the faintest glimpse of her red hair in the night. A moment ago, I was about to go to bed with my lover. Now I was chasing her into the dark. Not a good look.

"Gwen! Please, I need to explain. Let me tell you, -oh God. I didn't tell you everything, Gwen. Stop running!" But she was in the wind, tearing through the brambles and grasping branches over stony, uneven earth. I plunged after her, and Otis streaked out of the open front door into the forest behind me at a gallop, but the search was in vain. My chest was heaving, my breaths choking rattles by the time I made it to the parking lot. A squeal of tires and the reeling flash of panning headlights was all I got as she swung her Beetle around and tore off into the night. As I stood with chest heaving, cursing my stupidity and realizing she was likely going to the police, I glanced down and realized I was holding the shotgun. I didn't even remember grabbing it. I looked at the cold, heavy weapon with a sense of foreboding as I turned and limped on twisted ankles back into the dark curtain of the forest.

As I stepped into the trees, I drew my flashlight from its place in my coat pocket and clicked it on. The beam shone out dimmer than before, barely illuminating ten feet ahead of me. The batteries were low, but worse, the torch was jostled roughly in my feverish run downhill. It was touchy -the way used flashlights can get. My hand gripped it tight and tried to keep steady, for a sudden movement might cause the feeble electric glow to go out. Otis whined and growled somewhere in the darkness, but I sought for him in vain. I called out his name in a harsh, strangled rasp. The dog was unresponsive, but his growls and whimpers were alarming. I continued to sound his name in the dark as I haltingly moved up the dirt track. There was a snap of twigs under furtive feet that weren't mine. The frail beam cut out as I jerked toward the noise, and I gave the flashlight's head a little slap of frustration, urging it back to life. But the beam illuminated only tree bark, frayed ferns, and tangled ivy. I heard the laugh of a little girl and turned in time to see the hem of a black skirt slip out of the spotlight's edge.

Several other times on that walk, I heard the murmurs of children, and saw their furtive shapes slipping beyond the edge of my light. There were others, as well. As I followed the ever-distant noises of my dog over rock and root, the beam of my light caught a dreamlike and fantastic glimpse of a woman in green and gray garments covered in leaves, lithe and fairylike, but crowned with branching antlers like a stag. Her back was to me, and she was unaware of being caught in my light for a moment. But the moment passed, and when she turned, her face was concealed in a long papier-mâché deer mask, like something from a witch's masquerade. She froze for a moment in the light and bounded off. I was so stunned by her appearance, I froze too. When she left, I gave chase, unknowing if she was a person or a shade. The girl of leaves and antlers moved like a deer herself, flitting among the trees with astounding agility. I called out and ran after her. We snapped through branches and brush clawing at our arms and faces, and I was slowly gaining on her.

The stag fairy's breaths were quick and sharp, and as I reached out to grab hold of an antler, an unseen body tackled me full force from the side, throwing me off my feet, knocking the wind out from within my ribs, and ramming my skull hard into the trunk of a tree. The flashlight spun end over end out of my grip, flashing drunkenly before extinguishing in the dirt. The pain of my rattled head was blinding, and blood started from my scalp where some of my hair was sticky with tree sap. I gasped and groaned as I clutched to the tree for support and staggered to my feet. In the darkness, I saw a man in dark clothes rise unsteadily to his feet, clutching a battered shoulder and caked in dirt. His face was hidden by an elaborate fox mask in orange and white. I thought I might lose consciousness. The taste of blood was thick and metallic in my mouth as I looked at them through bleary eyes. My broken arm was screaming and battering at the walls of its cast. We stood there panting for a moment, and I realized my gun and flashlight had been lost in the fall. Immediately I dove to the ground, scrabbling blindly in vain for them. The Fox understood what I was doing just in time, and turned to run as my hand seized on the stock of the 12-gauge. I shouldered the gun with a gritty cascade of the dirt it lay in, lined up my bead and fired a spray of buckshot, but heard no other sound over the thunderous boom. Cursing under my breath, I fumbled desperately for the flashlight and seized on it at last, casting its frail, dust-coated light into the space where I had fired. A tree took the brunt of my pellets, and there was no Deer or Fox around. I spat a heavy, dark glob of blood and dirt, wiping my lip and sandpapery chin on my sleeve and giving up the hunt. As I trudged back up the hill, I had little time to contemplate the strange masquerade, because the gunfire was beginning.

I knew, this time, the muzzles flashing and rifles barking in the trees were some spectral display of the Pioneer and the Sailor. But this knowledge gave no comfort, and the bullets ricocheting off stones and burying themselves in tree trunks still seemed as real as they needed to be. Over the clamor of guns, I heard the forlorn howl of Otis. Gathering myself up and fighting to see, I took off at a run uphill, finding the trail once again. Bark shards and dust sprayed as bullets crashed near me. *They aren't real.* But other thoughts were intruding, grasping like paralyzing tendrils suffocating my reason. It was happening again.

I was clutching my gun, ducking bullets, heart pounding, fear seething, and '44 was bleeding into '63 until I couldn't see the difference. Talking myself out of it was useless. These weren't memories, it was happening to me again. I was there. Machine guns were rattling off belts of bullets shredding men into meaningless meat, pulverizing concrete and rock into dust. Luftwaffe dive-bombers were screaming low over us, their payloads leaving fields of pounded craters, twisted metal, and smoking ash where deer had once grazed. I saw one of those deer staggering lost and dazed across a blackened no man's land, leg garroted in slicing razor wire.

Nineteen-year-old boys screamed for their mothers and grasped in the dirt for blown off limbs, while some clutched at their own guts to keep them from wetly slapping the ruined earth. Skeletal Jews, gypsies, homosexuals, political dissidents, mentally handicapped people, the disposable casualties of a new world order promising to separate the wheat from the chaff of the human race; they were shoved like sardines into cramped, efficient, and punctual railway cars. They clawed at the unsympathetic walls of gas chambers as their lungs and throats burned with poison, were obliterated into belching columns of black smoke by crematoriums of hell or left in twisted heaps of pallid limbs and naked violation to freeze in the night.

I shot another burst into the darting shape of a Nazi in the trees and ducked behind a heavy tree as a panzer rolled past on earth-churning treads. An elephant screamed as I burst through the tree-line and staggered onto the lawn. The grass was lit in a false daylight by the column of consuming fire swirling about Usher's Fall Light. Bright electric light was spilling from all the windows and the open front door of the house, and a chill ran down my spine as a German soldier rose from his seat on the porch and took aim. I bolted to the side as he fired at me from fifteen paces and felt the bullet whistle by my ear as I lifted my own gun in answer. A burst of shot bit into the wood and shattered the window behind him as he collapsed, eviscerated. I racked out the spent shell and smelled the metallic, acrid smoke of gunpowder as I climbed to the porch and threw open the door. My box of shells was sitting on a low shelf in the mudroom. With practiced hands, I reloaded and emptied the rest of the box's contents into my coat pocket before battering down the second door and coming into the house. The gun was raised to my shoulder and I fired again when a German came out of the kitchen. As another lifted his submachine gun from behind an overturned couch, I threw myself through the doorway into the kitchen and shut off the lights as I crouched behind the counter.

Furtive steps of boots clacked on the floorboards, and I counted them as they grew closer. When I heard the familiar creak of a troublesome board from the doorway, I spun with shouldered shotgun and pumped a burst of fire through his face. The double clack of the pump action snapped fluidly in my hands. I replaced my spent shell, keeping the chambers full. The kitchen had two open doorways, and as I heard a scuffle of feet in the dining room through the portal behind me, I crept cautiously over. The footsteps drew to a halt, and I could hear furtive breaths on the other side of the wall. Slow and steady, I lifted my gun and pressed the muzzle against the wallpaper. Sheetrock and wood paneling burst in a shock of dust from the hole I blew in the wall. There came a moaning grunt and a scuffle of boots on the other side as my man clutched the wall in horror, and I saw his face through the hole I had made. Racking out the spent shell, I moved around the edge of the doorway and sprayed two more shots rapidly into the dining room, shredding two more soldiers into hamburger. The one I shot through the wall reeled drunkenly and drooled blood. A dry, empty click sounded as I pulled the trigger again. Gun empty, I hauled the Nazi down to the floor and rammed the stock into his face, over and over again, as his agonized grimace cracked and caved into a red pulp and sanguine droplets peppered my own face.

Breaths rattling from my heaving chest, I cast the blood-wet gun onto the floor and slowly picked myself up from the soldier whose own mother could not have recognized him. The house was a still ruin, walls peppered with shot, windows shattered, cushions shredded, furniture splintered. My feet dragged drunkenly over broken glass, jagged stakes of table legs, and inky pools of blood.

"What happened, Joe? You've made such a mess," Jean said, stepping carefully in bare feet over the ruins of the shot-up house. "What am I going to do with you?" Her thin lips parted in a cold, mocking smirk too cruel to have belonged to the woman I'd loved, and her hair was smoking.

"No, stop." I tripped and fell weakly back on the stairs, trying to catch myself with my forearm in its cast and groaning at the angry creak of healing bones. "Get away from me." She walked over scattered diamonds of broken glass, unflinching as blood started from her soles and left wet footprints behind her. I clutched my wounded arm to my chest and ran up the stairs to my bedroom, but as I opened the door, an elderly man and woman jumped hand in hand from the bed, and the house shook with the rending snap of their necks from the support beam gallows. I collapsed on the landing as Mr. and Mrs. Waters swung. The soldiers, Jean's voice, and deafening beats of bombs and gunfire all over the Cape, all went silent when the old couple's necks snapped. I crouched on the floor shaking with tears, pressing my aching forehead into the boards and begging for it to stop, when in the living room, the old gramophone switched on. At full volume, the silence was broken by the scrape of needle on vinyl, the faint crackle of the speaker. A familiar high twine of violins creaked out a melody, backed by low thrumming chords of piano. No. No. How could it know that? How could–

The lyrics to Hymne à l'amour blared over the tinny gramophone like an accusation.

"Please!" I wept through gritted teeth. "Please, stop!" As Edif Piaf's voice quivered richly over the crackling speakers, resounding off the thin walls of the ruined house, I crept down the stairs and saw the gramophone playing on its own.

I screamed as I hauled the antique machine heavily onto its back and fell with it into the floor. The record cut out with a needle's terrible scratch midway through the final line of the song, and I slammed the player into the floor with all my strength before staggering to my feet and heaving the whole thing through the living room window with a cathartic shatter of glass. As the crash tinkled out and the ruined gramophone wallowed on the porch, there came a loud and rhythmic banging from the kitchen. I swallowed dryly as I turned, and the wheeze of cold January wind drifted through the broken mouth of the window. The sound knocked dully through the house, slow and steady. I stepped over broken glass and wisps of cotton stuffing, feet moving to the rhythm of the steady hammerings from the kitchen. When I peered through the doorway, I saw a single cabinet door opening on its own and slamming shut, repeatedly even as the wood was cracking from the force. I stepped into the kitchen in a cold sweat and tentatively grabbed the free clattering door. It halted easily in my hand, as if inert. All was still for a moment, and then every cupboard door flew open at once, every drawer shuddered out of its place. Simultaneously a shockwave like a sudden gale rippled heavily out from the kitchen, shattering every single window in the house.

A clattering metallic hail of silverware pelted onto the floor. Heavy, new-bought replacement mugs and plates of tin, wood, and enamel rather than glass or porcelain showered from the cabinets in a clattering whirlwind. I crouched small amid the battering storm. Everything dropped to the floor at once, and I drew up carefully to my feet, heart in my throat, every rattled nerve racing. When I reached my full height and my eyes settled on the yawning emptiness of the cupboards, I saw a dusty bottle sitting squat and alone on the otherwise empty shelf. It couldn't be. It couldn't.

-*"Pour the fucking drink!"*-

-*"Christ alive, Crowley"*-

-*"You know what, Joe? You're the fucking joke. You miss your deadlines, you come into meetings drunk. You're drunk right now!"*

-*"You're drinking again. I found the others, too, in the woods out back. Did you think I wouldn't find out? Jesus, Joe. This has to stop."*-

-*"I don't drink. I... I'm a recovering alcoholic. I haven't had a drink in three weeks."*

"Oh dear... I apologize, my friend, I didn't know."-

It was the bourbon. The same bottle from Rupert Wycliffe's cigar room. The memory of it was unmistakable, and there was no liquor anywhere in any part of the old house. I would have sniffed it out by now in a moment of weakness if there was. A moment like this. My resolve gave out, and I snatched the bottle of sloshing whiskey from the shelf, cold and comforting in my trembling hands. The pulled cork gave a familiar old *thunk* as I lifted the open neck to my lips, gulping down four swallows of rich, oaky firewater with the desperation of a dying man. I told myself I would take enough in to calm my nerves and cool the edge off, but I didn't stop. I chugged longer and deeper as the bourbon poured down the murky hourglass. Already I felt exultant and heady as I coughed and wiped my burning mouth on my sleeve. The sound of broken glass crunching like icy snow underfoot lifted my gaze across the ruined kitchen to Jean. She looked on with strange approval as I took another draught, she who never approved it in life.

"That's it, darlin'. Take your medicine. Let it make everything better." She turned and walked out of the kitchen, looking over her shoulder in its thin nightshirt and saying, "Come find me, Joe." I nodded wearily, broken at last, all trace of courage or resistance purged. I was ready to be with my wife. It was over for me.

I watched her pale nightdress billow and dance in the wind. My eyes traced each lithe muscle and supple curve shifting beneath its fabric. And when she disappeared into the woods, I followed her. My little girl was holding my hand, or maybe it was one of the Usher girls. The booze was coming on quick, and it was getting hard to tell. I could feel Otis close by but couldn't see him. He was too afraid now to come close, keeping a furtive vigil from the underbrush as they guided me into the woods. The path, so confusing and chaotic before, was now clear. I held the child's hand as I trailed behind the slow, sweeping tread of my wife down the forest trail. As the moonlight filtered in spotty beams through the branches of pine needles, occasionally a beam of it would shimmer onto the path, and her black shape would show its transformation.

The shaggy blonde hair turned to inky black, long and sodden, hanging out from a wilted black bonnet. The thin, skimpy nightshirt was replaced with a thick, ruffling black dress of puritanical modesty, heavy and moldering with dampness, clinging with seaweed and shellfish. The Drowned Woman had been watching closely as I drank myself to oblivion. She was guiding me patiently now down the path, down to the water. I dimly came to realize our final destination as the path and the woman in black blurred in my vision. The overwhelming, pendulous wave of guilt and existential agony was still there, but the terror gave over to resignation now. Indifference. The ability of my mind and body to fight frayed to uselessness. She had me now. I recalled the light of recognition in Henry Usher's clouded eyes, the moment before he killed himself in front of me. But I was done trying to look away. It was always going to end this way for me.

The night was clearer than any I saw since coming to the coast, vivid with countless stars. The little girl pulled at my hand, guiding me after the flowing skirts of the Drowned Woman as our procession went out to the lonely little beach of Siren's Cove. Hard-packed, wet sand glistened in the moonlight, spotted with discarded and broken things, the little pieces the Pacific picked out of her teeth and cast back to shore when she had eaten her fill of the rest. Tonight, this trash collector of a vast and silent world had collected me, and I was as broken a thing as any husk of crab or shard of driftwood it gathered into itself. The ocean roiled and churned, inky black and spitting salt as it laid siege to the same bastions of monolithic rock that stood against it for millions of years. And as I watched, I knew I couldn't stand as strong as they. I could not linger abstaining at the brink for even a moment of their ancient lives without plunging in.

The Drowned Woman looked out at me from the water's edge with twin pinpricks of light shining out from the cracked, veined marble of her face and the lank curtains of her hair. *It's time to go for a swim, Joe.* I staggered out after her and lifted the heavy bottle to drain the last of its potion. The thick, dark green glass slipped from my fingers and thudded into the sand. There would be no message in this bottle. The heavy, wet brine of the air washed over me, tousling my hair and coat in its gust. I shivered and unbuttoned my pea coat, shrugging out of it and casting it away. My sweater and undershirt were pulled over my head and soon followed it, with all the rest. I stood there naked for a moment, shivering in the cold as I watched the Drowned Woman step into the water. Her dress billowed and spread underneath her, darker even than the oily gleam of the night water as she stepped further out, up to waist and pregnant belly, then to shoulders. She turned around expectantly, a translucent face above the rolling black of the water, and I knew I must follow her.

The first step was the hardest, but the next came easier. The brink was a downward slope, after all. Soon my toes were churning the cool sand, and sheets of white breakers were playfully licking at my feet before crawling back, inviting me to come in with her. They pulled at me like a lover urging me to bed, and I followed obediently, stumbling in the cold shallows like a sleepy child. The frigid water rolled and swirled about my naked body as I let myself be pulled by its insistent touch. The ocean roared with a tireless voice. She shifted and rolled before my eyes, always changing, never changing. How endless were her dark depths, her boundless complexities? I was captured by her mysterious, moody turbulence, her treacherous and seductive beauty. In my feverish admiration of those qualities, I could not help but compare her to the woman I once loved. With each step, her briny perfume intoxicated my nostrils, her rolling waves whispered in my ear. Like a siren, the ocean was calling me. The gaze of the Drowned Woman held me spellbound as she invited me to the depths. I longed for her adventure, the wild throes of her turbulent love. And with each step, the ocean rumbled with hunger, like a beast about to make its kill.

How many other men like me had stood on her beaches before, though she washed away their footprints like she would mine? How many men had my promiscuous lover taken down to her bed in the crushing deep? But it was no good to be jealous. The water was up to my neck now, and when I looked out, the Drowned Woman was far out to sea. Only the mask of her face in its inky curls and black bonnet were visible. I was too drunk and exhausted to swim. It was useless. My arm in its soggy cast was like swimming with an anvil, and the cauldron of the Pacific was stirring hungrily. I made my way deeper, saltwater burning through my sinuses as a sudden wave dashed in my face. I coughed and sputtered, and a sudden current pulled me in. The ocean noises were lost in a dull, sucking rush as I was tossed and spun under the surface, limbs giving out as my lungs instinctively held air. I tried to make myself open my mouth, but was afraid. I lost sight of the Drowned Woman, and the pale face of the moon was shimmering through the deep like a mirage somewhere far over my head. Remorse was washing over my drunk, bleary mind, but it was too late. I couldn't fight the current. Oh God, what have I done?

As my lungs burned and screamed in my chest, my heart thumped with a terrifying, stabbing throb. With thrashing limbs and wasted mind, I fought in vain to break the surface and claw my way back to shore. I kicked and grasped, thrashing upward for the distant silvery coin of the moon and the vault of the heavens so impossibly far above me. A cold hand against my bare shoulder turned me around, and another caressed my face as I looked into the eyes of the Drowned Woman. Her hair and dress billowed and danced like the bell and tentacles of a jellyfish, all inky shadow in the deep. My last vestige of self-preservation wilted in her eyes. I opened my mouth to the flood. My consciousness was flickering out to black, but I was spinning underneath the sea in the arms of the Woman. The floor of the cove came up out of nowhere in the murky darkness, and my head struck a sharp rock on the bottom. All I knew was blinding pain, my blood like a plume of red smoke in the ocean's murk, and the last darkness of all.

Part Two: The Delilah Suicides

Interlude

July 8th, 1961

The rustling, vibrating scream of hundreds of annual cicadas was thick and pulsating in the summer air outside of Raleigh, North Carolina. Heat was already radiating in oily, pulsating waves off the pavement. The shimmering mirage moved in rhythm with the cicada screams. An odor like rotting fish was wafting from the white flowers on a grove of Bradford Pear Trees. The blue Land Rover was parked outside a tavern called Devil's Due. The bar had closed at midnight, but the party hadn't ended with last call. The windows and back hatch of the vehicle were all open to air out the smell of spilled beer and guard against the windless heat already blistering the morning. Empty beer bottles were scattered in the floor of the cab. I hadn't slept but was about ready to pass out from dehydration and drunkenness. My mouth tasted like a toilet. A tapping finger pressed into my sunburned collarbone, and a girl named Kitty who was even drunker than I was yelled in my ear when she'd meant to whisper.

"Sing the Elvis one again! Show me how the King does."

I'd met Kitty the night before and we'd been drinking ever since. She was probably twenty-five. Last name unknown. No sex, but this was still a betrayal. I'd been too angry to care.

I feigned sleepy reluctance, but she stretched the word 'please' to the county line, and I broke in with a slurred, emphatic impression of Heartbreak Hotel. My deep, quaking Elvis impersonation broke into a series of red-faced coughs. Kitty cackled while she sucked down the last cigarette in my pack, leaning on my arm and singing along.

"Give me one of those, will ya?" I asked, and she mockingly crackled the crushed, empty packet in my face before I snatched the lit one out of her lips and took a drag off it.

"No fair, give it back!" She reeled into me, climbing onto my lap and drunkenly trying to wrestle me for it. We were sighing with bleary laughter when broken glass crunched under a boot outside. The sound made Kitty jump across the cab, and she stared sullenly at the floor when the policeman walked up to the rear window. The paunchy, elderly deputy looked over the vehicle and us in it with disapproval.

"Y'all havin' a party?" He eyed us with weary disappointment.

"Morning, Officer." I shielded my eyes from the sun with one hand while I held the cigarette with the other and took a drag.

"Red don't mind. He said he'd rather us park here than drive when we been drinkin', Officer," the twenty-something offered from my side.

"Miss Kitty May, does your mama know you're here carryin' on with a married man 'til the sun come up? You get on outta here before I call her and she slaps them earrings off ya dang fool head. Go on! Get!" The policeman chewed a toothpick beneath his drooping gray mustache while he talked. At these words, the girl meekly opened her side door and took off. The old deputy watched her go down the hot gravel road until she was out of sight. He shook his head ruefully and turned a withering stare on me.

"So is this what you do with your life?" he asked.

"I don't really know what I do. So what happens now?"

"Are you Crowley? Joe Crowley?"

"So I'm told."

"Don't you get flip with me, Boy. We've been looking for you all morning. You ought to be ashamed of yourself for cavorting around like this, you know that?"

"Looking for me? What for?" I rubbed my temples, trying to massage out a burgeoning headache. Nausea and weakness were giving way to exhaustion, and the cigarette dropped from my clumsy fingers as I struggled to stay awake.

"We got a call, out from Chapel Hill. Something you need to see, Son. And once I've showed it to you, I'm gonna have to arrest you." My eyes flickered shut, and my head nodded while he spoke. "You hear me, Crowley? Something's happened! You've gotta wake up!"

Wake up. Wake up.

They told me I'd come back from the dead. It was like being born. There was nothing, only darkness. A void disconcertingly identical to sleep. Two of my ribs cracked during the application of chest compressions. The rhythmic pressures on my chest massaged my heart to a slow and steady beat. The first feeling was suffocation, my stomach and lungs full of the sea. A mouth pressed into mine and overwhelmed my airways with breath, and my body sputtered up a vomit of saltwater before any kind of thought or perception was restored.

"Wake up, you crazy bastard. Come on. Wake up now." I heard it as if from a great distance. The feeling of waking from sleep with a stranger hanging inches over your body. Unable to breathe. All at once, horrified and claustrophobic, I jolted upright and collapsed onto my side. A torrent of water spewed out of my throat, mouth, and nose. I gagged and moaned, and a firm hand slapped my back as more came out of me. It was more water than could be in a person.

"Oh, Jesus, he's coming back. There you go. Get it all out." I clutched the man with one arm as I turned over and vomited some more sea water, whiskey, and bile back into the surf crashing over us in the shallows. The roar of it came back startlingly, all at once. My vision took longer, swimming shadows becoming more distinct. The next sensations were agony and disorientation. My head felt as if it had split open, and I was conscious of my blood everywhere. The pain meant I was alive. I coughed, gagged, and lay face down in the foamy sand, shaking with tears and ragged hacks.

"Oh my God. Joe! Joe!" Gwen's voice, terrified. The air was split by frantic, shrill barks, and I saw a shaggy shape bounding back and forth from Gwen to me. A wet nose quivered close to my face.

"Gwennie, back up. You too, dog. Give him some room." My foggy, throbbing brain struggled to put a name to his voice. As I looked into his face and the lights turned back up in my eyes, I saw Will Blake.

"Will, there's a lot of blood. Why is there so much blood?"

"Don't look at it. Don't look at it! Gwen, I need your help. Grab his feet there. We're gonna put him in my squad car.

Bastard's heavier than he looks."

"Is he going to be alright?"

"*Alright* is relative. But our first concern is to get him to the hospital. Even after spitting up that water. He's going to die if we don't get him some-"

I lost consciousness as I felt myself heaved upward roughly, sagging like a corpse in their wet hands as I disappeared into the dark interior of the police car. Outside the automobile, Otis let loose a long and forlorn howl in the night.

Chapter Nineteen: Lazarus

January 14th, 1963

Sunlight streamed in through parted blinds, tiny dust particles floating in the luminous shafts. As I came to, the first thing I felt was the metal nasal cannula running down the bridge of my nose and hooking into my nostrils like a strange fork. This device was affixed to my bandaged, blood-encrusted head by a thick leather strap around my forehead. I was heady and sleepy from the tickle of oxygen breathing into me through the tubing from a canister at the side of my bed. A blanket covered me, and a thin hospital gown clung to my frame. My chest was stiff and immobile, throbbing with dull pain. Straps across my chest kept me from opening the wound or disturbing my broken ribs. Medicine was dripping from a hanging bottle, routed through IV tubing and into the top of my left hand via hypodermic needle. My eyes followed the IV line to the point of entry, and I winced at the injection site... And at the manacle secured around my wrist on the same hand, chained to the metal railing of the hospital bed. *So that's how it is.* I rattled the fetter on my wrist with a jangling and scrape of metal, and stiffly laid my aching head back on its pillow. My right arm was laying at my side, without its cast. The plaster must have broken down to mush in the ocean. The arm looked small and pale, coated in flaky dead skin, foreign and unrecognizable to the limb I had known. My glasses were long gone, and I missed their clarity as I took in my surroundings. A bright bouquet of flowers stood in a vase on the bedside table with a card set amidst their petals. Out beyond them, Rupert Wycliffe perched on the edge of his seat, statuesque with quiet anticipation as he watched me come to my senses. At the sight of him, I jolted violently in bed.

"Easy does it, Mr. Crowley," his clipped, nasal transatlantic accent chided from his seat. "Thank heavens you are finally awake. You gave us all a scare with your little breakdown."

"You son of a bitch," I rasped from my restraints. "You put me here. You knew what you were sending me into. You knew there was something in that house."

"Tut tut tut, there's no need to get hostile. You are confused. Of course, you would be. But make no mistake. Your choices led you to that house, and everything within it. I merely handed you the keys. And didn't I warn you of the effect it had on people? Didn't I do my part to ensure you were not a risk for suicide? Well, I did not do enough, clearly. For that, I am sorry. You've made quite a mess of the house, Mr. Crowley. Keeping what happened out of the papers was impossible, I'm afraid. And I have to close the attraction to the public until such a time as it can be cleaned up. Not to worry, I will take care of it. I've brought your next paycheck, as per our arrangement, minus my estimate for the damages to the house."

"Fuck you. Fuck your money. I don't want this anymore. I'm done. Write your own damn book."

"Of course, I cannot force you to stay. But I have a feeling you don't mean that −not really. You're so close now, Joseph. And you are soon to find your quest for the truth is becoming more important than ever."

"I don't care what happened anymore." But we could both hear the quaver of the lie in my voice.

"I'll let you think it over. I'm uncomfortable with you renouncing my patronage in your unstable psychological condition. Particularly since you are still drunk."

"You put that bottle there. It was your bourbon."

"Oh dear." A lizard's smile and a basilisk's glint of beady eyes, lightless and cruel. "And what bottle would that be, Joseph? Can you produce it? No bottle was found in the house or near your body when you washed ashore. It was swept out to sea, never to be seen again."

"What do you get out of this? Why did you send me to her?"

"Who?"

"You know."

He laughed to himself and lowered his head ruefully.

"Surely you haven't fallen for the old ghost story too. The hardened skeptic who told me humans are only, oh −how did you say it? Apes with big brains? Don't tell me you've gone and become a believer in the Drowned Woman."

"No one calls her that. She's not part of the story as the locals tell it. And you know why. The people who have seen her are all dead. Except me." Wycliffe sucked in breath when he realized his mistake. I saw it, and he knew I saw it. The Timber King gathered his composure before continuing.

"If what you say is true, and there is some suicide siren haunting Cape Contrition and sending all who see her to their deaths... I would suggest you tread carefully. After all... Who would think twice if the aging, alcoholic writer past his prime threw himself into the sea, after so many months of living alone in that dreadful old house? Especially after what you did to your wife..."

I rattled at the shackle, IV lines, and straps immobilizing me in bed, a rush of dizziness washing over me as I tried and failed to sit up. I felt like I was going to pass out, but I bared my teeth like a beast and rasped my wrath through a choked and ragged windpipe.

"Yes, Mr. Crowley, I would suggest you tread carefully. Do enjoy the flowers. And consider sending me a draft of your manuscript soon. I cannot wait to see the talent I have bought." He swept elegantly out of the room. I laid back and groaned as my head swam. After a few dizzy minutes trapped inside my broken body, a doctor in a white coat entered the room with a clipboard in hand. His hair was strawberry blonde, thinning on top. Thick-rimmed glasses were squeezed between thick, permanently furrowed brows in their perch atop his long, notched nose. He unscrewed the lid of a coffee thermos and downed a swig while frowning at me in the doorway.

"What's up, Doc?" I asked as he wiped his coffee-soaked lip on his sleeve, leaving behind a little brown stain on the cuff. He looked like he was having a long day.

"Oh, Good. Mr. Wycliffe told me you were awake. My name is Dr. Adrian Cullen. How are you feeling, Mr. Crowley?"

"Like I got hit by a train at the bottom of the ocean."

"That's near the truth, I'm afraid." He pulled up a chair at my bedside.

"You want to tell me why I'm handcuffed to the bed? Can't say I've ever gone out for that sort of thing before."

"Those cuffs are courtesy of the Delilah Police Department

and are a safety precaution until you are deemed not to be a threat to yourself or others."

"A threat?" I laughed grimly, but it descended into a rattling fit of coughs.

"How much do you remember about last night?" My head was still raked with hot coals so painful I couldn't see straight, but I closed my eyes and tried to think. Murky glimpses of the dinner with Gwen, our argument, the nooses and her terrified flight from the house, the walking nightmare of the war flashbacks, the burning lighthouse, Jean, the moonlit beach, and the Drowned Woman swam through my mind. I felt myself disappearing in the churning depths of the water and pulled into the cold embrace of the dark and beautiful siren. Of my rescue and rush to the hospital, there were only the vaguest impressions.

"I can picture it all. But it's like pieces of a puzzle I can't put together. I died, didn't I?"

"For about a minute and a half. It appears, Mr. Crowley, that you suffered a severe nervous breakdown. *Combat Stress Reaction.* Have you ever heard those words before?" I didn't answer.

"It is a psychological disorder we are seeing in veterans of war with alarming frequency. I have some familiarity with your books, Sir, and the recent events of your life. Your depression and alcoholism, the difficulty relating to your family upon your return from overseas, failure to maintain your professional relationships, these are all possible manifestations of the trauma you endured. The science is catching up, albeit slowly, to affirming the difficult reality many like yourself have walked through. We didn't understand these things when we sent an entire generation of young men off to war. Since they have returned –the ones who got to return, anyway- we had to reckon with what we were seeing. And what we are learning is this: human beings are not designed to kill one another. The trauma of killing actually damages the brain and alters the personality.

"For years, we have been telling shell-shocked, trauma-tized men to pull themselves together, stand up straight, and go in to work like they might have before. When it became apparent those men couldn't join the rank and file of civilian life, couldn't cope with what they had experienced, we attributed this to weakness and lack of moral fiber. I fear that sort of scorn is still the prevailing thought among many. As a result of being conditioned to outwardly show strength, many men do not relish admitting this is what has happened to them."

As he spoke, I felt defensive and vindicated by turns. This information was so dramatically affirming and had such incredible ramifications for my understanding of my life, I was dizzy trying to follow its implications. But I did as I'd been taught to do and listened with a brave poker face; even after he told me our generation was facing this with the same empty machismo, and he saw right through it.

"So you're saying I have this disorder? That I'm *stressed* by what happened to me in the War? Do you have any idea how fucking meager that word is to describe what I'm going through?" A passage from Rosemary Usher's journal recalled itself to me. *'I am desolate, wretched beyond the description of words. I am struck by the poverty of the English language for words of anguish.'*

"I can't formally diagnose you, as I am not a psychiatrist. But Usher's Fall, I'm told, looked like the O.K. Corral. The whole ground floor is riddled with buckshot from a single gun. We're close to the same age. I was a combat medic in the Pacific Theater. And when you came in to the hospital last night, you looked as if you had been in battle. Tell me, do you experience periods of acute stress, where your senses become hypervigilant, your heart rate spikes, and your entire body is pulled out of the present into the sort of fight-or-flight body-terror you remember feeling in combat? And when that happens, do you ever experience flashbacks?"

"Yes... But comparing them to memories or dreams isn't close enough. When these... reactions occur, those things are *happening* to me again. I was *in* '44 last night in '63. The truth is, I never left it. Even though there were times I fooled myself into thinking I had."

"As I said, I am not a psychiatrist. But it is my sincere belief you suffer from this disorder, Mr. Crowley. And I believe the terror of your trauma manifested itself last night in one of the ugliest episodes of walking flashbacks you have ever experienced. You attempted suicide last night. You were drunk and tried to drown yourself in the ocean. Do you have any memory of this?"

"Yes."

"It is likely, while you were sucked into the current, you struck your head against a stone on the floor of the cove. You suffered a minor skull fracture. There was a dramatic amount of bleeding, but fortunately you were spared any brain injury more severe than a concussion. You came close to drowning, but losing consciousness and being limply cast back ashore actually spared you from that. For the most part, we drown because we are panicking and hyperventilating as we fight to stay alive. After the ocean spat you back up and you were struggling at the verge of a blackout in the surf, the acute shock to your system caused a cardiac arrest."

"You're saying after making it out of the ocean I had a heart attack?"

"As far as anyone who knows you can tell, your only hobbies are running, drinking coffee, eating fried chicken, and smoking. So yes, you had a myocardial infarction at forty-seven." I didn't have any witty response.

"Our police chief arrived on the scene within minutes. He found you unresponsive and administered the CPR that broke two of your ribs and saved your life. This suicide attempt nearly killed you three different ways. I cannot tell you how lucky you are."

Or unlucky. Christ. Of all the guys I could owe my life to. When I followed the Drowned Woman into the ocean, all I wanted was to die. The overwhelming power her specter held over my mind was cut when I lost consciousness. Now that I was awake again, the black wave of her overloading angst faded to a vague nausea, the unsettling disquiet of a nightmare remembered the next morning. I knew the hospital staff would want me to feel grateful I was alive, and God apparently saw fit to intervene with a miracle on my behalf after all these years of silence. But I hadn't arrived at gratitude yet.

"And he's the one who cuffed me?"

"Like I said, Mr. Crowley, it is for your own safety. We've had you on suicide watch since you arrived, but our resources here for keeping you out of trouble are limited. In the end, the decision must be up to you. However, your Combat Stress Reaction has gone untreated for such a long time, and has manifested itself in such a horrific way, you would benefit from close psychiatric monitoring. It is nothing to be ashamed of, Joseph. But your nervous condition is so frayed right now, a temporary institutionalization might prove best for your safety. Our state hospital-" my mind flashed with the dramatic gothic architecture of the Kirkbride Building, and the ghoulish red smile of Henry Usher when he bit off his own tongue in front of me.

"No," I said hastily, more gruffly than I meant to. "I'm not going back into that place again. Is he here? Will Blake?"

"No, Sir. I suspect he went to get a few hours of sleep before work this morning. But I'll send for him."

"Cullen, give it to me straight. How much trouble am I in?" He turned back in the doorway.

"Since you only harmed yourself, damaged Mr. Wycliffe's property, and scared Ms. Christiansen half to death, I would guess you are at the mercy of those two parties." I wasn't sure if that was a comfort or not.

I was in and out of consciousness for much of the day, with nothing to do during my waking hours but think. At one point, I sleepily looked up to see Thomas Forester praying at my bedside, with Hana Iwamoto sitting sullenly beside him. She wasn't inclined toward prayer, and her eyes were open when they caught a glimpse of mine peeking. But she didn't say anything, and I listened to the old man's mumbled benediction with a weary smile. I wasn't grateful to be alive yet, but I was grateful for them. At one point the old priest stopped murmuring into his hands to peek side-eyed at Hana.

"Why don't you join me, girl?"

"I'm pretty sure I'm... Buddhist." She looked at her shoes and shuffled her feet. Thomas sighed and looked at her, unsure of what to say.

"Well, let's get him on the line too. He needs all the help

he can get."

Hana chuckled, folding her hands beside him to pray. One of her brown eyes peeked at me one more time, but I pretended to be asleep again. It was long after sundown when Will Blake came into my room and woke me.

"Thanks for seeing me like this," I murmured as I stirred in bed, "And for the other thing, I guess."

"Saving your life? Yeah, you're welcome."

"When you found me, did it ever cross your mind I didn't want to be alive?"

"Yeah, well, most of us don't get what we want. Didn't see why you should be any different." He took a seat at my bedside. "You want to tell me what happened last night?"

"I didn't want to scare Gwen or hurt her. Only myself."

"There were two nooses hanging from the support beam in your bedroom."

"I didn't tie those. I wouldn't even know how to tie one. Not exactly a boy scout."

"Who did, Joe?" I knew I had to tell him, and he wouldn't believe me.

"Do you know who Tom and Mabel Waters were?"

"No. Are they dead?"

"They hanged themselves from that beam in 1949. And a part of them is trapped there still."

Will Blake let out an exasperated sigh and looked away from me.

"Come on, not this spooky lighthouse shit. Joe, you're not well."

"Believe me, I know I'm not well. But this is happening. It isn't a joke; it isn't a delusion. There is something in that house, Chief. I tried to tell you before, but I didn't think you would believe me."

"When you came to me before, you were talking about creeps in costumes. Kids committing break-ins."

"That's what I thought it was, too. I tried to tell myself for a long time I was seeing things with rational explanations. But that Cape... There is a power there, something predatory and ancient. It feeds on the worst regrets of your life. It lays siege to your emotions; it conjures illusions that feel real but aren't there. And once it has exhausted and isolated you, it kills you. By driving you to kill yourself. I wasn't just a lonely, depressed novelist who went crazy and attempted suicide. I know that's a true-to-form, comfortingly familiar explanation, but it's wrong. The Drowned Woman... It's all her. Every suicide, every tragedy. She's the author of the sickness, and one of its victims... I'm still trying to wrap my head around that. But, Will, you have to believe me." I felt more and more hopeless with each sentence as I watched his face. He looked at me with incredulous, tired sympathy. He at least had the courtesy not to laugh at me this time, but I knew convincing him was a lost battle.

"Joe, I don't doubt living out on that headland has been ... lonely, isolating, a place where your old demons have come back to haunt you; a place where stormy weather and disturbing history have a certain power of suggestion. But you're a smart guy. You have to know how this sounds."

"I know." My lip quivered as I bowed my head hopelessly. "All I can do is tell you the truth. I can't make you believe it." The police chief scratched the tight curls of his hair and rubbed his baggy eyes.

"Long day?"

"It's like your kind of crazy is catching all over town since last night. No offense," he added quickly, realizing his exhaustion caused him to speak out of turn.

"What do you mean?"

"No, it's just... There have been two suicides today. I responded to both calls. An old man electrocuted himself in his tub. The other one was a teenage boy, took his father's .38 and killed himself in front of his ex-girlfriend. Ugly. Neither of them were people you'd expect, so no one saw it coming. And with the story of your attempt in the papers the same day, the whole town is on edge." There was a dark feeling in my stomach, as if the bottom had dropped out. My head swam with nausea for a moment as I considered what he'd said, and I gripped the rails of the hospital bed as I waited for the moment to pass.

"Show me," I rasped weakly.

"Look, Joe, you can barely stand up. You can't be trusted on your own, you're on suicide watch. In the last twenty-four hours you've suffered a nervous breakdown, attempted to drown yourself, cracked open your skull underwater, and had a heart attack. You're not leaving here for a few days. And when you do, I really think you need to rest and focus on getting well. Let the police do their jobs. It's the off-season slump for tourism, times are hard, the weather is dreary, and a few suicides aren't out of the ordinary. I'm willing to concede we got off on the wrong foot and you're not a bad guy; just exceptionally, *and I do mean exceptionally*, troubled. But Joe, you're at the end of your rope. You're barely staying sober. Gwen told me what you were hoping to achieve in your life by living out here, your arrangement with Wycliffe, the comeback novel. My advice to you is the same as it was the day we first met: *'Best you move on someplace else, before you get yourself in trouble.*'"

He leaned over and squeezed my shoulder.

"This place isn't good for you, Joe. You've got demons, and they play havoc with a man in a place like Cape Contrition. That has nothing to do with ghosts and drowned women, that's just being a veteran and a widower with no friends in a house three miles from town. Give up this little town, this book. You don't owe that creep Wycliffe anything. Hitch up the wagons and head North up the coast a ways, like you said you would. Or better yet, head back east, and try to make things right with that daughter of yours. But don't stay here, Joe. I mean it."

"Alright." I had no fight left in me.

"I've got your dog, by the way. He's safe and sound. He was inconsolable when he thought you were dead, you know that? He howled and cried all night and hasn't stopped staring at my front door since I brought him home. I took him to the vet, and they took him out of that cast, finally. His foreleg healed crooked, so now that paw splays out to one side a bit. Doesn't slow him much."

"Thank you." I was fighting tears. "So that's it? I'm off the hook, as long as I get out by sundown?"

"It ain't like that. I'm not banishing you from Delilah. I'm saying you need to leave for your own good. But you don't strike me as the kind of guy who does what's good for him. I leave that in your hands. But no, I'm not planning on arresting you. You scared the hell out of Gwen, but she doesn't believe you would have tried to hurt her. She's not pressing charges."

"And how is Gwen?" It felt like a foolish question.

"How do you think she is? She cares for you, and saw you

take your own life. She stayed with you all through last night. She waited, heartsick, while the doctors put you back together. How could you do that to her?" He looked like he was going to lose his temper but checked himself.

"Is she angry with me?"

"What are you, fourteen? Of course, she's angry. She's terrified. Forget about her. Crowley, I'm choosing to cut you loose when I could have you jailed, or institutionalized instead. I get the feeling you don't know how big a favor that is. Let's just say from one veteran to another, you're not the only one who is haunted by what he did, and you're not the only one who has been overcome by that on an especially bad night. But Joe, don't make me regret this. Take your chance, cut your losses, and clear out of here. That's what's best for everyone involved. Gwen included."

"Alright. I will. Thank you."

"Don't worry about it. You rest, Joe. Here's my card. Once you've been released, I'll give your dog back. Then you've got your whole life ahead of you. Not a whole lot of guys who go into the teeth of the Pacific like you did get to say that."

Chapter Twenty: Confession

January 18th, 1963

The remainder of my stay in the hospital passed at a crawl. Four days of laying immobilized in bed, passing between fitful sleep and groggy, restless wakefulness. Because my right forearm wasn't fully healed, I was fitted with a heavy and clean new plaster cast. The itch was unbearable. There were also two dark, purple bruises on my chest where ribs had fractured. I was told these would heal on their own in about six weeks, but I would need to be careful not to agitate that process with any strenuous physical activity. When I finally walked out of the hospital on the morning of the 18th, Will Blake met me in the parking lot with Otis. The young mutt frantically leapt out of the squad car window and galloped across the way to me with unbelieving whines. When he reached me, the dog crouched and sniffed me as his wagging tail sent tremulous wiggles through his entire body. As the dog's quivering, inspecting nose confirmed it was me, he toppled me over and made me clutch my ribs in pain. I cried as I held Otis, and he licked the tears from my weathered cheeks as they sprang up. As I rubbed fingers deep into the mutt's shaggy, wiry coat, I looked out to Will Blake and nodded gratefully to him. The cowboy doffed his wide-brimmed hat with a sad smile before getting in his police car and rolling away.

I wandered around Delilah for a time in a mood of disquiet. I had no fight left in me, no desire to finish the book or try to unravel the truth of how the Ushers met their demise. I intended to take the police chief's advice and move on for good. But for now, I was on foot in downtown Delilah, weak from my convalescence in the hospital. My truck and all my worldly possessions were still at Usher's Fall, three miles distant. That was not a journey I felt up to in my condition. I knew if I was to make good on my promise to leave town, I would need to look up one of my few friends and convince them to give me a ride back to the old house. But I was loath to face the place again. And with my suicide attempt so recent, I was ashamed to explain myself to any of the bare handful of people in town who might have helped me. While I worked up the courage to ask for help and considered whom I should approach about a ride, I wandered the streets and took in the thick coastal air. I thought about Will Blake's words. A second chance when, by all rights, I should be dead. This strange saga of horror and mystery was over for me. I'd been beaten, but I hadn't been killed. I still had questions without answers, but who in this life doesn't?

When I finally convinced myself I could walk away, I passed a blue newspaper vending box and glanced at the headline. **Suicides Continue, Five Dead in Four Days**. That horrible dark pit opened in my stomach again. Five now. As I stared in horror at the vending box in the street and contemplated the headline of the *Delilah Caller*, I was seized by a black and unshakable conviction. Will Blake was right, in his way. My crazy was catching all over town. I had awakened something in Usher's Fall, and it was no longer content to stay sequestered on Cape Contrition. It had come into Delilah. If I made it so, I must unmake it. No one else could, because no one else even believed it was happening. And as this certainty squeezed my pained chest and fragile heart, I knew who I needed to go see.

The sun was setting over the ocean in the distance as I made my way to Lost Cove Books on Conch Street. It was closing time. A bitterly cold wind was knifing off the bay, and I shivered in my coat and scarf as I walked up and opened the door.

"Hey, welcome in," I heard Gwen's voice call from the low-ceilinged back of the shop beneath the loft, disembodied in a labyrinth of musty bookshelves. She hadn't seen me, only heard the bells on the door ring. There was an old man milling about in the religion section, but the place was otherwise empty. "We're closing in about five minutes, but you know. Take your... time..." She'd been speaking from behind a shelf, unaware it was me. Her last words stumbled and crawled over the realization before trailing off.

"Hey," I said quietly.

"Hey yourself." She set a book on the counter and crossed her arms over her maroon cable-knit sweater. "I didn't know you were out."

"Can we talk?"

"I don't know... I have a lot to do around here, so." She turned to walk away.

"Gwen, wait. Please." She stopped walking but didn't turn around. Her hands were balled into fists at her sides. "I know I scared you. I never intended to hurt you that night. Even if

271

you never want to see me again, I need you to know that."

"Scared me?" She hissed a harsh whisper as she turned around, glancing suspiciously at the only other customer in the place as he continued to thumb through paperbacks in the corner, pretending not to hear us. "Seeing you... seeing you *dead* on that beach, listening to your dog cry as Will tried to make your heart beat again... And all that water you spat up... It destroyed me, Joe. I was beside myself."

"I know." I met her eyes with a pained grimace.

"I waited all night at the hospital to make sure you were okay. But after that, I couldn't see you. I can't see you now." As we spoke in hushed tones, we both realized the customer from the corner had been standing close to us for some time. He loudly cleared his throat before impatiently droning,

"Miss, I'm ready to be checked out now. If you aren't too busy!"

"Okay, sorry about that, Sir. This way, please," Gwen shuddered and moved behind the counter, shooting daggers at the man and me with stolen glances as she assumed her position at the cash register. The drawer shook open with a rattle of change, and the man paid slowly and deliberately in painstakingly assembled stacks of coins. I waited, rocking on the balls of my feet as the money was counted.

"Have a great day," Gwen said in a deadpan, robotic voice as she tore the receipt paper out of its printer and handed it to the man.

"Yeah, enjoy your book, Pal. Hope it's a good one," I said over my shoulder as he walked out, and the bell rang behind him. Gwen flipped the sign hanging in the glass paned front door to "CLOSED" and turned to face me.

"So, what do you want to say to me?" She crossed her arms

and leaned with her back against the front door.

"I understand why you don't want to talk to me right now. That night probably ended what we had between us. My 'tortured artist' thing, it's not just me putting on airs. I've got real issues I thought I'd escaped, but they're closer than I could admit. And until I face them, it's probably best I'm not... *with* anyone. I wanted to be ready, but the truth is, I'm not."

"I agree." A twinge of regret as she said it.

"And that's the worst part of this. I really enjoyed being with you. And I never wanted to drag you into my problems or cause you pain. I know what we had was new and it's not like we were in love or anything, but... It felt like we could have been, before long. That possibility was, well, it was nice."

"It was. But, Joe, there's something you don't understand. You keep talking like you don't want to be a burden or upset me with your problems. But we were *together.* They weren't just your problems. I wanted to help you, but you wouldn't let me in. I'm not keeping my distance from you right now because you broke down out there, or because you tried to kill yourself. When I ran away from you, it was because there was a moment when I saw those two nooses and thought you were going to try to kill me too. —You weren't... Right?"

"No, never." She looked in my eyes for a long moment and seemed satisfied by what she saw.

"But anyway, I didn't leave because I couldn't slay your demons. I left because you wouldn't let me see them. What happened to you was horrible, but *that* wasn't your betrayal. Your betrayal was concealing what you were going through and not trusting me to stand at your side."

"I understand now," I said, "And that's why I've come here.

There's something I haven't told you. It's a big something. You're going to want to sit down."

With Otis in tow, I started up the creaky steps to the loft. After a long hesitation, Gwen followed us. She curled up on a sagging, comfortable couch with the dog, and I brewed a pot of coffee as I began my confession.

"You know all those stories folks tell about Cape Contrition? The way the Indians scorned it, old ships broke apart on its rocks, the disappearances and deaths that plagued the construction of the lighthouse? The lighthouse that burned with the Usher children inside. On the cliff where so many have jumped? You remember the stories of people losing their minds, or being overwhelmed by depression?"

"Of course, I do." Gwen was impatient and apprehensive. Coils of steam were spilling into the air as a steady trickle of piping hot coffee was pattering from the machine into a clear carafe.

"That place changes people. You said something like that when I first came here, tried to warn me. You were right. It did change me." I wasn't looking at her as I said these words but was pouring coffee into two brightly painted mugs.

"Joe, what is this? You're scaring me." Gwen stirred in her seat, recognizing the precariousness of her position if I was as unhinged as she feared. My hands trembled as I poured portions of half-and-half into each mug from a carton, plunked in a couple sugar cubes, and stirred both into swirling brown whirlpools with a loudly clinking spoon.

"But the *reason* that place has killed so many people, the reason it almost killed me, is not what the people of this town think. Cape Contrition isn't just some lonely place where people meet the demons they bring with them. There are demons there already."

"Are you sure the doctors cleared you to leave?" She tried to make it a joke, but there was fear of me in her voice. I looked to her with a hard frown, but the expression in my eyes was pleading. She reached out a hand and I passed her a mug painted with sunflowers. I thought I saw a blonde woman laughing in them, only for a second.

"I knew you weren't going to believe me, and that's why I held back. That's why I didn't say anything for weeks while this was tearing me apart. Will you please hear me out?" The question was loud, unhinged. She got quiet and gave me a frightened nod to go ahead.

"Usher's Fall is haunted, Gwen. By ghosts, and by something worse. Something older, darker. That's what I couldn't tell you. And I know you won't believe me, but it's true." I stopped to look into her eyes for a read on how this news landed. She sipped her coffee and swallowed nervously before murmuring for me to go on.

"In the time I've lived out there, I've experienced disturbing things I can't explain. Things would go missing and turn up someplace else, I would hear and feel beings near me without seeing anyone. It started with small things. But it got worse. When I told you I ransacked the house, the truth was, I returned home from our holiday trip and found it that way. I've seen the members of the Usher family, as real in front of my face as you are now. I've seen the lighthouse burn, so real I could feel the heat and smell the smoke; so hot it scarred my hand when I grasped the knob." I stopped to show her. "In 1949, Tom and Mabel Waters hanged themselves from the support beam in my bedroom. I've seen them too. I didn't leave those nooses tied there. I was as surprised to see them

275

as you." This was tumbling out so clumsily, so messy. As with Will Blake, I could look into her eyes as I spoke and see I was failing to convince her.

"Something tried to lock me in the storm cellar when I took shelter there on Columbus Day, during that terrible gale. There was scratching on the inside of the door, and there were people in there with me. When Henry Usher killed himself right in front of me, we weren't alone in his cell. His eyes were on another person behind me. I felt her there, but I couldn't look. And that's not all. This place has shown me horrors of my own memory, things I saw in the war, my... My wife-" I stopped myself, gritting my teeth and looking into my cup with feelings of impotence. *Pull yourself together, Joe. Focus.*

"Look, I should have told you these things a long time ago. All of it coming out at once like this, I know it sounds crazy. This isn't how this conversation should have gone. There have been so many things I've experienced; you couldn't believe unless you experienced them too. I could ramble here for hours and you wouldn't be any closer to trusting me about this. The reason I'm finally telling you all this and risking you looking at me the way you're looking at me right now... is because every horrible thing you've ever heard about that place, every suicide, every nervous breakdown, all has one source. The Drowned Woman."

"*Drowned Woman,*" Gwen started and broke off, trying to recall something. "You were talking about a drowned woman while you were recuperating in the hospital, after your car accident."

"That's right. I've seen several ghosts in the house and on the grounds, but... Well, as disturbing as it is to see something that defies what you think you know about the world, those unreal people and scenes I saw were like pictures on a projector. They played out with disconcerting clarity, but it was like the people I was seeing didn't know I was there. They were fragmented, stuck in time. Old memories trapped in the land. I'm not sure they had much power to hurt me. But there was something that trapped them there, Gwen."

"And that *'something'* was the Drowned Woman?" I got the feeling she was playing along, stalling for time while she thought up an escape.

"I'm still trying to understand what she is. But from what I can tell, she is the ghost the other ghosts answer to. They are slaves to her will and go in fear of her. She seems more complete than them, with the intelligence and malevolent power to manipulate them as she pleases. The things I've seen are the things she has intended for me to see. But that isn't the end of it. She can control the living in the same way she controls everything else on the headland."

"Are you saying she's controlled you? Made you see things?"

"The first time I saw her was the night of my car accident. She made the illusions and dark feelings of the house attack me all at once and drive me out. As I was fleeing down the road, she appeared in the path of my car. When I saw her face, I immediately felt this, this overpowering black wave of agony and guilt. It was emotional pain like I've never experienced before, and I can't describe it. While she had me in her gaze, all I wanted was to kill myself and make it end. But it all happened so fast, I was automatically swerving to avoid her as she stepped out into the road. I rammed that tree and blacked out. But the next time I saw her face was the night of my suicide attempt. She mustered all the powers of that house to shock and bewilder me until I was psychologically broken. Then she led me into the water herself. You feel darkness when her back is to you, or when you can't even see her but know she's standing right there. But when you look into her eyes, all the lights in the world go out. Like nothing will ever be good again, and you would never deserve goodness anyway. I think that's her power. She makes people kill themselves. It's the only thing she wants of the living, and every other distortion of reality she can conjure up is designed to push people to that point."

"Joe," Gwen started tentatively, sensing I was in a delicate place. "This isn't some kind of literary metaphor, or-"

"Jesus, no. The Drowned Woman is real. She lives to drive people to the brink and force them over the edge. I only have my own experience to go on at this point, but I think the other people who killed themselves out there saw her too. I think she had something to do with what happened to the Ushers. She bears the appearance of a pregnant woman in outdated, puritanical clothes, like what Henry Usher made his family wear. She looks like I imagined Rosemary Usher would look. The mother of the family who vanished the night of the fire. That's what she became, after she died.

"The manifestations of paranormal activity in Usher's Fall became more dramatic and aggressive as I learned more about the Ushers and got closer to learning what happened to them. I can't explain it but living out there and seeking the truth stirred her up; angered her. And since she forced my hand to try to take my own life five days ago, five more people have committed suicide in town. I woke something out there, and she isn't content to haunt Cape Contrition and plague those who come to her anymore. She's on the move, and people are dying here because of what I did. This is my fault, Gwen. And I need to put an end to it."

"How do you expect to do that? I mean, if what you're saying is true... How do you kill a ghost? How do you fight something that can turn you against yourself with a look? Something that almost killed you twice?"

"I don't know." I looked down at my cup, realizing I hadn't taken a sip, and it was cold. I took a swig of the old coffee and set it aside. "But if she is trying to prevent me from learning about the Ushers, maybe what I find will show me how to fight her. Or at least help me understand what I'm up against."

"But you know investigating that is going to send you right back to the house in the end, right back to her." Gwen finished her cup of coffee and set it aside as she leaned forward earnestly in her seat. I couldn't tell if she believed me, but she could tell I believed it, and despite herself, my certainty was infectious.

"I know. But people are dying, and I set that in motion. I have to be the one to stop it. No one else even believes it's happening, so I'm the only one who can."

Gwen sat for a long moment, looking into my eyes and weighing everything I said before responding.

"Look, I don't know if I can believe this. These kinds of things aren't supposed to happen. I can tell you believe this is happening, but you're also in an incredibly volatile place right now. I don't believe you are lying, and I find it hard to believe this is entirely in your head, but the alternative is so difficult to accept. And listen to yourself. This *being* on the Cape has had you isolated and tormented for so long, deprived of sleep, hardly eating, haunted by flashbacks and illusions... You've been run ragged. How are you supposed to figure out what's going on in this town when you don't even know what's real and what's a nightmare anymore?"

"That's why I'm going to need help from some friends. All I can get. Are you in?"

She didn't answer, but she also didn't throw me out or call the police. I guess we had to start there.

Chapter Twenty-One: Voyeur

January 19th, 1963

A camera whined and sparked a dizzying flash the second I opened the door of my ground floor motel room, and I instinctively lifted my hand to block my face.

"He's alive!" the lone paparazzi declared, ejecting the spent flashbulb and reloading.

"Hey, cut that shit out," I said groggily as Otis growled at my side and the man took a step back. As I flicked the wheel of my Zippo and puffed my first cigarette of the day to life, he primed his camera for another flash. "Kid, what did I say? This isn't a fucking zoo. Scram."

"Edwin Gaines, *Delilah Caller.* How does it feel to be back from the dead?"

"Let me get a cup of coffee and I'll tell you. Say, you're not that guy who made the lamp shades and furniture upholstery out of human skin, are you?"

"What? No, why?"

"Must've been thinking of someone else, sorry." I was staying in a small room on the ground floor of The Sandcastle, a beachfront motel with battlements along the roof and little towers at its corners. I was resolved not to stay another night at Usher's Fall, but it didn't feel right to impose on Gwen when our relationship was in such an uncertain place.

"Have you been back to Usher's Fall since your mental breakdown?"

"No." I opened the door of my beat-up truck so Otis could hop in.

"Do you care to comment on what happened that night, or why the tourist attraction is roped off from visitors?"

"Because I'm a dangerous lunatic on a murderous one-man rampage," I turned around and said in an urgent, confiding tone inches from his face. He was so surprised, he jolted backward in an involuntary flinch. "That's what you were going to print anyway, right? Go ahead." I climbed into the cab and shut the door.

"Mr. Crowley, Mr. Crowley," the young reporter badgered as I started the fitful old truck. He snapped another photograph and I rolled down my window, dragging off my cigarette and exhaling.

"It's tricky to get this truck going with one hand *and* have a cigarette. Here, hold this." I flicked the stub in his direction. As he fumbled to swat away the orange heat sparking against his chest, he dropped his camera on the pavement. "Ah, damn. How clumsy of me. Sorry about that, Pal." The young man stared at his camera in stunned disbelief as I backed up. He let out a shriek as I swung wide to roll over it with a satisfying crunch on my way out.

My first stop of the day was Usher's Fall. I needed to face the place myself again, by strong daylight, to prove to myself I could do it. After a long and foreboding drive, we crossed the Siren Creek Bridge, parked in the lot, and made our way up the zigzagging forest trail. The sun was high and smiling, and the verdant woods held no horrors today. The old farmhouse was visibly ransacked even at a distance. Every window was shattered and boarded up. A yellow sawhorse was placed at the foot of the porch steps, and there was a cordon rope across the door, which was locked. A sign on it read: USHER'S FALL IS CLOSED FOR MAINTENANCE DUE TO INCLEMENT WEATHER DAMAGES.

"Yeah, Hurricane Joe. That's me." I jangled my keys, fit one to the lock, and let the front door swing slowly open with a loud creak. "Hello? I was looking for a tour guide. Anyone home?" I called out into the stillness, masking my voice in an exaggerated Midwestern accent. Ten seconds passed before I glanced about at the empty grounds, lifted the rope, and slipped inside with Otis at my heels. The place was destroyed. Furniture turned over, cushions torn apart with stuffing strewn, kitchen chairs splintered, silverware and dishes tossed about, insulation and piping showing through gaping holes blasted through the walls. Shotgun shells littered the floor from the rampage. But there were no bloodstains, no bodies. The hallucinated soldiers felt so real the night of my breakdown and attempted suicide, I needed to see to this for myself. Standing in the ruin of the Ushers' kitchen, I was only feebly assured it had only been in my mind. Particles of dust drifted in the air through shafts of light from between the boards over the windows. In the time it took for the house to be sealed up again, the damp sea air breathed heavy over the walls and floors. The plywood barriers had been nailed in too late to prevent black spots of mold infestation from creeping across the wallpaper. The close, stagnant air had a fungal, sickly odor to it. Out of curiosity, I glanced in the refrigerator, but it was emptied.

The electricity had been shut off until the house was habitable again.

I thought of Wycliffe's visit in the hospital, his smug assurance I would not back out of finishing his book. Would he cordially invite me to move back into the house once the repairs were complete? It was mine, he insisted, until I finished the novel. Even if I *was* intending to hold up my end of Wycliffe's bargain, I never would have returned to live in that house. It was the domain of the Drowned Woman, and the Ushers. A house with such death in it cannot truly be possessed by the living. Only borrowed from the dead. After what happened to me, they could keep it. I shivered in the musty cold of the place, buttoned my pea coat, and gathered my typewriter and a few other essentials in a large cardboard box before stealing away.

As I stepped down the porch, I remembered something and ran back into the house. In my old bedroom, I untied the long rope knotted and wound about the support beam with a noose at both ends, and took the grisly thing down. When I exited the house again, I set the bundle of twin nooses on my typewriter at the top of my cardboard box, moved the sawhorse barricade back, hefted my possessions with a grunt, and started back downhill with them.

I was a dead man grappling with being alive, and an atheist grappling with undeniable experience of nightmarish beings that weren't supposed to exist. The other suicides were connected to mine. I knew. But it was something my mind rebelled against and needed to disprove. When it had been a matter of convincing Gwen, I was able to muster a knightly conviction to find the truth and appease the spirits of Cape Contrition. Now that I was alone, it was hard to find the same certainty what I proposed to her could even be accomplished. I told myself I was going to gather my possessions from Usher's Fall to establish a base elsewhere and continue the fight. Now that my things were packed, I realized I was ready to leave. And all the instincts of self-preservation were screaming for me to do just that.

During our brief time together, Gwen taught me I could come back from my past. I could leave Cape Contrition and all its dark memories behind me. And when I left, I could drift on to some other place and try to rebuild my life. The new book and its restoration of my writing career tempted me to stay longer than anyone should have. But I remembered that moment under the water when I knew I was going to die, and felt my lungs nearly burst with regret. The potential for money and fame was not worth my life. I could learn to live without them. At least I would *get to* live.

But where would that leave the people of Delilah?

I swallowed hard. I stood next to my old truck with the heavy cardboard box in my arms and my dog beating my leg with his tail, stuck at a moral crossroads. With a curse, I dropped the box in the bed and furiously lit a cigarette. I struck a fist against the door of my truck and gasped a primal, wordless scream into the space between knowing what is right and doing it. The parking lot and little cove where I had nearly died were empty, and my bestial howl mockingly rebounded back to me. I couldn't face her again, but I was perhaps the only person who had done so and lived. I knew I had an obligation to help others survive the darkness of Cape Contrition as well. *But you don't* know *the suicides are related to what happened to you. You don't* know *what happened to you was anything more than a psychotic break with reality.* Yes, I do.

No, you don't.

Compromise. If your suspicions are true, you must act. If people are in danger and you can help, you must defend them. But you don't *know* yet. Your motel is six miles away. If you see or think of a clue along that drive, stop and look into it. If no such epiphany arises before you reach your room, pack your bags and leave this town behind you. *Compromise. If I see a chance without going out of my way, I will do the right thing. And if I'm lucky, the chance won't come.*

But of course, it did.

My truck was chugging and rattling along Main Street when I heard shouting and saw people running toward the sound. I leaned forward in my seat, straining my eyes to detect the source of the commotion, when a balding middle-aged white man and the lanky, acne-pocked teenage Latino boy he was grappling with toppled into the street right in front of me. I cursed and brought my vehicle to a shuddering halt as the two hit the blacktop in front of my headlights.

"What did you do to her? What did you do to her, boy!?" The man shouted as he swung a meaty fist into the boy's face and a woman screamed. I heard the smacking impacts of his fists through the windows of my truck. Otis snarled in the cab and clawed at the glass, eager to get into the middle and break up the fight. I left him inside as I got out

"Stop! You're killing me!" The boy gasped through cracked, bloody lips.

"Whoa, whoa!" I called as I grabbed two fistfuls of the man's sweater and hauled him off the boy by the shoulders. Immediately, the man turned and swung a haymaker, which I thoughtlessly lifted my right forearm in its cast to block.

I let out a seething hiss as I clutched the screaming bones and stepped back. The pain was nauseating. The big man stopped for a moment, hesitating with conflicted honor when he agitated my broken bone. I bit down the pain in my arm before he realized the fight was still on and snapped my left fist into his mouth. When he staggered back against the hood of a parked car, I stepped between him and the boy. With panting breaths and fierce glares, we looked at one another and glanced around at the crowd forming around us. A tableau of male aggression framed in the spotlight of my truck's headlights.

"I'm, I'm sorry," the man panted, wiping a trickle of blood from his chin. "I shouldn't've done that. You were right to stop me." Blood was welling up on one knuckle I'd cut open on his tooth, and I sucked it up with a grimace before spitting and demanding,

"What the hell is going on here?"

"I'm calling the police, that's what," an older woman said from the sidewalk of the ice cream parlor the altercation had spilled out of. I realized the lanky teenager was dressed in the uniform of the parlor. His paper hat had been knocked off his head of curly black hair onto the road.

"Abuela! No! Wait," he panted, lifting a hand to still the old shop owner as he picked himself up woozily off the street. A car with an old woman in it slid to a halt behind my stopped truck and the commotion, and impatiently honked for me to move along. I broke away long enough to wave her around. By the time she was gone in a huff, the man leaning against the car was shaking with sobs.

"It's my, my little girl. Maggie. I found her in the bathtub this morning. She'd cut her wrists. Why would she do that?"

He roared the question out to everyone in a paroxysm of bewildered grief. My heart sank as I heard these words and knew what I had found.

"Sir, I had no idea you were going through something like that. You have my condolences. But why attack him?" The boy was spitting blood on the blacktop and clutching his knees as he also shuddered with sobs.

"Because my little girl was going steady with this, this fucking *spick*, and he broke her heart a week ago when he decided she wasn't good enough for him anymore."

"Hey, watch your fucking language," I growled before turning around to the young man. "What's your name, Son?" I extended a hand and he looked me in the eyes as he shook it and tried to keep his voice even.

"Luis."

"Is it true, what he's saying?" I felt the weight of the spectators' stares all around us. Luis' mouth twisted down in an agonized grimace.

"I don't know, man. It's not like that, okay? She," he stopped talking and tears welled in his eyes as he looked at all the people, his grandmother, and the father of his dead ex-girlfriend. "She wanted to take it to the next step with me. I was scared, I wasn't ready. I backed out of talking to her. And I was going to make that right when I got the news-" he broke off and covered his face with his hands, crying. Maggie's father, Gerald, stood bewildered for a moment as he put together what Luis hinted at.

"You son of a bitch! How dare you!" he lunged for the young man again, but I shouldered up and shoved him back against the car.

"I really do not want to break this hand on the face of a guy grieving his daughter. Back the hell up." Luis stepped past me with hands lifted, showing he came in peace as he stepped toward Gerald.

"It wasn't like what you think, Mr. Flint. She was a good girl. I didn't want to hurt her. She was my heart, you know?" The young man was sincere. He and Gerald held one another's gaze for a long moment before Gerald broke off, and his shoulders shook in sobs.

"Why would she do this if you didn't mess her up? She *was* a good girl. A fine student, a babysitter, a singer. She had nothing to agonize over like that. There was no hint-" he broke off, weeping. "How come I didn't know?"

"Look," I said, coming in close to the two and looking around at the murmuring spectators, "Seems like you two need to have a tough conversation. Can you put the fisticuffs away long enough to do that?" Both teary men agreed. Luis looked out to his grandmother to make sure he didn't need to come right back to work, and she nodded.

"Hey, Mister. Who are you to fight for me, anyways?" Luis asked me as the air was suddenly filled with the blue flash and wail of a police car skidding to a halt.

"Joe Crowley!" Chief Blake said as he got out of his squad car and closed the door. "Thought I told you to get out of here."

"Say, are you the only cop who works in this town, or what? We keep running into one another like this."

"Should I take you to my holding cell so you can get reacquainted with the others? They do miss you. What about you two? Gerald? Jesus, what are you doing in this mess?"

Gerald stepped forward and lifted his hands.

"It's alright, Chief. I lost my head. This man, Crowley... He was helping me find it again."

I stole an appreciative nod to Gerald and he winked at me. Will Blake stood there shifting his gaze among each of us, but he hadn't seen the scrap, and it seemed to be over in good faith.

"Shit." Will Blake shook his head as he realized. "This is over Maggie, ain't it?" Gerald and Luis nodded sheepishly. "And everyone's okay? No one pressing charges?" Gerald looked nervously at Luis, and I looked nervously at Gerald.

"No," Luis said first. Gerald affirmed the same, and we all breathed a sigh of relief.

"Look, I'm real sorry about what happened to Maggie. Whole town's upset. But I'm on my way to Walnut Avenue. We've got another one. Sixth suicide in six days." When Will said this, the people on the street broke out in gasps and a dark buzz of murmurs. My heart sank into my stomach, and all I wanted to do was get in my truck and drive back to pack up my motel. But I'd made a promise to myself.

"Chief," I said, breaking through my hesitation. "Can I come see?"

"Hell no," Will Blake scoffed. "Why in the Sam Hill would you want to see a thing like that?"

"I have to."

"You don't have a badge. I'm going to a crime scene. Not a damn peep show for morbid scandal writers."

I recoiled slightly at the sting and didn't feel like I could say more in front of the perplexed and gossiping mill of people on the sidewalk. I glanced down, defeated, before going back to my truck and closing myself inside without a word. Gerald and Luis picked themselves up, dusted themselves off, and ducked into a nearby coffeehouse to sit and talk. When the spectators dimly realized the show was over, they melted away from the scene of the altercation and returned to their various errands. And when Will Blake drove away toward the scene of the most recent suicide, I quietly tailed him.

The house was at the end of a long gravel road, cloistered on three sides in a screen of windblown cedars. The front faced the street and its long line of seasonally inhabited cabins. Its sloping roof was heavy-laden with decaying needles and pinecones, its square exterior coated in faded and peeling yellow paint. The scene around the house was one of bewildered grief. Police stood around their cars talking and smoking with a few curious neighbors. The coroner's men wheeled out a gurney with the shape of a large man draped in a sheet. As they loaded the body carefully into the back of a black car, an older woman in hair curlers and a nightdress wailed inconsolably in the arms of a friend. I parked a block behind and left Otis in the truck with the window cracked. Will Blake took off his cowboy hat and approached the woman in curlers, who turned from her friend to embrace him heavily. As I approached the house, I walked slowly with muffled footfalls, keeping an eye on the sightlines of the many people gathered on the front lawn. I tried to look unassuming as I drifted among the people like a curious onlooker.

With trained ears, I gathered the person who ended his life was a thirty-year-old man who lived with his mother. Both had reputations as odd and reclusive. The mother, I gathered, was the old woman in curlers and a night dress who was being consoled by the police chief. One of the policemen laughed confidentially to a fellow officer, "the stiff was a real pervert." Making sure no one noticed, I slipped into the trees about the property and strolled discreetly around to the back of the house. I stepped through wet grass over a hose and past a rusted bicycle onto a rotting back porch and glanced about cautiously before trying the sliding glass door and finding it unlatched.

The house was unlit and still, the air musty and close. A fluffy white cat yowled before jumping off the kitchen counter and scampering down a hall with a tinkling collar bell. The house was dirty and unkempt, giving off a strong suggestion its occupants rarely left. My heart was pounding simultaneously with the thrill of entering a forbidden space and the fear of having to explain my presence there. My conscience panged and protested my trespassing in a place of death, but another part of me was looking for something I couldn't articulate. Panic and doubt roiled within me, but I crept silently down the hall of the dim house anyway.

I couldn't believe I had broken into a victim's house, but my every step was driven by a need to know if what was happening to them was the same thing that happened to me. I knew Will Blake would bar me from participating in his investigation or talking to the house's other occupant outside. But perhaps, if I could not speak to those who knew the victim, I could come to know something of the victim by seeing where he lived. Somewhere in the room where he slept, I might find a glimpse of who he had been, and why he died. The next door was ajar. The glimpse through the crack told me it was the bedroom I sought. I was already here, no matter how repulsive that was. Might as well see it through.

The room stank of hot death, and dejected flies were still buzzing about, wondering where their meal had gone. From the smell, the body must have been here for several days before it was found. How squalid and lonely the life of this house must have been, for his mother not to know he was dead in his room until he started to rot. It was something I had not wanted to know and should not have known. My shame for entering the miserable house compounded. As I stepped on the carpet, I noticed the blood stain. It grasped out in a grisly, dried pool of rust brown near the toe of my shoe. A shamed disquiet rose in a rush of nausea I tried to keep down as I edged around the stain, deeper into the close bedroom.

Though nervous about touching anything, I thumbed through the shirts, slacks, jackets, and sweaters in the closet. Tucked away behind them, I saw a few large dresses hanging from hooks. Cheerful pink and bright yellow, floral prints and polka dots coated in a thin veneer of dust. On the nearby desk was the suicide note, squarely in the center. I hovered over the message. In a hasty, semi-legible hand that smeared ink, it lamented a life spent in hiding, a world where they did not feel comfortable in their own skin and were afraid to be themselves. Signing farewell at the bottom, the name Patricia. Known to the outside world as Clyde. Beside the signature, a photograph of a large, balding person in a flowing black dress of mourning, mouth set in a cracked frown, eyes bright with grief. A dark shadow stood out on the photograph behind them, indistinct like something the Polaroid instant camera was unable to capture. The hazy shape dominated Patricia in the photograph. A thought occurred to me and I leaned back to thumb through the dresses on their hangars. None like the one in this photograph. Could it have been the dress they died in? Could this picture have been a last self-portrait before they ended their life? A drawer stood not fully closed to the left of the desk, and it slid roughly open to my touch. Inside were several other photographs of Patricia in brighter colored dresses, taken in happier times through the years, going back to their late teens. The dresses were those neglected and dusty ones I recognized from the closet, untouched for so long.

"You looked happy," I whispered in the stillness, trying to process aloud. "Did someone make you ashamed?" I set the small stack of photographs back into the drawer and pressed the stubborn thing closed. I mouthed an apology for my intrusion on Patricia's domain, and was seized by a dark question about the nature of the shadow in the background of the suicidal self-portrait. As I realized a familiarity in the way the dark mass hovered over the one whose happiness and self-worth were fading in every successive photograph, I felt something standing behind me. I jumped halfway out of my skin when I turned around to see Will Blake standing in the doorway, and his voice boomed,

"What the hell are you doing in here?"

"Oh Jesus! Uh, Hey, Chief. I thought I was going to my motel and got in here to realize I must have automatically followed you to the wrong house by mistake."

"You're goddamn right you made a mistake." Will grabbed me by the throat and yanked me toward him, slamming me against the wall. "What did I tell you? This isn't the place for you. You're here to embarrass the community with a story about our worst family, right? Last I recalled that family was the Ushers and not the Collinses."

"Alright, let go of me, will ya?" I rasped, and he set me back down, taking a step back.

"You're a real fucking creep coming in here, you know that?"

"Yeah, I was feeling real guilty about it and turning around to leave when you found me."

"So why did you do it? Give me one reason why I shouldn't arrest your skinny ass and make you apologize to Darla Collins for breaking into her house while she's out there crying."

"You wouldn't understand why. But I'm not here to give your town a bad name or write about this."

"Try me. Last chance."

"Because since I went into the hospital the night of my suicide attempt, six people have committed suicide. Rumor has it, that boy Jake Reynolds killed himself too. You once told me Delilah has a suicide rate at nine times the national average. I already tried to tell you these suicides are connected. And I came here because I needed to *know* if I'm right." Will Blake took a step back and shook his head like he couldn't believe what he was hearing, pulling a cigarette out of his shirt pocket and lighting it.

"Look, Joe. I've been real accommodating to your troubles. I've tried to reason with you. I've gone without arresting you when I could have. I'd arrest you right now if I thought what's wrong with you could be fixed in a cell. But the truth is, you need to be in the state mental hospital."

"I'm not crazy, Will. I just needed to see for myself."

"Yeah, well, you've seen. More than you bargained for, I reckon. Ol' Clyde was as queer as Christmas, wasn't he? Damn shame he couldn't get help," Will said with a full puff of smoke and a mirthless, morbid chuckle.

"Maybe the shame is that a guy who wasn't hurting anyone was made to feel like he could only be himself in this," I said, glancing about the pitiful room. "If the town would've rather seen Clyde kill himself than step out of this room in a dress, maybe that's the *town's* shame."

"Oh, right," Blake rolled his eyes. "And you've come to dig up all our secrets and show us how ashamed of ourselves we should be, is that right?"

"I'm trying to make sure nobody else does what I tried to do."

"Then talk to the family members. Take notes. Do what you have to do. As long as it's within the confines of the law, I can't stop you. But Joe, don't you ever let me find you in someone's house like this again. I've run out of pity for you."

Chapter Twenty-Two: I AM WITH THE DROWNED WOMAN

January 23rd, 1963

Delilah was a shaken place. Doris Reynolds stopped show-ing up to her waitressing job at the Thunderbird. Her atten-dance had been spotty, her working behavior erratic since the death of her son. She had been reprimanded twice for coming to work drunk. But her co-workers and patrons knew she was grieving her little boy and held their tongues as food came to them cold, or not at all. The town was small enough, everyone knew what had happened and gave her the space to work through it. Their forbearance was increased by the fact the coroner said too much to some friends while in his cups at Melville's a few weeks ago. Dark rumors were spreading. Jake Reynolds had not only drowned but slashed his own wrists for good measure. Officials spared the Reynolds family the disgrace of announcing it, but the ten-year-old's death was confirmed a suicide and not an accident. Of course, discretion does little good when the local coroner is a drunk given to sharing scandalous gossip about corpses when it might get him some attention.

The rumor that a beloved scamp of a young boy opened his

own wrists into the salt of the ocean at ten years old, and this was kept quiet to spare the family, spread like wildfire. Of course, it would. But when Doris heard it from the lips of a customer, she dropped the heavy coffeepot she was holding and stood still amidst the broken glass and pooling coffee splattering her shoes and scalding her legs in their stockings. She didn't feel it but stood wide-eyed and rigid like one in a trance, staring out the window over the head of the loose-lipped man. She did not seem to hear as people gathered around, urgently murmured her name, and shook her shoulders to snap her out of it. The crowded parlor swelled with murmurs of concern. Tom called out for her to wait up, but Doris Reynolds turned and walked out of the parlor for the last time, her high-heeled shoes leaving wet tracks of coffee to the glass doors. That incident occurred on January 21st.

On this day, the 23rd, police found the body of Doris Reynolds twisted with rigor mortis and dusted in a thin coat of sand on the beach outside her cabin. It was the same beach where her son died in early October. She was still wearing her white diner uniform, and it appeared the Pacific had tossed her body about like a toying cat for some time before growing bored and discarding her on the beach. She died in the same way as her son, a combination of blood loss and drowning. In the sand and balding yellow grass closer to the house, seventy yards from where her body was found, was a bloody steak knife. In addition to a crust of sand and dried blood, high on the blade were traces of white dust, perhaps drywall. This theory was confirmed when police broke down the door of the Reynolds bungalow and saw the only suicide note Doris would leave. Carved deep and jagged into the wall over her living room couch with the same knife she would use to kill herself, these words: **I AM WITH THE DROWNED WOMAN**.

To the police, it was nothing but the cryptic suicide explanation of a disturbed woman, but I knew it to be more. While the body was carried reverently from the beach on a gurney and draped in a sheet, shocked onlookers gathered about the house of death and conferred among themselves, as they always will. I milled about them as unobtrusively as possible, asking questions of neighbors and relatives, taking notes. When I stole a glance through the window and saw the carved writing on the wall, though, I knew what I had found. With her young son Jake's death in October counted as the first, Doris Reynolds was the eighth person to commit suicide since then. Seven of those deaths occurred in the last ten days since my own failed suicide attempt. It was noted Jake Reynolds died right before I arrived in town, and the suicides started occurring at such an alarming rate after my suicide attempt. Their eyes didn't forgive me for living when their own perished.

The citizens of Delilah had by now marked that whenever one of their own committed suicide, I was frequently not far behind. I came to be regarded as a kind of vulture lurking about the grotesque scenes of their grief. And as I attempted to inquire about the victims of each new tragedy, I was finding it increasingly difficult to find anyone willing to speak with me. My habit of keeping to myself whenever I went into town was working against me in a community already mistrustful of outsiders. That I was living in Delilah only to write a book about its most shocking and shameful event was not well received. Living for months in the isolation of the accursed house of the Ushers also conferred more than a little of their own historic stink onto me. For the first time in more than forty years, the lighthouse on Cape Contrition had a new keeper for the people of Delilah to fear and loathe.

The police chief stepped out onto the low porch of the Reynolds house to shoot me a dirty look in the crowd, and as I trudged back to my truck, he caught up with me.

"Wait up, Joe." I rested my forehead against the driver's side window of my automobile for a moment with a murmured curse before turning to face him.

"Look, I'm keeping my nose clean, alright? I just wanted to ask a few questions, which, by the way, was unsuccessful."

"I'm not here to chase you off. I threw you out of ol' Clyde's house because you deserved to be thrown out for trespassing there. But like I said, I'm not going to stop you from showing up on the sidewalk like anyone else has the right to."

"I appreciate that."

"Well, if you're going to keep poking around, we might as well see what you see. What do you make of Doris?" He lit a cigarette as he spoke.

"You know what I make of it." I pulled one from my shirt pocket and let him light it for me as I took a few quick puffs. "And I know you think I'm crazy."

"Well, you have to admit, asking a lawman to believe a witch or a ghost is making people kill themselves is a tall order."

"So, what's your explanation?" I asked irritably, breathing smoke.

"Right now, I'm trying to keep up with the dead and console the families. I don't have a villain to point to, Joe. A cluster of suicides springing up is tragic, but you don't investigate it the way you would a cluster of murders. There is no perpetrator.

These things just happen, and they frequently follow after one another."

"But have you ever dealt with this many at once? In town?"

"Hell no. This is like nothing I've seen. But Delilah has always been a hard luck town. The canneries are closing, the fishing is drying up, and this off-season for tourism has been especially difficult. It's no secret folks are struggling to make ends meet. And then you turn on the radio. The Government is testing hydrogen bombs in Nevada. The Reds are loaded for bear with their own. We've got schoolkids being instructed by a damn cartoon turtle to duck and cover underneath their thin wooden desks when the big one goes off, like that will be anything other than kindling. Our boys are getting shipped off to Vietnam, blacks and liberals are marching in the streets, and folks are more divided and angrier now than they were when the Civil War was on the verge of breaking out. It's a scary time to be alive, Crowley. The whole damn world is changing or getting ready to burn into ashes around this place. And when the jobs are leaving and the cupboards are bare, of course folks are struggling to face that. When one person makes the decision to end it, others who were on the fence about it follow their example. It's the Werther Fever."

"The what? Werther?" I stopped him.

"What, you've never —wow, *you* didn't know what that was?" Blake cracked into a proud smile he couldn't contain and poised himself to teach me a literary reference. "Well, you see, Joe, back in the 1700s, Goethe wrote a novel called *The Sorrows of Young Werther*. Werther loves this broad, Charlotte, but she's already engaged to another man. Al, Alfred or something. Their love can never be, Werther is distraught, but he could never cause her or the man she loves any harm.

So, he writes to Charlotte and Albert, requesting they send him some pistols. He takes those pistols and shoots himself dead underneath a linden tree. Takes the poor romantic a long time to give up the ghost, too. Anyway, once that novel took off in Germany, all these fruity Europeans agonizing over unrequited love start dressing like the guy, Werther. Yellow trousers and a blue coat, it becomes like the uniform of a generation of depressed literary types. And then all these young men start shooting themselves. *Thousands* of men dressed in blue jackets and yellow pants, all using the same style of pistols, ending it all because of some guy in a *book*." He said that last word like he was suspicious of their power.

"Anyway, all that to say, these things have been happening for a long time. They don't exactly require a monster from nightmares."

"I saw the message Doris left, Will. *The Drowned Woman.* Those are the same words I kept saying when I was in and out of consciousness after my car accident and my suicide attempt."

"Or a woman who was about to *drown herself* carved it into her wall with a knife because she was out of her gourd," Will Blake argued, but there was fear in his voice.

"Has anyone else mentioned a Drowned Woman in their suicide notes? Have you found any other references to her amongst the deceased?"

"Only you and Doris. But suicide notes aren't exactly consistent from one person to another, if they're left at all, which has only been about half the time in these instances. The only thing these deaths have in common is they're driving the whole town crazy and bringing folks' skeletons screaming out of their closets." I thought about the cannibalistic feeding

302

frenzies of gossip with each new death, the grudges and private shames dragged into the open. Also, about the diary of Rosemary Usher, who once loathed those same smiling facades and buried secrets: a tendency toward gossip and judgment unchanged by time.

"I'm telling you, Chief. Cape Contrition is connected to this."

Will looked at me with exasperated frustration for a long moment, puffing his cigarette one last time before stubbing it out on the sole of his boot.

"You must think we're so stupid," he shook his head with amazement. "That's what this is, right? We're all simple-minded townies to you. People are here grieving their loved ones who destroyed their own lives, and what do you do? You lurk around whispering ghost stories in their ears, playing on their superstitions, scaring them into thinking you have all the answers for what's happening to them. Of course, this wouldn't have *anything* to do with the book you're getting ready to sell. That's pretty fucking low, Joe." I tried to protest it wasn't like that, but I knew what this was. Had I not once been as determined not to believe it as he was? What could I say? Thomas Forester believed me. Gwen Christiansen was at least humoring me as indulgently as she could. But Will Blake would never believe this unless he saw it with his own eyes.

"You should have left town, Joe." Will Blake shook his head in anger and flicked the cigarette butt in a storm drain. "You really should have."

Chapter Twenty-Three: Town Hall

February 6th, 1963

I did not take Will Blake's advice, but time passed with little meaningful progress in my quest. I was finally cleared to get my right forearm out of its cast. The limb was withered, pale, and weak, coated in dandruff feathers of ugly flaking skin. The bones healed properly, but it would take some time before my grip would be as strong, my fingers as coordinated, as before. The purgatory of the cast atrophied it considerably, and I was prescribed a regimen of calisthenics exercises to get my strength back.

I didn't know how I was supposed to confront the Drowned Woman and bring an end to the deaths she was causing. How do you fight something you can't touch? How do you face something that can kill you with a look? I told myself I didn't want to challenge her unprepared. If I was the only one who knew what was happening and had a chance to stop it, what good would it do to throw my life away in vain? But the heart of the matter was, I was afraid to learn *how* to fight her. I could not bring myself to return to that house and face its nightmarish control over my body and mind again, properly armed or not. A part of me preferred not to know how to do battle with her. At least, then, I had a good excuse not to try.

But as time passed, more suicides were uncovered. Between January 23rd and February 6th of 1963, four more people in town died. The harbormaster and his wife, Dick and Mary Wright, died of numerous knife wounds in what appeared to be a murder/suicide. Two days later, a local grocer named Manuel Estrada hanged himself. Among his personal effects was evidence he had been carrying on an affair with Mary Wright for several years. This led police to conclude the revelation of this infidelity led to the murder/suicide. In addition to grieving the grisly death of his mistress, it was revealed Manuel Estrada's small grocery store was going under, as increasingly bare shelves hinted for weeks.

I visited each of the scenes of their tragedies, talked to witnesses, took notes, cowered over my typewriter and punched out my thoughts on the keys so I felt like I was doing something. While I hesitated and kept my hands busy, more people were dying, to my eternal shame and regret.

Hours were spent going over the details of the victims, trying to see some connection between them, but they defied any attempt to see a pattern. I pored over their deaths by the dingy light of my motel room lamp. What sort of intelligence was I dealing with in this entity I had awakened on Cape Contrition and turned toward town? It seemed like a game to her. Random acts of suicide, and things would fall quiet long enough for the citizens of Delilah to take stock of it, perhaps even to catch their breath a moment and assure themselves it was not going to happen again. Then, two more victims would be found. Some were people who concealed years of private pain or hid sordid secrets from the world. Some were, by all accounts, happy and content with their lives. People were driving themselves mad trying to understand it. The torment was working its fingers into the brains of the community. I recognized the way she was psychologically torturing them, because it was how she'd tortured me for months on end. And it was working.

The people of Delilah were at their wit's end. There seemed to be no pattern to puzzle out, no way to anticipate who would be next. And while some of those who died left no skeletons in their closets, many did. And when they were no longer there to defend or explain themselves, those dark secrets were seeping out into the churning gossip mill of this small, conservative American town. The clean white-picket illusions of their lives were unraveling as righteous and clean-cut family members had to contend with the exposing of deep hurts, loveless marriages, beaten wives, cheating husbands; parents reluctantly acknowledging the homosexuality of their dead sons, the unwanted pregnancies of suicidal teenage daughters, for the first time. There were twelve dead residents now, with three additional attempts. People were bewildered and enraged by the things they were learning about their neighbors, the things they were learning about themselves, which all preferred not to let on about. Revelations of local mistresses and long-suffering family members were turning kith against kin.

On the evening of February 6th, a town hall meeting was called. The municipal building where it was held was an old-timey, broad-faced structure unchanged since the Old West. When I pulled up to it, my headlights shone on the gathering of huddled citizens making their way in beneath the American flag snapping in the wind. Though only a temporary resident and a local pariah, I was part of what was happening, and had a duty to find a way to help stop it. Or at least to witness it all since I lacked the courage to stop it. In my months of studying the Ushers and living beyond the pale of this small logging and fishing town, I must admit I'd developed a prejudice against them. Will Blake's words had been cutting the last time we spoke when he witheringly said, *"You must think we're so stupid."* At the time, I thought his characterization of me as an educated East Coast novelist looking down my nose at the struggles of those in a rustic community was enormously unfair. But he wasn't wrong. The way their elderly generation, many of whom still lived, knew of the abuse Rosemary Usher and her children endured for a decade and did nothing until it was too late, the characterization of them as supremely judgmental and hypocritical by Rosemary Usher herself, Alice Cole, and Gwen Christiansen, all these things worked on my opinion of an entire community.

My book did not paint a kind portrait of them, and they could sense it without having read a word. What had Alice Cole said that day in her shop, when she compared them to sea lions shoving and howling for their own piece of the rock? *'Happy, barking little fools.'* But now I saw hundreds of desperate people looking for answers, joining hands against the darkness. Crying children clutching to the sweaters and flannels of their parents; weathered laborers with callused hands choking back tears; stoic old women, molded by hard lives on pitiless coasts, set their jaws firmly against this communal threat as they gathered to listen to their elected leader. I had allowed myself to hold too small and uncharitable a view of these people, who were still rugged pioneers more than a hundred years after their ancestors settled there, living much the same way as they had.

Delilah's mayor was a man named Walter McCoy, a broad-shouldered, plainspoken cowboy who had made his living operating a ranch inland before passing the work on to his two sons and wading into local politics. His face was round and clean-shaven, and a monk's tonsure of short gray bristles clung to the back and sides of his head while the rounded and smooth crown gleamed with baldness he wore better than most for his refusal to hide it. As people gathered into the marble-floored atrium of the municipal building, Mayor McCoy raised his hands and tried to calm the surging wave of constituents.

"Folks, come on in. I appreciate you coming out tonight. I'll open up for questions in a moment, but I wanted to address everyone first. As you all know, there has been a rash of suicides in town. Two days ago, Dottie Jameson was found dead in her garage of carbon monoxide poisoning from her car's exhaust. An autopsy revealed significant bruising on her body, as well as evidence of former wounds indicating Dottie suffered abuse at the hands of her husband George for many years. You folks know old Cliff Murphy, her little brother, has something of a reputation for being a hothead. Well, he saw the bruises as the body was being taken away and attacked George Jameson. Beat him so badly, he had to be rushed to the hospital. Though many of you might agree with that, we had no choice but to arrest Cliff. Delilah police were planning to arrest George once he was released from the hospital, but we have now received confirmation that at 4:22 P.M. today, George Jameson committed suicide as well."

There were gasps and muttered curses boiling over, and Mayor McCoy let the tide of citizens swell and rock for a moment before speaking again.

"He is the thirteenth suicide since January 13th, and my understanding is we've had four other attempts in that time. I look out at you people and see a lot of folks who have known one another our whole lives. This is a close-knit community, but the old ones have been here long enough to know this stretch of coastline has never been a forgiving place. It was difficult for our ancestors to carve out a life for themselves here. And those hardships have not gone away. We're a people who work with our hands. The toil of anglers, lumberjacks, and ranchers hasn't changed much since Lewis and Clark days. The storms haven't relented. We pride ourselves on resilience handed down by our ancestors, but we are also reminded their strength is not all we inherited. Lonesomeness has been as much a part of this coast as the salt and the sea. Depression and suicide have always dogged this community.

"But none of us can remember seeing so many make that decision at once. We gather in this place frightened, bewildered, hurt, bereaved, and looking for answers. I have to admit I don't know exactly what the solution is. Like you, I am afraid. I've lost folks who were dear to me in this. All I can say is if you're lost and alone, if you're feeling unworthy, and are considering taking this step to bring an end to your life... I implore you to reconsider, and to tell someone you love so they can help you. And neighbors, if anyone comes to you in confidence, I ask that you do everything you can to convince them to stay and show them they matter. I ask that all of you would hold one another close and make an extra effort to be kind. There are things we aren't good at talking about around here. But as people labor under hurts not spoken of at supper, we must try to care for one another. I have reached out to psychologists from neighboring towns and counties, some as far out as Portland. Several have agreed to drive in and make their services available to you at affordable rates."

"I have a mortgage and a dead husband! What's affordable?" Someone heckled from amidst the crowd. A woman's voice. People stirred and muttered approval, and if anyone knew who interrupted, no one was giving them up.

"Shrink your own head, McCoy!" A man's voice snarled, thin and high.

"Now, folks, please. We'll take questions in a minute," Walter McCoy pleaded, but he was losing control.

"How am I supposed to feel like my children are safe?"

"How do you stop a person from killing themselves?" The questions bubbled in a mob turning from scared to angry. And then-

"Mayor McCoy, why was my dead wife keeping letters from you!?" All other noise in the atrium was brought to a shuddering halt as this question rang out over everything else. All eyes turned on the mayor, and his affable face turned down in bewildered fear.

"What was that?" He feebly offered, pretending he hadn't heard to stall long enough to think up an answer.

"I said, why was my wife, Susan Sullivan, who died by her own hand last week, holding onto letters from you? Why do those letters say you got her pregnant and made her get an abortion?" There were gasps and curses as a lanky man named Ira Sullivan pushed through the crowd and stood towering over the man who cuckolded him.

"I don't —I don't know what you're talking about!" Mayor McCoy stammered, stepping backwards as Ira matched him step for step, red-faced and fuming. Ira stalked forward like a haggard, territorial wolf.

"Heyheyhey, easy!" Police Chief Will Blake said, running to shoulder his burly frame between the two men and putting a hand on Ira's bony chest. "Remember where we are, Ira. This ain't the time or place for this."

"What is the time?" Ira demanded, letting himself be eased back a step by the pressure of Will's hand, but looking the frightened mayor in the face as he spoke. "All my secrets were ripped out of my house when Sue went. What about his?" As people in the crowd agreed, Ira tried to lunge around Will for the mayor, but Will Blake shoved him back into a stumble. As Ira Sullivan fell back into the arms of the first of the mob, they surged forward. Will Blake unholstered the big revolver at his side, lifted it high, and fired a shot into the ceiling with a startling crack. There were gasps and everyone fell back. A sprinkle of white dust fell onto Will Blake's hat and shoulders, along with a few small shards of plaster.

"A little overzealous, Blake?" the disgraced mayor scolded, and over his shoulder the policeman replied,

"Yeah, unless you want to see some real overzealousness, I'd suggest you clam up, McCoy."

Someone in the startled mob repositioned their feet or made some other innocuous movement, and Officer Cody Mitchell pumped a deafening shotgun blast into the ceiling with shaky hands. Everyone in the room turned to stare in disbelief at the awkward young man as a large piece of the ceiling plaster and some asbestos fell around him in a shower of white dust.

"Really, Cody?" Blake scolded.

"Can we stop blowing holes in the ceiling for a moment?" Mayor McCoy said from his position crouching on the floor behind his police chief. Will Blake took a moment to calm himself before clearing his throat and addressing the crowd.

"Before you all go, there is one last order of business. We got a call this morning from Alice Cole. Four college-aged boys took a fishing boat out yesterday and haven't come back. They were out of towners, amateurs at best, and they might've been doing some drinking out there. The seas have been choppy and there is a wide perimeter we need to search. I've notified the police of neighboring towns and the Coast Guard, and tomorrow there is to be a coordinated search effort for these boys. I want to ask any able-bodied sailor here to sleep on the prospect of joining me tomorrow as we search for them." Regardless of what people thought of Mayor McCoy after Ira's revelation, Will Blake still commanded their respect. Several mariners stepped forward, and among them was little old Alice Cole.

With the emotional and largely fruitless meeting disbanded, I walked slowly out to my truck where Otis was waiting, thinking about everything they'd said. There was an electric anxiety in the air, as palpable on the tongue as the coastal brine. As I contemplated the infectious disquiet spreading throughout Delilah, something occurred to me for the first time, though it seemed a trifle then. It hadn't rained once since I attempted suicide nearly a month ago. That wasn't just odd for coastal Oregon in winter, it was damn near impossible. The dreary constancy of drizzle and wet fog was continuing as usual up and down the coast, but the skies over Delilah and Cape Contrition were holding their breath, waiting for something.

Chapter Twenty-Four: Seal Sister

February 7ᵗʰ, 1963

It was a cold and overcast morning of heavy slate gray clouds, but the rain was still withholding itself. The uncanny weirdness of the weather was making the atmosphere pal-pably tense, adding to the nervous paranoia in town. Word from the next town to the north and the next town to the south was coming back that it was chilly and rainy as any February on the coast ought to be, but in and about town remained unseasonably dry. I puffed tersely on a cigarette while I crouched and fed Otis some leathery strips of beef jerky. We were lingering at the edge of a gathering crowd in front of city hall at the request of the police chief. As it was a Thursday morning, those assembled were largely snowy-headed pensioners, or the recently bereaved who hadn't yet returned to work but needed something useful to do. They milled about the square lost and groggy, visiting with one another and trying to steel themselves against what was happening. A frosty, pallid sunrise was lightening Delilah over the foggy hilltops to her back.

I rose to my feet and looked on at the olive-green pavilion set up nearby as a little command center. Will Blake bent his broad shoulders over a map of the local coastline spread on a small card table as he listened to the counsel of gray-bearded, cold-eyed old sailors standing around him. These veteran mariners were each being given search zones. Will was both explaining his plans as a field commander and seeking their approval like an apprentice, knowing there had to be some give and take. He knew the procedure of a search and rescue op, but they knew the Pacific. So, he told the plan, and they let him know whether or not parts of it would be workable. Each of them knew the forbidding cliffs, tidal caves, squat ocean rocks, and treacherous sandbars like the lines on their own faces. And the policeman knew he would need to lean humbly on their experience if he was to depend on their help. They were wily old sharks, after all, who cared little for rescuing foolish out-of-towners who got drunk and wrecked rented boats. Though they graciously listened to Will Blake's plan for the search and guided him when he needed it, his position and the authority it conferred did not cow or impress them into automatic subservience. They had known Will Blake since he was a baby. In coordinating this operation, he could not take them for granted, since they could just as soon be at home this morning, college boys be damned.

Alice Cole stood on the edge of the huddle, listening intently as she sipped from a tall thermos of coffee coiling steam from its stout open neck. We had spoken briefly before she joined the meeting, and I was mainly looking at her as I watched the proceedings. She was as experienced a boat pilot as any of the men in that pavilion, and a good deal more than some, but they would never admit it. Even now as I watched, she said little; at some intervals she spoke to Will Blake like a stern mother, but never engaged with her colleagues directly. I had a feeling Alice Cole did not like most people. I was far from convinced she liked me. One of the graybeards who passed under the pavilion twenty minutes earlier had muttered to a compatriot she was "a thorny old broad." As I watched, I had the distinct feeling her mind was processing the search plans on faster wheels and a more absorbent memory than the men about her who still joked it was bad luck to have a woman aboard. As if *women* had been the ones cracking open their ships like eggs on the coasts of the Pacific Northwest for more than a century. Me, I'd made up my mind. When the little conference broke up and it was "all aboard", I was volunteering with the little old woman who was tough as nails.

The aging circle of smoking, coffee-sipping volunteers broke apart, and as everyone went to scramble their boats, Otis and I hurried to keep pace with the rapid stride of Alice Cole.

"Mrs. Cole!" I called, and she didn't stop. "Mrs. Cole?" The second time, she looked over her shoulder, but didn't slow down.

"What do you want, Crowley?"

"I was hoping to come aboard and lend a hand. Do you need volunteers?"

"Have you ever handled a boat bigger than that little outboard I sold you?" she asked over her shoulder.

"Well, no. But I can help."

"Look, Mr. Crowley, the wind is picking up, seas are choppy, and I don't have room on my craft for another tourist. Tourists are the damn reason for this whole manhunt in the first place. What's it to you, anyway? Don't you have a book to write? You don't know these kids."

What could I say? I felt responsible for everything. I needed to feel like I could save someone, or at least keep busy.

"I want to bring those young men home." It was true, but it was a noble strand among self-serving, guilt-ridden ropes pulling me onto her boat. "I have to feel like I'm doing some good, helping someone." She drew to a halt and turned around, evaluating me with icy, bright eyes for a long moment before speaking again.

"Huh. Yeah, well, I just want my boat back. Oh, and as for saving the day and all... It's been two days. I've been living on these shores a long time. If you're going out there with me, you need to understand not many people here expect we're going to find them. Or my boat. Oh, we'll try our best to get some answers. See what we see. But the ocean takes a lot of things she never gives back. And not all shipwrecks are acts of God. Better men than these have vanished out there, with no answers for their loved ones except 'that's just how it is.'"

"Is that what happened to your husband?" It was a pointed question mentioned with careless offhandedness, a reflex of the old ex-journalist grabbing hold of a tight-lipped interviewee's momentary lapse into candor, hoping to unearth a story. She turned and slapped me across the face.

"Don't you ever say that again," she snarled, every inch the surly old dock cat.

"Yes ma'am." I was ten again as I bowed my head, held my stinging cheek, and followed in tow behind the coarse shipwright's widow, afraid to ask if I'd forfeited my spot on her expedition. As we made our way out onto the slimy surface of the rickety, crowded docks, we passed Thomas Forester and a few older members of his church. They were huddled by the harbor in a fervent prayer vigil, and a choir in flowing robes was wailing and harmonizing a haunting old spiritual.

"Wade in the water,

Wade in the water, children

Wade in the water,

God's gonna trouble the water"

Alice walked purposefully past heaps of crab rings, moldy coils of rope, and seagulls bickering over rotting fish heads, picking her way over the uneven, slippery boards with practiced steps. Otis and I trotted along in her wake, along with a small crew of other volunteers. There was a handsome young carpenter with wavy red hair named Garrett O'Connor, his sunny, upbeat girlfriend Marianne, and a brawny Siuslaw Indian fisherman named John Hicks. Garrett worked in her employ at the shipyard, and Marianne was her occasional bookkeeper, while I gathered John had been close with Alice's husband. In this company of experienced strangers, I couldn't help but feel as if I'd gone out of my depth. Alice Cole's vessel was a tub-bellied old 1930s gillnetter christened with the name *Seal Sister*. Old tire fenders hung at regular intervals around the gunwale and blue-trimmed capstan, and most of the boat was painted in peeling and diminished white.

Alice swung herself over the gunwale with surprising agility and lowered the gangplank for us, and we filed across the wobbling board in single file as John Hicks deftly unmoored the vessel from the docks. The *Seal Sister* bobbed gently underneath our shifting weight as we moved about the crowded deck, and Otis whimpered as he looked up to me for some cue. A rumble underwater sent a tremor through the craft as the engine coughed and sputtered to life, and the propeller began to churn. John leapt from the dock and vaulted gracefully over the gunwale, silky black hair falling about his shoulders as he found his feet on our side. From the wheelhouse, Alice deftly guided the chugging vessel out among the crowded sailboats and fishing rigs, out into the open bay. As the boat cut through the waters, ploughed up a foamy track into the ocean, and spattered my lips with salt-spray, a sinking anxiety weighed on me. My mind conjured images of towering waves sweeping over Main Street and threatening to wash away my automobile in the Columbus Day Storm months earlier. My Adam's apple bobbed in a dry swallow as I admitted my stay in this place had imparted a terror of the angered ocean.

The slate gray waters rolled in low hills and valleys, pitching the *Seal Sister* into a nauseating rhythm. With a cool hand, Alice Cole piloted the craft over the rises and dips in oceanic terrain, setting her jaw with the boat's rumbling churn as it knifed through the waves. Marianne smiled and talked like she was at a picnic as she unlatched the lid of a tin lunch pail and passed out ham and rye sandwiches wrapped in butcher paper to anyone who wanted one. Otis opened his black lips in a wide, tongue-lolling smile as the smell of human food mixed with the brine in the air. Everyone else ate and Marianne offered one to me as well, but I had to wave it off. I hadn't known I could be afflicted by such a thing, but the rolling motion of the boat and the twisting dread of the Pacific were spinning into a bout of seasickness. With droplets of sweat forming in the wrinkled creases of my forehead, I grasped a cold metal drum of the main winch and the prickly, soaked line coiled about it.

Though I only meant to steady myself for a moment, Garrett barked with a mouthful of rye and motioned wildly for me not to touch the winch. Once he swallowed, he apologized and let me know the winch was the most dangerous part of the boat. I nodded wearily and apologized before staggering over like a drunk and taking a seat on the deck between John and Marianne. Realizing it was Otis' breakfast time, I handed him the sandwich meant for me and watched him bolt it down greedily. As the dog tossed his head back and chomped up the last swallow, I wiped a gob of mayo from his mustache and let him lick it off my finger. Knowing I had better try to eat something small to settle my stomach, I accepted a cold hardboiled egg from Marianne's pail and chewed it slowly, closing my eyes as the spraying wind played havoc with my hair and all my energy went into keeping myself from throwing up.

Seal Sister moved beyond the sheltering arms of the jetties, and without their shielding presence, the sea was choppier than I had imagined. The prow of the boat slapped down on the waves in splashing spurts. Alice guided the tub in a southerly loop, and Marianne climbed into the covered wheelhouse with her to consult the map. We were assigned a wily stretch of cliffs and tidal caves South of Delilah. The plan was to start a few nautical miles out and slowly sweep back to our assigned stretch of coastline, taking the time to see what we might see in the open water of our sector before combing the cliffs themselves.

A small Oregon state flag snapped navy blue and gold in the wind by the mainmast. The gray waters held and shook us in a slow, steady rhythm of rolling plunges. A roving canopy of inky clouds swirled overhead, bringing a soft, chilly rain over us. Miles out in the distance, where the line between gray sea and gray sky blurred to meaningless distinction, other rainstorms could be seen as vague curtains of vapor. I watched these mirages drift beyond sight before glancing down at the thousand pinpricks of rain on the ocean's murky surface right around us. John ducked out of the rain into the wheelhouse, preferring to experience the chilly downpour through thick panes of glass. Otis, shivering and grumbling, tucked tail and went with the Siuslaw. I, however, stood against the rail and greeted it like an old friend. The heavy wool of my pea coat was damp and glistening with droplets, but I was contentedly warm within it. Soaked to the skull with my dark hair flattened against my head, I couldn't help but smile. I hoped some of this rain would find its way back to the strange town I couldn't help but think of as home.

Amid savoring the peaceful solitude, I glanced down to the surface of the water and was unnerved. A dark shadow passed underneath the boat, indistinct in the deep murk of the water, but immense in a way that made my stomach drop. It was a thing instinctively felt more than seen: the evolutionary sensation of an unseen body close at hand and dangerous. An antelope dipping its head to the edge of the Nile, marble eyes widening with fear at the vague tell of a crocodile's shadow concealed in the muddy bottom. The Leviathan passed in a smooth glide, the rush of its bulk in underwater flight creating ripples trembling in the hull under my feet. Darkness within darkness. I was so in awe of the thing my mind couldn't make the obvious connection of what it was. And so, with wide eyes and white knuckles, I glimpsed a sea monster with the awe of an ancient mariner.

Black and oil-sleek, its wide back crested the foamy water and rolled like the trunk of a serpent. A white plume of spray shot from the blowhole, and underneath the surface, mottled white fins undulated like impossible wings. My last glimpse as the Leviathan dove was the sight of the wide flukes of its

320

inky tail fanning the air for a moment before disappearing in the dark. I stared breathless, looking for more, but the water yielded no trace. It was the first humpback whale I had ever seen. My awe of its beauty was tempered by the healthy fear of such an enormous and intelligent animal passing within ten yards of the *Seal Sister*, invisible underneath our feet once again after choosing to reveal itself for only a moment. The whale dwarfed our tub-bellied gillnetter, a reminder of how small, fragile, and fleeting we were within its power. Even the most serene and holy moments a person can experience with the ocean cannot help but remind us of that.

An icy fog rolled over the surface of the waters, biting and cruel in the way it turned the pleasant drench of long-absent rain into chest-rattling cold. Giving up my post on deck, I huddled into the bridge with the others, sipping coffee from an olive-green thermos Garrett offered me. Alice Cole strained her cold, piercing eyes into the veil, keeping the looming cliffs ahead of us in the distance. Her knobbed hands guided the polished wooden wheel of the boat confidently. There was a small panel of switches, dials, and faded glass gauges she monitored and fussed with, but I understood little about the rudimentary and aged instruments of the gillnetter's bridge. The long, low blare of the foghorn sounded out jarringly at her command, making me flinch without warning. The forlorn sound echoed out in the emptiness, and we all huddled within the wheelhouse, straining to see through the smoky curtain over the windows. No one spoke, but the tension in the air was palpable. The nerves in the flats of our feet were pressing up against the soles of our shoes, listening at the deck, waiting to feel some horrid scrape against the hull as we watched our pilot navigate. Only Alice Cole showed no concern in the face of the fog bank. The inboard engine hummed low below deck, and she sounded the horn once more. The blare carried more than usual over the surface of the water, magnified by the density of the moist air.

"Well, what are you two lovebirds waiting for?" Alice asked, turning over her shoulder to cock an eye at Garrett and Marianne, who were whispering and giggling in the corner of the wheelhouse. "This ain't a pleasure cruise. We need to be seen, and to see what we can. Go man the searchlights."

"Yes, ma'am." Garrett sheepishly lifted Marianne off his lap and ducked outside onto the slick deck. Marianne turned the map over to John and followed. In a few moments, the teens were each turning on two mounted searchlights, one at bow and one at stern. With an electric hum, the two bucket-like torches flickered on, and their heavy beams panned over the surface of the water as the foghorn bellowed its grim dirge.

"Blanket under the seat there, Crowley," Alice said as I wrapped arms about my squirming mutt and tried to keep my teeth from chattering. As I obeyed and pulled out a thick blanket roll, she flicked open a crumpled packet of Lucky Strikes. "Have another cigarette and warm yourself up before you keel over." Like the teenagers, I was compelled to obey, pulling a bent, non-filter cigarette out and holding it between two fingers while John struck a match and lit it for me. After a few quick puffs, I returned the favor for him. The searchlights swung slow over the surface of the foggy ocean, and John cracked the door to the wet, howling wind as the wheelhouse got smoky. I leaned back, resting my head against the cold glass and closing my eyes as I pushed out a slow, hot breath, spat out a couple brown shreds of leaf from the unfiltered butt, and took a swig of steaming coffee metallic with the tang of its container. Otis was curled on the bench next to me, head in my lap, and the warmth was rushing back into my bones.

"Was that your first whale?" Alice asked.

"I didn't know you noticed," I smiled, "But yes, it was."

She took a drag, holding it in as she guided the boat's wheel with a knobbed hand that grasped a stubby cigarette trailing smoke. As I contemplated this self-reliant, headstrong, quarrelsome woman who sailed with the best of her bay's mariners and had little use for anyone but her cats, I was simultaneously amused and ashamed of a thought. If we'd lived in a more paranoid time, and people began dying in a mysterious outbreak no one could explain, the panicked citizens of an earlier century might have hanged old Alice Cole for a witch. That might have been what made her so intriguing to me. Outside, the fog let up, and the cliffs were looming close overhead. Garret's light was cutting over the surface of the water ahead of the bow, and Marianne was panning off starboard. With a few thoughtful puffs, I idly watched her work. I was sleepy from the warmth of the wheelhouse and the rocking motion of the boat when my heavy-lidded vision caught a flash of torn fabric and something red. Marianne's scream rent the air outside. The cliff walls and foggy air were still throwing the horrific noise mockingly back at her when the three of us spilled out of the wheelhouse and onto the deck.

Garrett rushed over to us as well. His jaw quivered as he glanced down into the spotlight on the surface of the water and took Marianne in his arms. The girl covered her mouth, and a shudder ran through her as she murmured something unintelligible and buried her face in her boyfriend's rumpled pine-green flannel shirt. John, Alice, and I exchanged looks before walking to the gunwale and peering over the edge. *Seal Sister* had pulled near some rocks in the shadow of the cliff. They pierced the surface of the water like the jagged bone ridges of a sea serpent's back. A torn sail spread bloated and baggy over the surface of the treacherous shoal, still clinging to a broken mast. In the beam of the searchlight, a dirty seagull was bracing padded feet on an orange lifejacket, spreading its wings for balance as it bent double to pull up stringy shreds of meat in its bloody beak. It took me a minute to realize the thing it was eating from in the tangle of lifejacket and sailcloth was the dead arm of a young man.

Chapter Twenty-Five: The Wreck of the Lucky Hour

February 7ᵗʰ, 1963 (Cont.)

"Christ," Alice muttered as her eyes settled on the dead boy. With a hand trailing blue smoke from a stubby cigarette in two of its fingers, she crossed herself at the sight of the body. But it was more like a distantly instilled, half-remembered physical tic than an inspired gesture of true piety. Alice Cole was only reverent of the ocean.

"Well, that's it," she sighed. "Garrett, take the girl into the wheelhouse. Get the chief and the others on the shortwave. John, fish that poor fool out of there." She produced a florescent orange flare gun from inside her aran sweater, lifted it to the sky, and pulled the trigger. With a pop of thick white smoke and a rushing whine, a sparking red comet shot into the overcast sky in a shimmering arc. A few seconds passed before a distant foghorn echoed across the bay in answer, followed by another bellow. On the horizon, other boats were turning their noses in our direction. Without a word, Alice and I watched as John lowered a fishing net into the water, produced a long boathook, and tentatively grasped out with the pole toward the body. The hook caught on clothing and bloated flesh, and he guided the corpse over to lap with the waves against the hull of the boat. Bending almost double over the bulwark, he gently poled the body into the snare of the fishing net and set the pole aside, muscles straining as he heaved the ropes upward with their ponderous dead weight. The young man's name was Bradley Zimmer. A strand of seaweed wove through his red hair and clothes, and his soggy, translucent flesh was lacerated by the constricting ropes of the net as the brawny Siuslaw hauled him aboard as gently as possible. As the corpse flopped onto the deck, I was horrified to see his eyes had been stabbed out. He stared up at the gray sky with two gory holes, disturbingly expressive even though each window to the human soul was gone from them. His tongue was also missing.

"Seagulls," John reported, disturbed but unsurprised as he turned the body over to find several other places slashed by piercing beaks. "They go for the easiest morsel first. Damn buzzards."

"Anyone should be damn grateful we were able to find anything at all," Alice said coarsely. I rounded on her with a look of appalled disappointment, but she didn't bother to see it. But her own husband had been lost at sea, and that was all the answer or explanation she would ever have. Her harshness, while shocking, was hard to interpret as unreasonable in her environment. She had to be harsh to make her living in the teeth of the beast who ate her husband. As John looked over the body, I noticed a horrible round hole in the side of his head, trickling a small stream of water into hair crusty and matted with dark blood. As the fisherman took a quizzical look, I crouched next to him with a grimace as I confirmed my suspicion.

"Bullet hole." I'd seen enough of them. That complicated things.

"There's nothing else for it," the shipwright's widow finally said, leaning over the bulwark to try and see into the murky swirl of inky water. "We'll need the suit. Johnny, would you be a dear and fetch it up for me?"

"The suit?" I asked.

"We keep it for underwater salvage. Some things need a man for doing, I won't deny it. I couldn't move in the damn thing. It's older, of course. No new-fangled aqualung has made its way to Delilah yet. But it'll keep a man from drowning, and that's all you can ask for out here." It took me a minute to realize what she was referring to. John opened the hatch, and heaved up a heavy, rumpled full-body suit of waterproof green canvas. The thing spilled out onto the deck like some dead creature, and John set a ponderously large diving helmet on top. It was something I had only seen in illustrations of *Twenty-Thousand Leagues Under the Sea*: brass and copper dull and stained with sickly green, thick glass porthole lenses on the front, sides, and top, each protected by thin crosses of metal wire. I whistled low as I glanced over the antiquated gear with an untrained eye that still had the sense to be nervous about its decrepitude.

"You're going down in that thing?" I asked, and he looked at me with surprise, giving me the first sinking feeling the others were in on something I hadn't grasped yet.

"He's working the pumps up here. *You're* going down in that thing."

"I don't know how, I've never-"

"There's nothing to know. You'll walk the bottom and see what's down there. The rest of my sailboat, maybe. Maybe not. We'll keep the air flowing. Your job is to scout out the bottom and let us know what we're in for. If we need to pull the wreck out, the other boats and I will coordinate that when they get here. What did you tell me on the docks? You wanted to help. And you remember what I said? *'I don't have room on my craft for another tourist.'*"

"No tourists," I mumbled reluctantly, letting out a hiss of nervous air as I looked at the heavy standard diving dress. "Alright, suit me up."

John helped me into the get-up. This was a more laborious process than I expected, due to the complexity of the apparatus. He put me into the exposure suit, checking it for punctures before putting me into a heavy harness with a bailout cylinder strapped into it. Once these were secured, several weights were attached to the suit. These were added when I still had some time to go standing on the surface, and my muscles ached while I stood there waiting for the complex assembly and testing of the equipment to end. I was assured even though the weights were cumbersome now, I would be grateful for them on the ocean floor. Last came the heavy helmet, which was lowered carefully onto my head. Much of the sound from the outside world was muffled as John secured the locking mechanisms on the neck dam and checked for obvious faults with the seal.

My first impression was claustrophobia. The thick canvas bodysuit was stifling, and I felt sticky with sweat within minutes of putting it on. My breath shuddered within the heavy, awkward copper helmet and rebounded within its walls.

"Oh, Jesus," my sigh echoed in the helmet, and she gave a far-away-sounding chuckle before coaching me on adjusting the back pressure of the exhaust valve to control my suit's buoyancy. John heaved a heavy weight overboard with a long rope tethered to it. There was a loud plunk noise as it splashed in, and John fed the rope in after it steadily. When the anchor weight hit bottom, the Siuslaw marked the distance on the rope and whistled low.

"Looks like about thirty feet deep, Granny," he reported before pulling the weighted rope back into the boat hand over hand.

"You'll know for sure if you call me granny again," Alice retorted, unfurling a rope ladder and hanging it over the bulwark.

"Yes, Ma'am," John replied dutifully, with the curl of a sly smile as he busied himself with assessing the manual pumps that would deliver air through the tube into my helmet. Through the small porthole, I saw him measure out the tubing so I would have enough of a lead to walk around on the bottom. Methodically, he put the surface air supply equipment through a series of checks at various stages, ensuring there were no leaks, and everything was functioning correctly. He set up a compressor so it would bring uncontaminated air flowing into my intake, checked filters, pored over the hookah cord for punctures, blew through it with his mouth to break up any clogs, and checked its connection to my helmet. Last in the laborious process, he put the non-return valve and bailout block through a function test. As he studiously performed these tasks I couldn't quite follow, he explained the function tests of the non-return valve and bailout block were to prevent something he called a "helmet squeeze" if my airline was cut. I was afraid to ask what that was.

As John's air supply equipment was confirmed to be in working order, Alice stepped into the wheelhouse for a few minutes, and I was alarmed by a sudden whine of static within the echoing chamber of my helmet. The noise was sharp and abrupt, jarring within the confines, but soon her voice crackled through with,

"Hear me alright, lighthouse keeper?"

"Loud and clear," I spoke aloud into the helmet comms link.

"This will be our communication channel while you're under," her crackling, metallic-grained voice replied. She emerged from the bridge to put me through a series of breathing checks, confirming my air supply was coming through properly. She walked me through engaging my bailout system, making sure I could reach the operating valve and turn it smoothly.

Alice guided me over to the gunwale and helped as I clumsily hung out over the edge, feet grasping blindly for the next rung of the ladder as my thick-gloved hands clung numbly at rungs I couldn't feel. As I picked my way into the cold water, John lowered in the anchored rope once again, feeding its line out from the boat at a steady pace. When the weight reached the ocean floor and the line went taut, I craned my neck up to look through the pane in the top of my helmet and saw Alice Cole's wrinkled face smirking down at mine. She walked back into the wheelhouse and spoke to me through the crackling radio console inside.

"You'll need to let go of the ladder, grab hold of the shotline, and establish negative buoyancy on the surface. Remember how I showed you to work the valve. Slide down the line, and grab hold of it when you need to stop. I'll feed out your umbilical as you descend, and John will keep you breathing with the manual pump. Go down there, see what you can see, and climb back up the shotline when you're ready to ascend." I wanted to ask more questions, but they didn't seem worried, and I was resolved not to be a tourist about this.

Reflexively gulping down an unnecessary breath, I leapt clear of the ladder into the cold ocean. Treading ungracefully, conscious of my top-heavy gear and restricted range of movement, I grasped out half-blindly for the shotline and grabbed hold of it. I bobbed with the motion of the choppy water, waves licking against the dome of my diving helmet and splashing its porthole windows. Finding the exhaust valve, I adjusted the pressure and felt myself sinking, pulled indelibly downward as if by a weak magnet. As the atmosphere within my suit changed and negative buoyancy was established, I drew myself downward hand over hand on the shotline, my helmet at last submerging completely beneath the waves.

The ocean gurgled and pressed in against the metal walls and thick glass of the diving helmet, and the heat and echo of my breaths within its shell reminded me of swimming up into the air pocket formed by a capsized rowboat as a boy. The murky green water was hard to see in, rich with the microbial life that allowed my friend the humpback whale to thrive so well in this part of the world. I felt myself tethered to the boat, and the umbilical cord fed out from the deck of the *Seal Sister* as I sank deeper into the dense darkness. It was as close to outer space as a man like me was ever going to get.

The near-Arctic cold pressed in against my sweaty, clammy flesh inside the suit, and I hung in the abyss with nothing in my vision but the rigid rope in front of me and hands in unwieldy gloves sliding down, down, down. As my eyes adjusted to the murky pickled green of the water, I craned my head upward in its bowl to see the broad belly of the boat, my oxygen cord trailing up to it. When I was hanging in the water ten feet over the ocean floor, the dark castle of jagged rocks that broke the surface and lifted the splintered mast into the air was visible in the dim soup swimming before my eyes. Bladed fingers pierced the surface above, but the wide base of the thing sat squat and resolved like an old toad. Littered broken about its feet was the wreck of a small pleasure yacht. The cream and navy-blue sailboat cracked open on the rocks above, and had not drifted far as it settled to the bottom. It spread before me like the shards of an heirloom smashed in anger. I thought about that bullet hole in the kid on deck and wondered what I would find.

Clouds of sand plumed as my boots touched the ocean floor. Crumpled paper streamers of kelp drifted upward like stalks in an alien cornfield. Not far from where the anchor of my shotline had fallen, the sandy floor of the ocean sloped downhill in a steep drop off. It was like the cliff of a dark Martian canyon, startlingly close but too inky and massive to comprehend. I stood there for a moment with one hand on the line, looking out from the brink of the world into the bottomless pit of the Pacific. The call of the void crept up my spine. I broke my gaze from it, turning around and walking across the sand toward the wreck. My arms parted the kelp as I walked through it like a curtain, feeling its slimy fronds run cold fingertips over me, almost grasping. The otherworldly movement of their lank, sodden strands reminded me of the black hair flowing from the wilted bonnet of the Drowned Woman, but I assured myself I was alone in that cold, still underworld. The only sound was the heavy echo of my breaths. The boat's name was *Lucky Hour*, and I could hear my own heartbeat in my ears as I walked along its bow. The rocks left long deep scratches along its sides, like the claws of some Lovecraftian horror. A startling flash of silver wriggled out of the jagged split in *Lucky Hour*'s belly as I approached. Only a fish, I smiled with a sigh of relief as I watched it take flight into the distance. Alice must have heard my start because her voice came graining through on the comm line.

"Alright, Crowley? Do you see it?"

"I see it; the whole boat is here, broken in two. I don't think you'll be getting it back, Alice."

I felt the serrated points of wood, marveling with a kind of sympathy pain at the sort of hole that was punched in the hull on the rocks above. Though a landlubber, it seemed clear to me what had happened. *Lucky Hour* strayed within the shadow of the cliffs and bottomed out on the teeth of some especially ruthless crown of scarcely submerged rock. Rather than simply running over it, the vessel got stuck, balancing precariously like a seesaw. Queasily, I imagined the boys with a few beers in them a-piece, cursing and collapsing on deck with alarm as the entire wooden pleasure yacht groaned and rattled. Water spilled in from the punctured hull, but they weren't sinking. The adrenal response slowly ebbed as the young men grew still, realizing the *Lucky Hour* wasn't moving. I'd only seen the face of the one before, but in my mind, they were boys like the ones I'd fought alongside in the War. Boys like I had once been. Maybe they held their breath, listening as the boat creaked and tottered slightly on its balance. I imagined a moment of relief as their eyes met, and bashful smiles curled on their lips. What a story to tell mom and dad.

Skewered on a rock a hundred yards from the shoreline, a couple miles outside of town.

Well, I guess we'd better get on that radio and figure out how to call ashore. Probably be a couple hours before the cavalry arrives, but it seems stable. Gee, thank God we didn't have any gals aboard to see us in this mess-

A gust of wind filled the sail, still unfurled, and its kite swelled as the hull tipped ever so slightly beneath their feet... And *Lucky Hour* broke in two like a stick over a giant's knee.

My heart sank as I imagined the two pieces drifting apart, water flooding in on the glossy panels and leather cushions of the furniture. Perhaps two of the young men in one half and two in the other, looking across the gulf of churning waves and salt-eaten rock, eyes wide in horror as they realized they were going to die.

But then, the bullet hole.

How did that make sense? Why would one of them even have a gun in the first place? Did the one on the surface shoot himself for fear of drowning? Taking one last choice out of the teeth of a cruel death by doing it on his own terms? I stepped into the gulf between the two halves of *Lucky Hour*. Ultimately, the two halves of the boat had not wandered far. After splitting apart on the rock, they more or less drifted straight downward, and settled in the dust of the ocean floor no more than eight feet apart. One crooked toe of the rock that killed them was stuck between it: a corner of the foundation they had fallen around. As I surveyed the damage, I imagined the mast snapped off in the grinding break of the boat as its two parts slipped beneath the waves. I stepped into the cavernous belly of the bow of the boat. Like any yacht of its size, the quarters were cramped, but the wood was of a polished finish, the furniture comfortable and elegant. There was no one in the fore half of the boat, so I stepped out into the eerie, alien field once again, breathing greedily of the thin air in the suit.

The stern end held the more spacious part of the cabin and was the larger of the two parts in the break. As I walked toward the darkened mouth of the wreck, I looked down to see a wriggling mass in one corner of the cabin. Heart in my throat as I wished for some form of illumination, I stepped closer to see the trembling bulk was a horde of Dungeness crabs. Carapaces of purple, brown, and gray skittered spider-like over one another, serrated pincers tearing at meat and pulling pale shreds greedily into their sideways opening mouths. It took me a few moments to understand the thing underneath the swarm of crabs was a young man, and the shreds of meat were being pulled from his face and arms. I gasped and reeled backward into the wall and low ceiling at the other side of the hull, feeling my oxygen line strain at the edge of the opening for a moment before I regained my balance. Oh, God. Oh, Jesus. The young man was pinned beneath something that crushed him into the sand. As I thought about the silent skittering of the bottom-feeders, the tearing pincers and shuttering mouths, I made a silent vow never to eat a crab again.

As my eyes adjusted to the macabre sight, I noticed something in the dirt at the boy's feet. I crouched to my knees and reached for the L shape, dusting off the thin coating of sand and holding up a Smith & Wesson revolver in my hands. The thing was already going back to nature, the wooden handle slimy with algae to the touch, corrosion already staining the metal. I turned the thing over in my hands with puzzlement before flicking open the wheel. Brass cartridges glinted dully in their places, one for each of the six chambers. Four of the cartridges held spent casings, with two bullets left. Four shots. Four boys. With a rush of nausea, I crouched over the writhing body of crabs and checked the torn-apart head of the victim. My eyes strained through the foggy glass as my useless hands fumbled with the young man's drifting curls of brown hair, and I swatted crabs aside with annoyed disgust. I nearly vomited in my helmet as my searching fingers fell into the shattered back of his skull. *In the mouth, then.* I laid his head back against the wall of the boat as tenderly as I could.

My stomach continued to roil with revulsion and disquiet when I turned around and saw a pale hand grasping out toward my face. With a horrified yelp, I fell backward onto the boy and the beam of wreckage pinning him down. Crabs scuttled, scratched, and pinched at my thick armor with annoyance as I stared through my porthole in horror at a ghoulish form hovering over me, translucent skin and dark, flowing clothes that made my heart jump into my throat. In a panic, I squeezed my eyes shut and rolled my head to the side in its helmet, desperate not to make eye contact with the Drowned Woman, for this was the encounter I most feared. For a long moment, I lay there in the echoing gloom of my helmet, listening to clawed feet scratching and scuffing at its surface as the arthropods climbed over me, seeking in vain for an entry. I waited in the darkness with my eyes shut, no sound at all but the crabs. As my pounding heart settled, I opened my eyes slowly and realized what I had seen. The third body floated up against the ceiling, trapped from rising to the surface. The bloated face looked at me with wide-eyed disbelief, curiously expressive as its lifeless hands grasped wide for an embrace. On the side of his head, too, was the tell-tale bullet hole.

"Talk to me, lighthouse keeper," came Alice's voice over the channel.

"Oh my God. They're down here. Two of them."

"Drowned?"

"Shot."

"We'll bring them topside during the salvage when the others get here. Don't worry about that. Do you see the fourth?" I glanced about through the dim twilight and moved deeper into the broken half of the yacht to check the further compartments.

"No."

"Well, the ocean likely got him. And she won't give him back. Finding three of the four bodies is more luck than we could have asked for. Can you tell what happened?"

I repeated to her my theory of the boat running aground, tipping when the sail filled with a gust, and snapping in two. Next, I haltingly reported the condition of the bodies as I found them, and the wheel-gun with four spent casings. Her voice sounded less surprised than it should have been.

"Alright, lighthouse keeper. You've done all you can for them, understand? Excellent work. Time to make your way back." I put hands to my knees and doubled over, breathing heavily as I closed my eyes and felt the pounding of my heart, the reel of my stomach. I held there for a few moments in the echoing silence of my helmet, between the two boys and the scuttling crabs. As the surging spike of adrenaline passed and I was able to gather myself, I turned and ducked out of the yacht's gaping belly. My umbilical caught on the broken teeth of the hole in the ship and was sheared off by a jagged twist

337

of rent metal as easily as by a dagger. At first, I felt a pinch of pressure as the line went taut, and a snap sent me stumbling forward as the air cord broke. As the chain of events revealed its grim meaning to me, I whipped around to see the cut line drifting away like the string of a lost balloon. A thin trail of small bubbles was trickling weakly out of its torn mouth. It was impossible, I told myself, as I replayed in my mind the events of the past few minutes. I had been careful, hadn't I? There was no way my line could have caught or torn like that. My thoughts were dispersed by the trickle of sea water glugging into my helmet through the torn cable.

Chapter Twenty-Six: Helmet Squeeze

February 7th, 1963 (Cont.)

Alice was on the radio as if she telepathically knew something was wrong.

"What happened, Crowley?"

"My line was cut! My air!" I echoed with loud alarm into the reverberating bowl of the helmet. The air pressure was already changing, and the lack of air in the helmet was immediately stifling.

"Alright, stay calm. I'm going to walk you through this, alright?" The pressure of water spouting through my air tube was increasing, and a shallow puddle was forming about my neck in the bottom of the helmet. "You have a bailout cylinder that is going to give you oxygen. Do you remember where the valve is?" My ears popped as the air pressure within the helmet changed and I staggered forward, barely able to hear her. My eyes burned with a terrible strain.

"What's happening? Alice!" I groaned as the rapidly changing pressure in the helmet began to squeeze my head. The pain was suffocating, disorienting, like I was about to be sucked up into the torn airline.

"Damn it, Joe! Turn the valve now!" A trickle of hot blood

poured from my nose and blood vessels in my eyes ruptured with a dizzying twinge of burning pain as my gloved hands found the bailout and engaged it with a desperate wrenching motion. The horrible squeezing pressure around my head was alleviated in moments as a flood of breathable air filled my helmet. I collapsed and struggled through bleary, pink vision to be able to see straight. Blood was trickling down my chin from my nose, dark droplets pluming red swirls in the water leaking into the helmet, rising steadily. I groaned on my knees and clutched my heart, helmet down on the ocean floor as the weak organ's chambers drummed and throttled in a paroxysm threatening cardiac arrest. The pop of pressure change in my ears was a deafening stab. My breaths came ragged and heaving as I gulped the air greedily. A long moment passed as I came back to myself once again, hands grasping the sands of the ocean floor as I tottered unsteadily to my feet. The seawater in my helmet sloshed and burned in my puffy, bleary eyes as I got up.

"Joe? Joe, do you copy?" Alice's voice was faint and petrified on the radio. It was the voice of someone calling out tentatively to a loved one they've found dead in their living room.

"So that was the squeeze?" I asked between panting breaths.

"Oh, thank God," she sighed with relief. "Joe, you're alright? What happened?"

"I got... I got to the bailout in time, I think." I blinked painfully, stepping forward on dizzy feet. "It felt like my head was going to explode."

"You were closer to that than you probably want to know," she answered with her usual frankness, but it was lightened with a grateful smile, audible in the depths. "What are you experiencing right now?"

"I can breathe again, and the pressure was relieved." The bloody water touched my chin and licked against the lobes of my ears. "The helmet is still filling with water."

"Can you see the shotline?" I looked out from my place at the bottom just outside the shipwreck, straining with pained vision to see through the waving strands of the kelp forest.

"It isn't far." It should have been through the stand of kelp. Privately, I worried I was too disoriented to find it.

"You need to get there and come topside, now." I nodded, too dazed to realize this gesture wouldn't get through the radio and staggered forward into the kelp forest.

The sickly green fronds brushed against my suit with slimy fingers, grasping more tangibly and aggressively than before. Heavy footsteps churning the sand, I brushed them aside with my arms and fought forward. Up in the murky distance, I could see the belly of the *Seal Sister*, and several others that had joined it. The line stood taut at a short distance from the barnacle-spotted hull, and I tried to keep breathing the emergency air supply as I reeled like a drunk in my sloshing helmet. The water had a rank iron quality from my free-flowing blood, and it was pungent in the close helmet. Dimly, I told Alice I felt nauseous, and she pushed me to keep walking. She told me if I threw up in my helmet, I would likely asphyxiate. Whatever fog descended over me in those stifling, squeezing, blindingly painful moments was banished by that harsh reality. I rallied all my faculties, focusing everything I had into walking in a straight line, keeping one foot in front of the other.

But the kelp stand was longer and thicker than it had been

before, and in that weird and uncanny forest, I began to feel I wasn't alone. My eyes were still struggling to function properly through their burning, swollen haze. But there were shapes drifting among the stalks of kelp and seaweed. Human shapes, walking along the ocean floor. I saw little children in dark home-made clothes, horrible burns crackling and raw upon their faces as they walked hand in hand at the bottom of the sea. Distant and indistinct, pale arms and ghoulish faces wriggled with pale flashes, like the underbellies of fish in the murk. These horrible, twisted forms staggered and lurched among the thick fronds at the edge of my view, and as I forced myself to see them and admit they were real, I saw they wore the garb of sailors. It was hard to tell how many there were. They were there one moment and gone the next, spread out over miles of drifting kelp, seen mostly in the distance or the periphery of my damaged sight. I had seen horrible specters now enough times not to repress or rationalize them, or even to give myself over to terror. But these damned shapes of lost souls had a master.

She, too, was walking among the cold fronds. I shuddered and turned to walk in another direction at the first glimpse of her, drifting aimlessly among the tall weeds. Her horrible visage was turned away, and she moved slowly along the ocean floor. The dress with its clinging starfish and scuttling crabs billowed and swayed with her steps, and the lank locks of dark hair coiled with an uncanny life under the water like the terrible writhing mass of Medusa's serpent locks. I shoved the kelp aside and ignored a dead-fish-eyed, shambling corpse that reeled drunkenly close and clicked its jaws in a terrible, mocking way. The thing made a grab for me I was somehow fleet enough to avoid, and it fell over on its face, struggling to get up. I kept moving away from the Drowned Woman, straining my aching eyes overhead to seek the salvation of the shotline.

But when I cleared a thick curtain of the horrible alien plants, she was standing fifteen feet directly ahead of me, back turned. She stood statuesque and inert as the dress and hair lifted in a lazy dance about her thin frame. I resisted the fascination to watch her as she stood apparently unaware of me, having crossed an impossible distance to check my path in a catatonic, disturbing trance. I turned again and walked to my right, feeling bewildered and turned about as I had in the surface-world forest of Cape Contrition. As I struggled to remain calm and keep my steps in the right direction, the dull trickle of water was continuing to swell about my ears and jawline. I had almost forgotten it amongst everything else, until it rose to my nostrils and forced me to lift my head with a sputtering cough. Alice tried to coach me through the radio, but the static whined and crackled, overpowering her voice as it became smaller and smaller. Determined, I pushed forward in the direction of the distant hanging hull of *Seal Sister*, but the dull static crackled with another voice that made my heart sink.

"Come find me, Joe. Come find me, Joe." It crept into my ear again, again, again, like a broken record in another room.

"I'm cold," it said as I murmured 'no, no, no, stop it' under my breath, holding my chin up as the blood-tinged water tried to force its way into my mouth. *"Hold me, baby. Don't leave me here alone."* The voices wouldn't stop, spilling in over the whining comm-channel in an inundation, whispering over one another. An impossible number of voices, none from Alice Cole or anyone on the radio on the surface. Voices

of all the Ushers I recognized, but how, I couldn't explain; voices of my wife and daughter, my parents, Rupert Wycliffe, Orson Welles, Larry Filbert; Crabtree, Perry, Horse, from my platoon in the old days. And the groaning trumpet of a wounded elephant. The Woman was walking among the kelp. I struggled to look away as my mind imagined her as Jean, smiling mischievously among the waving sunflowers of a world that knew light. The kelp was grasping at the hard canvas and copper armor of my suit, with pale horrid hands and the ocean's roar of all those voices. Alice Cole's voice broke through the uncanny noise over the channel, and her shout rang within my helmet, calling me back to myself.

"Don't look at her, Joe! Don't look at her!"

I ran forward through the kelp field, head craned into the top of my helmet as I desperately gasped for air amidst the rising well of leaking water, struggling to see ahead of me. At one point, my hands collided with a cold body and shoved it hard, bowling the thing over and trampling it down.

I moaned with joy as my hands closed on the line. The feeling of clawing hands and biting teeth on the hard surface of my diving dress propelled me upward as I cranked the valve to restore some of my lost buoyancy and clawed up the line. The push of my replenished buoyancy bore me up as I climbed in a frenzy, choking on water, lungs threatening to burst before I reached the surface. A writhing mass of pale limbs and grasping hands was forming about the base of the shotline, a dozen hands grasping at my feet and legs as I climbed. Blindly and desperately, I thrashed with my legs, kicking and stomping until I felt the grasp give way enough to pull myself up out of its reach. The surface seemed so far overhead. I would never make it. I would drown in the water of my own blood and be pulled back down by the cold hands of a hundred lost sailors, to dance with the damned in the garden of the deep.

But the weak sunlight glinted through the surface overhead as I put one hand over the other on the line, and I was holding my breath in an almost completely filled helmet when I burst up through the ceiling into the foam-flecked, rolling waves and rocking boats on the surface. Blind and desperate, I let go of the line and reached out for the rope ladder of *Seal Sister.* I coughed and sputtered on the pink water in my helmet when I could no longer hold my breath. There was a dull splash in the water next to me, and strong hands bore me up, pushing me forward into the shadow of the hull. A long boathook was there, and I grasped it like a desperate castaway. John and Garrett hauled me into the boat, and when they saw how full of water my helmet was, they frantically unlocked its mechanisms about my neck dam and lifted it from me with a gushing gout. I moaned and shuddered as I collapsed onto the deck, gulping the briny air with ragged, wheezing strains like broken violin strings. The two men looked at my face with horror, and I tried not to think about why as I gasped,

"Help me."

"Get him inside, now!" Alice commanded as the two men hastily stripped me out of my standard diving dress, bore up my sweat-soaked body, and carried me into the wheelhouse. I felt a rush of nausea and doubled over to retch on the deck before losing consciousness.

I don't know how long I slept, but I felt as if I'd once again slipped deep under the surface into that cool green envelope where Jean waited. The voices and grasping hands of the dead under the water couldn't reach me in here, but they were all I could think about. After a little while, John Hicks went and retrieved me. The Siuslaw averted his eyes when they came to my face, murmuring he hoped I felt better than I looked. When I asked why no one could look at me, John handed me a small pocket mirror. The whites of my eyes had gone a horrific shade of blood red. My mouth and sandpapery chin were streaked with the drying jelly of thick blood. Beyond that, well, I looked as if I had seen a ghost.

By the time I regained consciousness, other boats arrived on the scene and cranes were being employed to raise the wreckage from the water. I watched the huge machines and rolling cables for a few moments until the magnificent, broken yacht broke the surface and streamed frothy water down its contours and edges. The others were standing near the stern. A nearby tarp rippled slightly over its bundle in the wind, and I saw still feet beneath. It was the bodies of the three young adventure-seekers we'd recovered. The salvage operation continued until sunset, and I huddled with Otis under a blanket in the wheelhouse as we turned back to Delilah. I was alone with Alice in the bridge, and she glanced over at me from the wheel before venturing a question over her shoulder. She spoke with a feigned emotional disconnect, but her gruffness poorly hid her concern.

"What else did you see down there, son?"

"The dead."

"Those boys? That must have been hard for you."

"Not just those boys. So many bodies."

"Other divers went to secure the salvage. The ones you found are the only ones they saw."

"The ones I saw will never be found," I replied. "They live with her at the bottom of the sea."

She started to ask a question, but it fizzled out with a drag of her cigarette. Was she on the point of asking if I had seen her husband down there?

"With whom?" Her tone belied the question, for it held no uncertainty.

"You know who." I called her bluff. *"Don't look at her!"* she'd said. My dazed and haunted thoughts were going over a dozen conversations. I didn't know exactly what she knew, but Alice Cole knew more about the horrors I was experiencing than she let on. She knew the rules too well to give an impression of ignorance: not only the rules of a dangerous ocean, but of sirens, lost souls, and unexplained deaths that belonged in wives' tales. None of what was happening registered surprise in her eyes the way it should have. The malevolent power manifesting itself to the people of Delilah for the first time was one she was introduced to long before they. I recognized it as I recognized other men who had been at war without the need for words. We were two of a kind in this, both knowing more than the others, neither ready to speak about it. But words were unnecessary. We had marked one another.

The searchlight panned over the black waters and impenetrable darkness as we entered the bay, and the soft yellow lights of Delilah reached out to greet us. Far to the north, as far as I could see, the blazing automated beacon of Usher's Fall Light resumed its watch. As we drifted over the calming ocean toward town, John Hicks lifted his voice in a wailing traditional dirge of his people. He was at the stern, standing lone vigil over the bodies no one else would go near. The song was raw, primal, and grieved in an upsetting way no song of the English language could approach. It was the saddest sound I ever heard.

Though it was after dark, many people were gathered at the harbor to learn what the search party had found. Rumor already floated back to town from boats that docked ahead of us. The bodies were received with solemn ceremony by the police and overworked coroner as the townsfolk looked on with grim foreboding. Otis and I stood with the others on deck as the bodies were taken, and we listened to the police chief say a few words to the gathered assembly before going to notify the out-of-state parents by phone. When the thing was done and the crowd was beginning to disperse, I said goodnight to the crew and trudged the dock, nursing a pounding headache. The blood and vomit had been wiped away from my nose, mouth, and chin by a wet rag, but my eyes were still disturbingly red, so I cut a frightening image walking along in the dark with my shaggy black dog. My mind was so full of the disturbing events of the day, I didn't notice as Gwen stepped out of the dispersing crowd in the town square and came up to me near my parked truck.

"Hey, Stranger." she gave me a jolt.

"Hi." I turned to face her and watched as she recoiled at the horrible sight of my blood-red eyes.

"Oh my God, what happened to you?" She pushed down her initial disgust and stepped closer.

"Rough day. I think I almost died. I need to... I need to go get some sleep. I'm a fucking mess."

"Can you even drive?" She stepped between me and the door of my truck as Otis licked her hand warmly.

"I don't know."

"Talk to me, Joe. What's going on with you?"

"I went out to find those kids today. I... needed to do

something to help. Well, I found them, alright." My story came tumbling out, and she listened through to the end.

"Your airline was... Joe, the Drowned Woman has made you do things before. Did you... Did you cut your own cord?" I could tell by the way she spoke; she was trying to believe. Maybe she still wasn't convinced it was all real, but she was interacting with my delusions on my own level.

"No."

"But it wasn't cut by accident?"

"No." I flicked open my lighter and lit a smoke, but after a few puffs I started wheezing and my eyes burned. I had to stub it out. She turned away from me so she wouldn't have to look at my bloody eyes.

"What the hell is happening here?" I didn't have an answer. "Do you want to come over tonight? I can't think about you in that ratty motel."

"Are you sure?" We hadn't exactly ironed out what sort of relationship we were going to have since my 'death.'

"No. But I don't think any of us should be alone right now. Least of all, you."

"I don't know if it's a smart decision: us being together right now."

"Damn it, Joe, you can't shield me from this. This is my town. It's happening to me whether you want it to or not. Let me help you. We can figure out the rest later."

"Okay. Let's go home." There was a strange twinge in my voice as I said this; the painful reminder I could never go home again. But in my pain was also something new, something that felt right.

Chapter Twenty-Seven: Kazuo Iwamoto

February 11th, 1963

Within minutes of my return to Gwen's place, I drifted into a deep and dreamless sleep. It was almost twelve hours before I awakened the next morning to find she had gone to her bookstore and left French toast on the counter for me. After eating the rich pastry and washing it down with two cups of black coffee, I walked back to the town square where my truck was parked and drove to the Sandcastle to settle up with them and vacate my room. The woman at the front desk gasped when she looked at me, as if I were a dead man. My ghastly appearance softened over the next few days as the swelling in my face went down and the white and blue returned to my bloodied eyes. On the evening of the 8th, Gwen and I sat up late into the night, talking about what happened with *Seal Sister*, the diving suit, and *Lucky Hour* the day before. There was still an awkwardness between us. The renewed cohabitation came back before trust, before intimacy, and before we were both completely of one mind about the nature of what I was experiencing. Her gentle, humoring disbelief as she tried to help me process the terror was palpable and distasteful to me. But to her credit, she was trying her hardest to believe something unbelievable.

Nerves and body rattled, I spent the following several days at rest with Otis and Gwen's cat Lennie, alone in the small one-story house on the hill. My hours were divided between sleep, writing the book again, and nursing terrible headaches. During those long hours while Gwen was away at work, I thought about Alice Cole: the way she had sensed what I was seeing. The terror in her voice as she shouted over the radio, *"Don't look at her, Joe!"* Her confidence in navigating an ocean she spoke of with the grim reverence owed to a capricious pagan deity. Her husband, the shipwright lost at sea, his splendid yacht left unfinished in the workshop. And as the sun set on Monday, February 11th, I picked up Gwen from her shop and told her we needed to go to the library.

The squat brick building was, as ever, empty save for Herman Mast and Hana Iwamoto. Hana was reading Fitzgerald at the front desk and looked up with surprise as I walked in with Gwen at my side and Otis sauntering behind.

"We're closing in an hour," she said.

"Go ahead. But I need to do some more research here. Hello, by the way."

"Hi. I don't think we've met," she said, turning to Gwen and holding out a hand. Gwen shook it and introduced herself.

"So... How do you two know each other?" Hana asked.

"She's uh," I paused, trying to find the words. A friend? A lover? An ex-lover?

"Can you keep a secret?" Gwen asked, eyes darting side to side in a show of vigilance as she leaned over the counter and confided in the young girl with a conspiratorial whisper. "We're hunting a monster together. Partners in the chase."

Hana's eyes widened indignantly.

"What the fuck, Crowley?"

"Hey, language."

"What the fuck, -Mr. Crowley? You tell me to butt out, there's nothing to find; but there was a *ghost* all along, like I was telling you! Then you and she became *partners*?" There was a complex flavor of jealousy in that last word.

"Quiet in the library," Herman Mast said over his shoulder as he wheeled a cart of books between us with a slouching gait. I continued at a whisper.

"*Eesh*, look, kid, it isn't that simple. Last time we talked about this stuff, I didn't think there *was* anything, okay? Things have gotten ugly since then. Dangerous. I didn't want to expose you to that."

"Is that why you were in the hospital?" she asked. Gwen listened on with smirking surprise that this lanky kid was among my few acquaintances in town and was in on my quest -or delusion.

"Yes. And that's why I didn't tell you, okay?"

"And as you were getting yourself killed and the whole town was going crazy, you didn't think, *'gee, if only I knew a ghost detective who could help?'*"

Gwen came to my rescue.

"A ghost detective does sound like the sort of thing you need, Joe. She has a point," she confided to me, loud enough for Hana to hear.

"Thank you!" Hana elicited another hiss for silence from Herman, who was putting books away nearby. I looked between the two and had no choice.

"Alright, fine, you're in. On one condition. You don't go to Cape Contrition, ever. And if I tell you to close your eyes, I tell you to run, you do it. No exceptions. Can you do that?"

"Yes." She took the duties of her conditional admission seriously.

"Alright, let's get started. Give me everything you have on local shipwrecks. Mysterious deaths and disappearances especially. See if you can find anything on the disappearance of Caleb Cole and his boat. I don't know what year, but probably in the last ten."

"Shipwrecks," Herman muttered to himself while filing away books. His scalp pulsed beneath its long, thin hair as his brain worked. "September 3rd, 1881: *Twenty–Nine Souls Perish at Siren's Head.* April 8th, 1921. *Ghost Ship Drifts Unmanned Past Delilah, Crew Slain.*"

"You heard that?" I asked, turning to Hana. She nodded.

"Go with him. See what he's talking about." She turned to the work with gusto, taking the aging librarian by the hand and helping him up the narrow staircase. Gwen made herself at home, putting on a pot of coffee while we waited. When seven o'clock came, I took the liberty of locking doors and flipping the hanging sign to 'CLOSED.' Not long after, Hana and Herman came down the stairs with a sheaf of papers in hand. These were spread out on the table: a collection of faded and yellowing *Delilah Callers* dating back a century.

Handling each paper carefully, I scanned the contents of article after article. Many were of fishing vessels wrecked on the shoals and jutting stones surrounding Delilah. Some with no casualties, some with people swept overboard, some where people and their boats simply disappeared. I had lived on the Oregon Coast long enough to discern there was nothing suspicious about most of these articles. These shores were not far removed from the stretch of Pacific coastline from Tillamook Bay to Vancouver Island known ominously as "The Graveyard of the Pacific." Shipwrecks didn't have the uncanny frequency here they had to our north, but shipwrecks and drownings were a fact of life here. All told, the sheaf of papers Hana and Herman assembled contained ninety-six articles reporting shipwrecks.

Though most of these wrecks were no more obviously diabolical than the normal tragedies of this chilly coast, some were truly unsettling. I paused for a moment over one from October 12th, 1955: *Beloved Shipwright Lost at Sea.* Scanning the article, I saw it was indeed the fate of Caleb Cole, Alice's husband. Underneath the headline was a grainy black and white photograph of a round-faced, affable old man with a plain and pleasant smile. He had been out on the ocean alone one clear afternoon when the skies suddenly turned, and the winds churned the ocean to a turbulent froth. Neither he nor his sailboat *Rosemary* were ever found. Alice was hardly mentioned in the article. Despite the treacherous turn of the seas, the article lauded Caleb Cole as a sailor who had been confidently navigating the local waters for fifty years: a hometown mariner without peer. The Pacific had turned, but Cole braved worse mood swings of hers than this. Perhaps, the article surmised, his luck had simply run out. Perhaps, indeed. One could practically hear the journalist shrug at his typewriter.

There were far less ambiguous accounts. Between the burning of Siren's Head Light in 1919 and the construction of the new, automated Usher's Fall Light in 1931, there were thirteen shipwrecks on Cape Contrition. Some of these read as typical accounts. Weather turned nasty, fog concealed a dagger of stone that punched a hole in the hull, a rogue wave washed three men overboard and they were lost. But the survivors of some of these wrecks spoke of navigation equipment going haywire, of being turned in blind fog to be dashed upon the battlements of Cape Contrition as it leered out of nowhere like a living beast. One survivor in 1929 swore he saw a dark woman walking on the water. 'Like Jesus,' he'd said, but with fear and not holy comfort. Some of the shipwrecks had no survivors at all. I hesitate to make any claims of which of these accidents could be linked to the malevolent power of the Drowned Woman and which were simply the ugly realities of that other mighty and capricious mistress: The Pacific Ocean. It would also be impossible for me to take these decades-old articles after the fact and discern truth from tall tales among the accounts of mariners: a people notorious in equal parts for their superstition and their exaggerations. But I did recognize elements of numerous accounts that rang true to my strange experiences of Cape Contrition. Beyond that, there were *a lot* of shipwrecks occurring on this small five mile stretch of coast.

The most haunting were the ones Herman Mast first mentioned in his strange way. On April 8th of 1921, a commercial fishing trawler named the *Multnomah Princess* drifted unmanned and ominous past the sheltering arms of Delilah's jetty, missing the entrance to the crowded marina, and listing closer to the shore as it ploughed steadily southward. Locals hailed the vessel unsuccessfully. As it became clear the vessel was unmanned and destined to run aground, concerned boatmen sidled along it and boarded.

They found every one of the trawler's eleven-man crew dead, sprawled and twisted in horrible positions over every surface of the deck, fit together like human puzzle pieces. Each of them was killed by a self-inflicted gunshot wound. A single pistol had apparently been passed around by each of them in turn, calmly, one at a time. It was found with each of its rounds spent, clutched in the hand of the captain in the wheelhouse. The article was written sheepishly, sparing much detail, as if typed by someone who felt deeply uncomfortable reporting it. An improbable scenario of mutiny was hopefully suggested at the time of the event, and quickly discarded for the uglier truth. The article admitted the deaths appeared to be an unexplained incident of mass suicide. The paper wrote the piece as if they were reticent to come out and say this, but it was rapidly becoming public knowledge anyway. Too many people had seen the 'ghost ship' cruise out beyond the fingertips of Delilah's reach.

The second article Herman mentioned concerned the fate of the *Osprey*, a clipper ship that perished in 1881. This sleek, fast sailing vessel was discovered on September 2nd of that year. The *Osprey* ran aground on the stony knuckles of Siren's Head and tore its wooden belly open on the rocks. Siren's Head was the popular name of the peninsula before it was renamed Cape Contrition by Henry Usher in 1909. Immobilized, the clipper remained on the promontory for perhaps five days before being discovered by local fishermen. The beaching of the ship on the rocks gutted it, but it had been fortunate not to break apart or sink, and instead hung there immobilized. A frightful accident, but surely not a fatal one. The five-day wait should have found the sailors restless, sunburnt, and dehydrated (if they had lost the fresh water barrels in their hold). But instead, crabbers found the crew of the *Osprey* in a much different state. A grisly old photograph of the wreck was included on the front page, faded and out of focus. Hanging by their necks from the clipper's three masts, like a forest of marionettes dangling from varying lengths of string, were the entire crew of the *Osprey*. Twenty-nine souls.

Gwen and I exchanged dark looks as our gazes broke off from the horrible image of the twenty-nine sailors hanging from their own masts. Two documented instances of mass suicide occurring on maritime vessels near Cape Contrition, in addition to the mass suicide on the *Lucky Hour* several days before. And God only knew how many of the smaller disappearances and wrecks had been the work of that maddening siren. We talked about this at some length while Hana looked on, trying to keep the appearance of bravery as she realized she was on a real monster hunt after all.

"But Joe, there's one thing about all these shipwreck accounts that disturbs me more than anything else," Gwen finally said. "And I can tell by that look in your eye, you're thinking it too. The ghosts you saw on Cape Contrition were primarily of the Usher family. Rosemary Usher, the matriarch, is the one you believe is the Drowned Woman today."

"Yeah." My heart sank as I stared at the newspaper and came to the same dark conclusion Gwen was leading toward.

"If Rosemary Usher died in 1919, who was the Drowned Woman in 1881? And how long has there been a Drowned Woman?"

I shuddered at the thought, trying to remember what Thomas Forester said about these entities being fragmented, neither here nor there. This phantom appeared as Rosemary Usher. It appeared as my wife Jean when it suited her. It wore their faces like masks of human skin, like an immense octopus camouflaging the tentacles invisibly reaching out for its prey. If this being was not *wholly* Rosemary Usher, what was it?

"It's getting late." I swallowed dryly. "Come on, kid. I need to get you home."

"Aw, come on. Now?" Hana asked.

"Yes, now. Get your coat, come on."

A chilly wind was scouring over the house on the hill when we pulled up in the cloudy, starless dark. As the truck sputtered to a stop, I glanced at my watch and saw it was almost 10:00. On the covered porch, an old man was pushing himself back and forth on a wicker rocking chair. The thin blue line of his cigarette smoke trailed into the jangling, discordant wind chime flashing overhead.

"That's just grandpa," Hana said as she hefted her back-pack and got up. "Kon'nichiwa, Ojiisan!" she called as she slammed the truck door.

"Hana-chan, dare kore?" the old man asked in a deep, guttural staccato. I had never heard a conversation carried on in Japanese before, but I gathered he was concerned. '*Who is this?*' I guessed he asked.

"Kore wa Joe Crowley-san.   Orokana furui hakujin." Grandpa laid his head back against the wicker chair and laughed, and I smiled pleasantly, wondering what she'd said. He took a drag from his cigarette before stubbing it out in an ashtray and gesturing to me with his hand.

"Come in, Joe-san. I would speak with you." His voice was deep and clear, with a clean melodic timbre. His face had been bathed in shadow, but as I stepped closer, I saw it was round and kind, with deep laugh-lines about the mouth and crow's feet at the edges of his intelligent eyes. The wrinkles of an old man who laughed and smiled often. His short iron gray hair stuck up in a cowlick. I judged the old man to be in his mid-seventies. We shook hands, and he introduced himself to me as Kazuo Iwamoto. Otis raised a sharp bark behind us, clawing at the glass window on the passenger side of my truck.

"Otis is a good boy. Bring him too," Kazuo said, and I obeyed. The dog and I entered the house behind the two Iwamotos. The place was close and cozy, with smooth wooden floors and cream-colored walls.

"Take off your shoes," Hana called to me with irritation as I walked into the house. "Do you have any idea how disgusting that is?" I meekly obeyed, slipping out of my weather-beaten wingtips and setting them alongside the orderly collection of shoes tucked in the corner of the foyer.

"Quiet, girl." Kazuo spoke in English for my benefit. "Your parents are asleep and have a big day tomorrow. I said I would keep watch for them until you arrived. You enjoy keeping your old Ojiisan up late with your mischief?" Hana crossed her arms and listened impatiently.

"I'm on a case, Oji. Detectives don't have curfews."

"But little children do, and you have overstayed yours. Go on, Hana. To bed."

"But you invited Joe in."

"Not for you." His tone was firm and annoyed, but not unloving. The two had a stare-down for a moment before Hana sighed and walked the corridor to her bedroom near the back of the one-story house.

"A *case*," he chuckled, turning to me as we listened to her bedroom door slam shut. "She is a funny child."

"She was telling the truth, though. She's helping me with some research at the library. I'm sorry for keeping her out so late, Iwamoto-san," I ventured the honorific, having never used it before.

"Oh yes, Hana has told me all about her strange friendship with you, Mr. Crowley. Your mystery and your haunted house, your Drowned Woman. That is why I have stayed up late to speak with you. Come in here." Kazuo gestured with a liver-spotted hand into a darkened study, and he flicked on the light switch as I followed him in. The room had two leather couches, a cluttered roll-top writing desk, and several tall bookshelves lined with tomes in Japanese, English, and what I guessed from the characters to be Traditional Chinese. A record player and cathedral AM/FM radio, both made of wood, sat on small end tables at either side of a television set. There was a fireplace at the opposite side of the study, and on the mantle squatted a green ceramic urn. There were several Japanese art prints hanging on the walls depicting tranquil scenes: a crane fishing in the shallows of a river while a woman bathed behind the screen of nearby reeds, another of a yellow tiger creeping in a forest of bamboo.

"I know Hana's story must have been hard to understand, Mr. Iwamoto, but it's true. There is something evil happening in this town. I can't expect you to believe that, but I want to assure you I have no ill intent with your granddaughter. To tell you the truth, she reminds me of my own kid-"

"-I did not ask to speak with you because I fear your reasons for speaking with Hana are false. I asked to speak with you because I know they are true." I was taken aback by this. I was so accustomed to being seen as a madman; I didn't know how to respond to being immediately believed.

"You what?"

"You are not the only one who knows the ugly secrets of

this place. There are other histories these people are eager to bury. You fought in the War, is that so, Mr. Crowley?"

"Yes," I admitted, unsure of where he was leading.

"European or Pacific Theater?"

"European," I answered with a dry swallow. "I didn't fight your people."

"*My* people?" He raised his eyebrows with sardonic amusement. "Mr. Crowley, I left Sapporo for America when I was ten years old. I never saw Japan again until 1952, the first of only two return visits I have made in my lifetime. No, I grew up in San Francisco. Of course, my parents and I spoke another language at home, and adhered to the customs of another place. Our family friends were mostly other Japanese neighbors, and when I brought an apple-pie-American girl home to dinner as a teenager, I had to coach her through the customs of a strange table, with strange food. Eventually I married a good woman from my own community; one who made my parents proud and didn't wince at raw fish." He chuckled, and I smiled silently, urging him to continue.

"We came here to raise our children, away from the bustle of the big city. A quiet, comfortable American town of hard-working, pleasant people. Our family lived in a comfortable old world at home, and a promising new one outside. But this was the experience of many an American, before me and since. In a way, America belongs to the whole world, does she not? And make no mistake: that was how we saw ourselves, as Americans. Occasionally there would be some clumsy question from a co-worker, a vulgar cartoon in the newspaper, a vile thing someone would say to my boy in class. Some small pinprick to remind us not everyone saw us as we saw ourselves. Some needed to remind us we were less deserving of this place than them. But we never let them shake our faith in what we were building here, for those who would come after us. We were simply Americans. But the news from abroad was growing uglier. Our neighbors, crueler and more suspicious. Those of us with relatives in Asia saw the War coming long before our white neighbors chose to see it. Japanese forces invaded Manchuria in 1931. The Marco Polo Bridge Incident, the Massacre of Nanking, the Battle of Wuhan. We held our breath and kept our children close, feeling a shift in the wind long before Pearl Harbor.

"When the planes struck and the *date which will live in infamy* horrified the nation, everything changed. Our countrymen got a taste of the fear we had been quietly monitoring for a decade, and it drove them mad. Your Franklin Delano Roosevelt took pains to make it clear to us we were not Americans after all. In the spring of 1942, my family was told we were no longer welcome on the West Coast. We were forced into squalid camps. Barbed wire, crowded bunkhouses, rifles at the ready."

I listened with horror. Concentration camps for American citizens on American soil. I felt ashamed, disgusted that the outrages I avenged in another land had been permitted in my own backyard. The journalist in me wished badly for a tape recorder. Without asking, I seized a pad and pen, and jotted notes. Kazuo did not seem to mind.

"There was a camp in the mountains, eleven miles from here, surrounded by forests, desolate and hidden away. That was where my family was sent. We thought in this, at least, we were fortunate. Many had to travel much greater distances in the forced relocation. But our luck betrayed us. The place was small, nowhere near the size of Tule Lake or Manzanar.

Close to a thousand people, all told. But that was twice what the camp could hold. The soldiers told us we would only be there temporarily, until we could be transferred to another more permanent camp. 'Permanent camp' was hardly a comfort, but we bore the squalor and poor rations patiently, convinced at first, we would soon be sent away to a place better equipped for our needs. But we stayed there for three years. The soldiers would not answer us when we asked how much longer it would be. Soon, they stopped speaking to us altogether. Government agents in dark suits came and went from the facilities, conversing with guards in hushed tones. They established a base there and began conducting experiments with infrasound. We prisoners were cut off from any kind of information, of course, but there were rumors among the well-educated and connected of us. We believed they were conducting experiments with some kind of weapon, something involving radio frequencies playing sounds the human ear was not evolved enough to comprehend. These were supposed to create auditory and visual hallucinations, physical discomfort and anxiety, bewilderment, and terrible mood swings.

"As reality began to bend and distort itself, and our pleading went on unanswered, it became clear to us no one was going to come and take us away from this place; perhaps no one else in the internment system even knew we were here. There is no public record of the camp I am telling you of, Mr. Crowley. It is totally absent from all official accounts. After we have spoken, I can give you instructions to locate the ruins, but you will be disappointed by what remains. And you will not be able to corroborate what I am telling you with a shred of documentation or testimony. This is the first time I have spoken of this to anyone."

"From my experience, stories that can't be corroborated are mirages."

"Something you see but isn't there. Interesting choice of words from *you*, ghost hunter." I ignored the jab.

"Why are you choosing to tell me this now?"

"Because you know what it is like to have seen things you cannot prove, and no one else will ever believe. Don't you?" My Adam's apple bobbed in a nervous swallow as I relented.

"We were all plagued by hallucinations, hopelessness, loss of direction, and terrible fits of depression during our time in the camp. Our jailers observed the bedlam in silence. Whether or not the scientists found what they were looking for or were successful in their attempts to weaponize the illusions, I do not know. But they were not the only ones playing their games with us, feeding on our despair."

"What do you mean?" I held down a tremble creeping into my voice.

"There was something else in the camp. A demon was hunting us. She appeared as a dark woman with long wet hair, an expectant mother. This is beginning to sound familiar to you?" I gave a terse nod, urging him on.

"It is possible these infrasonic experiments were designed to control and harness her power or recreate it artificially. Imagine the power to harness raw emotion and direct it to make your enemies shoot themselves in the trenches, fling themselves from the battlements of the fort you are besieging. Then again, perhaps these experiments inadvertently attracted her to the camp like a moth to a lantern. Or a shark to blood."

"Did the guards see her? Did they know about her?"

"We tried to tell them, but they did not listen. In our culture, the closest word we had for a creature like her was Yūrei." He reached into a cleft between his desk and the wall and pulled out a secreted parchment. This he unrolled and showed to me, and it made my skin crawl. The image was a Japanese print of a pale woman in flowing white robes on a foggy night. Her hair was long, lank, and inky black. Her translucent hands hung limp from their wrists, and the expression on her face was agony.

"A troubled soul, taken from this world violently and denied its last rites. But when the suicides began, we learned Yūrei was not a strong enough word for the being who stalked our nights. Men, women, and children perished by their own hands, held by another will. We found them along the fences, or in their beds. Our guards did nothing but clear out the bodies. *'Isn't that what you Japanese do when you have been dishonored?'* one of them said when I tried to convince him what was happening. Their small minds had been fed on dramatic stories of seppuku. As if these deaths were Bushido." He spat the word, disgusted. "In three years, one hundred and twelve of us perished. My own sister was one of these. We cursed the creature who stood with her back to us at the edge of our sight, tormenting us and vanishing as if she had never been. When our people kept dying in the camp and we realized our dark woman was more than a ghost, we gave her a new name. Kuroi-Oshidashi: The Black Wave. That is how it feels to look upon her, yes? Like nothing in this world will ever be good or clean again."

"The Black Wave." I almost heared the ocean's roar in my ears as I said the words. "Yes, that's what I felt."

"Then you will not be surprised by what this old man must

say next. I forbid you to have anything more to do with my granddaughter. You are a kind man, and you humor her curiosity toward the darkness. But curiosity has given dead children back to their families more than once in this town. You are a grown man. Surely, you have your own reasons to look into the eyes of the Kuroi-Oshidashi. Perhaps you think you can stop her. That is your affair. But my Hana is only a child. Children believe the monsters will never catch them. We adults have to know better." I bowed my head, ashamed I hadn't taken a firmer hand in preventing the girl from assisting Gwen and me in our quest.

"Yes, Sir," I said. "I won't let Hana near the Kuroi,-" I fumbled over the words and reverted sheepishly back to English, "the Black Wave."

"Good," old Kazuo said, sitting back in his chair with weary approval. "Good."

Chapter Twenty-Eight: The Tub

February 14th, 1963

I waited in indecision for three days before making my mind up to go and check out Kazuo's story of a secret camp in the hills near Cape Contrition. I had avoided going anywhere near Usher's Fall since my suicide attempt, but this was something I couldn't pass over. Before I'd left the Iwamoto house, Kazuo handed me a local map, with an X in pen marking a point in the wooded foothills of the Pacific Coastal Range, two miles from the nearest access road. Otis, Gwen, and I went up the highway out of town, along the hilly heaths with their stunted lodgepole pines and hardy bushes, past the marshy wetlands of yellow grass and glimmering inlets, and away from the ocean into the foothills of the stolid mountains. The dense cover of trees shut out the light as we passed into the tunnel of their coniferous branches. The woods were dry and crackling with the freak drought, the smells of dirt and sap earthy and rich in the unseasonably warm air. I kept one eye on the map crinkled across my steering wheel as I jolted and rumbled onto the dirt access road snaking off further into the trackless woods with their cliffs that made Cape Contrition inaccessible by land in the days when Rosemary Usher and her children were imprisoned there. This narrow, uneven dirt road ran for two miles. The trees crowded in close on both sides. Sometimes the wall of trunks to my left dropped out entirely into sheer cliffs. As I engaged the clutch, shifted gears, and urged my vehicle along, I thought the track seemed more a goat path than road. "RESTRICTED AREA. NO ACCESS BEYOND THIS POINT. VIOLATORS WILL BE PROSECUTED!" a sign at the roadside read. Not far beyond, the road reached a puzzling dead end. I eased to a stop in the shade of some low branches as far off the road as I could manage. Satisfying ourselves the truck was concealed, Gwen and I got out with Otis and walked into the trees. Kazuo's map indicated our destination was ahead. We walked two miles in the stifling heat, following the ghost of a footpath nature had reclaimed.

In the end, we came upon a tall chain-link fence in the middle of the forest. More signs warned to keep out, and I stepped to the edge of the metal barrier. Coils of barbed wire bristled at the top like a crown of thorns. As I lifted a hand to touch it, Gwen shot out an arm to pull me back, and I yanked Otis' leash as well. You could hear the dull hum of electricity vibrating through the fence, though none of the signs gave warning.

"Nothing to see here, folks," I murmured, "just an electrified fence in the middle of nowhere, enclosing nothing at all. Government." We trekked cautiously along the perimeter of the high barbed wire fence, but if anyone was out there, no one spotted us. Sure enough, among the thick trunks of trees in the distance, we saw a lean-to collection of dilapidated buildings: long and low-ceilinged bunkhouses, a few decrepit guard towers. The small ghost town sat forlorn. A large, ruined satellite dish sat atop a squat concrete bunker coated in ivy. The place looked thoroughly abandoned, and yet... The electric current was humming close, and what was that satellite? We gave it up and turned back, unsure what we had seen. Kazuo's story of the hidden camp seemed confirmed. But whether there were any people still operating or watching the place was unclear.

"Bet you can't say you've ever been taken to an abandoned concentration camp before," I said as we pulled up the drive to her house that evening.

"I've had worse Valentine's Days."

"Let me make it up to you. How about Melville's tonight?"

"A bar? Are you sure that's a good idea?"

"I can handle it. Besides, where else are we going to eat this late?" Gwen looked at her dusty boots and sap-stained flannel shirt with a smile.

"Let me change out of my Meriwether Lewis get-up first. Then I'm all yours, lighthouse keeper."

"Deal." I walked Otis in the yard while she disappeared into the house.

Gwen poured some dry food for Lennie and rubbed him affectionately behind the ears before ducking into her bedroom for a dress and closing herself in the bathroom. As she shucked off the clay-spattered boots and peeled out of her sweaty socks, the sound of a drip from the faucet drew her attention to the claw-footed tub, screened off by a yellow curtain. The drip sounded again, unmistakably plunking into a bath someone had drawn and left. Perplexed, Gwen turned and pulled the curtain aside, recoiling with horror at what she saw. Another drop fell from the faucet, rippling across the glassy surface of a full bath. A bloated, pale corpse in a heavy black dress was lying fully submerged beneath the water.

Gwen shuddered as her knees grew weak, immediately understanding what manner of thing had come into her house. She tried to turn away, but some powerful magnetism held her entranced. She wanted to cry out, but no sound came as her body levitated rigidly into the air. Thrashing and shuddering in vain, Gwen felt herself float upward and hang horizontally in mid-air, suspended over the tub. Her red curls fell into the water as her face hung inches from the still death-mask of the Drowned Woman, who lay with eyes and lips squeezed shut. Black, all-consuming hopelessness overcame the body-racking fear as she waited, unable to move or close her eyes. There were strands of seaweed in its hair, and a crab needled over its distended belly.

Gwen's stomach lurched as her glasses gave way. With horror, she watched them tumble from their perch and splash into the water, striking the Drowned Woman's forehead before drifting slowly to the bottom. For a moment, nothing happened, and Gwen's blurred vision remained unbroken from the dead face, waiting for what would come next. The corpse's clouded eyes shot open, and her rotting mouth twisted in a horrid, enraged scream, muted under the surface.

I opened the door of the house slowly and urged Otis inside. The hackles on his back stood rigid as he growled low, stalking into the entryway.

"Gwen? You ready to go?" I called out into the silent living room, nervous that Otis was on edge. As I stepped cautiously behind him, there was a crash of breaking glass down the hall. I hurried toward the sound and saw the bathroom door was closed. Flickering light spilled from the bottom crack. Light and... Oh, no. Fuck. Fuck!

The frame buckled around the lock as I shouldered open the thin door, bursting into the blood-soaked bathroom. The electric lights whined and flickered off and on as Gwen slipped in her own blood, lying crumpled on the tile floor. A long dagger of silvery glass from the shattered mirror was clutched in one hand, and she had slashed open her wrists. Two shards of glass stood out from her forehead where she'd butted her head into the mirror, and her eyes looked up at me sleepily, half-blinded by the blood.

"Joe... What did I do, Joe?"

"Oh, Jesus, Gwen! Oh, fuck. Look at me, okay? Don't close your eyes." Frantic, I yanked a hanging towel from a bar on the wall and wrapped it tight around her wrist. I screamed for help as I slipped in her blood and crouched over her, holding her opened arms together with towels soaking through. "Hold these here, okay? Just like that. You can do it. I'm going to the phone, okay?" She nodded faintly, and I ran down the hall. I stained the old telephone with blood as I picked up the receiver and shrieked at the operator for an ambulance.

Within minutes, flashes of colored light spilled into the house as first responders screeched up the driveway. The rest was a blur, but soon they were rushing her into the ambulance, and I was following behind in my truck while the paramedics struggled to keep her alive. The hospital was like a bad dream as Dr. Cullen and his team of nurses operated in another room, and police interrogated me in the lobby with questions I could barely register. *Was she behaving normally? Were there any signs of this? Did she express to you she was feeling depressed, or contemplating suicide? Where were you when this happened?* As the night wore on, the questions faded, and I was left alone as hospital staff muttered darkly to one another. Will Blake arrived at ten o'clock as we learned the blood transfusion was successful, and Gwen stabilized. He walked in without looking my way and went straight to Gwen's room. When he came back out and walked toward me, his entire broad frame quaked with anger. I was staring at the floor when his boots came into my low gaze and looked up dully with tired eyes.

"She's okay?" I asked.

"Yeah." I knew from the tone I was in trouble.

"Can I see her?"

"No." We waited a moment of tense stand-off before he spoke again.

"She didn't ram her own forehead into that mirror, Joe. There was glass in her brow, in her scalp. She couldn't have done that to herself."

"Nobody is doing this to themselves. I've told you that." As he drew his revolver, I asked, "What are you going to do with that?"

"I let you stay here, you son of a bitch. Accidents just follow you, though, don't they? Every time one of my people turns up dead, you aren't far behind. I thought you were a vulture, or a victim... I should have seen it. I should have-"

"Will. Slow down a minute. This isn't me. This isn't-"

I heard the jangle of cuffs and knew I couldn't explain anymore. My heart jumped into my throat as I jolted from my seat, throwing a shoulder into his gut, and driving the wind out of him before tearing out through the hospital doors. Instinct and blind terror of arrest spurred me into a desperate run as I heard the police chief huff and bellow out behind me. By the time I cranked the key in the ignition of my truck, my adrenaline-high brain clutched a single, desperate play. Gears chugged and rattled as I shifted, engaged the clutch, and accelerated into a reckless flight from the parking lot. Two blocks behind me on Main Street, blue lights jarringly announced the siren of the Chief's car.

"That's right," I sped through a red light and a green car lurched to a skid with its horn blaring, "Come find me." I angled north and pushed my wheezing truck for all it was worth. The acceleration came painfully slow, but I maintained the high speed I earned on the straight lunge of highway out of town. Will Blake's squad car roared up at my tailgate, sirens and blue lights raging. *Like you'll outrace him in this tin can. Stupid.* With a jarring knock, he nudged my rear bumper hard.

"Pull over, now!" He shouted over the bullhorn. I flipped him off through the back window, and it shattered with a warning shot from his revolver. *And he's got a gun, genius. What do you have?* I gritted my teeth and floored it around a blind curve, careening in a tight hug of the cliffs. Will hung back and matched my reckless pace along the winding cliff face, knowing better than to try and pull alongside me on a road like that. It bought me some time. Black coast darted past as we careened by, and at one point a side mirror snapped off when I inched closer to the shadowed cliff than I thought. I cursed my recklessness as we pulled out of the cliff-hugging run, and I veered off the highway at the exit to Usher's Fall Light. Another warning shot sounded, but it wasn't a sincere effort to hit me. Will angled alongside me, gesticulating, and roaring something muted into the wind. I lurched my truck left in a bluff to hit him, and he skidded to the pebbly shoulder before recovering behind me. I led him through the pitch-dark forest road, over the Siren Creek Bridge, and skidded to a halt in the visitor lot. In a headlong rush, I left my cab's open door and ran into the dark forest. Will Blake skidded to a stop behind me, and his car's blue lights played fantastic shadows on the trees as I ran uphill, arms uplifted to ward off grasping branches. Will Blake shouted behind me, and he gave chase into the trees. *He's going to arrest you for attempted murder. It doesn't matter if you're innocent. By the time you're vindicated, IF you're vindicated, how many people will be dead? You can't tell him. You have to show him!* My mind raced as I ripped through the brush. The house loomed dark and silent ahead of me, illuminated in the panning electric beam of the tower beacon. *Your presence reminded the spirits in the house of Henry. How much more will the shaved grizzly bear shouting and waving his gun behind you?* A third gunshot sounded in the darkness behind me, and I vaulted over the yellow sawhorse and porch steps. With a frantic jangle of keys, I opened the door with its warning sign, cast the caution rope aside, and disappeared into the darkened house. My breaths came in shuddering gasps as I pressed myself into the darkest corner of the mudroom, hid behind the angle of the front door, and waited. I wheezed and clutched my hammering heart, and the rattling rasps of Will's panting sounded at the treeline. The house was still and inert, and I told myself I was about to die foolishly as the policeman's boots shook the porch steps.

"Crowley!" He burst in through the open front door with his gun drawn. "Don't do this, Joe!" Will slipped past me, filling the inner doorway to the darkened house. I strangled my heaving breaths as he checked his corners with the Colt, missing me behind him.

"What did you do to those people, Joe? What did you do!?" As the roar echoed into the deserted rooms, two bright pinpricks of terrible eyes glinted to life, and a terrible shriek chilled my bones as a swirling black mass of shadows lurched out of the wall at the far end of the living room. Will drew to a halt with a shuddering groan, and I angled in the doorway to see him without glimpsing the gorgon he locked eyes with. The air grew cold as the unseen beast glided forward, and I knew she had the police chief in her spell. The last thing I saw before I squeezed my eyes shut was the brawny man raising the Colt in his trembling hand, pressing the muzzle into his temple. He cocked the hammer with his thumb. I hurled myself blindly through the doorway with all my might, tackling Will Blake hard as his bewitched finger reached for the trigger. One hand locked his wrist and wrenched the Colt upward as it barked with a deafening flash. The bullet hit the ceiling as the Chief and I tumbled into the ruined kitchen, and my shoulder hit the doorframe hard as I drove him into the floor. I heard the gun skitter across the hardwood and fought with all my might to keep my grapple over Blake. He spat, thrashed, and seethed as I wrestled him, struggling in vain with all his bison might against my desperate Nelson hold. The Drowned Woman's scream died reverberating off the walls as her specter rushed past where Will Blake had stood and drifted out the front door. The chief thrashed in his mad, suicidal rage as images of his own past pain filled his thoughts. One warrior to another, I recognized the trauma of his battles in Korea rearing up and held him away from the handgun as I rasped, "It isn't your fault. It's not real, and it isn't your fault." He fought me for several more moments before pressing his sweaty forehead into the floor.

"Okay. Okay! Get off, damn you." I released my hold, rolling onto the kitchen floor next to him, taking his gun, and tucking it into my belt. Knowing where the hand towels were, I knotted one into a blindfold and gave another to him.

"Cover your eyes."

"What?"

"Do it!"

He obeyed, and we spent a long minute gasping for breath on the floor with our blindfolds on.

"Is she gone?"

"I don't know. Keep it on."

"Oh my God. Those eyes, Joe. Those terrible cold eyes. What–"

"The Drowned Woman. I tried to tell you. In the end, I had to show you. Had to make you feel it for yourself. That blackness when she had you locked in her eyes is what I have lived with for months out here. It's what's killing those people in town. So, do you believe me now?"

"Yes."

"I didn't hurt Gwen, or anyone else. If you arrest me, people are going to die, and you won't be able to help them. Are you going to help me kill her, or stand in my way?"

"I'm with you. I understand. Sorry I didn't sooner. It was a tall order," he panted.

"Are we about to be swarmed by your men?"

"I didn't call them. Stupid of me. Didn't think I would need back-up for the likes of you. –No offense. Say... How did you know you'd stop me in time?"

"I didn't. Come on, let's get the hell out of here."

Chapter Twenty-Nine: The Coven

February 15th, 1963

The police chief and I kept a vigil throughout the night, alternately dozing, sipping coffee, and talking of Cape Contrition in hushed tones. The nurses who witnessed our explosive confrontation earlier were surprised to see us return together but asked no questions. After sunrise, Dr. Cullen greeted us and let us know Gwen was awake.

"Hey," she said groggily as we stepped into her room. Her wrists were bound in thick bands of linen, and she was on suicide watch, bound securely.

"Hey, sleepyhead. Rough night?" I said with a kind smile, and she looked at her wrists to chuckle in spite of herself. It was only a moment, and when she looked back at me, her eyes welled with tears.

"I was so scared, Joe. So alone. It came over me so fast, and I thought... I finally understood what you were carrying in your soul, and I'd never be able to tell you, because it was killing me. Why would she come for me like that-" Gwen drew up short, marking Will's presence behind me.

"It's okay, darlin'. He knows. He's seen her, too."

"He has? Will... I'm so sorry."

"It's alright. I'm okay, Gwennie. We all made it here."

"So, I guess that makes us the only three people who have seen her and are still alive," I remarked.

"Wait, Will. When you saw her, did you try to-" Gwen started haltingly.

"Yes," he replied, lip quivering under his mustache. "It was a long night for both of us."

"What are we going to do, Joe?" Gwen asked. I looked out the window at the sunlight playing on the vegetation.

"We need to arrange a War Room meeting. Everyone we trust who knows about this. Thomas Forester, Alice Cole... I've hesitated too long to face the Drowned Woman again. People have died because of my cowardice, and I'll have to live with that if I make it out of this. But none of us can destroy her alone, if we can destroy her at all-"

A nurse burst in through the open door and nudged Will's shoulder.

"Chief. Telephone."

"Yeah, in a minute," he snapped.

"Chief! You need to take this."

We exchanged dark glances, and he nodded to her before stepping out into the hall. I held Gwen's hand while we waited for him to come back. He walked in unsteadily, his eyes wide.

"Three teenagers were just found dead on the beach at Siren's Cove."

"Jesus," I muttered, and Gwen squeezed my hand.

"Go, both of you. I'll be okay here. Maybe they'll let me make some calls and bring everyone together."

"Could we have the meeting here so you can be part of it?" She broke into a surprised smile and said yes.

"Great. Shall we say tomorrow evening?" She agreed as

I leaned in and kissed her lips. We held one another for a long moment, her bandaged wrist brushing my ear as she dug fingers into the hair at the back of my neck.

"I love you," I said for the first time, and it gave her pause. "I'm glad you're still here."

"Me too, Joe. And I love you. Now go on. Will's waiting for you." I looked about and noticed he'd stepped into the hall, and blushed.

"Yes, ma'am."

After swinging by Gwen's house to pick up Otis, Will and I took the drive back to Cape Contrition. We smoked and sucked down coffee, trying to stay awake. When we arrived, the parking lot was flashing with the lights of emergency vehicles. The teens were lined up on the beach side by side, in body bags. The other police looked questioningly at their chief when they saw us arrive together, and Will informed them I would be consulting on the case as a private eye.

"Crowley's a Dick? Since when?" asked Officer Hoskins.

"He was born that way. It's a condition," Will said, lighting a smoke as we walked up to the black shrouded bodies.

"Thanks for that," I muttered. Hoskins went down the line, unzipping each bag enough to show the cold face within.

"Rebecca Kelly, Martha Watson, and James Black. All students at William Clark High School."

"They drown?" Will asked.

"No. We found two bottles of sleeping pills in the sand nearby, empty. They took their medicine, then laid down and died together."

"You notify the parents?"

"Not yet," Mitchell reported.

"I guess that's where I'm headed, then. Christ, I'm tired of this."

"You want I should go instead, Chief? You look done in. When's the last time you slept?"

"Okay. Hoskins, you take the Blacks. Mitchell, the Watsons. I'm going to the Kellys. Anything else I should know before I notify them?"

"Oh, I almost forgot. They had these masks with them. The tide pulped them up a little bit, but they seem like some kind of animal masks."

My blood ran cold as something scratched at the back of my brain.

"Let me see them," I ordered. Cody Mitchell dug into his car and pulled out three papier-mâché animal masks: a hare, a fox, and a deer.

"Oh, shit." I remembered the strange vision of the woman in the wood, garbed fairylike in leaves with the antlered head of a deer. I remembered being tackled by the fox-faced boy and grasping in the dark for my gun.

"Something familiar, Crowley?" Will asked.

"Can't place it. But maybe." Otis strained forward to bury his nose in the inside of the deer mask, sniffing long and deep. Will started to ask a colleague something, but Otis snorted in the mask, and began to act strangely. He whined and caught my sleeve in his teeth, pulling me away from the others. Will asked what was wrong, and when I turned to answer, Otis loosed a shrill bark.

"What?" I asked, and he walked away, turning to make certain I was following.

"Looks like he's got hold of a trail. Who's coming with me?" We watched as Otis plodded along the beach, nose quivering along the ground as he got to the dark basalt rocks at the base of Cape Contrition's cliffs. The headland jutted out into the sea, but with the tides low, a stony footpath could be made out edging along the cliffs.

"Do you think they walked along this?" Otis clambered onto the rock ahead of us.

"It's a path more fit for a goat than a person, but... Otis sure seems to think so," I answered.

"And when the tide comes in, it's going to wash away their trail."

"Could do the same to us if we don't hurry." Will evaluated the foaming crash of breakers washing over nearby rock. "Looks like we have about an hour before the waves flood out the trail. Let's hurry. Hoskins, Mitchell, wait for us here. We'll go out together." His subordinates nodded, only too eager not to clamber over rocks pounded by sea.

Careful of our footing, Will and I edged out along the tidal path. Pock-marked battlements of dark stone held back the rhythm of waves only at arm's length. As we climbed on the sunbaked stone ledge farther out along the Cape, we were soon soaked to the skin. The wide brim of Will's cowboy hat hung low and misshapen over his brows as he huffed behind me. Otis sniffed over sand and stone, poring over the trail with flaring nostrils as the clawed pads of his paws gripped the stony path. As we rounded the point of the headland and hung out precariously over the churning froth ten feet below, an ambitious wave grasped at the path and threatened to shake us loose. Otis avoided the striking wave by scampering ahead, but I was pulled back. My heart went into my throat for a terrible moment as I almost fell backward into the cauldron of dull stone knives and roiling saltwater below. Will's mighty arm shot out to grab a fistful of pea coat and scarf, yanking me back to clutch at the cliff face with relief.

As we climbed around Cape Contrition's point, a beautiful cove revealed itself to us on this unmarked, forsaken far side of the headland. We edged carefully along the cliff as a glimmering green wave rippled past the towering monoliths of mossy rock and washed up the beach of black basalt pebbles. A distant tinkling sound like rain could be heard as the sea receded back through the pebbles, only to marshal strength and push forward again. Ranged along the bases of the cliffs were small tidal caves eaten into the stone by millions of years of patient shaping. At the top of the cliff more than a hundred feet over our heads, towering pines and aspens ranged themselves as a screen from view of the house.

"This entire cove must disappear in high tide, along with the footpath," Will said, "Look at these caves!" Otis climbed down from the rock onto the pebble beach, avoiding the foaming push of a wave as he plodded toward the gaping maw of a basalt cave at the foot of the cliff. Will and I rubbed out twisted ankles and scraped hands as we huffed up behind him. Otis had led us this far, but when we stood at the entrance of the dark cavern, he shrank back with a low growl, ears laid back against his neck. I reached into my coat pocket and clicked on the beam of my flashlight, shining it into the abyss. Will produced one of his own, and we advanced slowly as the beams cut back and forth over the slimy rocks. We stepped around dirty pools of uncertain depth as we made our way into the cave, and Otis sat on the pebbled beach with a whimper, refusing to follow us in. The cavern sloped downward in a snaking flow, turning inward toward the heart of Cape Contrition. When the waves washed in, they rippled in a tumbling stream down the middle of our path. At one point, Will's boot slid out from under him, and he tumbled hard down the rough floor of slick stone. I winced as he fell, and carefully picked my way after him, landing on my feet in some shallows where he hissed and wallowed in pain, khaki shirt and pants soaked through, hat floating on the surface of the water. I picked the Stetson up gingerly, shaking it out before setting it on his head.

"I can't carry you back, so you better say you didn't just break an ankle."

"Not yet," he growled, raising a palm for me to catch and haul him up. He was fairly banged up and in a surly mood, but too intrigued by our discovery to complain. Our light beams cut around in a circle as we examined the closed bowl end of the cavern into which we had ungracefully stumbled. The chamber was roughly circular, about thirty feet in diameter. We stood knee-deep in a shallow moat encircling a cold plateau of black stone, rising like a table in the center. As the beam of my flashlight crawled over the walls enclosing us, dread rose in me. Not a table. It's...

"An altar." Will sloshed out of the cold stream and set a hand on the slab. The flashlight illuminated thin, chalk-white pictographs covering the walls, terrible in their stark simplicity, appearing to be ancient in a way that made my head swim. I saw a forlorn castle of stone jutting into the ocean. A dark creature with long black hair and a horrible face crawled from the sea and grasped the rocks with long, clawed fingers. People gathered on the rock to worship her. Sacrificial victims looked on the dark goddess and slew themselves upon her altar. Their blood ran down the runnels of the rock and into the rushing sea.

The ritual was overseen by people who had the appearance of beasts. The sharp lines of their primitive figures were augmented with fanged snouts, antlers, wings, tails, fins, and tentacles. When the sacrifice was complete, the beastly acolytes left the cavernous temple, and it was daily submerged in the tide. There were other people in the pictographs, etched smaller and with softer lines. These more numerous people shrank away from the headland, avoiding it and its dark goddess. Her people and their cult, whatever they were, died out. Stripped of her human cattle, the dark goddess starved, shrieking on the rocks that had once been her castle and were now her prison. For years, she subsisted only on the occasional Indian who was drawn by some tortured inner magnetism to that forlorn spot, to take his own life and feed her diabolical power. The cave painting showed the Drowned Woman tricking a Native girl into serving as some kind of vessel for her, putting her own soul into a seashell and allowing the Drowned Woman to wear her skin and walk on the surface.

This form served her well, but she was still chained to the headland, unable to exert her power far from its confines. The pictographs ended in scenes appearing to show discovery of the headland and its tidal cave by white settlers. A tall man drawn with the likeness of a tree guided his disciples into the cavern, where they rediscovered the Drowned Woman. Rather than make them look upon her and claw out their own hearts, she let herself be worshiped again. The cult of the Drowned Woman re-formed itself. The worshipers donned fearsome animal masks for their dark orgies, black magic, and human sacrifices. And the man like a tree stood exalted at her side, watching over it all. As the coven of the Drowned Woman's witches carried on through the years, they conspired to send more people to the Headland through guile or intimidation. And as each person driven mad by the Drowned Woman's power threw themselves into the sea, her terrible image grew taller on the cave wall, with a stride stretching farther into the surrounding land.

"Oh my God." My light quavered on the towering image of the Drowned Woman, with the man like a tree at her side, and the coven of mask-wearing witches at their feet. I got lost in that glowering visage until a spilling rush of water gushed into the cave from above, filling my ears with its roar.

"Joe, we have to get out of here! The tide is coming back in. Come on."

"Will... How old are these cave paintings?"

"You seriously think I'll know if you don't? Move, now!" The trickling stream from our descent became a waterfall as we clawed our way out of the cavern. Will limped and grunted as he tried to keep up, and soon we burst out into the dizzying glare of sunlight. Otis barked from his place higher on the warm rocks, where he sat watching the tide roll in. Together, the three of us climbed back onto the stony path and edged along the outline of Cape Contrition as mist and spray from incoming waves made the air heavy and wet around us.

We hardly spoke on the drive back into town. The heat was heavy and oppressive, eerie in its unseasonable intensity. Was it February or August? Word crackled in over the police scanner. A wildfire had broken out ten miles inland. Lightning, a rarity in the climate of Western Oregon, struck down in a wrathful lash, setting the dry old growth ablaze. Forest rangers and the fire brigade were responding with a perimeter and were confident they would soon have the blaze contained. Who ever heard of a forest fire in February?

I mulled over the pictographs on the wall. The man like a tree and his bizarre acolytes were dancing in twisted, ghastly movements through my mind. I thought of those dead children on the beach: fourteen, fifteen, and seventeen. What had they gotten themselves into?

We pulled to the Kelly house slowly and an old woman was waiting for us on the porch. Mildred Kelly was the sole guardian of her granddaughters, Rebecca and Tabitha. Her countenance sank as Will stepped up the creaking porch steps, taking off his wilted hat and resting it against his chest as he looked at her with tired eyes.

"Ma'am... I'm sorry-"

"No! No!" Mildred shouted, "Don't you do that to me, young man!" she balled a wrinkled fist and threw it into Will's chest, and he took it, and another, as he continued to climb the porch steps.

"It's Rebecca." She collapsed on the hardwood, screaming in agony.

Teacups clinked quietly in the cluttered living room, as we sat with our cups and saucers on couches too low for us and talked at length with Mildred about what happened. Will led the conversation, gracefully navigating the pertinent and sparing her the unexplainably weird elements. She sat back in a corduroy chair and fanned herself, struggling to breathe and yet still playing hostess in spite of everything. Unsure how to comfort someone so bereft, I got up and mumbled I needed to use the restroom, and she directed me back into the hall. As I disappeared into the corridor and heard Mildred murmur the question "what is *he* doing here?" I passed a cracked door and heard a small voice sobbing. For a moment, I looked ahead to the restroom in indecision, and against my better judgment,

386

nudged open the door that hid the sobbing. A little blonde girl was sitting on the bed in a cluttered, darkened room, weeping into her forearm. She rubbed her eyes and sat up as I entered, looking incapable of surprise.

"What's your name?" she asked.

"I'm Joe. What's yours?"

"Tabby. –Tabitha," she sniffled, jamming a fist into her eye. "Are you here because my sister is dead?"

"Yes. Yes, I am. Do you... know anything about what happened?" My sentence skipped a beat as I glanced about the room. There was a framed painting of Usher's Fall on the bedside table, and the walls were fairly papered with sketches of the lighthouse, people dancing with animal masks on, and heavily shaded drawings of a dark-haired pregnant woman in flowing black garments, with fiery children clutching at her skirts.

"Did you draw these?" Nervousness fluttered on my tongue.

"No, this is Becca's room. I come in here sometimes."

"And Becca... Did she tell you who this woman was?" Tabitha looked at the crude, heavy-handed drawing of the Drowned Woman shyly for a moment.

"The Timber King knows. He's the teacher. Becca told me they were going to see him for the answers."

"Who is the... Oh." I stopped and sat next to her on the bed as it hit me. "Tabitha, I've got to go. I'm... I'm sorry this happened."

"Me too. Hey, Becca said she was going to take me soon, to meet the Timber King. Do you think I'll still get to–"

"No," I cut in, harsher than I meant to. "Tabitha, listen to me very carefully. Don't go near that place. You understand?"

She looked at me with big, frightened eyes, and shook her head yes. "Good. Good girl. You and your grandma need to take care of each other."

"Yes, Mr. Joe," she mumbled, and I stepped out of the room. Words were so small. I forgot myself as my head swam with betrayed anger, and I staggered out into the living room.

"Chief, we need to go, now."

"The hell are you talking about? —Sorry, ma'am. Hold up. Joe?"

"I know who the tree man is," I called over my shoulder as I stormed out onto the front porch. Will winced and made his apologies, squeezing Mildred's shoulder and murmuring he was there for her before following me out the door.

"Nice fucking manners back there, Joe," Will said as he slammed the door to the cab and turned the key, jamming the cruiser into reverse.

"Just take me to Wycliffe Manor as fast as you can." He looked at me with disbelief as he engaged the clutch, switched gears, and accelerated.

The sprawling lawns of Rupert Wycliffe's estate were yellow as Kansas plains as we rolled up the drive. The palatial family home smirked in the flashing blue light of the police car, so small against its façade. Hayato greeted us at the door, and I growled for him to fetch his master. No, we wouldn't be having any refreshments while we wait, thank you. Rupert Wycliffe walked down the stairs with a bemused smile as his hand slid on the polished banister.

"Mr. Crowley! I must say, this is a surprise. And you've brought your delightful dog with you. Oh, Sheriff Blake, how nice to see the two of you finally getting along."

"*Chief* Blake," Will said, squaring up in the entryway.

"Quite. Mr. Crowley, *how is* my book coming along?"

"It's coming. Not sure you'll like how it ends."

"What can I do for you gentlemen? I was about to have Hayato pour me a whiskey and lemonade for this dreadful heat. Shall I have him mix two more? Oh, Joseph, that was quite silly of me. You must forgive that–"

"Enough with the *Gone with the Wind* bit. Rebecca Kelly. Martha Watson. James Black. Mask of a hare, mask of a stag, mask of a fox. Two bottles of sleeping pills. What do you know about that, *Timber King*?"

His perplexed grin was infuriating.

"I'm– quite sure I don't know what you're talking about, Joseph. Are those names supposed to... Oh. Oh, dear. Those names do ring a bell. Has something happened to those dear children?"

"You son of a bitch. Yeah, something happened. They committed suicide this morning during low tide. We followed–"

"Joe. Joe, stop talking," Will growled, pulling my shoulder, and murmuring in my ear. "You're playing your hand. You can't tell him everything we know and have an interrogation with any integrity."

"Oh, dear. Did you two not discuss tactics before you came in? Civilian consultants do have a way of mucking up police work," Wycliffe simpered. "Especially ones with such resentment of authority figures. Mr. Blake, it would be an honor to assist the constabulary of our dear little town. As you know, I have maintained Usher's Fall for its iconic place in the history of our county. Rebecca asked to interview me about Usher's Fall a year ago for a school paper. I had her and her friends over and regaled them with stories. It was a delightful evening! Having no children of my own, it meant a great deal to see youngsters with heads for learning sitting around my fire asking questions. There is not enough of that in this generation, with the *marijuana*, *rock and roll* music, and other such mind-numbing tomfoolery. We have not had a chance to reconnect since, I'm afraid. If their interest continued after the assignment was turned in, or developed into some kind of dangerous game, I don't know. It's a tragic thing. But if they took their own lives, as you say, I'm not sure I understand how I might be suspected of any wrongdoing."

"Can you tell me where you were between the hours of five in the evening last night and five this morning?" Will asked.

"I took dinner at seven o'clock, as is my custom. Retired at nine with a bad bit of heartburn. Tossed and turned all night, I'm afraid. But I never left the house."

"And you have people who can swear to that?"

"Of course! Hayato and May were here, and Clarence, my mechanic and groundskeeper. They will readily attest to my poor night's sleep. Shall I fetch them?" His beady eyes gloated as he smiled, and I knew his henchmen would have their lines memorized perfectly.

"No. Not right now, anyway. I'll be in touch."

"Anything I can do to help, Mr. Blake. Please do not hesitate to call."

"Of course, Mr. Wycliffe." Will doffed his damp hat and turned to take his leave.

"Do mind that blood pressure, Joseph. Rage isn't a good thing for a man of your weak constitution to carry around in his heart. You need all your strength right now. How hard it must be to see these suicides happening all around you, when you failed to do even that to assuage your pain."

"Don't worry about me. I've got all sorts of outlets for my anger in mind." I turned and followed Will out, clicking my tongue for Otis to come along.

Chapter Thirty: Séance

February 16th, 1963

The town was in hysteria. A death toll of sixteen suicides, news of the forest fire creeping forward and spreading to new acreage faster than the fire brigade could contain it. And perhaps worst of all, rumors the last three suicides were teens practicing black magic, worshipping a heathen god with a name tied to several other suicides. I drove through streets where Pentecostals raved and Baptists accused, waving signs warning of the dangers of Satanic influences on the minds of the young. Some turns of the wind were now bringing the faint whiff of wood smoke, and people were at one another's throats. I arrived at the hospital early with sandwiches to split between me, Gwen, and Otis. One by one, the others on our council arrived: first Hana Iwamoto arrived with Herman Mast. I winced, remembering my promise to her grandfather that I wouldn't involve her further. I realized too late I'd forgotten to tell Gwen we were leaving her out of it. Then Thomas Forester came, and lastly, Will Blake.

"Is this everyone?" I asked, glancing about. They filled the small hospital room, but our ragged band of ghost hunters was smaller than I had imagined. I feared we were not equal to the quest.

"Alice Cole didn't let me finish telling her what the meeting was before she hung up the phone. This is everyone," Gwen reported.

"Ladies and gentlemen, you have been asked here this evening because you have come to know the Drowned Woman is real, and she must be undone if we find the power to do so. My investigation of Cape Contrition and residence at Usher's Fall appears to have prompted her excursions into Delilah, where sixteen people have now fallen victim to her. The people outside this room don't understand what is happening, and they will not believe us. There is only one way to save them: for us to return to Usher's Fall and confront the Drowned Woman.

"Here is everything we know about her at this time. Yesterday, Will and I found a tidal cave at the base of the Cape, bearing pictographs and an altar that indicated the Drowned Woman is a far older being than we realized. Her existence on the Headland goes as far back as indigenous history can record, and it appears the cavern we explored was a temple for ritualistic human sacrifice. Research into local history with the help of Herman, Hana, and Gwen also indicates instances of mass suicide years before the slaying of the Usher family. Whatever manner of being she is, she is far more than a ghost. Her power appears bound to the headland, but I have seen her exert herself to appear as far away as Salem. It would seem the more people fall victim to her, the more powerful she becomes, and the more freely she can move into the surrounding countryside.

"As most of you know, she possesses deadly telepathic abilities to overwhelm people with their own memories and emotions to the point of suicide. My interactions with the ghosts of the Usher family have led me to believe those she kills become bound to her in death. The pictographs and my own sightings indicate she chooses to bind herself to the physical forms of young women who have committed suicide through the years, using them as vessels. I still don't understand the nature of that... arrangement. Most of the times I have seen her, she has been a black-haired woman in modest, hand-made black garments like the Ushers would have worn. She has also appeared to me as my wife. I can't say for sure how she will appear to you.

"My time on the Cape has led me to believe the Ushers were not murdered by Henry. Rosemary Usher was trapped in a horrific existence ruled by her husband. He savagely abused her and their children, ruling over them in their isolation like a god. The haunting showed a gunfight between Henry and another man. I don't comprehend that part yet. But Henry was wounded in the woods and went back to the house. I believe Rosemary, ever meek, ever underestimated, seized her moment. She trapped Henry in the cellar and locked him inside. But... Where could she go? Her husband pounded on the doors and bellowed while the ocean raged on all sides of her. Delilah was three miles away through impassible cliffs and frigid waters. The Ushers had no boat. What would the people of Delilah do for her anyway? Her children traumatized by a life in hell, her husband perhaps minutes away from escaping to take his vengeance... She made an act of desperate mercy to free her children from the man who made them his child brides, his slaves. She rounded them up into the lighthouse with quiet words of comfort. She urged them to say their prayers and sing a hymn as she anointed them with oil... poured it all over the stairs and the floor. She lit the tower on fire and had them lock themselves inside. Children's songs turned to screams. When it was over, she realized the full extent of what she had done and threw herself from the cliff into the sea. And now she walks the world in torment, worn as the skin of choice for the Drowned Woman, bound to be her hands and feet."

I stopped for a moment to survey the faces of the others. "It's not perfect, but it's as much as I can understand from the visions I've seen out there. I also believe the cult of her worship has continued, and the three teens who died yesterday got in over their heads. Rupert Wycliffe got them interested in Cape Contrition and the Drowned Woman, just like he got me interested in them. I believe he brought me to Cape Contrition with the intention of using me to feed her power. Her acolytes have been doing that for some time. Whether the current outbreak of suicides in town was their endgame or they lost control of their hungry goddess, I don't know."

Next, I related to the council what Kazuo had once told me of his time in the secret internment camp, and the way experiments with infrasound inflicted a similar depressive power on the test subjects and attracted the Drowned Woman to them. Hana sat in horror, hearing this for the first time. The room sat with my words for a while before Will spoke in a struggle to keep the threads straight.

"Ghosts, abusive cult family, ancient pagan deity from the sea, teenage witches, and government black hats testing experimental weapons... Am I missing anything? Oh, the forest fire coming closer to town every day. That was it."

"How do we stop her, knowing all of this?" Gwen asked.

"I might have something to contribute," Thomas spoke reluctantly. "Joe, I've been thinking a lot about you since we first spoke. You have been so hounded by the power of this creature while you lived in her domain. The visions of supernatural phenomena were so constant and vivid for you, but you were so alone in experiencing them. It was as if you were uniquely vulnerable to her power, uniquely susceptible to communication from the other side. When we first spoke, I thought you were so full of regrets and memories, she had plenty to draw from. But then I thought about all the visions of your wife, your friends in war, your old agent; and how long you have been followed by dreams of the dead in your life. Your Biblical namesake is Joseph, the Dreamer, and like him, your nights have always been riddled with troubling visions. What you might have thought of as an especially vivid imagination... Well, I've never believed in this sort of thing before, but..."

"Just say it," I said.

"I believe you are a latent Medium. A powerful one, but you never learned to control it or had a name for what it was. You have a unique sensitivity to contact from the dead. Perhaps you also have a better chance than any of us to reach back through the curtain and contact *them*."

"Whoa, cool," Hana said breathlessly as I came to grips with it. I was frankly beyond surprise or skepticism.

"You're talking about a séance?" I asked.

"Séances were mostly parlor frauds. I'm talking about a *real* one."

"We would need to go into Usher's Fall to make contact," Gwen said, "the lion's den."

"I can't protect any of you, and I can't ask you to do this

with me."

"This is our town. Our neighbors. You can't protect us from this on the Cape, but you can't protect us from it in Delilah either. We're going with you," Hana said.

"Hana, what did I tell you when I let you tag along? What did I tell your grandfather? You aren't coming. I don't want dead kids on my conscience."

"There are already dead kids. That's just the world. I'm in this. I know the score." I hesitated, looking into the grim faces of my compatriots for a long moment before leveling eyes on her.

"Alright. You're in. Gwen?"

"Yeah... I'm in," Gwen said, looking me firmly in the eye. "Let's put an end to this bitch."

"Count me in, too," Will added. Herman agreed. We all looked at Thomas expectantly, and he faltered for a moment.

"Shit... This stuff wasn't supposed to be real. Alright. Get the damn Ouija Board."

The coast was dark when we reached the wooded path to Usher's Fall, hands linked in a human chain as we kept an eye on the waving sword of light from the distant tower. No one spoke as we stepped out of the trees into the biting wind and walked to the desolate ruin of the darkened house. The maintenance work to get it up and running again never materialized. Wind whistled through teeth of broken glass and splintered wood. The door stood yawning open. Each of us had on thick industrial goggles, lenses painted over in black to reduce us to near blindness. I hoped they would obscure the vision enough to prevent the Drowned Woman's gaze from having its full effect. At my insistence, Hana was also bound in a straitjacket. We must have cut an interesting figure: a cowboy cop, an Episcopal priest, a schoolgirl in a straitjacket, a thin-haired, acne-pocked librarian, a red-haired shopkeeper, and a sleep-deprived, irritable veteran in a cardigan, walking hand in hand toward the forlorn house like six blind mice.

I went inside first, glancing about the rooms with their tossed furniture and walls pockmarked by black mold to make sure the coast was clear.

"Quickly, now," I said with a low whistle, stepping aside as the others made their way up the creaking stairs and into the darkened house. I closed the storm door behind us and glanced about nervously with a hand on my lifted goggles. In the dining room, a round table was being dragged upright and set in the middle of the floor, six chairs set evenly about it. Thomas Forester cautiously lifted his goggles as he lit twelve wax candles, setting them about the table as well as around the room. Their warm glow softened the mystique of the house, pushing the shadows back and giving us the comforting illusion of a protective barrier. On Thomas' advice, I walked about with a bag of salt and cast a thin coating of it over the floorboards. He set his largest white candle in the center of the table and instructed me to pour the salt in a thick circle of protection around the table and chairs. Gwen set up the talking board, and each of us took our seats. A draft of briny wind whistled through the rooms, but all else was still. We all lifted our goggles and joined hands. Thomas began with a prayer.

"Lord, you are the king of the living and the dead. Guide us in this evil place and cast your protection over your children in this hour of our desperate, perhaps stupid attempt to reach these tortured souls, and bring your peace once again to our hometown. Amen."

"Amen," we all muttered, and it was my turn. I took a bell out from its muffling cloth in my coat pocket and rang it gently.

"We wish to communicate with the spirits of Usher's Fall. Are you with us?" All was still. We waited in tense silence, and I asked the question again. A frigid gust of wind swept through, and I felt Gwen's hand tighten around mine. I held my breath as the sound of footsteps scuffled on the floorboards, and small shoeprints appeared in the white salt. The planchette rattled and jolted a few inches across the board, and the jerky motion began a steady scrape as it moved to a word on the board.

YES.

"How many of you are in this house?" There was silence for a moment. The planchette lifted from the board and rapped hard on the table in a steady rhythm. I stared in disbelief and surprise for a moment before realizing it was counting, struggling to keep tabs on each new rhythm as I reached back to recall the number I had let pass. *Tap. Tap. Tap. Tap. Tap.* I listened to the frantic sound, simultaneously trying to recall the death toll as I knew it.

Seventeen workers in the construction of the original farmhouse and light

Twenty-Nine souls aboard the *Osprey*

Eleven on the *Multnomah Princess*

The six children of the Usher family, Henry, and Rosemary

Twenty-six from the cliffs between 1932 and 1960

Sixteen in the waking nightmare of the Delilah Suicides

Tom and Mabel Waters

Caleb Cole

110?

TAP. TAP. TAP. The number came and went. We shuddered in our seats as the noise rumbled on, mounting higher. And higher. I lost count, pressed my forehead into the table in disbelief as terrifying thuds resounded on the walls all around us, a percussive chorus of unseen pounding that shook the room. At last, the rhythmic impacts halted, and the planchette spelled the total out plainly.

"Nine... Nine hundred and nine," Thomas breathed. *"My name is Legion, for we are many."* Beside me, the bell jangled a jarring report, clanging rapidly for ten seconds before collapsing inertly to the floor.

"Who speaks for you?" I asked, and the planchette scrawled across the board in a steady rhythm. Gwen scribbled fast on a pad of paper, tracking the letters.

A-N-N-A

R-U-T-H

P-E-T-E-R

E-L-I-Z-A-B-E-T-H

N-E-T-H-A-N-Y-U-L

On this last name, the planchette scrawled with uncertainty from letter to letter. As I tried to make sense of the crude misspelling, I remembered Nathaniel was only two years old when he died.

"Do you know you are dead?" I asked.

N-O-M-O-R-E-Q-U-E-S-T-I-O-N-S, the planchette rattled.

S-H-E-I-S-C-O-M-I-N-G

S-H-E-D-O-N-T-L-I-K-E-T-H-E-S-E-G-A-M-E-S

"Wait! How do we stop her? How do we free you?"

The planchette rattled violently on the talking board before rapidly darting from letter to letter.

C-O-M-E-F-I-N-D-M-E-J-O-E

As soon as the phrase was spelled, the planchette hit the word "Goodbye" and spun in place rapidly, whistling into a blur before shooting off the table and clattering to a corner of the room. At the same moment, all the candles guttered out simultaneously. We sat bewildered in the dark silence and trailing smoke. We listened to our own breaths fogging in the meat-locker cold, and my heart froze as I looked about the dim silhouettes around me and counted seven seated figures when there had been six. Between Hana and Gwen sat the dark shadow of a woman in black, a heavy veil over her cracked, pallid face. Piercing pinpoints of light gleamed hungrily through the fabric.

"Goggles!" Everyone reached for them at once, but they had been delicately lifted from our foreheads without our noticing. The Drowned Woman smirked and stood at the table, and I shouted, "Close your eyes!" My head swam with visions of a burning house, of crabs scuttling over a dead teenager pinned to the ocean floor, an elephant cradling the red stump of its leg, and the Black Wave caught my soul in its claws as I panicked for it to end. Will screamed and thrashed, and I turned to clutch him as much for my support as his.

"You will not take another of God's children to the deep, Demon," Thomas murmured as he pulled a crucifix from his coat —a violation of my rule not to carry anything that could be used as a weapon. It appeared Thomas Forester had suggested a séance and secretly planned for an exorcism. The old man defiantly rose in his seat and lifted the icon of Christ before the veined face and mottled eyes of the creature, and the wide corners of her mouth twisted into a rotting smirk as she locked him in her gaze. Thomas' eyes welled with tears and he averted his eyes to the floor. My heart sank, for it was as if the light had gone out of him.

"Are you there, God? Are you listening? Do you care?" he mumbled, and the hand holding the crucifix dropped to his side. "Lord help my poor soul." He clutched the crucifix like a dagger and shoved it upward toward his own neck.

"No!" Will bellowed, knocking the cross from his hand and shouldering him hard into the wall.

"Gwen!" I shouted as the two of us ducked below the table, and the air filled with the terrible two-voiced scream of the Drowned Woman. "Get them out of here, now!" She shuddered and nodded as our eyes locked in the middle of the chaos, steeling ourselves. With her head down, she scooped up Hana where she screamed and thrashed in her straitjacket, grabbed the whimpering Herman by the collar, and ran for the door. Thomas passed out and crumpled, and Will grunted as he hefted the old priest outside. In the shadowed woods, rifles cracked, and the lawn was illuminated by a horrendous pillar of spectral fire. Alone with her all-consuming agony, I squared up in the doorway protectively while averting my gaze and trying to keep my voice steady.

"I know who you are. You were once a mother, imprisoned here by an evil man. Forced to live as his slave, you watched your children grow stunted in the tiny world of his making. You longed to show them there was something more, beyond this place. You watched your daughters squirm and cry in his grasp as he forced himself on them –like he'd once forced himself on you. You watched your sons play cruel games with the farm animals and defy you as they looked more like Henry with each passing day. You longed to escape and save your

402

daughters from becoming you, and your sons from becoming him. But your world was surrounded by cliffs and long falls on every side. The only way out was to jump –so you jumped. And you took your children with you the only way you could."

She stood still in a surprising way, as if considering my words attentively.

"Since then, you've become part of something else: this old and terrible blackness that has led so many of us to this place. It uses you to walk in the world and hurt others. It wears your face. But it isn't all you are. I have to believe there's redemption for you, even now. Maybe then, there will be some for me. See, I've also hurt people I cared about. And I've been dead, too. Rosemary..."

I was struggling not to look at her dead on, but in the periphery of my vision, I saw the inky, rolling cloud of her skirts shift backward as the name caught her with surprise. I remembered what Thomas Forester said about the power of uttering a spirit's true name. Back straightening, I gathered my courage and shouted.

"Rosemary Usher!" The words echoed on the walls and there was silence. I stood waiting, but nothing seemed to have happened.

"Rosemary?" she asked in a voice carrying the eerie dual pitch of woman and demon. Then, she did something I never would have expected. She laughed. It was a terrible, shuddering sound mocking and reverberating from the walls of my brain. The guttural laugh of the pit shook the house while the high wheeze of an earthly woman shattered my hopes. I stood and stared at the grotesque lines of her contorted, scornful face as the bottom dropped out somewhere inside me. A voice called my name over the rushing swell of hideous laughter,

403

but it sounded so small and far away. *Joe. JOE!*

Gwen grabbed my collar roughly and shielded my gaze with wrists still bound in gauzy linen.

"Come on!" She dragged me in my stiff-legged hopeless trance, one foot after the other until we stumbled out onto the grass. As soon as we hit the ground, the front door slammed shut with a thunderous crack. The fire of the lighthouse snuffed into blackness, the shouts and rifle shots in the woods ceased, and the terrible laughter was silent. The six of us were sprawled and heaving in the grass in front of a silent, derelict house, the moon and stars twinkling overhead as the cold tower and forbidding trees loomed all around us. Thomas tore off his white collar, and was hyperventilating as the others huddled about him, whispering he would see light again. We said not a word as we picked ourselves up and descended the trail. Throughout the long drive back to Delilah, and as Gwen and I silently made ourselves small on opposite sides of the bed, my mind was consumed with one thought.

That was never Rosemary.

Chapter Thirty-One: Firstborn

February 19th, 1963

The Thunderbird was dull as waitresses milled about listlessly, refilling coffee cups of old men and women who didn't speak. Gwen, Hana, Herman, Will, Thomas, and I sat in an exhausted reverie. The old priest was still shaken from the disastrous séance. Desperate for guidance, I attended his church on Sunday, and it was painful to watch him struggle to find any hope or reassurance for the families in his parish. He broke from the lectionary to preach on San Juan De La Cruz and *The Dark Night of the Soul*. It felt like all of us were in that night, together, but alone. Looking about the table, each of us was wrestling with our own stranger in the night. Gwen's best instincts were to support and encourage those around her, and she was struggling for the words. Hana sat dejected, the cracked case she'd once dreamed of a lost and childish thing. Herman looked blankly and spoke not at all. Wherever he was, not even Hana could reach him. Will had a two-way radio occasionally crackling over with updates from his men, and chain-smoked cigarettes beneath his frowning mustache as the world outside went mad.

Mayor Walter McCoy had called a press conference the night before to announce his resignation and shot himself in the head on the steps of City Hall. The forest fire caught on unfavorable winds and spilled beyond what the fire brigade could hope to contain. One fireman and two forest rangers died in the inferno, which spread across the forested coastal mountains to consume over five thousand acres. The conflagration devoured through the dry foothills where I'd seen the ruined concentration camp, and word floated back over the police radio this morning that Wycliffe Manor was burning on the wooded outskirts of town. Of the eccentric millionaire and his household staff, no one had heard a thing. Outside, people were packing their old automobiles and hosing down their houses, in disbelief the flames could carve out such devastation with the traditional fire season still five months out. Few people were working, and school was closed with the fire looming so close.

We were paying for our coffee and pastries when Will Blake had to turn to his radio. Over the static, we all heard a report come in of some trouble at Cole's Harbor. Something about an angry mob.

"It's too damn early for anarchy, but that's my cue to head out," Will said as he put cash down on the table for his breakfast, donned his bomber jacket, and put on his hat.

"Cole's Harbor. That's Alice's shop." I threw on my black pea coat. "I'm coming with you."

Otis wagged his tail as I untied his leash from the post outside and ran eagerly for the truck as we moved to follow Will. Gwen hopped in the cab beside me, while Hana, Herman, and Thomas rode together in the priest's Oldsmobile. The sunlight was an unreal, gold-washed, hazy shimmer. I didn't want to think about why the air was so warm, because it wasn't from the sun. Will turned on his emergency lights and our cars rolled out in a grim procession. As we drove through town, ashes fell from the sky like a mocking parody of rain, coating everything in a layer of dust that was once trees, animals, houses, and people. Glowering over us all was an uncanny, blazing blood-orange sun like something from a pagan apocalyptic myth. It reminded me why the ancients believed we live in the grasp of terrible and capricious gods. Perhaps we do. We would have wept with joy to see rainfall, but there was none in sight. How long until the fire crested the peaks at Delilah's back like an invading horde? I operated the truck's gears and clutch mechanically while my mind calculated how much rain it would take to drown the fire, and how far away that deliverance could be.

As we drove along the harbor, it became clear Alice Cole was in grave danger. Her shop was ransacked, windows shattered, and the unfinished yacht pulled down onto its side. Several boats burned in their moorings on the open water. A pluming burst of flames exploded from *Esperanza* as her fuel tanks caught fire. Police were lining up handcuffed culprits against the wall of the shipwright's shop where they had won the skirmish. But on the docks, there was a terrible brawl in the works.

"What the fuck is happening?" Will demanded of Mitchell and Hoskins, but I didn't stop to hear. Otis snarled and bounded off, and I ran after him with Gwen and Hana while Thomas and Herman assisted the outnumbered police in subduing the vandals. The dock was crowded with roughly a dozen screaming men and women, pressing forward along the narrow dock as they bore back Alice Cole and her workers

407

toward the end of the plank. Lost in the jostle of heads and shoulders, I could see John Hicks and Garrett O'Connor standing shoulder to shoulder, the two men streaming blood from busted noses and cut mouths as they fought to protect Marianne and Alice at their backs. The crew of the shipwright's shop had been borne back along the docks to the mooring of the *Seal Sister* and appeared to be making their last stand there. The narrowness of the dock forced the brigands into a bottleneck, allowing John and Garrett to box three or four men at a time, but it was down to minutes before they were overwhelmed. As I ran, Marianne closed her eyes and fired a flare into the mob, and the smoking projectile whistled into their midst before bursting into red flames of phosphorous, scattering people to fall into the water or trample one another in their haste to retreat. One man screamed and struck frantically at his clothing as flames ate into his overalls and the smell of burning flesh grew pungent. Otis snarled and bit a man's leg, and when he reeled back to kick the mutt, I punched him in the teeth. The man who took the impact of the flare fell from the dock and splashed into the water with a hiss. White smoke was heavy in the air, and in the distance, I saw Alice Cole disappear into *Seal Sister*. When she crossed back over the gangplank, she was carrying a double-barreled, breech-loading shotgun.

"Alright," she declared, loading two shells in the breech, snapping it closed, and drawing the hammers back. "You bottom-feeders think I'm a witch? Well, I traded in my broomstick!" The cowards stumbled backward as she fired a shot into the air and leveled her muzzle toward the mob. The ones who hadn't already swam for shore were clawing over one another to flee back down the docks, where the police chief and his men were waiting. As they were hauled ashore and arrested, Garrett and John shook my hand with bloody smiles.

"Our erstwhile shipmate returns," John Hicks smiled, wincing at his cut lip.

"Good of you to come to my rescue, lighthouse keeper. Been some time since I was saved by a dashing heroic type." Alice snapped open and unloaded the shotgun, nestling the butt in the crook of her elbow and letting the barrel hang over her forearm as she lit a cigarette and puffed it to life.

"What the hell happened? Nice shot with the flare gun, by the way." Marianne sent a shy smile my way as she took the two battered sailors aside to tend their wounds.

"You know the sea lions when someone riles 'em up," Alice replied. "Gossip says the folks killing themselves are being controlled by some evil woman. Word got around; my shop was untouched by the suicides when my neighbors weren't so lucky. They've never liked nor trusted me. Said I bewitched my husband or sabotaged his boat, and I did the same for those tourist boys. Said I knew too well where to find them. Once word got out, it was torch and pitchfork time."

I glanced about at the burned ships and the ransacked shop with surprise. When I'd met Alice Cole, I'd thought in a more primitive time, a stubborn and self-sufficient woman like her might have been hanged for a witch. I'd apparently fooled myself with the thought we weren't living in such a time.

"It's a shame anyone would jump to the conclusion you had anything to do with this after you've been so careful to conceal that... Rosemary..." I made eye contact with the old widow as I intoned the name with the slow gravity of a Hollywood picture detective's accusation. It was a theory I'd been chewing on

409

since the night of the failed séance, but I'd told no one. The truth was, I didn't *know* it was true until I ventured the name, and saw her eyes widen with disbelief and contempt. The old woman finished her unfiltered cigarette and flicked the stub into the ocean.

"Alright, Lad. You'd better come inside."

The old woman moved more slowly than she had the last time we'd been in her shop. With ruins littered about us and a CLOSED sign on the door, she brought a teapot to a boil and lit me a smoke as she helped herself to another. Gwen knocked hopefully at the door with Thomas and the others behind her, but Alice waved them off like salesmen with an irritable swat at the air. As she turned to stir sugar into the piping hot tea, I lifted a hand to them signaling it was alright, and I'd catch up with them later. Our group had been through so much together since forming our unlikely alliance, they were loath to leave me alone; but Alice Cole would not be denied.

"Do they know?" she asked as she set a green enamel cup before me on the counter.

"No. They don't even suspect it."

"Good." Alice blew gently, rippling the surface of the tea before taking a draw from the cup. "How did you find out?"

"We had a séance in the old house to make contact with the dead there. I almost missed it, but... when the children identified themselves, there were only five of them. Rebecca, the eldest, wasn't with her siblings. When I confronted the Drowned Woman and spoke the name 'Rosemary' in her presence, I saw her face and knew I'd had it wrong. And I thought of your husband: a shipwright and skilled sailor beloved by all in town, lost at sea in a sudden storm few believed could have taken him. Caleb Cole. The name was familiar, but I hadn't placed it. But when I'd read the diary of Rosemary Usher, it spoke occasionally of a young sailor, strong and kind, who took pity on her and her children. The only decent man who took notice of the lighthouse keeper's wife in her hell of salt and stone. His name was Caleb." The old woman lowered her eyes as they brimmed with tears and wiped them away with a muffled snarl. No, she would not cry in front of this meddler. What tears did she have left?

"That man was the only goodness that ever came into my life. For years, he kept a close eye on us. Went out on every single supply run to the Cape and was as kind and gentle with me and the children as he could be without Henry seeing. Sometimes he would slip me letters, and I would read them in the lighthouse while Henry slept. I wrote a few back to him when I could. Our friendship grew slowly into love. He saw the cruelty and possessiveness of Henry and hated him for it. The two men came to blows once over his treatment of me. Henry beat him almost to death and sent him home with his mates, broken. We didn't communicate again for a year after, and the silence killed me. But... There was so much about my life I couldn't tell him. Henry controlled everything: what I wore, where I could go, even what I thought. These letters and longing looks we shared were forbidden: I knew that long before I knew they were love. Caleb was patient with me. He took his time and tried to understand.

"I was little more than a child when Henry brought me to the headland he named Cape Contrition. As the years went by, farm labor and childbirth aged me. What Henry once desired in me was gone. I underwent a slow death when I realized Henry was casting me aside as his mate. It might have been a relief, but... I watched him grooming our daughters – my daughters, to replace me at his side. And it reminded me how when I was a girl, I had replaced another as his woman. I'd feared one day I would be old and used up, cast aside for a pretty young thing I could never compete with. How could I have imagined she would be my own daughter? Rebecca, our firstborn, was his favorite. She looked the most like me but behaved the most like him. I – I tried to reach her. She was the one he had the strongest hold over: the one he abused the most cruelly. From the time she was a little girl, she seemed unable to form an emotional connection with me or her siblings. There was a gulf I didn't know how to cross. She looked at me like I was a stranger. As I tried to teach her right from wrong, I watched and learned she had no conscience. There was a darkness in her, like a part of my daughter was missing. She was so angry and powerless, and I didn't know what to do to help her. I was angry and powerless, too. When she was young, I would find her hurting her siblings –especially her brothers. Touching them... and herself. Bedwetting, setting fires, harming the animals. Once, I found a whole nest of baby birds, each of them killed. I asked Rebecca who did it, and she told me she'd freed them. At night, she had nightmares of her father falling on her as a baby and... hurting her. 'With a part of himself', she'd said. When Nathaniel was a baby, she pinched his penis so hard I thought she might tear it off. When I reached out to stop her, she stabbed me in the shoulder with a knife.

"So, you see, Rebecca was abused and an abuser, a violent and remorseless child. Henry kept her close, and she played the obedient little princess, gloating in her power over me and the other children. I know you have felt the aura of that place... The guilt and shame plaguing our thoughts. But she was unaffected because she had been molded into a girl without conscience. In the end, it was as if she had been made for that place. I came to fear her as well as my husband, as it became clear I was no longer needed. In my heart, I knew she was going to take my place in the family, and she would kill me herself. I knew our paths were on a collision course when she became pregnant with his child. God forgive me – I wanted to stab that baby in her womb to spare it the life it might have had with them. Henry's first wife, Catherine, once tried to do the same to me with my Rebecca.

"Though she was incapable of feeling for me, and I had grown to fear her, I knew my daughter, Joseph. There was goodness in her. She melded to Henry's side for her own survival, but in truth, she loved him no more than she loved me. I believe for years, she harbored intentions of taking her revenge upon him, and freeing her brothers and sisters from him as well... But don't you see? She couldn't see the difference between setting those chicks free and snapping their necks. There was a cave, at the bottom of the headland. When the tide revealed the doorway into that dark hell, she went down to meet strange people who rowed there in secret. I followed her once and watched as she took part in their evil profanities. Something waited for her there: something that had always been unseen, but close. She found a power in that dark place and gave herself over to it. She thought this creature would give her the power to face her father and save us all. But this... Demon... who possessed her was beyond her control, and answered her wish in a way she did not expect... In the end, her good intentions destroyed us."

"April 8th, 1919... What happened, Rosemary?"

"Caleb recovered from the beating that had almost done

him in. After a year of healing and regaining his strength, he sailed out to Cape Contrition alone. In his boat was a rifle, and room to carry us all away. He confronted Henry in front of the house for my hand, shouting he didn't deserve to keep me and our family after what he'd done. As the sun set, they tore at one another like wild animals. It was a horrific fight, like none I had ever seen before. In the end, Caleb sent Henry crawling back into the house. He took me by the arm and asked me to collect the children and bring them to the boat, but... Henry came out with his gun and fired shots, forcing us to flee into the woods. Henry and Caleb exchanged gunfire in the darkness, wounding one another. At last, Henry was forced to retreat a second time. But Caleb and I were alone at the beach of Siren's Cove, cut off from my babies.

"When Henry staggered back to the house, Rebecca had given herself over to the power of that creature once and for all and seized her moment. Taking advantage of his wound, she trapped him in the cellar. While he clawed at the door and screamed, she rounded up the other children and guided them into the lighthouse – Henry always said it made us like a shining city on a hill. My babies... poured the oil, locked the door, and lit the fire themselves. We had been watching the commotion from the beach, trying to understand what was happening, asking ourselves if we should risk turning back. When I saw the fire break out in the tower, I screamed, and we ran back to the farm... The tower still burned, but there was no more screaming. In the distance, Henry bellowed and rattled the doors of his trap. And Rebecca stood alone in the ruin of our family. She looked back at me from the brink, and her eyes were filled with horror. It was as if, for a moment, the real Rebecca had awakened. Even in her, there was a shard capable of remorse, and in the end, she realized too late what she had done. I had given her a necklace when she was a little girl: a nautilus shell wrought in silver. She'd told me a peculiar thing once, near the end: that it was the only part of her left. She'd loved it since she was a girl, but in the last days, she became unnaturally possessive of it. She clutched the pendant for dear life as she looked at me in that last moment, winning a breath of lucidity over the monster clutching her soul. I called out to her, but she shook her head and stepped backward. 'I'm sorry, mama,' she said, and threw herself from the cliff as I collapsed and screamed, and Caleb held me back from following her.

"Caleb picked me up from that place of ashes. Carried me to the boat and rowed us away from that column of smoke. We fled, and never spoke of what we saw. He married me, and we lived a long life together in Delilah: thirty-six years. I changed my name to Alice and told people I came from back East. The people had seen so little of Rosemary Usher, no one recognized me in all those years. I grew old with that remarkable, brave, gentle man. He was lost at sea seven years ago, despite being the most skilled sailor I ever knew. I suspect Rebecca couldn't let me keep him in the end."

I sat in awe and agony as the old woman stubbed out her last cigarette and took a final swig of her tea.

"I've spent my entire life hiding. What's the use, now? Who is there left to hide from?"

"Alice... I don't know what to say. I'm so sorry."

"Save your 'sorry.' My house is gone. You are the last lighthouse keeper of Cape Contrition now. So, what are you going to do about it?"

A snowfall of ash was falling over my hair and shoulders as I walked with Otis up the stairs to Saint Nicholas Episcopal Church. The red door was open, and the sanctuary was lit with candles where my friends awaited the news. With Alice Cole's reluctant blessing, I told them everything. When I finished, they had the same question as Alice: *'what are you going to do about it?'*

"Maybe the monsters we fear in the dark are the people we banished from the daylight," Gwen murmured. "The worst part about the story of the Ushers is we allowed them to die the way they did. We whispered our stories about them while they lived and died in a prison to which we had banished them. The Drowned Woman is a being far older and more powerful than any of us, but whatever she is, she can't walk, touch, and destroy without a body to inhabit. The body she uses once belonged to a frightened girl: a girl who was molded to cruelty, warped without conscience, true. But also, a girl who wanted to take revenge on her father, and free her brothers and sisters from his grasp."

"The séance didn't work because we didn't know her true name. Now, we do. I don't know if we can defeat the blackness that has always existed there, the force personified through her. But the part of her that was human once... I have to believe it can be human again. Even for just a moment. If I can break through and reach the part of her that is Rebecca Usher... Maybe I can save her and break the spell."

"You're going to talk to her and make her... feel?" Will asked with disbelief.

"It's not as crazy as it sounds... Crazy being a relative term, I guess," Thomas spoke. "I've been doing some research to keep busy since I got a clearer picture of what manner of creature we're dealing with. I believe Rebecca Usher, the Drowned Woman, is not just a ghost or evil spirit, but a being known as a Lich. In folklore, a Lich is the product of a transformation when a powerful sorcerer or king attempts to unnaturally prolong his own life by sealing away a part of his soul in an external object, such as a phylactery. A Lich can only be killed when the object containing part of their soul is destroyed, and because this item is their greatest vulnerability, they frequently hide it away or carry it on their person for safekeeping. Liches are represented as cadaverous beings: not only wraiths, but creatures inhabiting a physical body. From what 'Alice' told you, it sounds like Rebecca played the good little girl while privately practicing as a witch and stealing away for secret rites in the cave. From her testimony and what we can tell from the pictographs, Rebecca bound herself to the old, dark power of Cape Contrition like other women in other times, allowing it to take over her body in the hope she could use its supernatural abilities to grant her revenge against her father and save her siblings. Like many demons of lore, it kept its bargain in a way she did not expect. It freed the children by burning them and took revenge on Henry by keeping him alive. When Rebecca Usher understood what she had done, she threw herself from the cliff in grief. This shows for a moment after the transformation, a part of her remained lucid and fought its way to the surface. But suicide could not undo what she had become, for her consciousness was now joined to the Drowned Woman. Joe, I don't know if any part of this girl remains to be reasoned with. But if there is, you will be able to break through and speak to it. I just... don't know how you can speak to Rebecca without being consumed by the Drowned Woman. We could try another séance or exorcism, but–"

"No," I interrupted. "I can't face her and protect all of you. Besides, I'm the only one who can reach back across the curtain and speak to her. I'm sorry. In the end, this is something I'll have to do alone."

"And what's going to happen when she makes you throw yourself off the cliff?" Hana demanded.

"What evil part of myself can she show me that I haven't already seen and made peace with?" I looked each of them in the eyes to let them know I was prepared to return and face her one last time, no matter the cost. "We have to try. This is the only play we have. I'm not afraid of dying... I've done it already."

Chapter Thirty-Two: Hell and High Water

February 20th, 1963

My hands trembled as I parked the Ford and pressed my forehead into the steering wheel, murmuring a clumsy, out-of-practice prayer and steeling myself for what I had to do. My back was stiff from a long, restless night on a church pew. After our counsel and the reluctant agreement I would make the final attempt alone, each of us was too afraid to return to our own homes, and we bedded down in the sanctuary. When everyone else slept, Gwen guided me into a prayer alcove, and we tenderly made love like it was the last time. The day passed in restless anticipation, a mechanical pantomime of evacuation preparation I wasn't planning to go through with. As the terrible orange sun sank low over the Pacific, I'd said goodbye to Otis and Gwen, and turned my face toward Cape Contrition. The sky was darkened in a towering curtain of smoke, and with the fire visible from town, Delilah was totally evacuated.

I closed the door of my truck and choked on the fumes of smoke in the air, wheezing and leaning against the fender as I looked at my surroundings. The fire had crested the nearest hills now and was surging downhill in a mad plunge for the open water. The dark woods of pine, fir, and aspen lit the night with smoldering orange and billows of hot ash. Glowing orange hills reflected their light on the black water. The sight made me sick to my stomach. No matter how much pain this place held, seeing this Eden of America burning around me was an abomination. The air was filled with the crackle of old trees breaking to pieces, intermingled with the swells of the Pacific. Atop the distant cliffs, the electric beam of the lighthouse panned slowly across burning hills and orange-lit ocean. As the ashes rained, fire and flood seethed to the right and left of my path, and I made the plunge into the forest of Cape Contrition one last time.

My body was racked by horrible coughs as I navigated the switchbacks, keeping an eye on the approaching glow of fire at the farthest point I could see through the trees. Billows of dark smoke rolled across the path and half-blinded me. I knew this path would be ablaze when I needed to cross back over. No gunshots rang out, no spectral lightshow of burning tower greeted me as I stepped out onto the familiar lawn of Usher's Fall. The house stood dark and lifeless, and the pallid spire of the lighthouse diligently worked its beacon as if there was anyone left to see it. The whole scene was lifeless but lit by the encroaching blaze at my back. Through the rolling smoke and falling ash, I saw a silhouette backed against the edge of the cliff and went to it. Instinctively, I reached for the blindfold in my pocket. The others had pressed it into my hand, insisting I wear it. I thumbed the fabric tenderly for a long moment and cast it aside as I walked toward the edge of the cliff. The fire was going to consume me if she didn't. What use was blindness anymore? But I was resolved to destroy the Drowned Woman along with me if I could.

As I approached the silhouette at the cliff, it turned to face me. It was the dim form of a man. He stepped out of the shadow of the tower and into the flickering orange light spilling across the lawns, and I saw he was Rupert Wycliffe: glasses cracked, black suit torn and dusted with ashes. He smirked like a madman as he staggered forward, eyes reflecting the glow of hell.

"The last lighthouse keeper has returned. You couldn't resist her call even now."

"I'm choosing this. I have to destroy her, Rupert."

His eyes widened in disbelief.

"You couldn't destroy her before."

"I was alone before," I said. He smirked and gestured around me, wordlessly remarking that I was alone *now*.

"You still think there is hope?" He lifted his hands to the inferno, perplexed. "Don't you see? She's more powerful than any of us now. My family has been feeding her people like you for three generations. I was her high priest! But you gave her power to move beyond this place and take vengeance for her suffering in a way I never could have imagined. She's going to burn it all down, Joseph. Not just the ones I send. Everyone. Even me. We are living in the last days. And you can't save anyone, Mr. Crowley. Not even yourself. Entropy is the fate of all things."

"Then I'll live abundantly, experience everything, love recklessly; and when death comes, I'll meet him like an old friend. I know something I didn't before. Life is a gift, even when life is pain. Fuck entropy."

"How much can you even live, Joseph? What is left of you that you didn't bury in Jean's grave?"

"I guess we'll find out."

"Not 'we.' Goodbye, Mr. Crowley. And good luck."

"Rupert! Rupert, god damn it!" I shouted as he spread his arms wide, looked out at the Ragnarök around us, and let himself fall backward off the cliff. I ran forward and clutched at the guard rail, but knew he was gone as I looked down into the black abyss that had swallowed so many. The wind howled and stirred my ash-streaked hair, and the heat of it made me turn in time to see a house in Chapel Hill, crackling and groaning as the first flames licked its foundations and touched the eastern wall. Usher's Fall caught quickly, roaring and crackling with flames as the terrible heat and consuming glare inched slowly across the lawn in an undulating dance. Somewhere in my mind, there was the faint sound of an elephant's scream as I watched the house burn. The front door opened, and a vision of Jean in a nightshirt walked through the flames spilling across the porch. I watched her measured tread across the lawn with the wall of flame towering at her back, felt the familiar despair and longing rush in. But this specter didn't have the same power over me it once did.

As the phantom walked across the lawn, a weird cry sounded in the burning trees behind the homestead. I looked with horror to see a towering elk gallop out of the trees, wreathed in flames and tossing its antlered crown from side to side as it barreled forward in desperate, blind fear. I threw myself aside as the great elk thundered by and leapt from atop the cliff, falling like a comet into the ocean below.

My breaths came fast as I picked myself up in horror and disbelief. Jean looked at me sadly as she passed by, and murmured "Come find me, Joe," as she walked toward the door of the lighthouse and opened it. I followed her into the tower, closing the door behind me. Without a word, I mounted the spiral of echoing metal stairs, and followed the sway of her hips beneath the thin fabric as she guided me to the pinnacle. The light hummed powerfully at the top of the stairs, rotating on powerful machinery as it twirled slowly in place behind its thick glass. The beam swung slowly through Jean without casting a shadow, a last reminder she wasn't real as she stepped out onto the whipping winds of the narrow-railed balcony.

She stood at the rail looking out to the Pacific. When I stared over her shoulder into the outer darkness, huge storm clouds were forming. Out in the distance, an electric vein of lightning webbed across the sky, and the thunder rumbled low and menacing behind it. *Rain. The rain is coming back.*

"You came back for me," she said at last, turning to look me in the eyes. I flinched for a moment but held her gaze. The black tide of agony roiled inside me, but I had faced it before. The Drowned Woman's gaze was a mirror, and it could only show me myself. But I had already chosen to confront what I saw there. "I'm glad you're here, Joe. You've been hurting for so long. Come away to the water. Lie with me and rest."

"No." I looked fully into her eyes. "Not yet. Maybe one day I'll meet you there, when my time comes. It took living in a house of the dead to show me I've been dead, too. For a long time, now. But I came here to say goodbye, because I'm going to live, now. I have to let you go."

"Baby, you're... You're not making any sense. We talked about this. You know there's nothing out there –"

"Stop using my wife's voice. You're nothing but a shade, because she's dead, and that was my fault. You're the best copy my memories could piece together, but... you're not enough. My idea of you could never do justice to the person."

The façade dropped for a moment as she stared at me, aghast, and her true face bled through the illusion.

"Rebecca Usher," I declared, and the creature stumbled backward in horror as blonde hair turned to black, and sun-kissed skin turned to translucent ivory shot with purple veins. Now *she* stood locked in *my* gaze. "I didn't come to play games with you. Step into the light. Show me your face."

The creature growled and surged forward on undulating billows of black fabric, and the smell of saltwater and rotting flesh filled my nostrils as her dead, mottled gaze met mine, and the Black Wave surged to overwhelm me. I gripped the rail and held her gaze with our faces inches apart, and our spirits churned as each grappled for a foothold. After an agony of dizzying, bewildering pain, she stepped backward, and the light swayed between us. Each of us trembled from the psychic effort, but when we broke apart from one another, it had been with a tiny snap of metal. The Drowned Woman clutched at her throat uncertainly for a moment, and her mottled eyes widened with horror as she looked to see the thin silver chain hanging from my balled fist. I opened my palm to show her the nautilus pendant. While she hung at the railing in horror, I glanced to the raging inferno below us that crawled within ten yards of the tower. Her mouth twisted in impotent rage as I tossed it over my shoulder, letting it sail like a comet into the flames.

"**No! What did you do?**" the beast demanded in a voice deep as the Pacific.

"There's a part of yourself you locked away, and I'm setting it free."

My words strained with effort as I struggled to stand up straight and keep my eyes locked on her. The Drowned Woman poured out all her malice and screamed with the exertion, but the soft silver was scorching in the furnace, and the humanity trapped within it had been freed. The Drowned Woman staggered back and nearly fell over the rail as a gust of wind rushed up from the blaze, and she thrashed back and forth as she clawed at her dead face, struggling to regain control over a broken soul re-forged. The cadaverous form of swirling shadows and ocean water swirled and wrestled with a radiant burst of white light welling up within her translucent chest. It began to spill out of her body in rippling bolts of energy. While the monster struggled to maintain control of the girl, I found my voice and spoke.

"This blackness isn't all you are. Your name is Rebecca Usher. You're a girl who deserved better. These people were afraid of you, and let you be imprisoned in an evil place, under the rule of an evil man. You did what you had to. You survived and longed for the power to save yourself and your family. You made a bargain with a monster you didn't understand, and it destroyed everyone you hoped to save. When you realized what the blackness had done, you threw yourself from the cliff in agony. But your pact with it could not be undone so easily. For years, she has walked on the earth in your body, hurting others the way you had been hurt. And you allowed it, because the small part of you that remained had been drowned and locked away. With each passing year, that part of you seemed smaller and farther away. But I know there is redemption! Even for you! Remember it, Rebecca! Remember who you are!"

The creature buckled down and howled a terrible dual-toned scream before lifting off the ground in a billow of undulating garments and hair. She opened her mouth wide in a scream and the black water spilled out of her mouth, bursting forth like a sickly fountain and spilling down her dress. The creature coughed, sputtered, and moaned a deafening scream as the dark forces animating her vaporized with a snap and distant roll of thunder. As the brackish water spilled and slithered away in a disgusting waterfall, the levitating form of Rebecca Usher collapsed onto the catwalk inertly. I dropped to hands and knees and crawled to her side, moving the dark curtains of wet hair from her pale face and caressing it gently. Rebecca Usher's corpse looked peaceful, finally asleep. The last part of her soul had purged herself of the Drowned Woman, and as she rejoined herself, she died at last.

"You did it, Kid." I wiped a tear from my eye before laying her thin wrists across her bony chest, straightening out her legs and adjusting her dress as the light beam passed over us. Noticing my wedding ring as I worked, I wrenched it off my finger with a grunt and rolled it over in my hand before kissing it and setting it neatly on the lighthouse railing.

With the Drowned Woman's defeat, the suffocation of smoke and the radiating heat of the flames came sharply into focus. I hurried down the coiling spiral of echoing steps and burst through the door to stagger to the cliff, collapsing on the brink wreathed in smoke and racked by horrible coughs. Beads of sweat rolled down my face as I looked back at the wall of encroaching flame backing me to the ledge. The smoke and heat were blinding, and there could be no escape. The battle was won. But now, I was minutes away from immolation or suffocation. My first impulse was to make a run for it through the flames, but I drew up short of the solid wall of fire. *Run where?*

I cursed and glanced over the edge, considering my options. Hell, or high water. Lightning split the sky and thunder boomed as I dug in my pocket and lit the last cigarette of my life. A few fortifying puffs steadied my breathing, and I made my choice. I took a long look at the blackened frame of the farmhouse in the hellfire, seeing it as two places at once. My downfall and redemption, both found in a burning house.

"Goodbye, Jean." I flicked the cigarette end over end into the darkness, took off my pea coat, scarf, and cardigan, and tossed them onto the encroaching fire. As the first tongue of flame licked my shoes and caught the hem of my pants ablaze, I turned, ran, and jumped.

One hundred and thirty feet. My research told me of a handful of people who weren't killed in the fall. Each of them drowned. The darkness rushed and whistled by as I let dim recollections of distant paratrooper drills guide my body in the fall. Four seconds. My left foot shattered on the surface of the water as I plunged into the freezing ocean. The cold and excruciating pain shocked the meager air out of my lungs, and I screamed underwater. Before I consciously knew I wasn't dead, I was clawing my way to the surface on lungs threatening to burst. My head breached the surface right as a wave snatched me up and slammed my body hard into a jutting stone I'd missed by mere feet in the fall.

The impact broke several ribs, and I made a horrible rasping sound as one of them punctured my right lung. As the wave receded, it dragged me down the spongy face of the rock and shoved me under. I took in water, coughing and moaning as I fought to the surface again. The water was peppered with falling ashes, and the acrid salinity burned my sinuses as I choked and looked up at the next wave. As the rolling darkness crested to break me on the rocks, I sucked in breath and dove under, feeling it pass over me in the blind dark. Throwing one arm in front of the other in a desperate crawl stroke and kicking with one leg, I moved underwater and navigated around another great stone before bursting out onto the surface. The first raindrops began to fall as I bit down the agony and forced my broken body to push through the gauntlet of wave and stone. I coughed and sputtered in tiny, stabbing breaths as I hit open water.

A glance behind me showed Cape Contrition and Usher's Fall Light burning against the starless night sky. As the frigid sea racked my broken body with shivers and my breaths came in harsh barks, I crawled along the inky surface of the water for a hundred yards. Two hundred. My sight of Cape Contrition told me I was three hundred yards out into the sea when my body started to break down from the damage it had taken. My left leg was crushed almost to the knee, my right side pierced by hot knives of pain with every stroke, breaths giving almost no air. As my desperate efforts flagged and the ocean roared in my ears, something large loomed ahead, pushing forward in the night. I coughed and choked with surprise and lifted my arms in a frantic wave as I realized the coming metallic bulk was a boat. The gillnetter ploughed the waves to a white froth, and I howled out to it like a madman as my vision blurred and threatened to black out. My last confused thoughts were fear as the slowly panning beam of a searchlight leveled its glare on me, and in its light, I saw the silhouette of a dark woman with a little child clutching her skirts, waiting for me.

Epilogue

November 24th, 1971

"Attention: This is the final boarding call for passengers Donald and Melinda Marshall, booked on Northwest Orient Airlines Flight 305 to Seattle, Washington. Please proceed to gate..."

"She just landed!" Gwen smiled, taking a seat at the table and sliding me an Americano in a paper cup. "How do I look?" She fussed with her bob in a pocket mirror, and I closed it in her hand. More of Portland International Airport's announcements droned overhead, but she had all my attention now.

"Beautiful." I leaned in for a long, tender kiss. I took a long pull of my coffee and adjusted my glasses as I glanced nervously out across the airport. My hand fumbled for a packet of cigarettes that hadn't been there in eight years. "Damn, I'm nervous." I strangled the trembling in my hand. Outside, rain was falling in sheets against the windowpanes. My leg pulsed with old throbs of pain as I stretched it out uncomfortably in its brace, adjusting the lean of my black cane.

"Don't be." She gave me a bite of her cinnamon roll. "Is my big, bad ghost detective scared?"

"Cut it out." She tousled my gray hair with a laugh. Otis

stirred slowly from his place at my feet when he saw Gwen tearing apart the cinnamon roll and lifted his quivering gray muzzle to take a small shred she snuck under the table. "It's just... It's been so long, you know? What am I going to say? Christ. Ten years."

"Start with 'hi.' You're a writer. The rest will come to you. Say, do you think I should be here for this?"

"What are you talking about? You're my best girl. Who else should be here?"

"I know, but maybe you should do this part alone."

"Come on, don't bail on me, Ms. Christiansen." She got up and kissed my forehead softly.

"I won't be far. I'll be snooping around in that bookstore pretending not to watch. Now go on, Soldier." I smiled wearily as I watched her go, turning to wink at me as her curly, frosted red bob disappeared behind a display of books set in the doorway: rows and rows of dark blue paperbacks, emblazoned with a lighthouse shining into the inky pall of a storm.

Between the Devil and the Deep Blue Sea by Joseph Simon Crowley.

I smiled with secret pride as I tousled Otis' ears. Hard to believe it had been eight years since 'Alice' Cole and Hana Iwamoto fished me out of the Pacific on that terrible night. Hana had ignored the evacuation order and gone straight to Alice with Gwen and Otis in tow; begged her to unmoor *Seal Sister* and make straight for the Cape. Hana was in college now at Portland State University, and Alice had died four years back to lung cancer. It was only with her deathbed blessing that I moved forward to publish the book, which was a stunning success amidst all the controversy over whether or not any of it had really happened. A heavy storm blew in off the ocean that night, halting the fire in its tracks and sparing much of Delilah. The green things have come back, as they always do. Will Blake left. He's a park ranger at Mount Hood National Forest, the last I heard. Thomas Forester retired from the priesthood, and rediscovered his spirituality in time with his grandchildren, and the penning of several books.

It was a long road, but I've been sober for three years. These days, I'm living in Cannon Beach with Gwen, where we own a bookstore together and she's finishing her first play. We never married. I don't know if I ever will again. But what we have, it's good for us. I don't think I would have made it without her. We live close to the ocean and have learned to find comfort in its savage mystery, its turbulent beauty. But I've never been back to Delilah or seen Cape Contrition again. And I never go out on the beach at night. Sometimes, I wake up in the middle of the night, unable to breathe, overwhelmed by the weight of what I almost did. She holds me close and brings me back.

The Delilah Suicides have ended. As much as it's possible, the Ushers have been redeemed. But it all still keeps me up nights. I read the paper and worry the ugliness of American life that made them still lives on. Despite the good-natured dismissal many made of the claims put forward in my book, I'm not without my believers. In the years since I walked away from Cape Contrition, several readers have asked me to investigate other... events that defied explanation. Sorry to inform you, few claims turned out to be substantial. One or two of them, though... Ah, I don't know if those are stories I'll ever tell. Maybe Hana should be the one. More than a few of the best breakthroughs were her own. We became quite the team. My experience with the Ushers led me to study cults and familial abuse more closely, and that led me to consult on a few cases of purely human evil I'll never be able to forget... The Mansons, most recently. The older I get, the more I wonder if we're ever going to learn.

Otis stirred under my feet, drawing me out of my reverie. Leaning weight onto my cane, I got up slowly to my feet and looked out into the crowd. A woman was tentatively walking up to me, wearing a black turtleneck with her long chestnut hair cut with heavy straight-across bangs. A little boy pressed his forehead into her corduroy skirt, and she stopped to adjust his bag for a moment as I found my trembling feet. For a moment, I wanted to run, but that ship had sailed. She looked so much like her mom. Older than I dreamed she'd be when this happened. God, I'd lost so much time.

"Emma?" I ventured, surprised to hear the tears in my voice as I said it.

"Hey, Dad." She murmured an introduction to her son and pulled his fingers out of his mouth to look at me.

"Hi," I smiled, looking from one to the other. There's so much that needs to be said. Ten years. I don't know how to reach back across time. Across hurt. I don't know what we can say to become a family again, or if I can ever truly make things right between us. But it's a start.

April 8th, 1974

"Will the circle be unbroken?

By and by, by and by?

Is a better home awaiting

In the sky, in the sky?" the boy sang to himself as he climbed over a fallen log in the new growth of the forest. Soft rain

432

was pattering on the evergreen fronds and the ocean was roaring dully in the distance. A golden retriever nosed along the ground and growled, bolting up the switchback trail after a darting squirrel. The boy flashed a gap-toothed grin as he gave chase, climbing the rugged slope and getting sap on his hands as he went. He'd only seen the headland from a distance but was determined to know what it held. The road to it was permanently closed, but no one would tell him why. From the beach, all he could see were tall fences, a massive satellite dish... and an old lighthouse, blackened and hollowed by fire. The dog whimpered and reeled away as the boy panted up to a tall chain-link fence, topped with coils of razor wire and humming with electricity.

FEDERAL TESTING SITE
DEPARTMENT OF ENERGY
KEEP OUT
DANGER –HIGH VOLTAGE

The child was startled from his careful reading when he looked down from the sign to see a little girl holding hands with a toddler on the other side of the fence. Her clothes were rough-spun and dark, and she looked as if she'd been burned. She gave off an air of cold and her sudden appearance scared him. But she and her brother smiled reassuringly as they closed their fingers around the metal of the fence, and nothing happened to them.

"What's your name?" the girl asked.

"Billy. What's yours?" she didn't answer.

"Want to play a game?"

"What kind of game?" But she was walking away, leading her baby brother stumbling behind her.

"Come find me, Billy!" she teased, turning to run as

he walked up to the electric fence and called out to her, thoughtlessly reaching out to touch it.

The End

Acknowledgments

Cape Contrition started as a ghost story my wife Lauren and I came up with together on a trip to Florence, Oregon, in the Autumn of 2016 right before the presidential election. We stayed in a cabin on the beach with our dog Jack London, and he and I started walking out on the beach at night (for safety reasons, I warn you: this is inadvisable and very bad form for a Coastie). I guess that was where this book first began, in that absolute pitch darkness with the ocean rolling in our ears, and that creeping sensation we might not be alone. The following day, we visited Heceta Head Lighthouse for the first time and were absolutely spellbound by its forlorn beauty. Heceta Head Lighthouse is notorious among locals for a haunting of its own. The house and grounds are believed to be haunted by a lady in gray named "Rue", the ghostly wife of a lighthouse keeper grieving the death of her young child who fell from the cliff. Bundled up against the cold, we sat on a bench in the shadow of the lighthouse after reading some information about how isolated and difficult the lives of lighthouse keepers were, and we began to tell one another a ghost story. What started as a way for two horror fans to spook one another came to define our whole vacation. From the beach cabin to long night drives along remote coastal roads, we fleshed out the idea and I went on to spend the next two years writing it. As a person who has dealt with depression since childhood, this book also became a way for me to confront my own demons and find healing. All gratitude for the achievement of finishing this book starts with Lauren, my partner, the co-creator of this story, my constant sounding board, supporter, and friend. I couldn't have done this without her support.

I also want to thank my mom, Janelle Irwin, my dad, Tim Irwin, and my little brother Will Irwin for their indulgence and support as early listeners to my rants as I wrestled through what this was going to be. I'd like to thank my friends Matthew Schultz, Mollie Meyer, Dr. Arthur Kelly, Kerlin Richter, James George, Samantha Mitchell, Jacob White-Duong II and Anela Farrar-Ivey for their mentorship, interest in this project, and feedback as it was being written. Hannah Kloefkorn, Hannah Spencer, and Rie Tanabe Vigeland were early beta readers whose feedback was crucial to my editing process (Rie also assisted with Japanese translation for passages in Chapter Twenty-Seven). Caleb Switzer and Scott McKay are friends and fellow writers whose support and frank critique mean a lot to me, and I'm grateful to have had their commiseration in this. Tracy George of Sunday Portraits is a dear friend, and took the author photo which appears on the back of this book.

Next, I want to thank the people of Florence, Lincoln City, Cannon Beach, Newport, Seaside, Nehalem, Manzanita, Tillamook, and Astoria, Oregon for their hospitality and unknowing support as I visited their towns as often as I could, asked a lot of questions, took notes, and holed up back in Portland to write. This book was colored by the personalities and stories of numerous Oregon Coast residents, who are among the kindest and most welcoming people on Earth. Delilah is a fictional town, but is based on Florence, Lincoln City, and Newport. Sights that awed me in each of these towns found their way into Delilah, and if I did a decent job writing about them, you may recognize a few. Usher's Fall Light is unambiguously and exactingly modeled after Heceta Head Lighthouse outside Florence, with a little inspiration also drawn from Yaquina Head Lighthouse and Tillamook Rock Lighthouse, AKA "Terrible Tilly". Research for this book was aided substantially by volunteer tour-guides at Heceta Head Lighthouse, Yaquina Bay Lighthouse, and Yaquina Head Lighthouse, who are knowledgeable and dedicated historians and put up with a lot of questions from someone who wouldn't tell them what he was working on.

Oregon, my Oregon, I thank you last and most fondly of all. Thank you for being my adopted home, and for being my healing. One day, you'll also be my grave. Until then, I'm yours.

About the Author

Benjamin Connor Irwin was born in Nashville, Tennessee, and grew up in the Southeastern and Appalachian regions of the United States before moving to Oregon at age sixteen. A childhood spent on the move as the perpetual new kid in town led him to a life-long love of fiction, especially fantasy, horror, and science fiction. He graduated from Warner Pacific University with a Bachelor of Science in History and Human Development/Family Studies and works as a funeral director. He loves coffee, books, rain, dogs, cooking, hiking, playing guitar, and weightlifting. Ben lives in Portland, Oregon with his wife, Lauren, and their dog, Jack London.

You can connect with me on:
f   https://www.facebook.com/Benjamin-Connor-Irwin-Author-102028345391664

Made in the USA
Coppell, TX
27 June 2021

58185800R00246